G000075662

James Gabrian is a humanitarian, having worked with the homeless and vulnerable adults for eighteen years. Previously working in sales and marketing for the food industry, he has helped to raise funds for wildlife and habitat conservation charities via product endorsements. Born in Sale near Manchester, he now lives with his partner in Norfolk in the East of England. *One Step Away* is his first novel.

To Ali, for believing in me.

James Gabrian

ONE STEP AWAY

AUSTIN MACAULEY PUBLISHERS™

LONDON • CAMBRIDGE • NEW YORK • SHARJAH

Copyright © James Gabrian (2021)

The right of James Gabrian to be identified as author of this work has been asserted by the author in accordance with section 77 and 78 of the Copyright, Designs and Patents Act 1988.

All rights reserved. No part of this publication may be reproduced, stored in a retrieval system, or transmitted in any form or by any means, electronic, mechanical, photocopying, recording, or otherwise, without the prior permission of the publishers.

Any person who commits any unauthorised act in relation to this publication may be liable to criminal prosecution and civil claims for damages.

This is a work of fiction. Names, characters, businesses, places, events, locales, and incidents are either the products of the author's imagination or used in a fictitious manner. Any resemblance to actual persons, living or dead, or actual events is purely coincidental.

A CIP catalogue record for this title is available from the British Library.

ISBN 9781528980500 (Paperback)
ISBN 9781528980524 (ePub e-book)

www.austinmacauley.com

First Published (2021)
Austin Macauley Publishers Ltd
25 Canada Square
Canary Wharf
London
E14 5LQ

A tale of adventure and love in worlds beyond death,
in a quest for the meaning of knowing.

– James Gabrian

The Last Ride

"John, let your clarinet sing to you. Trying to make it sing, will not allow you to feel the ebb and flow of waves created by the very essence of your inner being. Breathe in your instrument and blow through it, with your soul."

Her musical metaphors were not always entirely clear and my music teacher, Mrs Daniels, a creative, yet somewhat eccentric woman, spoke a language, my mind struggled to grasp.

Imagining what she was trying to say appeared straight forward, but connecting the parts together to make me feel or experience any difference when playing, was another matter. It all seemed too elusive. What was essence anyway and connecting it to a difficult piece, whilst trying to concentrate on the notes, was really hard to do!

"It's a little like trying to catch a butterfly with a saucepan, whilst running through meadow grass, in your wellingtons," I proposed.

"Yes, but do not chase the butterfly, simply be it."

"Gosh, why didn't I think of that?"

Mrs Daniels fixed me with a perfect guilt inducing stare. One honed by her years of teaching and I felt the precarious glimmer of pride fall to lie amongst the anxiety already sitting in the folds of my stomach.

"Sorry."

I had to admit, I was making progress, but it was frustrating and fraught with a big chance of failure. Succeeding or winning wasn't one of my strong points. Imagining I could, was easy.

Winning was about feeling guilty, about letting others win because their feelings were somehow more important than my own. A message had been burnt into my consciousness from an early age that 'I should be aware of the needs of others and put them first'. It was this message that compelled me to take part in watching rather than competing. Music practice was a place where I could hide but still try, because the ones that impacted upon me, dare not attend such an uncool pursuit.

I wasn't sure, whether the message was purely parental or an echo from some sensed but elusive memory. There were times when I felt that I had somehow done it all before, but just could not realise my skills. The echoes however allowed a temptingly arrogant 'observer' feeling to emerge and provide me with a fantasy, upon which to reason and gain reprieve. Unfortunately, the fantasies always came with guilt and the compulsion to allow others to find their way without taking their limelight.

With a media world populated by super heroes, the competition was fierce, especially when I had not quite sourced the powers, but felt they were there somewhere. In the 'I need this to be true' part of my imagination, they simmered just below the surface, in a state of poised inertia, tempting me to find the key to their engagement and my salvation. I really needed that key, or to find someone who could show me where to look. In truth, I was convinced it had to be me alone who unlocked and unleashed, as a result of my own discovery, as this would be more powerful. After all, what holds more power, having your own idea or using someone else's? Being what seemed to be half aware was tortuous and tested my patience constantly. Like the recoil of an elastic band, my mother's voice of wisdom reverberated into my mind for the endless of times, 'the prize of patience, is in fact patience.' Not that she knew of my secret desires.

It was the feelings of loneliness that were the hardest for me. In my difference, I felt I was holding a hidden responsibility or purpose that felt grand, that somehow kept me from truly connecting with others. Another key I had also not yet found. I was a prisoner, unable to prove my innocence through actions and I did not think I was safe enough, to dare speak of how I really felt.

Another of my mother's messages was about remaining humble and deeply considering risk. The learnt sense of humility that I felt, had capped me from an early age and turned me into the outward passive observer with a burning desire to be otherwise. This constant mind dichotomy was an inward battle between mind and emotion, desired highs and restricting lows. Constant shoulds and coulds fought for the upper hand over a loyalty to an ever elusive and hidden pathway. I hated being human and often wondered upon intergalactic star systems and the possibility that I might in fact be half alien. However, it may just be a simple case of abduction and brainwashing.

I didn't feel human, because others did not think as I did. They didn't link all of the scenarios of a debate or discussion. The amount of times I would hear, 'I hadn't thought of that,' or being told by an adult, 'don't be silly, that's a minor reason and could not possibly be the cause,' of some behaviour or other. How did they know? People are all too ready to accept the obvious as the reason and why? Because they are lazy? I did not believe this, I believed that they were programmed to overlook the hidden and to not complete the jigsaw. I needed all the pieces in place to truly see the whole picture and getting it wrong was painful.

The internal battle, won and lost at the same time, had kept the part of me that was afraid, hidden from the view of others. This is because I felt that if what was hidden took hold of me, I would be overwhelmed and lose my ability to hide in the world. That part, 'he', fears being noticed and becoming an object for criticism and at the same time, wonder. I, the not so afraid part of John, long to become who I really am. Not knowing, which of the parts is truly me, creates anxiety and I am worried that there seems to be two Johns in my head, who maintain the status quo through this constant battle.

At 15 years old but feeling much older, my legacy is an awareness beyond my understanding and although I may have the will to change, the frustration is not to have the conscious experience to direct it, without becoming caught in what it is for. Without the ability to access the wisdom that makes me feel this way, I can only feel things without knowing why I do. Some say, that after my dad left my mum and I, when I was ten, it was Mum who felt it important that I should grow up quickly to help and support her. I suppose I have done that, but something has been missed along the way.

Others my age seem to live in another world, happy in an existence of innocence, although bound by their electronic screens and governed by silliness, something I cannot get. Being lonely is something I have never got used to. Being a misfit is hard and unfair, but blame is an easy way out of responsibility and my mum's needs, I feel, do not fully account for the magnitude of my locked-in potential.

Although I say it myself, my main strength is a brilliantly cut and multifaceted imagination. It mirrors, reflects and projects thought and feeling, from the most quintessential point to the most elaborate alchemic synthesis. It finds and bounces off the edges with ease from extreme to extreme, never balancing, as this would be a loss. However, to others I guess, most would experience this loss as peace. Whilst considering myself to be a trainee master of the schema, the work is still difficult in finding the meaning of connections seemingly disjoined. My imagined world is a place of safety and is one very much without peace and residing within, I know, are undiscovered depths and a hidden purpose. Well, I hope.

When I think about my music, inside my head, I know I can play well, well enough to succeed and one day show myself in my true light as a skilled clarinet player. Imagining the scenario, I am playing to a packed classroom, spontaneously enthralling the captivated audience of my classmates. Mrs Daniels stops outside the classroom door and listens, rooted to the spot in absolute amazement. Becky Roberts, a girl of dreams, finally reveals that she has loved me for some time and it was my playing that connected to her feelings, so freeing her voice. The headmistress consequently invites me to play at assembly, where there just happened to be a visiting reporter who takes my photo, printing it in the local newspaper after the rendition goes viral on the net. With a 253,022 following, I am consequently talent scouted and invited for an audition with the London Philharmonic Orchestra. Everyone would like me then and stop calling me Clarice or Toots.

"Don't ever hit back, just understand what they fail to admit to themselves and soar above them." I guess my mum had never been bullied at school or was too ashamed to say.

With after school music practice over, I kicked the snow from my shoes and unchained my racing bike from its corrugated and rusting dormitory. Checking my Casio, I calculated that there was enough time to ride the longer route home before 5.15 pm, when tea would be ready and waiting. Preferring a racer to a mountain bike, I bought my steed, from some money my grandfather had left me when he had died two years ago. This man, I loved and missed. He was the one who stood up and led me on my path after Dad left. Never once did I use the words, 'you are not my father', and his 'a spade is a spade' teaching really helped me to ground my imagination, when it needed to be. The memory of him connected with my schemas and by swallowing hard to fight back my tears, I acknowledged the art, I thought I had mastered well. Hero's don't cry, because there is always someone watching or judging what I feel, even though they appear not to be there.

Refocusing on my journey, the longer way home took me down what I called 'Unwind Hill.' I had named it as such because the speed I could reach during its course, helped me to shrug off a particularly frustrating day, a day when too many others were on my case. Today had been flat and routine, but who was I to argue with what felt right.

Unwind Hill was a relatively steep descent from the corner of Wind-Willow Cross, down past Pie Feast fields and eventually terminating at Crispin Woods. The road then ascended leading to Marshfield Common and home.

In order to get to Wind-Willow Cross, I had to ride down the main road from the school, take a sharp left past the village stores and over the road bridge which crossed a stream. I always managed to cycle a further 500 metres up a steep hill before being forced to dismount and walk the remainder, pushing my bike up to Ashe Cottages. From here I could cycle the rest of the way up to the cross.

Ashe Cottages are set on the road's edge, each sporting a stable door. In summer, they would have their top halves flung wide to capture the earthy sweetness of the evening woodland air. In late November, the doors were shut tight to repel all expected elements. Snow had come early. Their small mullion windows projected a warmer winter expression. I imagined the inhabitants sitting around their open log fires, relaxing before their evening meal. I suddenly felt cold and on their outside.

As I passed the last of the row of cottages, a face in the upstairs window unexpectedly focussed my attention, hairs raising on both forearms and on the back of my neck. I skidded, as I lost my concentration to the eerie experience. Frightful split seconds flashed through my mind at the thought of falling to the ground painfully. Luckily, I managed to regain balance and steer the bike towards the pavement, which stopped me with a jolt. Looking back at the same window, the person's face had gone. In waiting a few moments, I expected them to come down the stairs into the front room, but no one came. I dismounted and checked to see if the front wheel had been damaged.

I found the face in the upstairs window unnerving, as I could not remember having seen him before and I know the owners of that particular cottage. Perhaps he was a burglar, but there had been light and movement downstairs; but maybe they had not heard him. I checked my shoulder holster and realised I had left the 9 mm on my bedside cabinet. However, as in my mind, I was trained to be a black belt 3rd Dan in Shotokai, there was still a good chance I could overpower him, if he appeared and his intentions proved menacing.

The little voice inside my head, which was not grandfather's, but some irritating voice of rationality, told me it was most probably a visiting relative. The headlines reporting my heroic capture of the dangerous criminal quickly faded. Although it was now dark, the snow on the ground seemed to lighten the surrounding countryside in natural artificiality. I peddled on and the crossroads came into view.

Wind-Willow Cross was named as such by the local people of Denby Dale for two reasons. It was situated on high ground and thus open to all the elements and also, at the centre of the crossroads there was a small green, upon which stood a magnificent willow tree. In summer, this tree would shade more than twenty revellers from the Coach House Inn across the road. At 5 pm on a late November winter evening, the pub was deserted, apart from the flickering shadows dancing on the inside from newly lit coal fires. Come 6 o'clock, the place would start to fill with thirsty work folk from Jamison's textile mill, a half a mile's walk down the hill.

I turned right onto Barnsley Road and into the start grid of 'Unwind Hill.' Setting the stop watch mode on my Rolex to zero, I twisted the accelerator grip in my right hand and the red Ducati 990 roared its eagerness beneath me. Wind-Willow to Marshfield common in four minutes dead would knock five seconds from my previous record. Kicking the bike into gear, I let out the clutch and in reality, pushed the peddle hard with my right foot. The bike sprang from a standing start. I knew I would have to drive hard to reach the gates of Herne Farm in 30 seconds, if I was to beat the record.

Herne Farm was the first timed check point and I needed to be in the top range of my twenty-one gears to create the chance. The annoying and doubtful inner voice made me conscious of the icy road and although I was concentrating my effort on speed, my periphery kept my wheels in the vehicle tracks already cut.

I knew that the humble John was afraid of many things that were unseen, unknown or misunderstood. Hence much mind work was spent on prediction. However, the other part of me was not afraid of taking risks and riding edges. Right now, riding to the tracks, made it more of a challenge with less margin for error, just as my imagined world liked it.

At this point the first adrenaline rush hit me and powered into my legs. I screamed past the entrance of Herne Farm at 28 seconds and on past the mill. Suddenly, I was on the track at Brands Hatch and I my chances were good. To me, this was what 'Unwind Hill' was all about, I could be anything I wanted to be, transport myself to anywhere and achieve anything. It also helped me to come closer to who I believed I really was.

As I approached top speed, something shifted. I was suddenly encapsulated in silence even though the wind was rushing past my ears. Everything around me crystallised into the finest of detail. Even at speed, I seemed to become aware of every ice crystal hanging from each twig in the trees, the hedgerows and those on the surface of the snow lying in the fields. I could smell the earth and water beneath the snow and almost taste the ions in air. The realisation of a simple, yet awe inspiring beauty dramatically made its purchase.

A cold ecstatic sensation moved from the base of my spine and through my entire body. A feeling not dissimilar to the well reported sense of someone walking over your grave. This feeling energised each nerve ending, all firing in unison, sending wave after wave of ecstatic power right through my body and into my mind. I felt totally connected to everything around me, almost like I just knew how everything was linked together.

This feeling of knowing met me at different levels, the bike becoming an extension of my body and the surroundings merged with my own sense of myself. Suddenly, Mrs Daniels musical reference became clearly apparent. I felt as one with everything and in my realisation, the second adrenaline rush hit me just prior to a second energising wave to push hard. My eyes were watering in sheer emotion and I shouted at the top of my voice in sheer release, "Go! 'Go! Go!"

I was flying, the sensations were coursing through me, channelling power to my legs, through the gears and eating distance from the road. Pie Feast fields flew past on the right, summer memories hit for a split second and disappeared as quickly again, as I sharpened my mind and downloaded my imagination. With the peripheral part of me shifting to reality, it was planning how to negotiate the next bend, whilst I maintained the speed. 'Slow down, you'll be sorry'. 'I can do this, get out of my head!'

Unbeknown to me at the time, two headlights were growing larger behind me.

I leaned into the left-hand bend, imagining myself to be banking the Ducati. With my knee almost touching the road surface, I steered wide, cutting across the camber. Realising my mistake too late, the tyres now had no grip on the fresh snow outside of the tyre tracks. For some reason, probably because of the way action scenes are played out in the movies, you think that a slow-motion sensation will take control and you will be able to contemplate how much time you will have off school with a broken arm. It is not like that at all.

As my front wheel shot towards the right, I automatically stiffened to receive the full impact of the road surface on my left shoulder and instinctively stretched out my hand to break the fall. The harsh tarmac and ice removed most of the skin from my palm and my momentum snapped my arm beneath me, bones cracking as they twisted under my body. I was thrown into a roll, rather than a skid, rolling over and over with each extremity thumping into the road surface. Finally, I came to rest in the middle of the road lying face down and dazed. Every limb burned with a deep grazing and my left arm was numb from the shoulder down. The pain seemed blunt and bearable.

As I pulled myself up into a sitting position, the screech of breaks behind me seemed dimmed and distant.

The lorry's front bumper hit me squarely across the shoulders, snapping my head backwards, then forward violently, my forehead hitting against the ground.

I felt nothing more, or did I imagine my body had been dragged beneath the chassis before the lorry had managed to stop a further fifty metres down the road. Somewhere during that final scrape, I felt freed, like life had somehow shifted from the reality of non-reality and into a place between. The feeling was like evaporating, but without the intense cold. I was not floating, or looking through a screen at the trail of carnage which was easily traced on the luminescence of the snow. The bright red scar, was right there in front of me, starkly screaming from the whiteness. Yet I was standing on the road side, miraculously unhurt, just holding my breath and frozen to that spot.

I watched the lorry driver jump down from his cab, imagining his heart to be racing wildly. I guessed he knew exactly what he had just driven over and yet I was over here? He looked back and saw what looked like a pile of rags lying in the road. Nausea must have overwhelmed his feelings of dread and shock as he vomited into the snow.

In a short space of time, three people had emerged from a courtyard of cottages just opposite to my nightmare scene and were cautiously approaching the pile. The lorry driver started running to meet them. He was frantically trying to explain that the accident wasn't his fault.

"I didn't see him until it was too late, he…, he was just sitting in the middle of the road, he must have fallen off his bike, it was an accident… I didn't have a chance."

"Neither did he," said one of the men in the group staring down at the body. A woman member had rushed back into her house.

"Is he…"

"Yes," said the man who had spoken previously to the driver.

"Oh my God, why, why me?"

The woman returned from the cottages and gave a blanket to one of the men to place over the body. She then placed another around the lorry driver's shoulders, informing him she had called for the emergency services. He was sitting by the roadside, with his face in his hands, telling the unhearing others that he had two children of his own.

The second man had driven his car into the road behind the group and had switched on his hazard warning lights to alert approaching traffic. The headlights illuminated the scene revealing the extent of the impact. The body lying under the now blood-soaked blanket was crumpled and inert.

"Wake up, wake up!"

No, I felt awake and aware and I stood on the opposite side of the road, watching the group in absolute disbelief.

Desperately searching my memories, I was computing quickly through the possibilities of an out of body experience or hallucinations due to a head wound.

"Over here, I'm over here!" Not one of them responded.

There was an eerie, unsafe feeling to this place of muffled silences. Its emptiness shrouded what felt like an imminent threat, concealed yet expected. I was in the nightmare, like the one where you have no control over your movements to evade something that is stalking you from the shadows.

The feelings of panic emerged in the realisation, that what I could be experiencing, was not my imagination, nor a dream. I was somewhere else, yet in the same place, disconnected from everyone else and vulnerable to what my imagination might conjure next.

Caught Just in Time

Oily terror rose from my stomach and although I could stifle the scream, I couldn't keep back the howling wail as everything imploded into whiteness. Tears streamed down my face as I sank to my knees in the snow. My next thought was to run, to run home. Just as I was about to take flight, a woman's voice cut through me, restoring consciousness.

"Hey you! Don't think you are going to get into heaven after pulling that stupid stunt. That was your fault, that accident. Look at that poor lorry driver, do you think he will ever be the same again. He's got two small children and who do you think he is going to take his guilt out on, not you, selfish boy, them. He will make their lives miserable, his wife will leave him and he will grow old on his own. You, stupid idiot."

I had no idea who she was, but I felt that she had spoken the truth, it was my fault.

"I didn't mean to fall off my bike, I didn't do it on purpose."

"Makes no difference, you have ruined his life and you will not get into heaven. The best thing for you is to come with me. I will introduce you to others who are here and we will look after you. Anyway, as I've said, if heaven isn't an option and it isn't one for you, that leaves the other place and you don't want to go there. You would rather stay here near to your family, wouldn't you?"

"Yes, I suppose so. I don't know what is happening, will you help me?"

"You are in deep trouble, but we can help you. You will be fine."

I felt so guilty about what I had done and it felt like I should somehow pay for it. What she was suggesting, I thought was the only option open to me. I put my face in my hands and sobbed, thinking perhaps, I was already in hell.

"Pull yourself together, you sissy. Come on, no time to feel sorry for yourself, let's go."

As I stood up, a man's voice called my name from behind me.

"John, shh, shh, shh, it's alright, you will be alright. Don't be scared."

I looked up from my watery veil and instantly recognised his face as the one I had seen in the upstairs window, the one at Ashe Cottages.

"Back off Clara and leave this young man alone. You know you cannot win this fight, so don't even try. Unless of course, you want to come with us?"

"I almost had him and no, I'm not coming. I hate you do-gooders, all full of promises. This is where the real life is John, don't trust him, his kind are full of crap."

Clara disappeared into thin air and left me with this other man who had given me no reason, other than a gentle voice, to trust him either.

"Who was she? She said things that made me feel awful, that this situation was all my fault."

"She is a Leaf John, a low flier. They are people who trap themselves here in their confusion after they have died. Don't worry, you are safe now."

"I saw you before, before I got here."

"Yes, I know, I have come to meet you." He extended his hand for me to shake, smiling warmly.

"My name is Peter."

"I am John Kenton." Fighting to gain any sense, I very hesitantly offered my hand in return.

As our two hands met and gripped, I felt what could only be described as a feeling of wellbeing enter me and I somehow knew I was in no danger. Although I no longer felt scared, my sadness and state of confusion still remained.

"Is, is that me?" I was pointing to the blanketed form lying in the road.

"It's your body yes, but you are where you stand now," Peter replied.

"I don't understand. You mean I'm dead and I am now a ghost?"

Peter placed his arm around my shoulders to comfort me.

"You are neither John. Your body has died. Therefore, you had to leave it and without it, you will move on to the next stage in your life. Do you feel dead?"

"No."

"I can also reliably inform you that you are not a ghost either. When I first came over, I must admit, I thought I was a ghost too!" Peter was smiling.

"Came over? I don't understand, over to where?"

Peter's voice softened and told me that there are many things for me to learn and although everything must seem very strange, things would become clearer when we reached our destination. This immediately increased my anxiety as home was just up the road and the feelings of needing to run were gaining in strength.

"Why, where are we going? If I am dead and I am here, not there, pointing to myself in the road, then where is here, if we have not got to where we are going yet?" I think I confused myself and Peter at the same time.

Peter was quietly thinking to himself, having unravelled John's words that, this young man's awareness and agility were much sharper than many he had caught in a long while. Most did not question and accepted a few words of direction and empathy in reserved judgement. As he started to explain where 'here' was, my attention was drawn to the blue flashing lights making their way along the road towards us.

Alighting from their respective vehicles, two police officers and two paramedics rushed over to where my body lay. Their sense of urgency diminished when they realised I was dead.

Then a strange thing happened, bearing in mind everything that had just occurred. A man walked through the side of the ambulance and towards the group by the road side. Linking this man to Clara, I grabbed hold of Peter's hand as the fear started to well up inside me. Again, with a single touch, the fears evaporated. This other man was wearing scruffy, torn clothes and was wide eyed, as if desperate to find something.

"Don't worry John, you are safe."

"Who is he, is he another Leaf?"

"Yes. Leaves are like us, but they have trapped themselves in the plane which exists between the Earth world as you know it, and the after world where I live and we are going to shortly. We call spirits like him, low flyers, or Leaves because they stay close to the Earth."

"Why is he here. He is not going to try and take me with him too is he?"

"He may wish to come with us to the other side. Keep quiet and watch. If he sees us he will probably come over to talk. If he does, say little and let me do the talking. Remember, and don't be scared, he won't harm you, not while I am with you."

The man watched the paramedics lift my body onto a stretcher and place it into the back of the ambulance. He then started looking around intently. An instant later, he caught my eye and I tightened my grip on Peter's hand.

"He's seen us!"

"Yes, quiet now."

In a blink of that eye, the man was standing right in front of us. He was about fifty years old, unshaven and was wearing very old-fashioned clothes.

"Greetings brother. Does this world bare kindness upon you?" Peter said the words but knew that this world did not.

"Can't grumble, 'tis lonely at times. Is this the boy laid yonder?"

"Yes."

"Nasty," he tutted and shook his head.

"Fall off your bike boy?"

I froze, not sure of what to say and squeezed Peter's hand gently for comfort. Peter appeared to be listening to something else.

"…yes sir."

"Need not call me sir. By looks of your dress, I should be calling you the same young master. What's your name boy?"

"John sir…sorry…John."

Peter interrupted. "Is there some way we can help you, Simon, isn't it?"

"Yes." He scrutinised Peter's face in mistrust, before confirming his name to be Simon Johnson.

"Simon, I am taking John to the other side, why don't you come with us? You know that Sarah lives on the other side."

"How do you know about Sarah? Don't answer, I forget you other worlderers think you know everything."

"Not everything, but I know that Sarah was your woman when she was here and I know that love can last. I understand you have met many like me who have told you similar. If you come with us, all will be well."

Simon's mood turned to anger.

"I don't know that! I know I gotta pay for what I've done and I'm scared of coming over because I know they're gonna get me, I killed him y'know."

"You know it was an accident, you know you didn't mean to kill him and what's more, he will have forgiven you by now."

"I don't know that!!!"

"Come on Simon, take my hand. They, whoever they may be, are not going to get you."

"NO…no, I can't trust anyone, they'll send me to hell."

Suddenly, a pink haze appeared around Simon's head. Peter immediately dropped my hand and a blue and white pane of light appeared between where we were standing and Simon. A red ball of light shot out from Simon's form and flew above our heads.

"Hold your fire other-worlderer and look behind you!" Peter, with a red glow about his head, span, as I did, to see Clara lying on the ground in the snow. She also had the remnants of a red halo.

"Is she dead?"

"Yes, but not in the way you are thinking, she is just stunned. She must have been sneaking up on us to get to you."

Before I had a chance to blink again, Simon was gone. Peter's 'thank you,' projecting into empty space.

"So, you've got laser guns over here and alive-dead people battling it out. This was not quite my idea of heaven."

"I know. You must have lots of questions, but hold them for the moment, please." Looking up at Peter, he seemed to be deep in thought and I heard him say 'no he still isn't ready to come yet.'

The two police men were sweeping the bloodied snow into the gutter.

"Come on John, we must cross over now."

I no longer felt afraid and knew I must go with him.

"Don't worry John, you will visit the Earth plane again soon. Anyway, there is someone waiting to meet you."

"Who?"

"Wait and see!"

"Peter?" Hesitating before I took another step. "I don't want to go." Sadness welled up inside me as I thought about my mother, my friends and my home.

"You don't have to explain John, but you must realise, you have nowhere to go other than to wander between worlds like Simon and Clara are doing, not being able to talk to any of your friends, or your mother. It is a very lonely existence."

Something, which I can only describe as strongly instinctual, told me I must go with Peter, but the loss and sadness that fought to counter its command to leave my life behind was like an anchor reluctantly leaving the sea bed. I took one last look along 'Unwind Hill' and up onto Pie Feast fields. The scene glowed orange under the sodium street lights, diluting the natural appeal of this world that had been mine and adding to my anchor's lift. *More like Wind-Willow Cross to Marshfield common in four minutes and dead,* I thought to myself.

My bike lay crumpled and twisted by the roadside and I imagined it's picture on the front page of the local newspaper with an appropriate headline. As I looked left, I could see the ambulance making its way up to Marshland Common, sirens silenced and light's extinguished. Mum was going to be heartbroken, as much as she was when my dad had written from New Zealand five years ago, whilst on shore leave from the merchant navy. He told her he had got another job and would not be returning home. That was when I was ten years old and she had cried buckets for weeks. I could do nothing but hope she would be alright, but somehow, I knew, she wouldn't be. When you are dead, but not really dead, it seems unfair that those left behind have to suffer what is essentially a lie. I wondered who made that rule or law?

"John?"

"Yes, sorry, I am ready."

"Ok, hold my hand, you have nothing to fear."

"How long will it take for us to get there?"

"No time," Peter smiled.

As we turned away from the road and faced into a small wood, I could see the trees move out of focus and start to divide. They appeared to create the entrance to a leafy tunnel offering a way though from this world and into what was to become. This was familiar to me, having read a number of stories about near death experience. Maybe this tunnel thing was true, but if it wasn't your time to die, nobody met you to guide you, so you came back. I had always thought of the tunnel concept to be a bit twee, but come to think about it, we all travelled through a tunnel when we were born into this world, so it appears we do the same to enter the next.

The tunnel was paved with a golden coloured pathway, which seemed to wind along until it disappeared out of view. Golden light was emanating from it, lighting the way. I felt peaceful, although a little anxious, but the fear which gripped me previously had gone. Hand in hand we walked onto the path and after a few steps into it, I stopped and looked back wanting to leave a message in that world. I was leaving it behind, perhaps never to step into it again. I had to somehow leave a message for Mum that I was alright, so I imagined all that my mum was, her love, holding and kindness. I pictured her in the kitchen and willed my thoughts to connect with her.

"Whoa, whoa. Hang on a minute. You are not going to split, are you?" Peter was looking suddenly anxious, the calm demeanour replaced with concern.

"What do you mean, split? I am not going to run." His manner had wrenched me out of me projecting my thoughts.

"I am going to ask you something strange. Do you have any memory of having died before?"

"That's crazy. No, I've just died, what do you mean?"

"What you were just doing in connecting with your mum, had started the split process, where a part of you, your consciousness, can be projected to another place to observe what someone is doing or to view a place you may wish to see. Your form and it is now light based; remains in the place you are projecting from. Your consciousness, which is projected, can only observe, it cannot interact and you cannot leave a message."

"You mean I can see my mum, before I go with you!"

"If you had died before, you may have unconsciously connected to the process."

My concern now, wasn't whether I had died before, it was to see my mum one last time and make her aware that I was alright and not really dead.

"That will not happen. She will not be able to know you are there."

"Please Peter, let me do this, I won't stay there, I promise."

"You cannot anyway, because the rest of you will be here. I am closing the entrance, don't worry, you can still project from inside. I know you are going to do this anyway and I can bring you back at any time. OK, surrender to where you were before when you were making the connection and focus on that part of your mum that makes her who she is, not what she does, her essence."

I sat down and let my imagination move to where she was, wrapping my mind and heart around all she meant to me. The draw from her, engaged me and I left my body, travelling quickly through the air and above the village. I could see Simon standing on the opposite side of the road, his arms folded. A tear rolled down his cheek as he muttered the words, 'Forgive me lass, I'm just not strong enough. Please don't give up on me, I will come, I promise.' As I sped towards our home, I had no form, I was just me. I had no body, I was just there and then entered our kitchen at home with the familiar smells of laundry and cooking.

After-Shock

Mum was busily tidying the kitchen. She wasn't one of these overzealous cleaning people, she just hated clutter and the order seemed to give her more purpose in her life. Well, she told me to tidy up a lot. The large round kitchen clock showed 6.15 pm and I was aware that this was the first time, since the accident, I had been conscious of time. I was an hour late. The sensation of my presence was like being trapped behind a screen and even though I so desperately wanted her to know I was there; I could do nothing. I tried shouting, well beyond what would be a necessary level and again it turned into one of those nightmare scenarios of the living being left for dead, unable to alert those around them.

"Come on John, you are an hour late, your tea is going to spoil if you don't hurry."

I could detect in her voice she was concerned, as although I could be late at times, I was never this late. As I calmed down, I started to hear what I thought, were her thoughts. Just audible whispers creeping through the silence of her contemplations. She was searching her memory, trying to think of whether I had told her I was staying on at school after practice for something or perhaps visiting a friend on the way home.

Picking up her mobile from the worktop, she hesitated about ringing me because we had had a talk, just recently, last week in fact, about her being too protective towards me. It wasn't really that. My head is always in something and at times, her voice arrives from nowhere, requesting, telling or reminding me of something, when I have more important things to think about. She acknowledged I was growing up, but was struggling with the inevitable increase in my calls for a greater degree of the freedom to choose. She decided to text me instead.

"Have I forgotten you were doing something after practice today xxx?" Her finger tapped out the letters and symbols carefully, punctuated with little cringe thoughts of not wanting me to think she was intruding. These thoughts took me by surprise because she was actually feeling about how I might feel. Not that she was unfeeling, quite the opposite, but it made me sad that I could not have read her thoughts at other times when I needed her to understand how I felt and explain in words to reassure me.

She pressed send.

"I am not going to get that you know." How could she.

As she went into the living room to draw the curtains, both she and I saw a police car draw up in front of the house. In that moment, everything changed. Her heart stepped over the next beat as a Police Constable and Woman Police Constable got out and started to walk up the driveway. The speed and magnitude of her thoughts leapt into my mind as they fought for rationality and settled precariously in denial. I could hear the officers talking.

"I hate this part of our job, especially when there is a child involved."

"Yes, me too, but it is not as though we are doing it for the first time. Remember what we have rehearsed."

I watched them arrive at the front door, the WPC knocking gently. She was half hoping nobody was in. As my mum opened the door, the WPC cleared her throat.

"Mrs Kenton, Mrs Jennifer Kenton?"

"Yes?"

"I am WPC Davis and this is PC Pearson, it's about your son John, may we come in?"

Her memory connected her focus to similar scenes she had seen countless times on the television. I could feel her heart was racing, numbing the reality of not wanting to hear the next line. She told herself that I must have got into some sort of trouble and in the same moment, dismissed it as unlikely. Her whole sense of being was hanging in a nowhere place, senses purposefully dimmed in avoidance, yet highly tuned. She chose to connect to the mundane.

"Would you like some tea?"

Her mind was desperately trying to avoid the impact of the next line. She already knew what it would be and was shrinking under the threat of harm from this next blow. It came like a sledgehammer.

"No thank you, I think we'd better sit down."

It was at this point, I wanted to bounce through the front door, crying hi to my mum and explaining I was late as I had fallen off my bike and had to wheel it home. That I was sorry, my phone was out of battery and couldn't call and I'd give her a cuddle and ask what was for tea. I had no power to stop the proceedings. I could only watch as her life changed in an instant as mine had done before and yet we were both alive.

She led them along the hallway and into the sitting room. She was now in a daze and worrying whether everything was tidy.

"Mrs Kenton, I'm afraid there has been an accident and John has been knocked from his bike. I am sorry Mrs Kenton; John was killed in the accident."

"John dead, but that's not possible, how did it happen?"

She was staring fixedly into the fireplace, avoiding the WPC's expression and not wanting to believe what she had just heard. She came over and knelt beside the armchair in which Mum was sitting and took her hand.

"It happened on Barnsley Road opposite to Lantern Mews. It seems that John fell from his bike and then was knocked down by a lorry. It would have been instant."

Bitterness rose inside her as she searched for someone to blame.

"Have you arrested the driver? He must have seen John before he ran over him, there must have been witnesses, what are you doing about it? It can't be true; you have made a mistake… I… I…" She burst into tears. "No, no, not John, please, he is so precious to me."

Having to face the shock of something you know is true, but on a different level is not, when your hands are tied or your voice silenced, silenced me. I just cried, not for me, but for this desperate drowning woman, who was and is my mother, who I could not hold in her time of need, as she had held me on so many occasions before.

The WPC sat on the arm of the chair and gently pulled Mum towards her. She was sobbing spasmodically and trying to catch her breath between sobs.

"It was nobody's fault Mrs Kenton; it was an accident. The lorry driver came around a bend and John was sitting in the road, he must have been dazed from his fall. Is there someone who can be with you? Do you have a husband or a partner?"

"My husband no longer lives with us, it's just John and I who live here."

She had stopped crying and had fixed her gaze on the flames from the fire again. They somehow numbed the pain and detached her from reality. She watched them as they danced amongst the coals. How short their little lives were. Her tears welled and obscured their detail.

"Where have they taken him?"

"He's been taken to Huddersfield Royal Infirmary; he will be safe there."

I heard the PC cringe at his own words and chastise himself; 'of course he will be safe there, it's not as though he is going anywhere is it, idiot.' Nothing had registered anyway.

"Mrs Kenton, is there anyone who can be with you?" the WPC repeated gently.

"Yes, there is my mother, she lives just around the corner in Beachwood Drive. Her name is Mrs Audrey Harker."

"Will your mother be in?"

"Yes."

"Well Jennifer, is it alright if I call you Jennifer?" she nodded. "Would you think it would be alright if PC Pearson went around and brought your mother back here to be with you?"

"Yes, but be gentle, she is an old lady."

"I will stay here with you until they arrive back."

PC Pearson picked up his helmet and quietly left the room. After the front door shut, mum looked at the WPC and asked her if she had any children of her own. She shook her head and I heard Mum wondering how she could understand how she felt, how anyone could understand?

The minutes dragged. Moments of what seemed like detached peace were separated with tearful interludes as Mum wrestled with the thought of me gone, never to return and the loss of her sense of purpose. In the peace, I was able to see more of who she was. She was kind and loving with a strict edge, supported by principles and values she hoped were the right mixture to provide me with a framework for life. But she was also insightful and creative, qualities that she subdued with caution and a wounded sense of self belief. We were alike in this sense, except mine was a battle, where she had seemed to resign herself to needing to live in an unassuming and repressing way, really afraid of who she might be.

I felt sorry for her because she would probably live out her life in this way, too frightened to stand in the light of her own reflection, whereas I was different because I was now dead. Suddenly the unknown took its purchase in my realisation that I had lost my life and the fear of what I was to become, crushed my hope to a glimmer. I sobbed and Mum sobbed in unison seemingly connected to my grief.

The WPC gently rubbed mum's shoulders and distracted her by asking her about Grandma's mobility, saying they shouldn't be long now. The minutes continued to drag and the clock made its presence heard, creating an echo as it marked the seconds. The knock on the door, pulled us all back from our suspense and reality returned with a vengeance. The WPC went to answer it and took a pitiful look from her colleague. Grandma went into the sitting room, the two police officers remaining in the hall. Although I wanted to hug them both, I was resigned to watch and listen to them suffer.

"Oh lovey…lovey…"

The two of them held each other and wept in mutual consolation. Grandma, I sensed was the stronger of the two. I could hear that she was as upset as Mum, but she reminded herself she was a war child and to remain in control for the sake of others.

"Why did it have to happen, Mum, John was such a good boy, it's not fair, is it me? Have I done something to deserve this, I just cannot believe it is true." She was sobbing deeply again.

"No one knows when the Lord will reclaim his little children Jenny, it's nobody's fault and you cannot blame yourself. He will be well looked after. Dad will be there to take care of him."

Mum sat down and cried hauntingly, not just out of loss, but also with the frustration of her mother's belief which always attempted to make everything alright and purposeful. Grandma went back out into the hall to where the two police officers were waiting.

"Thank you for your help, I will be able to manage from here onwards. It has been a cruel blow for both of us and we will just have to put things back together a little at a time."

PC Pearson told her, there were people, counsellors who can help in situations like this and that he had left a card on the hallway table. She thanked him.

"Right, we better be on our way and we are so sorry we have had to be the bearers of such sad news," finalised PC Pearson.

She shut the door behind them and leant against it to steady herself.

"God, please be merciful with his soul and Tom, I know you are listening, look after John for us, I love you and miss you my darling."

As she closed her eyes she imagined Grandfather and I standing hand in hand in a beautiful meadow. I had never known her true beliefs, but it seemed she was firm in them. As I watched from behind her in the hallway, she turned slowly and I knew she was sensing something. As she turned her head, I gently called her name. She shivered, drew the heavy front door curtain and returned to the sitting room. The feeling of being cocooned and grief stricken was becoming unbearable as no message could be heard. There was a tension in the link and I could hear Peter's voice calling me. Focussing on Peter, I surrendered back into myself.

Over and Through

Peter was gentle in his opening line as I arrived back. He had kept a watchful eye on me as I had directly experienced the helplessness and horror of another in the reality of their grief and wrenching loss.

"You don't have to speak if you don't want to. Feeling powerless to affect any difference gnaws at the very fabric of the soul and creates an emptiness that only time can help replenish again. Therefore, take yours."

I was in that emptiness and numbed beyond tears. I sat motionless in this spirit's presence trying to make sense of the need for such a tortuous infliction when in my reality, I was still alive. The event seemed to deconstruct security for those left behind. The lie with its permanent intent, alters the course of the lives of those involved, changing viewpoints and tainting future emotional expression. My sense of truth was suspended in nothingness. Confusion now altering it by my perspective verses that of my mother's. Above all, it was the powerlessness and desperate frustration in knowing I could not change the impression which was causing so much anguish and pain, for everyone caught by it, including me. Within the emotional cauldron, my anger rose to the surface.

"You are a mind reader, so you know how I feel, but I feel like people on Earth are being deceived. They have to go through all of that grief, when it's not true. I could hear the thoughts and feelings of my mum and grandma and they were all about loss, sadness, despair and helplessness."

"It's not deception, it's the way it is for good reason and at this time is not fair for me to provide any answers. You must trust and be patient. I am impressed though, that you can split and hear their thoughts. There are not many newly passed spirits who are able to do that."

"You sound like my mum with your patience. I can't hear your thoughts though."

"No, I know. Spirit, which is what we are now, communicates on a channel you are not used to. On Earth, you will have been trying to think about what others are thinking from a very young age, but you remain unsure. With awareness and when released from the body into spirit, you are free to listen once you know how. I am blocking my thoughts because the journey we are about to make is best done with an open and unassuming mind. Come on, let me help you to get up."

The touch of his hand soothed to a degree, then he gently touched a spot just above and between my eyes with his middle finger. I sensed colour, like indigo travelling through me to my feet and with it a feeling of being washed through or cleansed, lifting some of my trauma and making my mind clearer. I asked him what he had done.

"Insight. I have just helped you to balance your perception of what is happening, that's all. How do you feel now?"

We started to walk along the pathway and away from my world.

"I am not really sure what I am feeling, it's all mixed up. I know I am safe with you and that I will be alright, which is something I cannot explain. But, if I am dead, albeit in a living sort of way, why did I have to die? You were here to meet me, so you must have known I was going to die. And it's left me wondering if I will ever go back there again?"

Peter was silent for a moment and during the silence, I looked around. The walls of the tunnel were no longer trees. They were still green in colour, but it was like being inside a wave tube without the walls being water. They were more like smoke or mist with green and white light shining through them. The pathway had disappeared being replaced by the same substance as the walls and yet it felt I was walking on solid ground. I was sure I could smell the ocean, but wasn't sure if I was imagining links to what I was seeing. The lights in the walls were constantly moving forward, creating intricate patterns which appeared to be motioning us along the route. In some way, it was like being in a giant kaleidoscope, beautiful and like nothing I had ever seen on Earth. When Peter answered, it made me jump.

"Some things, John are…um…predestined. Do you understand what I mean?"

"No."

"Well, it means that sometimes, things that happen to you are part of a larger picture in your life's journey, as if you are following a plan that has already been written. However, there are occasions when certain actions don't seem to make sense and seem to go against what may have been planned or expected by yourself."

"So, was I meant to die?"

"Yes."

"But why?"

"Why and whether you will return or not is a matter for you and the greater power to decide."

"What power?"

"Some call it God, others Allah, Jehovah, Elohim, Yahweh, The Divine or The Collective. There are many names, all meaning essentially the same thing."

"Oh my…!"

The thought of God linked to judgement, had somehow slipped my mind. My first thought was about what Clara had said, then I trawled my life for negatives and panicked. How could I have been more concerned with what was happening around me, when I should have been devoting my entire energies to prepare myself to meet God. Trivial, selfish and cruel acts materialised in my mind's eye and their collective potency weighed heavily on my conscience. I suddenly felt very small and very conspicuous, a bit like staring up at the universe on a clear night with the feeling that you are incredibly insignificant, yet are being watched. Peter squeezed my hand hard.

"Your thoughts relate to experiences you have had growing up on the Earth plane, which are all party to making you who you are now. You have nothing to fear."

"But when am I judged?"

"When you are ready and what's more you will know who judges you, if it comes to that, which I doubt? How would you even know if you had been judged already? In the state of all these confusing feelings you are experiencing now, did you find anything condemning in your search?"

"I can't tell, it cannot be that simple but I have caused that lorry driver and my mum and grandma a lot of pain."

"It was an accident John. Now calm, you will be fine."

As I looked up, white light cascaded towards us from the end of the tunnel. So bright and yet it didn't hurt my eyes. Bright light was another thing that had been reported in near death experiences and is synonymous with 'heaven'. I felt that we all look for comparisons when experiencing new things. There seems to be an instinctual need to anchor them into our realities, so we compare them to past experiences to make sense of them. It occurred to me that I may be building my own experience based on my knowledge and expectations and that someone else's journey over may be totally different. After all, familiarity breeds comfort and security but dying and going into heaven wasn't something you did regularly. *Quite rightly*, I thought, I was starting to feel anxious again. Thoughts with feelings had always confused me and thinking I was feeling something, seemed more logical than feeling I was feeling something. Intercepting emotions with thought somehow made them easier to deal with or avoid. Peter caught my attention, shaking his head and smiling at me.

"What?"

"Your mind is constantly in reason. Do you ever just experience and feel things?"

"Yes, but only after I have thought about them, you know, why they are happening or why I should be experiencing them."

"What do you think you are afraid of?"

"I don't know."

I let go of his hand to wrestle with my bravery on my own and refocussed my attention towards the light. It was like looking into a shower of splintered blue and white diamonds which seemed to penetrate but not harm me. Still feeling solid and experiencing this was interesting not alarming, as their affect was like taking short but rapid inhalations through your nose on a frosty morning. Almost like they were refreshing. Then, every sense was stimulated simultaneously, a little like the feeling I had experienced riding down 'Unwind Hill', just before the accident. Except this feeling was a thousand times more powerful. Elation, joy, love, wellbeing and total oneness, were all feelings inadequate enough to express what I could only describe as the feelings you would expect to think you would feel at the entrance to heaven. Was this real though, if real was possible when you are dead, or am I imagining all of this from a coma? I was probably trying to make sense of damaged neurons firing randomly from within this dream whilst in my unconsciousness.

"Master Kenton, it's not often you get the chance to experience this, unless you do a job like mine. So, enjoy the experience as the tempo and waves connect with your very essence."

"You are a mind reader!"

"Yes, of course I am. No questions, just breathe it in."

As we walked on, the end of the tunnel grew in size and I stopped as we reached the lip. The sight that met my eyes was simply beautiful. We were in a meadow looking down a gently sloping hillside towards the bottom of a small valley. The views were breath taking, with undulating hills, dotted with poplar trees, rolling beyond the valley top as far as the eye could see. The sky, a radiant blue, in a shade I had never seen before, was scattered with wispy tuffs of brilliant white clouds. Everywhere was lush and green.

Grasses softly whispered, their ears competing with each other to nod in time to the gentle breath of the sweetly scented breeze. Flowers shone in a fabulous display of phosphorescent colours, the subjects of dreams, rather than experience. Butterflies and bees floated and hummed their way from flower to flower in an orchestrated dance collecting their nectar. As they took flight to visit their next host, a shower of luminescent dust followed, caught by the sunlight as it was lifted and dispersed in the air.

My feelings were of peace, serenity and safety. All of my previous worry lifted to a manageable spike, somehow changing my density and yet my feet remained on the ground. Memories of Sunday school teachings flowed into focus as I wondered if this must be like Eden.

"Not quite," Peter interrupted, "but it is beautiful isn't it? Come on, take your first step."

The thoughts of Neil Armstrong arrived as I was about to step onto the grass, then of the thought of being born into a new life, having travelled along a daunting passage between worlds. The grass was soft beneath my feet and remembering to breathe, I took in a lungful of the sweet, warm air.

"I cannot describe this place to an extent that justice would be done. It is beyond perfect beauty."

"Nicely put!"

I was left wondering where these words and some of the descriptions I had been using, had come from. Then the questions came all at once without me being able to separate or vocalise them. "I…um…where does…how come?"

"Later John, you have plenty of time to ponder and question. Look towards the bottom of the valley."

As I lowered my gaze, I saw a group of people leaning on a gate on the far bank of a stream which ran along the bottom of the valley. Although I could not make out their faces, a tall man in the centre of the group was waving at us.

"Who are they?"

"They are members of your family and friends who have passed into the after world before you and who now live here."

Yet another near-death experience. The thought sliced into my perceptions. Could this be the moment I would be pulled back into physical life? Would it be my choice that sealed my fate? I was reassured by the small voice inside my head. 'It's OK, we are dead.'

I was off, sprinting down the hill as fast as I could run. I knew exactly who the tall man was.

"Grandfather! Grandfather, it's me, John!"

As I got to the bottom of the hill, Peter was waiting with the group. My grandfather opened the gate, another near death experience, and clearing the last few stepping-stones, I threw myself into his arms and hugged him as tightly as I could.

"I missed you, I missed you so much." Tears were rolling down my cheeks as I fought for my words, expecting to be dragged back at any moment.

"I thought you were dead?"

Grandfather let go one of his familiar chortles and hugged me close.

"Of course, I'm not. My old body just got worn out, that's all and I had to come and live over here. Look at you; you have grown so much in the past two years and into a fine young man. We are all very proud of you and love you very much. In a way, I am sad that you are here, but I have missed you too and have watched you grow since my passing. You are a credit to us all."

"I love you too, Grandfather, Tom."

I was aware of the other members of the group who were standing around us, smiles across each of their faces.

"I have so many questions, I don't know where to begin?"

"I know John, but keep them a while longer, you have plenty of time to ask them, let me introduce you to everyone."

Before he did, he turned to Peter.

"Thank you for bringing him across safely Peter."

"You are welcome Tom, all part of the job. He has had a bit of a rough ride, but seems to be someone who will settle here quickly, if he can learn to take things in his stride a bit more."

He and Grandfather appeared to hold each other's gaze for a short while, followed by a nod, before my grandfather turned to face me.

"You chose to see your mum before you left."

"Yes." I could not help my chin dropping to hide my feelings. He placed his arm around my shoulders.

"That was a tough call, are you alright?"

"Just hurting, that's all. It's a bit of a shock this dying stuff, I'll be OK."

I looked up and shook off the feelings gripping me. The others in the group consisted of two women, one of middle years, the other older and a young man, I thought to be about twenty. Not immediately recognising either of the women, I did think that one was familiar. However, there was something about the man that seemed to resonate with more familiarity, especially more so when he spoke.

"John, let me firstly introduce you to Hazel, she is your great-grandma and my mum."

She did not look old enough to be who she was. She was a kind faced old lady who smelled of what old ladies usually smell of, lilies I thought and weren't lilies a flower of death? I moved towards her and kissed her on the cheek.

"Pleased to meet you great-grandma," my politeness authentically engaged.

"Lovely to meet you, young sir and please call me Hazel if you wish."

"And this is your grandma, Edith, you won't know her, but –"

"You are Dad's mum, aren't you? I recognise you now from the photographs we keep at home. You died before I was born, I think?"

"Yes, that's right. Thank you, it is nice to be remembered. I see you share the looks of your father as well as his sense for adventure. I am sorry he had to go away. Sometimes people do make choices that are regretful, especially when they hurt their loved ones in doing so."

"I don't really know why Dad decided to stay away, but it does not stop me from loving him and I do miss him."

"You are a good boy John and I think your father could learn some things from you!" She hugged me closely and it felt like I was feeling her sincerity.

"Finally, this is Tony."

"I know you from somewhere, don't I?"

Tony grinned widely, and shook my hand.

"Yes, probably as much as I know you. How's the Ducati?"

As soon as he spoke, I felt the hair on the back of my neck to stand on end. How did he know about the motorbike, it was one of my personal fantasy's I had shared with no one?

"How do you know about that?" My curiosity sparked, yet knowing I knew I could trust this man completely, because in some way I knew him.

36

"John?" Grandfather interrupted. "Tony is what's known as a guide. He has been with you for about five Earth plane years. This means, that over those years, you have been sharing thoughts and ideas with him. Although you may not have known it, Tony has been there in your thoughts when you have been alone and had no one else to talk to. I have been a guide and companion to you too at times. I know it is difficult for you to understand, so don't try too hard, all will become clearer."

I was fascinated and turned back to Tony. "I misjudged the bank on the bend."

"Err, slightly!"

"The bike is pretty smashed up, sorry Grandfather, but do they have them over here, Tony?"

"Wait and see," he replied.

"By the way, how long have you been over here and how did you…um –?"

"I have been here for about twelve years and put it this way, I was riding a Kawasaki…too fast!" I knew the rest but was confused by the apparent ages and time references.

As I looked up and around, I could see a golden green light emanating from each of the members of the group. It seemed to create a complete ring around me.

"What's that, Grandfather?"

He smiled and said, "Love John, love. Emotions have colour over here, as does music, you'll see, but it is time to go, we must take you to hospital."

"Hospital! but why? I am not hurt or anything?"

"No not physically, but you have just gone through a very traumatic experience. You must rest your mind and acclimatise to this world. Don't worry, it is not hospital as you know it, it's more a place of adjustment."

"Did you go when you first came?"

"Yes, but only for a short while, because I knew I was coming and I was ready to come."

"What! You mean you knew you were going to die, but why didn't you tell me?"

"Only your grandma knew. No one knows exactly when they will pass until the moment arrives and there was no point in upsetting you beforehand."

"I understand… I think?"

In that moment I became aware of the behaviour of the tribe. I realised that when you meet parents or relatives, they tend not to see the real you. I had projected a less aware image, without strong opinion and one who responded easily to love and affection to generate reciprocal feelings and protection from the elders. I did this to feel part of the group. I did this because, frankly, this was another of the growing list of really weird experiences I had encountered so far in my death. Because of these, I was finding it difficult to imagine that this whole series of events was nothing more than my imagination. Apart from the Leaves, occurrences fitted with my knowledge of near death and I couldn't anchor in any form of reality. I was nowhere near panic, thankfully, but I still had my doubts that I could be dreaming all of this. I decided to roll with it. My grandfather appeared to search my face for a moment before speaking.

"It's been two years since you and I have talked. We have much catching up to do. I know it all seems strange, it did to me when I came over and acceptance takes a little time to engage fully. Right then John, we'd better be on our way, thanks again Peter."

"Thank you for making it easier for me Peter?" I said.

"You are welcome and take care my young friend. Try feeling before you think, you will learn more about who you really are." He shook my hand, turned away and vanished.

"We must be going as well. Lovely to meet you at last and we will see you soon." Both Edith and Hazel kissed me on the cheek and also disappeared.

"How do they do that?" It was Tony who answered.

"You see, you don't have to walk over here if you don't want to, you will learn how to do it soon enough. Right, I am off too, I'll come and see you shortly. Bye Tom, bye John."

He waved and disappeared. I was searching for the lost words.

"Do you remember reading Jonathon Livingston Seagull and how he used to travel?"

"Yes, I remember, you mean you think where you want to be and you are there."

"That's it, but there are a few rules. Take my hand John, we must leave now."

I held my breath expecting to vanish down some worm hole, or take a weird elevator ride. Without pause, we had arrived.

Recovery

We rematerialised on a lawn beneath a chestnut tree. It wasn't a journey we had just undertaken, it was instantaneous, like blinking and being somewhere else. In front of us stood a large white manor house, which was set in its own grounds and surrounded by well-kept lawns and flowerbeds. Beyond these were green fields, then rolling countryside, similar to before. Perhaps heaven was just one big field, as there did not seem to be other buildings near to us. Within the grounds and in the fields, were many trees some of which I had not seen before. The gardens stretched beyond the house down to a lake, which reflected beautiful gold, green and blue light as the sun shone upon its surface. There were children playing happily by the water's edge, chasing each other around and making lots of noise. The scene was surreal, however, gave me the impression that things were happy and peaceful here at the same time as being strange. A lady in a blue dress walked from the entrance doors to meet us.

"Hello Tom, how are things?"

"Fine Catherine, let me introduce you to my grandson, John. John this is Catherine, the lady who looks after many of the children here. She is a bit like the old-fashioned ward sisters we used to have on Earth."

"But not so stern! Hello John, nice to meet you."

"Hello…um…?"

"Call me Catherine, we are all on first name terms here, we have your room all ready and waiting."

"Hello Catherine, nice to meet you and thank you."

I squeezed Grandfather's hand in an attempt to say I wasn't sure about this.

"You have nothing to worry about little mate, you will find everyone very friendly and kind and you will not have to spend long here before you are back with us."

"How long will I be here, Catherine?"

"A few Earth days, I think, but it's up to you. You will only stay longer if you need to, but I think that is unlikely. You can have visitors during your stay as well, if you wish."

"I think you will enjoy it here John, I know I did when I came over to stay in the adult part. There are lots of people to answer your questions and lots of children to play with, who like you, have just arrived."

"When will you come to see me?"

"Remember John, I am only a thought away."

I held onto Grandfather's hand on the way up to the house. It wasn't that I wanted him to think I was still a child, but this was all new and I was fighting with loyalty and trust. By the time we had reached the entrance, I felt a bit better. Everything had moved so quickly and there was much I didn't understand. My senses had somehow altered, they were sharper, my mind reacting to the source of their affect much more quickly than they had done on Earth and the content of their information had greater depth.

"That's partly why you are here and I know, this is what you need right now."

"What is?"

"To learn to trust in a whole new way. See you soon."

"So, you are a mind reader as well?"

He smiled, winked and gave me a hug before he vanished.

"Come on, John, let me show you around," said Catherine.

She led me through a reception hallway, capped with a high ceiling and ordained with ornate plasterwork. A staircase swept up in a clockwise direction with a number of children scattered amongst its flight, chatting or reading. Entering a large light and airy room, the furnishings, included comfortable looking sofas and armchairs, some occupied by small groups of children speaking with adults. There were tables at which various activities were taking place, like drawing and painting. Walls were covered by pictures and collages and everywhere I looked, there were flowers. I was disappointed, as I could see no devices, phones or electronic games.

"We don't need them over here."

"You can hear me too?"

"Yes, we can all hear, some more clearly than others."

"Even over distances?"

"Even across dimensions, which you will learn about in time."

"Time travel?"

"No."

"That's a shame."

Catherine smiled at me and told me I would also be able to read into other spirit's minds, after I had become accustomed and receptive to the difference in the speed of thought and to filtering out other noise to focus specifically. I told her about splitting and hearing my mum and grandma's thoughts, so I hoped I would be able to pick it up quickly. She scrutinised my face in an instant before assuming her smile. I knew she was searching for something. I was searching for a similar affirmation to that of Peters', but it didn't come. I felt guilty in the realisation of my need to impress. Well I didn't, it was that annoying little voice again, who had somehow made it here with me. Catherine laughed.

"What?"

"You are going to like living over here, your mind will especially."

"There is a big part of me that's still living back there," I said remorsefully.

"I know. That's why you are here with us now, just be true to yourself and go with the flow."

A corridor led off from the main room to the bedrooms or rest rooms. The change of light from daylight outside to the main room and this corridor had intrigued me, as it was purplish in colour.

"It is violet light you can see. Quite simply, violet light is used as an aid to healing spiritual and emotional distress or upsets. Different colours of light, have different healing properties. As you become more accustomed to spiritual light you will be able to choose to see and recognise light emanation from different sources. Day light comes from the sun."

"What, our sun, the Earth's sun?"

"Yes, of course, I gather you walked over to our world here and you didn't catch a star ship which travelled at warp speed accelerating you to light years from Denby Dale?"

I liked quick humour and risked my response.

"We surfed in on a tube actually."

"Well, we'll make sure we put another shrimp on the bar-bee for you this evening then!"

We both laughed. I liked Catherine already, she was smart and funny.

"Another source of light comes from people. What you see in the light that surrounds us reflects our state of being, whether it is sourced from emotion, thought, intention or spiritual wisdom. Light is both potential and kinetic reflection in the spirit world and it is one of the many ways we can communicate. We call the light process 'reflecation', which is a combination of reflection and emanation. It sounds complicated, but reading it is easy to pick up if you choose to live with it."

"I understand potential and kinetic energy from physics at school. I think of it as 'can do and is doing'."

"Yes, pretty much."

"But reflecation? I am not quite sure," I questioned, my brow lowering.

"Well, on the Earth, colours are seen by the light which is reflected from them, for example grass is green. Light also emanates from different sources. But in Earthly terms, we may reflect colour, but as dwellers on Earth, we are not known as sources of light. In the spirit world, because we are light, we are both a source and a reflection of colour and light."

I rubbed my hands together and struggled with the concept of matter and light as I thought I was feeling flesh and bone. Surely if I was light, one hand would pass through the other. Catherine was smiling to herself.

"I know what you are thinking, and you can feel yourself because we instinctually imagine we are solid matter. On the Earth plane, we are spirit in matter and our senses are attuned to that world. It takes a little time to become accustomed to what new senses are available here."

"You speak of the Earth plane and the spirit world –"

"Hold your horses, John, I am not going to blow your mind, by providing you with an explanation of the existence, relationship and communication between worlds and their locations in relation to each other. Being straight with you, you need to ride a Shetland to start with, small steps. There is plenty of time to learn to ride thoroughbreds."

"I prefer motorbikes myself."

"So, I have heard and um…I notice you are here. A perfect example of my point in question!"

"When will I be able to read your mind, you have an advantage?"

"On your pony, Mr Wayne."

"You're funny!"

"Thank you." Catherine smiled warmly and the infectiousness sealed the bond.

My room, was simply furnished with a bed, a sofa, full-length mirror on one wall and two vases filled with flowers. The back wall had glass doors, which opened out into the garden which led down to the lake. Again, the light filling the room was of the same violet light that filled the main room. I was told that flowers also had healing properties, which was why there were so many around the building. We sat on the sofa and Catherine told me of some of the things to expect during my stay. I was to have a helper who would be working with me.

"When will my bags be brought up?" I asked, keeping my face as straight as I could.

"I suppose you will want room service as well? Good John, I am glad you can use your sense of humour, it's really important for everyone including yourself."

"There is another important thing, your helper's name is Monique and she doesn't speak a word of English. How good is your French?"

"Not very good. I have been learning it at school, but it isn't one of my favourite subjects."

A young woman of about 20, walked into the room.

"Ah! Monique, this is John."

"Bonjour Mademoiselle Monique."

I was hoping she wasn't going to reply with a complicated phrase. However, as I was anticipating her response, it felt like I was remembering my lessons and the meanings of words.

"Bonjour John, vous parle Francais, bonne. Comment alez vous?"

"I only speak a little and I am fine, thank you. Wait a minute, I can understand you, it's as though you are speaking French, but I am hearing English!"

Both of them were smiling at each other and Catherine was chuckling away to herself.

"Lesson one John, there are no language barriers over here. It does not matter what country a person comes from and what language they speak; you will always be able to understand them."

"Wow, that would have been handy at school!"

"There are a lot of things you will discover over here which would have been useful on Earth and for some people, listening is one of them. Anyway, I will see you both a bit later as I have some things to do."

"See you later, Catherine, thank you," I said.

"Catherine, can I just have a quick word?" Monique gestured. As the two of them chatted just outside the doorway, I had an opportunity to think. How could I prove I was in a coma or not? I knew I had an active imagination, but how could

I be thinking up all of these people and the experiences also. Perhaps I was still in the process of dying? I had heard of research, demonstrating that brain activity carried on for up to ten minutes after the heart had stopped beating. So, all this could be due to electrical discharges and an endorphin overload, as my brain was shutting down. There again, I am in a hospital of sorts, so I may be experiencing some sort of psychotic episode as a result of the accident. Monique came and sat beside me.

"*Je sais que tu es mort.*"

"How do you know I am dead? You could just be a part of this elaborate delusion that I cannot seem to wake up from?"

"Let go John. You have been fighting yourself all of your life."

"And if I let go, what will happen? Will I die and cease to exist in reality? It could be my imagination that is keeping me alive; going with the flow is not something I do well?"

"If it is any comfort, it took me a couple of months to accept that I had passed. I was afraid too. When I was a young girl, I heard a story about a very old coffin exhumed from a crypt, which had scratches on the inside of its lid. I imagined that I was somewhere I was not able to get out of, where nobody could hear me and my mind had sent me into this dream to sooth my distress."

"That's a nasty one."

"Fear protects us, but our fears are exaggerated until we are able to face them and understand the reality of the truth behind them. Very few expect the reality we are in now and you have just been wrenched from your body's death, with one of the strongest of instincts still intact, which is fear and you are clinging to life as you have known it."

"I have never found acceptance to be easy. It feels like I am cheating and betraying myself for the sake of some programmed status quo."

"Then you need to continue to wrestle with trust and acceptance until you find the fear. Wrestle gently John and seek others to spar with, who can teach you their truth."

I wondered why Monique's character was emerging from my memories within the psychosis.

"Could you be thinking of Grace Darling, John?"

"You mean the saviour of sailors?"

"I mean a guardian of those presently lost at sea."

"Like me, you mean? Is it alright if we draw a line Monique?" I was consciously trying to believe I was existing in two worlds at the same time, which was hard work.

"Yes, good idea and don't worry, the line is not like going with the flow. It is more like sitting on the bank watching the movement, because you don't feel safe enough to be part of it yet. Something I feel you know well."

In that moment, I was kind of pleased she had seen that part of me, even though it was a part I didn't trust.

"First things first, are you happy with your room?"

"Yes, it's really nice, but why do I need a bed? Do you sleep over here?"

"Not if you don't want to."

Monique explained that in the home, they furnish the rooms to create familiarity and security. By creating familiar environments, people are eased into the spiritual existence and most, whilst living here, surround themselves with things they would have had on Earth. Sleep to the physical body was necessary for rest and to refresh, but spiritual light does not tire. If a person wishes to go to bed for a rest, it is usually because they are used to that routine and choose to maintain it.

"Come on, I think the first thing we will do, is to join one of the working groups. These are made up of children who have recently come over and they work with adult counsellors who help them."

"What are counsellors?"

"They are people who will offer you guidance on what to expect in the spirit world and how you have come here from Earth. They will also be able to answer many of the questions you may have."

We joined a small group of children and their counsellors who were in the midst of a discussion about how they had passed over. Locating a couple of comfy armchairs, we sat and listened to a little girl who was talking about how she had been ill with leukaemia and had known she was going to die. As the time drew closer she said that she was no longer frightened because she knew she was going to be alright. She felt her parents were more worried and upset than she was.

One of the counsellors replied to her saying that sometimes the person who is dying accepts what is happening and in so doing, opens channels between themselves and the spirit world. Love and feelings of well-being comes through this channel to the person, reducing the feelings of anxiety. Rebecca, the little girl, said she felt as though someone was with her, who would occasionally touch her hand or stroke her cheek. She wasn't scared because she felt she had known this person and they were familiar. Her parents seemed to be more upset as time went by and they almost became angry with her because they felt she was giving in and accepting death.

"When the spirit lady came to fetch me, I knew I was ready to die and I had had enough of fighting anyway, but it was the look in my mum and dad's eyes when I was slipping away from them that I will always remember. I wanted to stay for them, but I just couldn't because my body was so weak and could not hold me there any longer." She looked down and started to cry.

"I miss my mum and dad. I hope they will be alright."

This reconnected me with my feelings and a tear rolled down my cheek. Weirdly, I could see the colour of light changing inside the circle. Each counsellor was creating blue, orange and yellow light which was directed towards Rebecca, who seemed to recover gradually from her distress. One of the counsellors, an older lady, with kind eyes and round cheeks, knelt beside her and placed her arm around her shoulders.

"Rebecca, I think you know it will take time for your mum and dad to not be sad and they will never get over losing you until they see you again. Even for you, who knew you were about to die, it is so difficult to say to those you leave behind that they shouldn't worry. How do you feel about coming over?"

"Sad and happy, at the same time. Sad that I am not with them and I will not see them again for a long time, and happy I am here, because it seems such a beautiful place and the people are so kind."

"You may see them, after you have been here for a little while. You can go with someone to visit them, but they will not be sure you are there." Rebecca started crying again.

"Don't worry, it is early days yet and there are people to look after you. You just cry when you want to."

Another boy, Aspen, had jumped from a window whilst escaping from a fire in his family's home. He said he had been burned and could feel the pain from the burns yet, he felt nothing when he had left his body, the pain had gone and why was this? Monique answered by saying that the physical body; nerves, bones and flesh, is designed to live in the physical world of the Earth plane. Our senses help us to feel our way through life and all five are physically related. By separating from our physical body, we separate at the same time from our physical senses and they become spirit senses, which operate in different ways. The reason we feel pain through the physical body is to act as a warning to avoid or limit physical damage. It is also present to slow us down so our bodies can heal faster.

"How are you now, Aspen?"

"Unless you have been in a fire, you don't know what it is like. The fire is like a hungry wild animal, whose sole purpose is to hunt and kill you. When we, me and my little brother, were trapped in the upstairs bedroom, I could see it eating through the door and I had nothing to fight it with and the smoke was filling the room. I had to smash the window because I couldn't find the keys to the locks and when I had smashed it, the flames were in the room in seconds. I was holding Dougie, my little brother, close to me and I wasn't sure whether he had passed out or was dead. I just knew I had to try and get out. There were people on the ground below shouting at me to throw Dougie down and jump. The flames were burning the backs of my legs and my hair and the pain was just so bad."

"OK Aspen, take your time."

"I couldn't throw him and I just couldn't think clearly anymore. I pulled this box to the window, the clothes on my back were on fire and I was so frightened, and I stood on the box, put my foot on the window frame and jumped, taking Dougie with me. Next thing I knew, I was standing just outside the group of people, looking at myself lying on the ground, my neck twisted oddly. Dougie was still alive but in a bad way. I so wanted to help him but I couldn't and then the catcher came and calmed me down and brought me over."

"How old is Dougie?" asked Monique.

"He is three, or was three, I don't know if he is dead or alive."

I watched Aspen intently whilst he spoke. I had experienced the change in pain like him, but I was glad I hadn't had to suffer being eaten by the fire. I could also relate to the powerlessness he felt in not being able to help his little brother after he had died.

"You did all you could Aspen and it looks like you may have saved Dougie."

Whilst this was going on, a side door to the main room had opened and a young man had approached one of the counsellors. As soon as he had spoken, each counsellor, including Monique looked up and acknowledged each other. The young man then left the room.

"We think you have been very brave. What happened to you was so awful and so distressing and you could have done nothing more to change things. Now Aspen, I want you to look at me because I need you to be even more brave."

At that point the side door opened again and the same young man came in, only this time he was holding the hand of a small boy, who looked lost and sad.

"Aspen!" the little boy shouted.

Aspen's face lit up in surprise. In that moment, I wasn't sure if he was pleased to see his little brother or sad that he had also died. Aspen ran across the room and picked Dougie up into his arms. They hugged each other and cried.

"Dougie, what happened to you, I wasn't sure if you were alright or what?"

"I couldn't breathe, I don't member what happened. I woke up in a room with nee-naw people in it and a kind and pretty lady held my hand. I was watching a boy who looked like me, he was lying on a bed and the grown-ups were pushing his chest and blowing in his mouth and then they stopped and everyone told the time? Aspen! I've been in a big tunnel and some grown-ups met me when I came out, they said they would look after me, but I don't want them to, I want you to."

"I will look after you Dougie."

"Did you see Mum and Dad?"

Dougie's face dropped and he looked down to the floor.

"They didn't speak to me, they were watching the boy and I called them, but they didn't hear me. Mum was really crying and calling for me to wake up, 'wake up Dougie' but she was looking at the boy. I said I'm awake, I'm here and I shouted and shouted, but they just didn't look at me and the lady picked me up and said we must go. I didn't want to go, I wanted to stay with Mummy and Daddy, but the lady said we must go and find you and I knew I must go with her. Mummy always said don't go with strangers, but the lady wasn't strange, she was kind."

"Do you know where you are now Dougie?"

"No."

"This is heaven Dougie, you and me are in heaven."

Dougie thought hard and looked up into his elder brother's eyes. "When can we see the angels?"

Aspen held him tight, tears falling down his cheeks. "I love you."

"I love you too Aspen…can we see the angels now?"

"Soon, little brother, soon."

There wasn't a dry eye in the room. One of the counsellors walked over and whispered in Aspen's ear and he and Dougie left the room. As he turned before going through the door, I put my thumb up and he smiled and nodded.

"Now John, what happened to you?"

I thought what had just happened was a hard act to follow, so I swallowed and said:

"I fell off my bike and a lorry ran me over."

"Do you want to expand on that?"

I told my story, including details of how I felt, the bike ride, the catcher in the window and Clara and Simon. I chose to leave out how I had split, because I knew that it would be too emotional to re-experience in a group of strangers. The other children seemed disturbed at the mention of Clara and Simon, but I said there was a difference between them and I would like to help Simon if I could!

"What do you mean by a difference?" asked Monique.

"Clara lied. She wanted to take me with her and blamed me for ruining the lorry driver's life because I had caused the accident. Simon was concerned about me, talked about coming here and protected Peter and me when Clara was about to attack us."

The counsellors seemed to be of the opinion I would have to undergo some training before I attempted to do what they called 'rescue work'. Low flyers like Simon, they said, could be dangerous because they feed on negative energy and can create some pretty frightening feelings in the person attempting to help them. I knew for some reason, he wasn't like that and he genuinely wanted to come over, but he was just scared. On the subject of feelings, I had more I wanted to say about pain.

"I still felt pain when I left my body."

"What sort of pain?" asked Monique.

"Like I was very sad I had died and I felt sorry for my mum because she would be upset about what had happened."

"There is a difference here because you were feeling emotional pain as opposed to physical pain."

"But it still felt as though my stomach was knotted up and my chest hurt."

Some of the children were agreeing with me and I felt proud I had made a good point.

"OK John, this is a good example. The feeling you are experiencing now is one of slight elation? Where you feel your heartbeat increase, giving you pleasure and a sense of pride?"

"Yes," I confirmed sheepishly.

"Well, those feelings are emotions and you experience emotions from a very young age because they are a form of communication to others. You become accustomed to the physical feelings associated with each emotion because these can help you to recognise what you are feeling. For example, if you have a knotted stomach, it could be that you are worried, angry or scared and by recognising the physical symptom, you learn to understand what may be happening to you. In the spirit world, we still get those feelings even though we do not have physical bodies. This is probably because we are genetically programmed to associate emotions with physical characteristics, even though we may not be aware of the link between them."

One of the girls in the group then asked Monique, how she knew what John was feeling just then?

"Well Hillary, firstly, because I have experienced the same feelings of elation myself, when other people have agreed with what I have just said and I have felt good about it. Secondly, I can read John's body language and the different energy he is giving off. Energy changes are detectable in an energy field that surrounds a person, this is called an aura."

"Excuse me," a boy, wearing a football shirt who had remained quiet during their learning session suddenly spoke.

"Yes, Jason."

"Emotions with physical characteristics and aura energy fields! I am ten years old and I know nothing of this stuff, I played football, gamed and back chatted my mum, and yet I understand you, how come?"

"And you are smart, nice one Jason," said Monique.

I could see from the reaction of the other kids, they agreed with Jason and that this discussion was on a level of grown-up talk.

"We have what's called a facilitator in the room and he is here to enable you to learn and understand at levels which are currently beyond what you have understood during your Earth development."

"What is a facilitator?" I asked as I was half expecting a computer type box with flashing lights and then, the wizard in my Oz dream arrived.

Facilitation and Colour

"I am a facilitator." The wizard, a tall dark-haired man in a multi-coloured robe rose from an area encased by books, just adjacent to the main room. As soon as he had spoken, I felt a tingling sensation rise through my body which made my eyes water. Looking directly at me he said,

"I feel we have a sensitive in the room, good to have you amongst us young master."

He then spoke into my mind without moving his lips. "And, Dorothy, this is neither Australia, nor an illusion. Believe it or not, you are in fact already back home in Kansas. All journeys end up here. Although some may see me as a sort of wizard, there is no magic here, other than that we create from knowing ourselves."

I felt immediately embarrassed and confused. At the same time, I also felt I had been recognised for something I had suspected about myself for some time, that I was somehow different from others. Not that I was better of course, but because I felt afraid of that difference and also, alone in it.

"Slow down John. Do you know why you are lonely and afraid?" said the man, reading and speaking back into my mind.

No, not the reason behind it! I thought.

The facilitator walked across the room and joined our circle, whilst holding me in his attention. I felt exposed and wary of what he may say next.

"Then this part of the journey will become a choice you may wish to pursue, when or if you feel so inclined and believe. I say 'will' because life and life after life is about the choice of how you believe you belong."

The word *awesome* flitted across my mind and I hoped it was fleeting enough in its two guises of total respect and playful factitiousness, even for the facilitator to catch.

"Fast, but not fast enough James, my apologies, John," was his response, again without moving his lips. He closed our conversation with a smile and a thought that we would meet again. I dared to think he couldn't be that good, because he got my name wrong. A further smile and a muffled chuckle, met my gaze.

The facilitator engaged with the group, welcoming us to the world of spirit and explaining he had many functions, one of which answered Jason's question. He introduced himself as Tarquin, a being like us, but from a higher plane or realm. He was a bit like Father Christmas, but without the red costume, the white hair, beard and sizable stomach. A poor negating description for a spirit who appeared larger than life, filling the room with confidence, grandeur and presence, almost a super human. Whilst the mention of higher realms raised many questions, he fended them away, saying that these would be answered in due course.

"One of my main functions is to facilitate knowing. Knowing is 'spiritually guided intuition'. In our lives we acquire wisdom through knowledge which develops over time. This helps us to facilitate the acceptance of personal truth in relation to what is being communicated by others, or thought by ourselves. Wisdom opens the person to knowing, the ability to tap into a sort of collective intuitive source of truth, which is beyond our current knowledge."

I thought back to the times I struggled on Earth with the feeling of knowing things, but not being able to access them.

He explained the reason the concept of knowing was introduced at this time so soon into the realm, was to help the newly evolved spirit to overcome the sometimes-traumatic transition. What is unknown, may be met with fear. Knowing enables acceptance and it is in acceptance, where we know without doubt and fear. He summed it up for us new fledglings by saying that sometimes you just know, even though you don't know how or why you know.

Tarquin said that he knew from Rebecca's account that she had developed more of a sense of knowing as she approached her passing. Therefore, her arrival here was less of a shock and she would be more likely to settle easily in this world. Jason on the other hand had arrived in a traumatic way. One minute he had been playing on his phone, whilst sitting on the back seat of his parent's car, the next, he was standing at the roadside looking at himself lying head first, part way through the back window of the car in front. It was he who first spoke of the knowing in the group. Aspen and John had also arrived via a very traumatic passing.

"I know nothing of the stuff we are talking about, yet I do know. I think that knowing more, is making it easier for me to accept where I am. Will I remember what I have come to know here?" asked Jason.

"Yes, but once you have left here, you will revert back to your own unique personal ability, to process information leading to knowing. Meaning, you will learn at your pace you learned at on the Earth plane, but with one big difference. That is, you know there is life after death and you can choose whether you wish to increase your knowledge or stay where you are now."

I didn't think Jason was going to be one who was into personal development. I hadn't been allowed a phone I could game on and had tended to judge people who played on them and with other computer games, as small-minded techno-bots. Tarquin caught my eye and spoke to me telepathically.

"Maybe, but how long did you bug your mother for one? I hear judgement based on jealousy! Interesting traits John, how do you know, Jason may be the next Ghandi?"

"I am sorry but I doubt it and I know because you are facilitating my knowing."

I had delivered my third challenge upon this wise being and it felt scary and risky to do so, but something deep inside of me questioned his authority and this reality?

"Quite true, however, I invite you to observe the teachings inscribed at the entrance to the temple of Apollo in Delphi. 'Know Thyself' and with that, if you must judge, do so with compassion."

"Will you teach me?"

"Yes, if I need to, but you seem to be doing fine in that dream of yours."

Missing the gift of 'if I need to', I was more caught with the realisation that neither of us had spoken during our short conversation. I was learning quickly and I hoped this new talent would remain. As for the dream, although I could not prove I was existing here in this experience of consciousness, I could not prove otherwise. Accepting reality was not one of my strong points, as there were always so many other possible scenarios. However, this knowing stuff was changing the way I saw things.

Tarquin steered the conversation around to body language and in particular, colour. One of the children, Sam, asked Tarquin why he wore a green robe? This stirred up a commotion because each of the children saw Tarquin wearing a different coloured robe. I saw his robe as multi-coloured and what's more the colours appeared to be constantly shifting, not only between colours but also in their brightness. The only thing remaining constant was a glow of white light which edged the fabric. I decided to keep my observations to myself. Monique took up the direction.

"Just before we heard from Jason, I was talking about the energy fields which surround our forms and these being known as auras."

"Do people on the Earth plane have auras as well as spirit people?" asked a tall, skinny girl, with blond pigtails, called Michelle.

"Yes, they do, but relatively few people who are more spirit sensitive can actually see them. In spirit, once you know what you are looking for, they are quite easy to see, however, the colour of the aura is changeable depending on what the person is feeling."

"When I was speaking to Catherine earlier, she was saying that Earth people do not reflecate, when what you are saying is that they do?" I asked.

After Monique had explained reflecation to the group, she said that most Earth dwellers could not see auras, therefore conscious aura projection and sensing was not a wide spread and accepted form of communication between Earth people. In truth, I was testing my internal management of my pride in mentioning reflecation, which I guessed not many would know about. I was a little disappointed to see Tarquin looking downwards with a wry smile on his face, slightly shaking his head.

"How is reading auras useful over here Monique?" asked Jason.

Monique explained, what is communicated in the aura, is in relation to how that person is feeling both consciously and unconsciously. In addition, for Earth bound people, physical feelings can also be projected into the aura, whereas in spirit this cannot happen. She continued by saying; in the spirit world you can detect what a person is feeling emotionally and therefore be in a position to offer empathy, guidance or healing if it is needed. Colour and its state of vibrancy, is also an indication of a person's spiritual development. Spirits who are more developed have auras containing more white light.

Everyone's eyes fell upon Tarquin and in an instant, it was as if someone had turned on a floodlight. Bright light flooded the room and blinded all present and as quickly, it was gone again. What remained was a white and shimmering screen around Tarquin's form. An air of awe and respect befell the audience, with all questions momentarily suspended.

"Thank you, Tarquin, your presence is always met with love and appreciation. I take it that you will be with us for a couple of days?"

"Thank you Monique, the pleasure is all mine and yes, I will be here. There are a few people I wish to catch up with, so call when you need me."

"Goodbye children, I wish you love and happiness during your stay here. You will see me around and if there are any questions you might wish to ask, please come and find me. There is one piece of advice I would like to invite you to take during this time of rapid learning and that is to allow and listen to your own heads and hearts, as you listen to others."

After Tarquin had left, Monique continued to explain what message the colours gave out when they appeared in an aura and how colours could be used to heal conditions both in the spirit realms and on Earth. Whilst aura light is generated from the individual, those people who worked as healers were able to generate different coloured light to treat various conditions in the person.

"On the Earth plane as well as in spirit, the body contains energy centres or chakras. There are seven main ones in total and these are responsible for maintaining a balance of energy throughout the body. When balanced, each chakra resonates to a particular colour and this balanced vibrancy can be seen in the aura. If the energy centres are not balanced the resultant coloured emission will be a degree of the most vibrant colour and the degree of deviance is an indication of the negative dis-ease or illness the person carries."

Monique began with red, which is the colour of the base chakra at the bottom of the spine. It deals very much with the physical nature such as senses, sensuality, survival, aggression and self-defence, but also appears in spirit aura. She added, that it would appear in the auras of 'low fliers', like the ones I met before coming over. This was particularly so because they are still very much connected to Earth. Red light was used to heal, to restore the person when they were lacking in energy, spiritually and physically.

"The sacral chakra is situated between the base chakra and the navel and deals with creativity and how we express ourselves sexually. It is also the centre of joy. Our sex or gender, male and female is a big deciding factor in how we are identified by others. Some, who have an imbalance in this chakra, need it not to be corrected or healed, but supported to transform to their true identity to achieve the vibrant balance."

At this point, Jason and one of the other students decided to leave the group saying they would rather go and play outdoors. Their choice was accepted and I was tempted to join them, but thought that what was being taught was going to be of use to me, plus I was enjoying the teachings.

Monique said the balanced colour of this energy centre was orange and orange light was used to heal emotional unhappiness.

"The solar plexus chakra deals with negative thoughts and feelings. It is anxiety or worry which are based on fear and insecurity, as well as anger and jealousy which are felt and also generated here. Someone who has not matured emotionally because they have experienced some sort of emotional trauma during childhood, would show a disturbance here. Therefore, the balanced colour of brilliant golden yellow would be seen as pale or darker yellow, dependent on the condition experienced. Yellow can also show when a person is mentally distressed or disturbed, which demonstrates the connection that this chakra has with thoughts and feelings. Yellow light, like that from sunflowers, can make us feel more optimistic, less nervous and stimulate higher mental activity.

"The heart chakra is where it says. It deals with issues concerning love and affection and higher emotions such as unconditional love, empathy and compassion and is therefore not affected by thought. However, the emotions can be conditioned by thought. The heart's colour is green. Deviations from the balanced colour can show that a person is very individual, competitive and preoccupied with self-protection and ego. Green light is used to heal feelings of insecurity and for regeneration. Physically it helps with growth and general health, as well as with physical complaints around the heart and lungs, chest and arms."

"How does the healer actually heal the problem then?" I asked and one of the counsellors called Greg answered.

"If the healer recognises a chakra is out of balance, they imagine in their mind's eye, the colour that is needed to heal the balance and allow this colour's energy to flow through them towards the person. Sometimes they will touch the person and use their imagination to transfer the colour to them. Therefore, it is also possible to heal from a distance."

"Imagination and allow, what does 'allow' mean exactly? That's what Tarquin said when he was giving us his advice?"

"I know it sounds complex John, but to enable yourself to 'allow' on the Earth plane you must disidentify from your body, emotional feelings and thoughts and in the spirit world, from your emotional feelings and thoughts."

"Disidentify?"

"Quieten them, by acknowledging their presence, letting them come, accepting them and letting them go. This can be done usually through your breathing, so what is left is an emptiness and fullness at the same time, to enable intuition to happen and imagination to create and transfer the colour. Have you heard of the expression 'pregnant pause'?"

"Like suspense?"

"Almost. What comes through and into you is spirit energy from a higher power. Do you remember just before your accident when you experienced the beauty of your surroundings crystallise in your mind and this feeling was 'more than' what you just saw?"

Greg looked up at the other counsellors who nodded and transmitted the experience I had had to all the other children in the group, so they would have an opportunity to understand. There were gasps and acknowledgements from most of them who confirmed they had experienced this or a similar type of feeling in different ways.

"I remember the feeling of being as one with everything, a beautiful feeling," I added.

I then burst into tears, remembering my mum in the same moment and was all of a sudden very alone and knew how alone and unhappy Mum must now feel. I remembered my life, thought of my future and then of my death.

"I was only 15 and I had lots to live for, who will look after my mum? We lived alone and my dad left ages ago."

As I spoke of my thoughts and feelings, I felt better and as the tears subsided I could feel those around me holding and loving me in my grief. The other children had gathered around me, some crying and others just stroking and trying to sooth me. A sky-blue light surrounded my body, which appeared to come from me.

"It's coming from your throat John," said Rebecca.

Having all of the others around me was a bit too much. I felt ashamed for having broken down in front of them. It wasn't that I didn't appreciate their actions, it was just I felt uncomfortable with so much loving attention and ashamed I could not control my feelings.

"Thank you, thank you for your help, I am alright now, it's just that I am finding it hard dealing with this grief thing."

The light emanating from my throat lost its luminescence and ceased to shine so brightly as a dark red, dull green and yellow light started to gather around me.

"What's happening?" I asked.

Bethany, one of the girls spoke and then started to sing.

There was an instantaneous round of applause and Monique spoke.

"Can every one see the colours surrounding John?" Everyone could.

"What's happened John, is when you reconnected to the 'allowing experience' which Greg was speaking to you about, you opened up a channel which connected you to your higher emotions and you started to speak your truth. This caused your aura to become visible for all here to see."

I felt embarrassed and in the spotlight. "I feel like a traffic light!"

Everyone in the room fell about laughing. My comment had totally diffused the intensity of others' speculation and my own embarrassment. This was one of my better defence mechanisms for taking negative attention away from me, but Monique saw through my disguise.

"Is it alright if we speak about what happened to you John and why the different colours appeared in your aura?"

"Yes, I suppose so, it's just... I feel a bit embarrassed."

"We are working with truth John. Sometimes the truth hurts, but we are not here to hurt you, we are here to bring awareness to what hurts and why it should continue to hurt, when it no longer needs to."

"OK, so why was there blue light coming from my throat?"

Monique described to the group, the throat chakra as the energy centre dealing with the issue of truth and the true expression of the soul. It also deals with communication and the way it is expressed, whether through language or the arts, for example, dance, art and music. Physically it is the chakra of the ears, nose and throat and when balanced it resonates and omits a sky-blue colour.

"When John was speaking, it was of his mother, home life and the fact that he had so much to live for. This connected emotionally for him and he spoke from his heart, he spoke his truth. This was why the blue light had come from his throat. The other colours, however, were created by his reaction to the attention he received from those of you around him, creating his dis-ease. You said that you were embarrassed by what happened, can you say more?"

Monique leaned towards me, her elbows resting on her thighs.

"It was just, everyone was showing me sympathy and crowding around me and touching me, I couldn't stand it."

"You couldn't stand it?"

"No."

"To me, it looked like they were trying to comfort you because you were in distress?"

"But it's my pain, nothing to do with anyone else, I could have dealt with it in my own way."

"In your own way?"

"Yes."

"What was so painful for you when the others were trying to comfort you?"

"I don't know, I just want to run away when things like that happen."

"But you didn't run away?"

"I did in my head."

"What happened in your head when you could not stand it anymore?"

"When the feelings in my head get too much, it's like a hundred ball bearings bouncing around in there. So I just detach from what's happening around me. It's like I knew the others were there, but I put up this barrier or force field until I get control over my feelings and am not worried or embarrassed anymore."

"You shut yourself away from other's feelings for you by defending yourself with a barrier?"

"Yes."

"Do you know why you do this, John?"

"Because it gets too much."

"How do you feel afterwards, when you have things back under control?"

"Relieved, but I feel alone and I am afraid that no one will like me, because I have pushed them away. I also feel strong and proud, at the same time, that I was able to deal with it on my own."

"But you are afraid of being on your own."

"Yes."

"So, when you defend yourself by rejecting other's love and compassion and you find yourself alone, aren't you making yourself afraid?"

"I am strong and proud enough to keep the fear away."

"Why be afraid?"

"…they may leave if I like them and they probably don't like me anyway, so what's the point in trying."

"In trying to what?"

"…to love someone who's going to leave anyway!"

A bright blue light exploded from my throat making the others wince and blink as the colourful wave hit them. The children in the group shifted uneasily.

"Why has John got a purple whirlwind coming from the top of his head?" Monique looked at Sam, the enquirer and held her fingers to her lips.

My head dropped to my chest and I slumped forward, my sobs came in waves. I cried deeply and I sensed Monique's approach. She sat beside me, placed her arm around my shoulders and eased me towards her. The other children, having heard my truth sat hesitantly, waiting for me to calm. Monique returned to her seat and spoke gently.

"Do you miss your dad, John?"

I floated in a momentary place of stillness in my mind, with a sense of being freed. I was sure it would not last for long, it never did. I took a deep breath.

"Yes, but I know I could not make him love me and Mum enough for him to stay. Even when he returned from one of his trips, I felt as though I was somehow protecting her and that I was like the go between. I feel it was my fault because I could not keep them together."

"How old were you when he left?"

"I was ten."

"You were ten years old. You were a little person John, caught in a difficult situation between two adults. You are not to blame. It sounds as if you were wanting what was best for them and you were trying to be their parents."

"But it feels like I am to blame."

"Well, I am inviting you to feel and think differently each time you think of your dad leaving. It will take time to heal and there will be many who will help you. How do you feel now?"

"A bit lighter."

"Good, now I also want to invite you to look into the eyes of each and every person in this group."

I felt immediately embarrassed but did as I was invited. As I looked, my eyes were met with a smile from each who were present. I returned each smile and as I reached the last person I felt loved and held by the group.

"You are loveable John and don't you ever forget that."

I felt warm and pleasant and glad to be alive.

"Thank you, to all of you." I wiped my face with both hands, drawing the tears back into my hair and rubbing my neck.

I was still intrigued about the traffic light and after Monique had checked out to see if I felt alright enough to continue, she explained what had happened.

"First of all, there was red in your aura because you were defending your difficulty with emotional attention. The yellow showed anxiety, insecurity, mental distress and fear. Finally, the green represented your individualism and self-protection. It also indicates your capacity for unconditional love. These colours were all present in your aura when you were struggling with your emotions," Monique addressed the group.

"What tends to happen is, as we grow as children, we sometimes learn how not to speak the truth. We learn not to follow our hearts and behave in a way we think is best to cope with what is happening around us. We do it to survive. The problem is, we may stop ourselves from loving and worst of all, we forget how to love ourselves. During your time here, there will be many occasions when you may be invited to face yourself, like what has just happened to John. When this happens, remember to be compassionate with yourself. Be forgiving, loving and joyful and the divine will meet you and show your self or your personality, to your Self; your spirit. This is so they can reflect upon each other, like a mirror and reveal the truth for you to accept or not."

"You mean like truly seeing who you are, revealing the bit you sometimes hide which is important to you, but seemingly unimportant to others?" asked Rebecca.

"That's it Rebecca, well summed up. Before I talk about the vortex of violet light we saw coming down into the top of John's head which is to do with the seventh chakra, the crown chakra, I want to tell you of the ajna or brow chakra. The ajna is situated in the middle of the forehead. It is the seat of intuition and soul knowledge and balances the power of mind and mental reasoning. It enables the development of a high level of perception to lead us to develop and trust intuition and knowing in our lives. When balanced, it resonates to the colour indigo or royal blue. You will hear some talk of the 'third eye' and this is what they mean by it."

I thought about what Peter had done when he increased my insight to settle me. I guessed it was my ajna he had touched.

"Now for the final seventh chakra and after I have finished talking about this, we will break for the rest of the day."

Cheers rang out from all of us and then apologies, as we didn't want Monique to think we had been bored with her lecture.

"The crown chakra is situated on the top of the head. It is the receptive centre for spiritual energies and allows a direct link with the divine. It deals with all spirituality issues and when balanced vibrates to the colour violet. Now, did you all see the violet vortex entering John's head before when John and I were talking, just before he had to cry?"

All of us acknowledged, apart from me, as I could not see it from my position.

"Well, John had got to a point of realisation, where something that had remained out of awareness for a long time or something that has been previously denied, was suddenly realised. Some call it when the 'soul drops in'. It does so in connection with the divine, where divine energy links with our own soul or Self and we realise more of who we truly are."

"Why is it a vortex?" I asked.

"Well I am not entirely sure, but I think that vortices are tremendously powerful structures which are drawn to ground. It is a structure of knowing, whose connection is catalysed by the realisation or 'the becoming known' that the person experiences. The process is spiritual, healing and beautiful."

"What is it that it actually connects with in the person?"

"In spirit we consist of light. Our personalities, thoughts and feelings including our memories, are intertwined with our souls or spiritual Self and are held by the frequency of our light body. Imagine many threads bound tightly together. The vortex, which also replicates the twist of the thread, makes a connection between the divine, or the 'Collective' as we call it over here and the Self. The Self is an integrated component of the Collective, providing us with our own sense of a separate individuality and at the same time connectivity. It is a part of us that comes to realise that whilst we are separate beings, we are also part of something universal or collective, which is the Divine."

"And for those on Earth who are still spirit in matter?" I asked.

"Bodies are vehicles of perception made from matter which physically hold memories and knowledge, which in relation with our sense of Self on Earth, create our personalities. All of the information gained is backed up on a sort of light drive which returns interwoven with our spiritual Self, over to here when we die."

I think the silence in the group reflected the complexity of what had just been delivered, even with facilitation. I sat with the battle of uncertainty I had experienced during my time on Earth.

"OK people, I think we have covered enough for today. Learn to read colours, they can tell you a lot about the person you are with. We will get together later but until then, the afternoon and evening are yours and there is plenty to do. We have the gardens and the lake or the library and for those of you who wish to eat, see Mark, one of the tutors, afterwards. There are your rooms as well if you wish to rest. Everyone has worked hard today and I want to thank you for your contributions. See you later."

Sniffed Out

I hung around while Monique spoke with some of her colleagues. She sensed my presence and turned to face me.

"I just wanted to say thank you for helping me before, I think I see things a little more clearly now. It was a difficult time when my dad left. I have had a lot of time to think things over and even after what just happened, there is still a part of me which feels responsible for him going and not being able to make Mum happy after he had gone. She hasn't met anyone since."

"You know John, the territory comes with being a sensitive individual and even though you may feel as though you failed, you are not responsible for your dad's failure to be able to keep his relationship together with your mum. Also, you could never replace what your mum lost and although you may have tried to support her, you could never be the parent or a partner to her. At some stage, you can choose to mourn your loss and what you lost as a result of being caught between them. I sense you are pretty angry with your dad and you will again have a choice to work with that anger which you seem to have directed against yourself."

"Not all of what you say sinks in, but I think I know what you mean, thank you."

I then caught sight of Tarquin walking across the lounge in our direction.

"Hi Tarquin."

"Hello, Monique and John."

"Did you mean to shake your head at me before?"

"Yes, I heard you. John, come and see me a little later and I will attempt to answer your questions if that is alright." I nodded.

"In the meantime, go and cool your jets, relax and have some fun and even if you take an eternity doing so, I will still be waiting to hear you."

"Thank you, there is just so much I want to know."

"That's my boy, now off with you!"

That's my boy, that's my boy, I wonder what he meant by that? The thoughts echoed as I walked into the garden. *Cool my jets, right, that's what I have got to do.*

I walked down to the lake and sat down on a grassy bank beneath a willow tree. Staring at the water and losing focus, I watched the peaceful blue light reflecting from the surface. A few of the children were playing skimming stones, which were making fabulous patterns as they propelled from touch to touch. As the ripples moved outward little splinters of light reflected from their concentric peaks, creating a peacock display of colours. I was so absorbed in what was going on, the sensation of something cold and wet on my left ear took me totally by surprise. I recoiled and found myself face to face with a golden retriever.

"Hello boy, I didn't know they had dogs here in the spirit world."

As soon as I had said this, a voice in my head said, 'Yes they do.' I didn't credit any importance to the voice and carried on petting the dog.

"I wonder what your name is then boy?"

The voice again, 'Don't you recognise me John?'

I stopped in my tracks as all the memories came flooding back, but this couldn't be Tinker, he died shortly after my dad had left.

'Listen John Kenton it is me, take a closer look.'

My eyes welled up and I hugged the dog, I felt so happy I burst into tears.

"I've missed you Tinker."

'I've missed you too John.'

Tinker licked me all over my face and wagging his tail, offered up his paw to me. I took it and shook it saying,

"It's good to see you again boy, so good to see you, but are you really talking to me?"

'No, not talking to you, but I am sending you my thoughts, hence you hear a voice inside your head which you have translated. It would have been easier if we could have done this on the Earth plane, I reckon I would have been taken for more walks. Do you know how important it is for dogs to sniff stuff?'

I suddenly felt guilty, but detecting the humour in his mind, I followed it with,

"Well there's one good thing Tinker, you smell a darn sight better over here than you did back there!"

We both fell about laughing, well I did and Tinker jumped on top of me, licking my nose, trying to bite my ears. Monique stood at the window watching, allowing herself to enjoy John's happiness.

"Where do you live over here and who looks after you?"

'Well, nobody really looks after me because they do not need to, simply because I don't need food. As to where I live, it's quite far from here as the dog walks, in a place I cannot really describe, but I live with six others.'

"What do you do then?"

'I do a lot of travelling and spend most of my time with people who need company or a friend. Take for example this place, I visit many of the rest homes where children and adults re-adjust to this world.'

"Will you come and live with me again?"

'I will certainly visit you John, but I am afraid I have work to do which takes me all over this realm, so I can't live with you. Please don't be upset, we will see each other from time to time.'

"I understand Tinker and I will look forward to when our path's cross. Anyway, how did you know I was here?"

'I was thinking of you as I quite often do and there was a difference in the link. I detected you were no longer on the Earth plane, which shocked me, so the only place you could have been was on this side. I then tuned into your scent and pin pointed your energy to here.'

"That is one hell of a tracking system, can I do it too?"

'Got four legs, a waggy tail and a big nose? You may be able to, but nowhere near as fast as I can.'

"Anything you can do!" I blew him a raspberry and he jumped on my head and farted.

'I think I will retract my last statement, funny how some things don't change!' Tinker pleaded with a 'who me', followed by a muttley chuckle.

We spent a couple of hours together catching up with our news and playing in the garden. Tinker explained, like people, animals also come over to the spirit world, as do insects and other creatures. He described the spirit world as being so large, it can accommodate everything without appearing overcrowded. When animals come here, they tended to live among their own kind or choose to cohabit with people.

"What about wild animals like lions and tigers which are dangerous on the Earth?"

'They are no longer wild over here. They had to be wild on Earth as their way of living was to survive and breed. Therefore, they had to be ferocious not only to feed themselves and their young, but also to protect themselves. Over here there is no need to feed and there is no threat to them from other creatures or humans, so they lose their basic aggressive and defensive behaviours.'

"But, where are they?"

'There is a part of this realm that is like a sort of animal kingdom, which is where my base is. Most of the animals go there after they have passed and remain there out of instinctual choice. There is no need for them to cross the boundary into other parts of the realm, but they can do if they wish to. Humans can cross that boundary freely as well to visit or live amongst the animals and there is no danger in them doing so. What you tend to find here is animals who have cohabited with humans on the Earth plane, seem to do so again after they have passed. I spent fourteen years with your mum and ten of them with you and learned how to communicate during that time. I could not speak on the Earth plane, but I had learned enough to be able to do so here.'

"Do you speak to all of the people here?"

'No, not all of them can hear me.'

"But I can."

'Yes, I think because we know each other, or you just speak dog exceptionally well.'

"What about insects, can you talk to them?"

'They are very limited, but non-the less are spirit and tend to communicate through their acceptance of other spirit here, sort of 'you're OK, I'm OK'. They are trusting and show no fear. I guess, what happens, is the majority go to live in the animal kingdom, although I see plenty of insects in this realm, bees for example.'

"So, you can't hold a conversation with your fleas then Tinker?" I said, scratching myself under my armpit.

'I'll give you conversations with fleas!'

He jumped on top of me and bit my ears again. After we had finished rolling around and exchanging insults, it was time for Tinker to say goodbye.

'I'll come and see you soon, but in the meantime, if you are feeling lonely, just think of me in a way of wishing to talk and I will link in with you.'

"OK, I will remember that. It's been great seeing you again Tinker."

'You too John, take care,' he licked my nose and disappeared.

I sat leaning against the willow tree with my hands behind my head thinking that I was beginning to like this place. Closing my eyes, I rested and dropped. I was thinking of Mum and the next thing I knew was, I was looking at the inside of a bus.

Aftermath

It was impossible to see John before the autopsy had been conducted. The loss of life had been reported as a sudden death and the coroner's decision had to be upheld. The delay was like a reprieve from the inevitable. The next few days disappeared in a haze as Jennifer moved from room to room picking up objects relating to John, reflecting on them and spilling tears upon her way. She had spent three hours in his room tidying his things, as if he was going to return home again. She didn't want to change things too much just in case.

It was hard to find a reason why he had been taken from her and even harder to accept her mother's belief that some things are in the Lord's hands and happen beyond our control. Nothing could console the fact that he was so young and had everything to live for. If there was a God then surely, he must have been able to see that John had so much more to give. Her beliefs were such that she could not allow herself to hate God, but she was really angry with Him and so miserably perplexed by his decision to take John from her when she needed him so much. She paused over her word 'needed', it somehow felt selfish, but the meaning was lost in her loss.

The school had been informed and this was succeeded by a string of callers all showing their sympathy. Jennifer received them out of duty and silently wished they would leave her alone. John's classmates had made a card depicting all of the things he liked and enjoyed in his life. Mrs Daniels had brought this with some flowers and a selection of pictures that John had painted. Jennifer knew how difficult it must have been for her and the other visitors and she showed as much kindness as she could for their loss, in the face of the magnitude of her own.

It was necessary to sort out all of the formalities and of course see his body in the chapel of rest at the funeral home where John had been transferred. Jennifer had to force herself to register his death and make the necessary arrangements for the funeral. Everything became a mammoth task, even though her mum gave her as much support as she could.

It was the actuality of seeing him that she most feared and didn't know whether she could keep herself together. She had been told by the hospital that his face and skull had been damaged by the accident and that it may be kinder to her, if she did not view his body. The police had initially identified him from the contents of his school bag and a silver identity bracelet she had bought him last Christmas. She had confirmed to them that these were his. The task of identifying the body was too much for her, so the police had taken her mother to the hospital to confirm it. Even though she knew from the expression on her mother's face, when she had returned, that he was dead, something inside her refused to accept it.

Holding a photograph of him and lovingly taking in each detail as if to etch them deeply in her memory, a tear rolled down her cheek.

"Oh John, I do love you so much. How am I ever going to get along without you?"

His smiling face looked up at her, so perfect, with his short blond hair, blue eyes and round cheeks and she gazed into his eyes. He was such a good-looking boy and had his father's smile. She thought about her husband and wondered about his grief. She had no way of contacting him and envied his ignorance.

Taking the bus to the funeral directors with her mother seemed to make things more final. They sat in silence looking blankly out of the windows at the bleak countryside, both holding each other's hands in the anguish of their own desolation. She thought about all the things she would do if she knew she was going to die and decided there wasn't enough time. She wondered what John must have been thinking before he was killed and whether his mind was on her and home.

Two small children were playing noisily on the back row of seats. Although this would have irritated her in the past, she thought of their oblivious innocence. Soon she was going to see her own child lying there, cold and lifeless, her own flesh and blood, whom she had brought into the world, never again able to hug her and call her Mum. She felt cheated and suddenly jealous of the woman who was shouting to her children to sit up and behave.

"Are you alright, Mum?"

"Yes, just had an odd feeling, you know, the one where your hairs stand up on the back of your neck and forearms."

"You're not going to die too, are you?"

"Don't be silly lovey, someone walking over your grave doesn't mean you are going to die. I just felt I was being watched. I can't feel it now anyway."

I was picturing them from the vacant seat behind where they were sitting on the bus. It seemed likely to me that I had inherited my sensitivity from my grandma, or someone in her line. The bus came to a halt, as we reached their stop. Reconnecting with them both was like stepping into leaden boots, everything depressed, repressed and sad.

Mum's steps towards the entrance of the funeral home were slow and heavy, but it was her heart that was even heavier. She waited in the reception area whilst Grandma reported to the sincere looking receptionist. Returning to Mum, she took her by the arm, shocking her back from a moment freed from reality. After nodding appreciatively at the funeral director for fifteen minutes and with Grandma having finalised the details of my funeral, they walked down the short corridor and arrived at the chapel of rest.

"Do you want me to come with you Jenny?"

"No Mum, it's alright. You wait here. I would like to be alone with John if I may."

"Try to be strong lovey, won't you?"

Aligned with her thoughts and feelings, I felt her bite her bottom lip in an attempt to fight back the tears. She nodded to Grandma and walked through the doors. A tall man met her on the inside and humbly asked who she had come to see. He directed her to a door on the right. Her heart thumping in my mind, she pushed the door open and walked inside.

I was lying in a coffin on the far side of the room beneath a coloured glass window. Light from the window was shining into the coffin illuminating my face and giving me colour. I automatically translated the colours learned from Monique's chakra lecture, but knew it was impossible for my dead body to emanate anything. As Mum approached me, her impression was that the colour spoke of health and life. I had been cleaned up and reconstructed by a sympathetic hand, but she connected to the damage that had been done and hoped I had not passed in pain. I wanted to tell her that I hadn't suffered, that I was alive and well, but the screen was unbreakable.

"Well my little man, I guess I never expected to lose you and although I don't understand why, it is hard to accept that you have gone. I just want you to know that I love you so very much and I am going to miss you."

She stroked my hair gently and her tear fell onto my cheek as she leaned forward to kiss me.

"God, please let me wake up."

As her lips brushed mine, their coldness returned the finality and she knew I was no longer there. Gently lifting a small lock of hair from my temple, she snipped it loose and quickly bound it with blue cotton, before placing it in her purse.

"Look after yourself my love where ever you may be, I will always remember you."

She straightened my tie, smoothed my jacket, kissed her fingertips and held them to my lips.

"I will always be your mum, so never forget me John, because I just love you and I always will."

She turned quickly and walked towards the door. Before she went through, she looked back just in case I had woken up. She recast her gaze to the floor with her tears rolling down her face.

"Come on Jen, you've got to be strong," she told herself and in her next breath responded by saying that it was alright to say that, but it was damned hard feeling it, when a big part of her life had just been ruthlessly torn away. She wiped her eyes, coughed, walked through the doors and out into the corridor to where Grandma was waiting.

"Are you OK, love?"

Mum nodded. "Come on, Mum, let's go home, I am so tired and empty."

On the bus journey home, I followed her mind as she ordered the final preparations. She paused in her diversionary process of prioritising, to mentally ask me if this and that was alright and answering herself as best she could. Her motions seemed to be conducted remotely, as if someone else inside her was going through the actions and completing the mental tasks, whilst she remained in the background observing.

From their occasional conversation, I established the day was Saturday and the funeral would be taking place on Monday. I found this confusing, as I had not been in the spirit world that long. Grandma was planning to go to church as usual tomorrow morning, but Mum had decided not to. She felt guilty because she had not been a regular visitor, tending only to go at Christmas and other special occasions, but also because she hadn't encouraged me to go after I had finished Sunday school. Her mind anchored into reasons why I would not be allowed into heaven and then as quickly, blaming herself for my lack of religion. As Mum was not a member of the church, it was Grandma who had spoken to the minister, who had arranged for the ceremony to take place at the church in Denby Dale.

Once at home alone, Mum chose to go to bed early. Although she was exhausted, she took two sleepers, hoping they would take her quickly. I watched her laying in the dark, imagining me to be asleep in the next room. It somehow comforted her, but in her heart, she knew Monday would mark the ending of my time on Earth. She screwed up her eyes in an attempt to stop the flow and pulled the covers over her head. I heard her whispers as she slipped into sleep. "I love God and I hate God, I love God and I hate God, I…" She repeated the mantra of ambivalence over and over until sleep met her mind and, in its delivery, she cared not for the words written upon the last petal to fall. I could feel something touching my cheek and Monique's voice distantly calling my name. Suddenly feeling guilty and caught out, I fell back into myself and with eyes still shut, yawned and stretched my arms.

Insight

"Oh, hi Monique, I thought you said spirit doesn't tire over here. I am sure I have just had forty winks. I have had a conversation with my pet dog Tinker, he was here, he knew I had come over."

I was trying to hide the fact that I had just split and visited my family on Earth. Eyes filled with concerned enquiry, met mine and then she smiled.

"Yes, I saw you both playing together from the window. Tinker is a regular visitor to this home."

"You know, I feel that since our conversation, he is much more than just a dog. I really respect and admire him for doing what he does and how he has chosen to work over here."

"Can you imagine the Earth plane if people felt as you do now?"

"Yes, less need for animal rescue."

"Exactly! You had a conversation with him?"

"Yes, he explained about the animals in the spirit world and how some of them work with people."

Monique was not sceptical, as she could see his mind, but speaking with animals wasn't usual. She kept her thoughts to herself.

"They also work amongst their own kind, helping new arrivals to adjust to life over here."

"Why do people work over here?"

"People do not have to work if they do not want to, it is up to them. It is not like the Earth plane where you have to work to survive, unless you are lucky or unlucky enough not to. It is a matter of choice and some people choose to help others because they want to give. After all, time has less importance here."

"Why do you work here Monique?"

"Well, before I came over, I used to work in an infant's school where I looked after young children. I enjoyed this very much, so after I had been over for a couple of Earth years, I decided I would like to look after children and young people again and started working here."

"How long have you worked here?"

"Nearly nineteen Earth years."

"That's impossible, you only look about twenty!"

I was totally bemused, as Monique looked so young. She smiled and said,

"In Earth years, I am forty-one years old. I was only twenty-two when I passed over and chose not to age. You already know we exist as light and spirit over here, not flesh and bone, therefore there is nothing to age in the same way that our bodies do on Earth. One just hopes we become a little wiser, that's all."

"You said you chose not to age. Can you age, will I grow up?"

"If you want to yes. It is up to you what outward age you want to be. For example, if a young baby passed over, it would be cared for by spirit helpers and would grow naturally, but in light and spirit form only. Growth seems to follow a blueprint which is apparent on both the Earth plane and in the spirit world, so as the Earth years pass, the child naturally projects its age stage in its outward form. When the child has grown to a stage where it can take responsibility for itself, it can then choose whether to carry on growing or not. For older people who come here, they tend to regress in age to what is considered to be their prime physical age. You will find a lot of people in spirit to be in their twenties or thirties."

"A whole bunch of Peter Pan's then?"

"Yes, if you like, but do you remember older people on Earth saying, that although they were seventy or eighty and their bodies were old, they still felt like teenagers inside. This is because the spirit you carry does not age, it can only grow in experience and wisdom and it allows you to feel young even though your body isn't. This is just one of life's great paradoxes."

"Paradox?"

"Self-contradictory, or it seems to be one thing and yet it is another at the same time."

"Have you seen my grandfather as a young version?"

"Yes, I have, normally he is about thirty-five. He would have projected the age you last saw him on Earth, so you could recognise him."

"It's funny why youth and image remain important after we have left Earth?"

"We remain relational beings and with so much beauty and perfection in nature on the Earth world and also in life over here, we instinctively try to create attraction, not only to continue to draw others to us, but on Earth to continue as a species."

"You want to see the anti-wrinkle cream adverts on the TV these days. I am sure the girls are getting younger. They have got to be about twelve at a push?"

"How old are you John, fifteen going on forty-five?"

"But, even over here, I am sure they all think they are worth it?"

Unfortunately, my joke fell on deaf ears and I had to explain, much to Monique's confusion.

"It makes me wonder, though about the Earth people's preoccupation with beauty, prolonging youth and immortality. If they knew about this place and how you can choose to be younger, would it be so important?"

"This realm is very similar in a lot of ways to the Earth realm, including the people in it. However, like Earth, this is also a realm which enables us to truly get to know ourselves, but with the exception that here, the inhabitants now know that they exist after death."

"Truly knowing, meaning?"

"On Earth and here, there are a lot of distractions that keep us from knowing more about who we are in authentic relationship to others as well as to our Selves. There are many who choose to project an image or way of being which they want others to believe is actually who they are. Take you for instance. When your dad left, other than sadness, what feelings back then have defined the way you are now?"

"I know because of the facilitation link and also from what happened in the group. Rejection and abandonment."

"And what have you done to manage these?"

"Controlled my emotions, avoided close relationships, isolated myself, risked my life in my sports and created an imaginary world where I am different and somehow special."

"Very good. Can you see how all of those pursuits have kept you away from accepting that it is alright and perfectly acceptable to feel vulnerable. And if you had done that, how you might have been more aware now?"

"Ummm. Experientially verses knowingly, I am not quite there yet. I feel that I do have a purpose, but I just can't see it yet because it remains concealed from me, but I do think my skills will help me find it."

"Just remember, if you conceal things, like you did when I stirred you from your 'forty winks', when actually, I had brought you back from a 'split' to visit your family; the energy used in denial to maintain the concealment, denies you the gain in energy from being truthful."

"I didn't want to admit it."

"Why, because you miss your family or are you feeding the feeling you had when Peter told you he was impressed with a new spirit being able to split and listen so early after death?"

I looked down, not quite sure what to say and then negatively interpreting her authority, I told her, 'Both'.

"Lower your defences, I am not judging you, feel my authenticity."

"It's alright, I believe you." I did not enjoy the spotlight of what I sensed as inquisition.

"This is not about belief. You have spent years detaching yourself from emotions, because they are too painful to connect with. I am inviting you to learn how to feel again."

"How?"

"Start with accepting who you actually are at present. It won't be easy, so don't expect a 'poof' moment where everything is instantaneously fixed. This may be the after world, where things can appear magical, but personal development, like on Earth, is hard work and repetitious because you are deconditioning your self or your personality you have created on Earth to defend yourself. This will be part of your Self-development."

"What were you caught in, that you needed to develop?"

"People's expectations, judgements and my self-esteem. That's why I worked with children to escape, because children didn't make me feel worthless."

"But you still do."

"It's all work in progress. Anyway occasionally, you get a fifteen-year-old who thinks they are forty-five and I get to practice working with both children and adults at the same time!"

Monique smiled and winked and I laughed and thanked her for helping me.

"On the subject of splitting, be mindful that you need to rest and take yourself away from the distress of those left behind. You are worrying the wound and can do nothing to change what has happened. I know you are grieving, but don't get caught by theirs. I am not trying to feed you, but it is unusual for a new spirit to achieve a split so early and it is not something that is encouraged at this time."

"Why?"

"Because in grief as with any strong emotion, we are affected by impulse. The impulse in grief is to try and change the source of it and you cannot affect others directly across worlds, where one world, the Earth world believes you are dead and gone. You can however, get caught and not want to let go, instead of accepting life over here as a natural progression of all of life's journey."

"You say directly affect, do you mean we can affect Earth people in other ways?"

"Directly means changing things by voices, materialisations or by changing or creating events that have no Earthly logical explanation. All things that would distract people from experiencing being grounded in Earthly life."

"I have my views on that already."

"I can hear them and I know you have lived the latter part of your short life trying to work out the hidden connections, but you are in the minority. Yes, we do need the minority, but as a species we must be allowed to evolve at a pace where consciousness evolves collectively, otherwise the species divide."

"Do you mean slow down progress?"

"I mean by showing acceptance and compassion for difference within the species and through transparency of action or motive. Human history is splattered with actions where one group of people have decided that difference is intolerable and genocide of the 'different' is the only solution to create, what, peace in their own society? Or is it to achieve a more powerful influence in the world?"

"And this still goes on and we are obviously still divided."

"Yes, but as a species we are slowly evolving to learn by our mistakes and lack of insight."

"Not fast enough in my view."

In my view, I had caught sight of Tarquin, who was standing on the veranda facing in our direction. Monique looked up and waved and he made his way down to where we were sitting.

"Can I join you?"

"Why didn't you just transport down to us?" I asked.

"Small steps are sometimes better. They afford you time to reflect and take in more viewpoints."

Tarquin narrated a story where in WWII, the troops coming back from combat in the far east, were on board ship with other soldiers returning, for a journey that took six weeks or more. That meant they were able to process parts of their trauma with others and gain a sense of comradery and compassion for themselves and others as well as, some sense of meaning. In the Vietnam war, an American soldier could be back on American soil and into civilian life within thirty-six hours of active duty. He asked me which of the soldiers had a better chance of adjusting to the change. I think in sensing the direction of the conversation, Monique excused herself and told me she would catch me later.

"You know I know, which I think is correct."

"And yet having made your transition to this world, your current pace slows your progress of readjusting. Knowing something is one thing, but we truly judge ourselves by our actions and your knowing and actions are disjointed at the moment. I am just saying what everybody else is, slow down a bit, time is on your side."

"I have always had this head, that knows stuff, but it seems I cannot always access the answers. I have spent a lot of time sensing things. Since dying and coming here, it's like I am starting to peak through the curtains, realise things and it's kind of exciting for me because I feel I am starting to become who I really think I am."

"And do you know who that is?"

"Not yet."

I had an idea that he was going to speak to me about allowing. "I am. Pace dictates allowing."

"And the prize of patience is the patience to allow?"

"All fixed now, call your grandad, off you go!" Tarquin laughed out loud. I joined in too, as I could see he had seen my engineered twist of discovering my wisdom whilst following his, then attempting to please him as I knowingly stumbled into the message he wanted me to grasp.

"Brilliant analysis! Can you see what you are doing? You have an agile mind that can twist and discover points of wisdom in a moment, as you are thinking along with the conversation. Yes, you project confidently, with that end point of realisation; in your words, 'patience is the patience to allow', but your aim is to create a feeling in the receiver, that you have known of that wisdom for some time. The listener is left with the impression that you are much wiser than you actually are, but you are not, because you haven't yet based action on that wisdom. You create an illusion. Do you know why you do this?"

"Shit."

Tarquin burst out laughing in response and informed me, it was less of a literal problem over here. I had never been seen like this before and whilst I felt exposed and a bit shameful, I was not going to back down easily.

"You know this Tarquin, but I don't know if you have ever experienced this yourself. I have always felt older inside and as I have said, I am aware of things I can't quite access. However, put me in a debate and things drop in which I seem to pretty much immediately grasp the meaning and relevance of. Possibly a bit like allowing knowing? I find I can be instantly versatile with their meaning. That is not an illusion, that happens. I project the illusion of long-standing wisdom because I want to be accepted, I want to be valued and people are less likely to reject wisdom that makes sense to them personally. Being a young person or a child, seems to give adults a permission to dismiss. The expression, 'out of the mouths of babes' was recorded for good reason. In my view it was saying listen to your children more."

There was a long pause and I wanted to read his mind so I could see how he processed. I thought about the truth of what I had said and had to admit my omission, that the illusion also gave me some sort of power and self-importance. He must know this because this man was present on many levels. There was the awe stuff admittedly, because he was a high planer, but I could see he was able to relate and understand me. I dared to think that he was someone I would wish to be like one day. "Why do you pause, when you are all knowing, you know, not being disrespectful?"

"For you, so you can reflect on what you had just said. I have learned that wisdom and the authentic guidance of others cannot be achieved without integrity. Power and self-importance serve only to distract you and support, not who you are trying to become, but supports the illusion of deceptive security in yourself and others."

"I have never lost sight of humility and so will battle those feelings against what I believe to be right."

"Sounds tiring. Why don't you just choose to accept and trust?"

"I don't know; I guess I am afraid." I knew Tarquin could have explored my fear if he wanted to and I felt he was purposely leaving that part for me to explore on my own.

"Why do you think they built the pyramids with the point at the top?"

I shrugged my shoulders.

"Because if they had built them upside down, they would have fallen over. Meaning, be aware of your pace and build a foundation that supports truth, not illusion. Remember the temple of Apollo teaching and even the building your house on a rock story. Cool your jets, slowing down isn't giving up. I also have another message for you."

"I'm *not The One?*"

The laughter from both of us was instantaneous and we smiled and chuckled for what seemed like a long time.

"That was funny and timely. However, although I can see you are not keen on waiting for anything, you are on the right track."

"Just one thing that Monique and I almost got into. We were talking about communication with or affecting people on the Earth plane."

"Yep, she was about to tell you about 'seeding'."

Tarquin told me that there was a research centre onsite, where people work specifically on medical issues and techniques that were also being investigated on Earth. The people involved were professionals, but the working groups also included people who have suffered with particular conditions. After collating their findings and proposing their ideas they presented them to Tarquin seeking his support to go ahead with a seeding. Seeding, it seems, is the direct or indirect suggestion of ideas to the Earth-bound person who could play a part in furthering the research and treatment of a particular disease. In the majority of cases, a person's guide is used to indirectly be the messenger. Occasionally, seeding is done directly from a member of the team. It takes the form of suggestion. It is never a direct order and is always placed in the unconscious part of people's minds. That is the part we are not aware of but contains a lot of the information we would need to enable us to become or realise who we really are. There is always a choice to reject this information once it becomes conscious.

"Why can't you just tell them the answer?"

"We are not allowed to instruct, directly affect or order the lives of Earth-bound people. The seed may lie in the unconscious for a long time and its retrieval has to be catalysed by the person's thought process connecting along the same lines as the seed's content. There is no power in having an idea that is someone else's. However, having your own good idea, brings positivity, motivation and a whole series of thoughts which connect into other areas in a knock-on effect. Have you ever heard of *de-je-vous*?"

81

"I know the translation as 'already seen,' and it has happened to me. It was like when something happens, it is as though I have felt it or seen it before, but it does not seem possible that I have."

"Am I right in thinking that it left you with a sense of intrigue and investigation?"

"Yes."

"Well, de-je-vous is the reaction to information emerging from the unconscious into the person's conscious. A person feels they already know the information or that it is familiar in some way, but as you say, cannot see the link to their own knowledge. It can create two reactions, intrigue or angst. Either of which presents the person with an opportunity to investigate further or dismiss. The power is in the meaning, but not just the meaning of the information, it is in the meaning of why 'I should know this' and the significance of why this has happened in that moment."

"What are the success rates?"

"One of the well-known religious teachings states, 'some seed falls on stony ground'."

"Yes, I know it. 'and some by the way side, in thorns and lastly on good ground'. I think I get the idea. Are all ideas spirit ideas?"

"No."

"So why do you do this? Why not let things just happen?"

"We help because Earth is part of the whole system. Many on Earth may think they are alone in the universe, but you now know they are not. This world and Earth are closely connected and we encourage the resources coming from Earth after they have died, to continue to feed into research that will help solve issues. It's not just medicine."

"I thought you would know all of the answers here, well especially you."

"No, we are still limited by our evolving and personal progression. You see, the Earth does not know of the after world without doubt and that's because they need to develop individually and collectively at the same time, but with them steering the ship. If they knew of us, it would change the whole concept of mortality and the feeling of being contained to one lifetime's achievements. Yes, it is different for me because I have a more developed sense of knowing because I come from realm five. You know that realm five exists only because I and others have told you. In the same vein, because this realm, like Earth, is a development realm, I am not allowed to provide you with information about life in my realm. If you want to access realm five, you will need to develop your relationship with knowing."

"I am battling at the moment because I want to ask so many questions, but I am going to choose not to ask them yet and cool my jets."

"Right choice."

"Thank you for talking with me."

"Keep on track."

Tarquin disappeared and I walked back up to the house.

Discharged

I found Monique sitting on the veranda wall reading a book of French poetry.

"Are you hungry?"

"No, but I could do with a drink, can I have a cup of tea please. Should I be hungry?"

"No, but I was wondering, because a lot of new arrivals miss eating, not that you need to."

We found a bench on the sunny side of the walled garden. Within an instant two mugs of tea had materialised in the space between us, accompanied by a bowl of red cherries.

"How do you do that?"

"Just visualise what you want and concentrate on it and in your mind, bring it to you and place it in the space you wish it to appear."

I concentrated and a bowl of bread and butter pudding appeared on my lap.

"Well done, John!"

"I was trying to visualise a banana!"

"Ok, so what's the link between bread and butter pudding and bananas?"

I looked down and explained that my mum used to cut up a banana and share it between us on the top of two bowls of pudding.

"Is my mum going to be alright?"

Monique took my face in her hands and looked into my eyes.

"She is going to be really sad for a long time John, but she will be alright and will still find things to be happy about in the future. Losing someone is really hard, especially for those left on Earth because they don't really 'know' this world exists."

"I think they should know without doubt."

"The way it is, is fundamental to our existence and I do not have the answers for you."

"Obviously Tarquin does, but I felt obliged not to push him when we broached the subject during our talk."

"You will have to let it be until it is made known to you, but don't hold your breath because the answers will not come to you. You will have to find them and they will not let themselves be found, until you are ready to hold them for the good of the whole of existence. Those who hold the meaning are those who are very spiritually advanced. At this level or in this realm, we mostly accept the meaning which is out there and is held for us for the greater good."

"What do you mean mostly?"

"Like many on the Earth plane, we in the spirit world would still like to know what it is all for? You have to accept, some spirit people who live here do not believe or accept there is a meaning or a bigger picture, much as they did on Earth."

"But what about the existence of other realms, like Tarquin's fifth realm. Their presence must mean something? How many realms are there anyway?"

"I can only share a limited view with you from my own understanding. There are eight realms in total, including the Earth plane. In terms of pace, I am not going to provide you with detail. I have a feeling you will find out soon enough. Basically, this realm, if we think of them as numbered, is the fourth and is very much like the Earth plane in the sense that most people who pass over, come to this realm. You will find a lot of similarities between this and the Earth. Including the right to choose your own spiritual path."

"Do people go into the first, second and third realms?"

"Yes. These are what we call the darker realms. On Earth there are basic codes of conduct such as 'respect of Self and the respect of the other' and 'whatever is hurtful to you, do not do to any other person'. Therefore, if you betray yourself by betraying or abusing others, then this shows that you have little Self-awareness. The degree of spiritual awareness and will, the personal power to change things, determines the level at which you can exist in the spirit world and the levels are realms."

"Does this mean that not so nice people go into the lower realms and are the lower realms hell?"

"Yes. Whether it is hell or not depends on your interpretation of what hell is. It's not all fire and brimstone and people being tortured like Dante's Inferno vision. The lower the realm, the more successively darker, colder and less pleasant it becomes to exist in. There is less communication and more hostility.

Although people who live there exist as light beings like us, light does not emanate as brightly from them, because the spirit within them has been denied."

"When I was coming over here with Peter, I was worried about being judged, but it seems people are judged before they go into the realms."

"They are not judged by another, each of us judges ourselves in a moment of truth that cannot be denied. It is at that point of clarity where self-denial is impossible. There are those who choose to forget this judgement encounter with themselves, as denial is a popular pastime for many, even though at that time, they can see the truth. People's own personal awareness of Self and will, determines the amount of spiritual light they reflecate. If you think of the full range of the realms as a spectrum, where the highest realms are the brightest and the lowest realms as the darkest, the amount of light you give off determines what part of the spectrum you match and can exist in."

"What about the higher realms?"

"Spirit access higher realms as they spiritually develop. People from this realm and higher, do visit the lower realms. It is possible with help, for people in the lower realms to become more spiritually aware and tap into the divine will. With development, they can move into the next realm up. Which is what we can do, if we choose. It's all about choice."

"But other than what Tarquin says about him coming from the fifth realm, what proof does anyone have that the other realms exist?"

"Well, I know people who visit the darker realms, so they exist, but no one on this realm can visit the higher realms until they are ready. So there is no proof, only belief."

"So this realm is much like Earth, except here there is a greater likelihood that there are realms above us. Whereas on Earth, death separates belief from knowing there is more life to come."

"Yes. Life can be a struggle punctuated with points of safety and possibly peace. Knowing yourself and others, helps you to navigate a path through it and at the same time increases the frequency with which productive choice points happen, which lead to increasing knowing."

"I admit, I have had my doubts, but now I feel I have reached a point where I can accept the reality of this place. On Earth, I accepted my feeling that there must be a bigger picture, but the truth is more visible here because we know more. How can so many here deny there is a larger picture and a meaning to all this. What's the point in people like that being here?"

I caught myself almost immediately and apologised.

"I am going to say this anyway. Be careful and show compassion Master Kenton. Knowing is the prize. Just in the moment, as you caught yourself and thought twice about it, if you knew, you would not have even thought it. All people and spirit in this realm are at different stages of development and knowing. Where is the value in us all being the same?"

I could feel I was not being told off, but guided and humbly accepted Monique's words.

As for Monique, she realised in that moment of John's speed of correction and acceptance and in his ability to split and read thought, he had revolved a number of times before and was a returning spirit not yet awake to himself. She closed her mind, so there was no chance of him reading it. It was for John to find or be found and he was ready to continue his journey.

"So, do you want a banana?"

"Yes please."

Monique took the pudding away and told me to focus on just a banana. Not to allow my mind to connect to other things associated with bananas like custard, monkeys or pudding. She explained, things were associated with other things, whether they be objects or memories, which are part of a schema. She described this as being like a spider's web coated in dew. The dewdrops represent associated items such as objects, thoughts and feelings and the web is what allows each item to be connected together. I concentrated and the most beautiful white flower materialised in my lap. Monique looked at me laughing and asked how it had happened.

"This is meant for you, because I can see how special you are and I want to say thank you for being my guide whilst I have been here."

"Then, this is for you."

A complete bunch of bananas, looking as though they had just been cut from the tree materialised at my feet and we both laughed. Monique placed the flower in her hair and I stuffed a banana in my mouth. I suddenly heard a voice inside my head.

"John, it is Great-Grandma, Hazel, is it OK if I come and visit you?"

"Yes please, when are you coming?"

"John, can you hear me it's Hazel?"

"Monique, I have got my great-grandma talking to me in my head and I can't seem to answer her, how do you do it?"

"Picture her in your mind and ask her again in your mind if she can hear you, you don't have to speak out loud."

"Hazel, it's John, can you hear me?"

"Yes John, I hear you, is it alright to visit you in a little while?"

"Yes, please do."

"OK, see you shortly."

"Monique, I was just thinking about listening and what I had been talking about with Tarquin. Why can't the spirit guides make the doctors or scientists on the Earth plane listen to them? Surely, it would get the information through to them quicker?"

"Well, you have to consider the form of the message, as well as awareness and belief." Monique explained that on the Earth plane, hearing voices in general, was not a positive thing. It is associated with being mentally ill by most, other than those who understand clairaudience, or clairsentience in hearing spirit voice.

If a guide suddenly made himself or herself aware to the person through speech, the effect may be random and negative because the person would be thrown into uncertainty by what they were experiencing. Scientists are renowned for attempting to rationalise everything and if you were to introduce something that could not be rationalised, the chances are the information would be ignored, or they would start to question whether it happened or not.

The risk is they may lose focus on their work, which is not what is wished to happen. Although the method of seeding may be less direct, you have to understand that people have a faith in their own ideas and it is faith and passion which together, drives ideas to the next stage. Ideally, they need the help of those who can bridge the gap between matters of the soul and matters of science.

"Since the start of science's drive to provide evidence based explanation and peoples dwindling faith in religion, people seem to see science and belief as opposites, or that there can only be one answer. In fact, we are the proof."

"But we are not allowed to prove it, are we? All this is pretty complicated stuff, but the strange thing is, the more I try to understand, the clearer things become. Is this all down to Tarquin facilitating?"

"No. Being a spirit person helps because there are no physical restrictions. Communication is direct and instantaneous, but there is something more personal going on. I know you want to learn and because of that, you help yourself to understand. However, with you John, as Tarquin said, you are a sensitive and part of being a sensitive is, you instinctively allow 'knowing' more naturally and so learn at a level where knowledge is integrated intuitively as well as cognitively. People say there may be a sixth sense, I believe 'knowing' is that sixth sense. How fast you learn is up to you."

"It's a pretty neat place this, isn't it?"

"Yes, for those who allow it to be."

"What do you mean?"

"You will meet all different types of spirit person over here John, as you would on the Earth plane. People's attitudes don't always change when they pass over as I have said. You will see. The best piece of advice I could give to you is to keep an open mind and try not to pre-judge. No matter how the person may come across, there is a place for them in the grand scale of things and a reason for them to be the way they are."

Both Monique and I span around simultaneously to the sound of a bump, to see Hazel sitting on the ground next to a bench. She was chuckling away and chastising herself for being foolish. I rushed over and helped her up.

"Are you alright, Hazel?"

"Yes John, I am fine. I have been trying to perfect the art of transporting myself sitting down. I had visualised the position of this bench in my mind and somehow ended up missing it by three feet! I think I will stick to doing it standing up."

I started laughing at the scene and in no time all three of us were giggling away together. Monique noticed the orange light now shining in John's aura and smiled to herself, he was ready to leave. She also noticed the yellow surrounding his head and the pale violet vortex spiralling up from his crown. He was a bright boy and she knew he would have much to give as he became wiser.

"I will say goodbye now John, as you will be leaving shortly. I wish you every happiness in knowing what you come to know on your journeys. I can tell you will have fun. Just remember, go gently at times when others or your needs call for compassion. It has been a pleasure."

"*Au revoir,* Monique and I do hope we meet again. Thank you for making things easier for me and for seeing me."

I kissed her cheek and in return, she kissed both of mine.

I walked for a while with Hazel and then sat down on another bench. Scents of honeysuckle and Jasmine filled the air completing the serenity of the garden's beauty. Breathing in the fragrances, I felt calm and relaxed.

"As it will be time for you to leave soon, Tom and I would like you to come and live with us, if you would like to," said Hazel.

"Yes, very much."

I felt very grown up in that she had asked me if I would like to live with them, rather than telling me I was going to.

"Where do you live?"

"Only a short distance from here in a watermill cottage by a stream. It's very nice, I'm sure you will enjoy living there."

"Why do people live in houses when they have no real need for shelter or somewhere to sleep?"

"You are absolutely right. Some people choose not to have a home and are constantly on the move. However, a feeling of security is important to others and to have somewhere I can return to and call home, is important to me."

"How did you find the cottage?"

"I didn't, I built it from a dream I had when I was a little girl which always stayed with me. I could not have a house like it on the Earth plane, so I decided to live in it when I arrived over here."

"How?"

"How did I build it, wait and see? However, there is something sad you must do before we go there, it is about endings."

"What is that?"

"Tom will come and collect you shortly, to take you to your funeral on the Earth plane."

I was shocked to a place of a million questions around my mum, my friends, why I needed to go and how I was to get there and back.

"Why do I need to go?"

"It's not only for you, it is for the ones you leave behind. Tom will explain; however, it can be a saddening time for you."

"How long have I been dead, you know, over here?"

"I am not that good with time comparison, but I think about a week now."

Grandfather arrived and I greeted me with a big hug. I explained to him I was worried about going back. The knowledge disrupted my feelings, like I was being pulled between the two worlds. He explained it was because I had recently passed and connections to Earth were still strong.

"Why didn't you warn me?"

"Well, you must have remembered that most people who die have a funeral, so you knew it was coming?"

"Yes, but I didn't know I would have to go!"

"I know you trust me. The funeral is best experienced unprepared because it is a ritual of endings and new beginnings. It is important you feel and experience the relationship that Earth-bound people have with their departed and most importantly, how you feel in that separation. It is a necessary rite of passage to enable you to move on."

"Ready? Instead of holding my hand, see what I am seeing in my mind?"

"Just outside the entrance to the church?"

"Yes. When I say, step towards it in your mind."

"See you later Hazel, off we go."

Grave Concerns

The December day was cold, crisp and bright. A hoar frost had taken hold during the night and everything had a shimmering white crystalline cover. To Earth eyes, the scene would have been bright. To my eyes the sun reflected upon the millions of minute faceted prisms, splintering the white light into rainbows, too numerous to wish upon. Squinting, I found I could adjust my vision to see less of the reflection and more of the form.

"Beautiful, isn't it John?"

"It's fantastic, if only we could have seen what we see now when we lived here."

"If only' are two words which come to mind a lot when you revisit this plane. Now I need to explain a few things to you, we have arrived early so we can spend a little time chatting."

Grandfather explained, it was important for me to attend my own funeral for the sake of others, such as my family and friends who came to grieve and say their goodbyes. Most people consider death to be final and whilst they would not be able to see or hear me, there would be a few who would think they had felt my presence. This feeling gave people hope and some comfort because it left a question rather than a full stop and the question opened the mind to possibilities as part of their belief.

It was also important because death is seen as a ritual of transcendence to spirit people. Representing the movement from one state to another, from spirit in matter to pure spirit, like water to steam. It marked a necessary transition of existences along the journey of life. It is also about honouring the time and life on the Earth plane as a necessary time spent as part of existence. The funeral, whether a burial or a cremation, represented an ending to Earth people and it was important for this to be witnessed by the spirit person and seen as severance from the world of matter.

"Letting go is important because it is a poor existence to try and remain attached to matter. I will introduce you to two desperately sad individuals shortly, so you can see what happens when you don't let go when life ceases on this plane."

"Grandfather, do you know if I am going to cremated or buried? I was hoping to be cremated, like a phoenix from the ashes."

"What planet do you live on?"

"Well, not this one, that's for sure." Whilst I loved and accepted him, he could be boring at times.

"You will be buried here in the graveyard. Your mother wanted to be able to come and visit you."

"I think people should be cremated. It takes up less space and I think really symbolises the release to spirit. Either that, or drill a bore hole and bury them standing up and the not so nice ones' head first."

"I don't know where you get this stuff from, but it's not from my side of the family. Anyway, you are going to be buried in my plot."

"Excellent, I get to be with you in more ways than one!"

I did respect Grandfather and was pleased to be with him again, but inside I felt the pull of the Earth plane, which was still strong and binding.

"I feel torn being back here. Now I have been in the spirit world, I know I now belong there, but there is much I have left behind here and I miss people and the things I used to do."

"Hold that feeling of tension. Now in your heart, surrender or give in a little to the attraction of what you have left behind here."

As I let myself think and feel about the things in my life I had left behind, my heart began to ache and I wanted more to be connected to the Earthly existence. The sensation was as though something was drawing me back to where I felt I belonged.

"I feel I want more of what has been lost, my mum, grandma, my friends, my life."

"And if you allow that feeling to deepen?"

"I am feeling; I don't want to leave those things behind."

"Come on, let's go and meet a couple of people."

We walked into the graveyard to be met with a strange sight. There was a man sitting cross-legged on a grave, his hands supporting his chin and he was staring downwards at the ground. Occasionally he would look up, as if he was reading the inscription on the head stone. As I watched, he was mumbling to himself as if he was having a conversation with another person. We were standing right next to him before he looked up.

"Go away! I have told you lot before, I am not interested."

Sensing a threat having detected anger in the man's aura, I remembered Peter's guard when he thought Simon was about to attack and imagined covering myself in white light as protection.

"Please," he remarked sarcastically, "you don't have to use your armour around me, I am no threat, I just want to be left alone."

"George, its Tom, you remember, from the mill. We used to play darts on Tuesday nights at the White Hart back in the old days. I want to introduce you to my grandson John, they are burying him here today. He was killed last week on Barnsley Road in an accident."

I thought Grandfather was being quite abrupt in the way he was talking to the man and I softened my tone, dropping my guard.

"Hello George, nice to meet you. You must have been over the other side, what did you think about it? I think it's amazing."

"Amazing! There is nothing amazing about a world of light, the real life is here on Earth. Everything I had and have is here and that's all I want."

"But what is here for you, life moves on and things change?" I said tentatively.

"I am here! The real me is here. I had a look over there, but it wasn't for me."

Grandfather squeezed my hand, wished George well and said goodbye.

"Glad to see you can defend. It's a good thing to be so when you are in between worlds, just in case."

"George seems so miserable, he would be much better off on the other side, why doesn't he go over?"

"If you knew George during his life time, you would have found he was miserable then. I do not know why he was so miserable, that just seemed to be the way he was. People gave up trying to cheer him in the end and he got the nick name of 'Grumpy George'."

"But if he went over to the spirit world, he would have met people who were his family and friends and they would have shown him a different life?"

"That's just it, a different life is a different way of being. Maybe George was not happy being miserable, but it was what he was used to, it was what he knew and what he knows. From how I remember him here, I guess if he woke up one morning and found he had nothing to be miserable about, he would probably get worried and spend time trying to think why he wasn't miserable until he was miserable again. Some people tie themselves or are tied into feelings and find it difficult to feel anything else. What is not familiar, may not feel safe. Although a feeling may be negative, some cannot change it to a positive one, because positivity is alien, overwhelming or fearful."

"I was depressed once and it took a long time to shift from being negative about everything to being happy again."

"Tell me about it! Everyone on our side was really worried about you. Poor Tony was racking his brains trying to break you out of it. Do you remember what started you on the road to recovery?"

"Yes, I had a weird dream about a canoe…"

"…and a waterfall?"

"Yes, how did you know?"

"Tell me what you remember."

"I was in this deep rainforest and it was so thick that I could not find my way out. Although I remember it being beautiful, I was also very frightened because I thought I was going to die and I suppose that didn't seem such a bad thing at the time. With every step I took, everything seemed to trip me up or snag my clothes. Then the forest opened up and I came across this river. Whilst I was looking at the water thinking, *would it be better to starve, get eaten by something or drown*, I noticed this canoe. It wasn't a hollowed-out tree or anything like that, it was a bright red racing kayak, with a spray deck and paddle. I remember thinking, *I must be dreaming*. I climbed aboard and sealed myself in. It was a familiar feeling because I had done it many times before and I felt confident I could stay afloat."

"Was there a lifejacket?"

"No, but there was this back pack with a harness and I remember thinking that it was strange because it looked like a parachute. Then I thought if I capsized, it was going to get all wet anyway so I left it behind on the bank. As I paddled downstream feeling better with myself, I noticed this really big crocodile. It spotted me and came into the water. It was large enough to sink me, so I sped up to put some distance between us. It was no good and it was right behind me. I paddled faster and faster, but I couldn't shake it off. I didn't want to risk stopping and trying to hit it with my paddle and I wouldn't have had enough time to get out of the canoe if I had headed for the shore. As I paddled for my life, I remember the current getting faster and the sound of the river getting louder and suddenly, I realised what I was facing a short distance downstream."

"A waterfall?"

"A waterfall! It turned out to be the mother of all waterfalls! I was about a hundred metres from the edge and looked back to see the crocodile had stopped and got onto a rock in mid-stream. I span the canoe around facing upstream and paddled for all I was worth. There was nowhere I could pull myself out onto and although I was paddling at full strength, I was making only a little headway. The crocodile opened its jaws and moved towards the water. In that moment, I thought I was going to die, but at least I had a choice and I figured, if I got in the water, with the speed of the current, I was not going to drown before I went over the top. I didn't want to be eaten, so I span the canoe downstream and paddled at full speed into oblivion."

"The parachute?"

"Yes well…as I shot over the edge I realised my fundamental mistake. It was an awful long way down to what seemed like deep water. I had time to think and I knew I had one chance. I threw myself forward into a pike position and grabbed the underneath of the canoe and immediately went into a vertical spin, stern downwards. My only hope, was the water being deep enough for me not to hit the bottom and smash on the rocks. Heaven knows what speed I hit the water, but over time the water had gouged out a basin deep enough for me not to hit the bottom. The canoe and I slowed down beneath the surface to a point where the buoyancy stopped my descent. The upwards journey was at terrific speed and beyond the surface, I was catapulted out of the rainforest and back into my bedroom. The really weird thing was, I woke up to find the parachute on my bed. I stored it underneath thinking it could be useful one day and then I woke up. It was strange, I had dreamed I had woken up twice."

"Would you say this was the turning point to you starting to recover?"

"Yes, yes, I think it was."

"Why do you think that was?"

"Well, the dream stayed with me and I was able to think about it and what it meant. I felt really alone in the depression and it didn't seem to make any difference what people said to try to get me out of it. I felt the dream symbolised my struggle and the crocodile and even drowning were ways in which I might die."

"You mean suicide?"

96

"Yes, it was crossing my mind, I might be better off dead."

Grandfather placed his hand on my shoulder and kissed my cheek.

"I also felt the waterfall could have been a way to die but it wasn't, it was a way to live or die. In the end, it was me who survived because of what I did which got me out of the danger and I chose to live. So, I had helped myself and then I understood that I had to help myself, if I was going to get out of the depression. I realise now, the parachute was a gift, but I didn't need it. I thought many times of how the end of the dream would have turned out, if I had used the parachute and where I might have floated off too. You knew about the dream then Grandfather?"

"Yes, we knew about the dream. I helped Tony with some of the symbols and he seeded it into your mind. We were really worried about you after Tony had seen you looking up at the viaduct with the death question in your head. We put a parachute in the dream because we wanted you to know someone was looking out for you and we wanted to slow you from falling deeper into depression. When we heard you hadn't used it, but had chosen positively yourself, we knew that your achievement would start to bring you out."

"Were you or Tony always with me or watching me?"

"No, of course not, just now and again when you needed someone or we wanted to see you."

"Cool dream, Grandfather, thank you."

"You should know; you are the one who rewrote the end. Spectacular pike!"

We both laughed and hugged each other, then Grandfather became a little more serious.

"Come John, you need to see this also."

He led me across the graveyard to a grave which was marked with the inscription saying, 'To a woman who loved life so much, she vowed to sleep only after death.' The stone was marked with the year of her death as 1974 and her age at 37 years. Grandfather told me to stay close to him and not to be frightened. He closed his eyes and whispered 'Pippa', the woman's name. In an instant, a spirit form rose up from the grave and stood before us.

"Hello, hello, is that you Susan, Peter, Lillian? Oh, it's not. I know you, don't I?"

"Yes, that's right, I'm Tom Harker, and we have met a couple of times."

"Why did you call me?"

"This is my grandson John, he is to be buried here today and I wanted him to meet others who were here."

"Oh, that's lovely. Hello John, you will like it here. They keep the grass neat and tidy and there are always people who come and leave beautiful flowers and the trees are beautiful. There are not many who stay though. In fact, there is only one other, a man who lives over there, but I don't talk to him because he is grumpy. Will you be staying? It would be nice, but if you don't, that's OK, because I am happy here, because this is where I am."

I thought Pippa spoke like a posh moth repeatedly hitting a light bulb. She had obviously spent much of her life away from ordinary folk and to be honest, I thought she was a bit dippy.

"Hello Pippa, why do you say this is where you are? I don't understand, surely wherever you are, is where you are," I said a little too cockily.

"No silly, this is where I really am, me, myself."

"You mean your body, but you were buried over 40 years ago."

I did not see the glance and frown from Grandfather, in meaning to say, 'show a little more empathy'.

"La, la, la, I am not listening to you. I know I am right. I was beautiful, desirable, men loved me and everyone wanted to be my friend. I had the perfect life and I had everything I wanted, but I always wanted more, well you do, don't you? This place, on Earth is where it all happened and I am not leaving this world for anything."

I was starting to feel a little sorry for Pippa. She was high pitched, her joviality seemed forced and she definitely seemed confused.

"What do you do all day Pippa?"

"Well, as I have said, I look at the grass and flowers and sometimes sit and watch for visitors, but mostly I am in me."

"In you?" I asked quizzically.

"You know, down there where the real me is." She was pointing to her grave. "I lie in me and will and will and will!"

"Why do you do that?"

"So, I will come back to life, silly!"

"But you are alive."

"Not how I want to be!"

Pippa spoke vehemently and directly at me, her face seething. I wasn't prepared for the attack. After lowering my guard to George, I had forgotten to raise it again. The ball of red light hit me square in the solar plexus, making me step back and grab for Grandfather's hand. I immediately felt afraid, threatened and vulnerable. Grandfather shielded both of us in white light to counteract any further attacks. I felt drained of energy, but managed to keep eye contact with Pippa, but before I could speak, Pippa interjected sarcastically.

"Oh, I am sorry John, I didn't hurt you, did I? It's just that, I know I am right and I will rise again complete and I will make it happen."

Not to be put off, but rather wishing I had been taught how to shoot back, I responded.

"Thanks for that. That was my first psychic attack and I could not have wished for it to have come from anyone more delightful than you. But I warn you, you will not catch me again." I fixed her with an equally sarcastic grin.

"Idiot!"

"Nasty woman!"

Pippa disappeared back into her grave without another word. After she had gone, Grandfather turned to me and spoke quite sternly.

"Lesson one, never leave yourself unguarded when you are communicating with spirits who dwell in between worlds and lesson two, you don't have to retaliate. These dwellers are here because their mind-sets confine them to a way of thinking that denies them the truth. I sensed you searching for a weapon just after she hit you with that ball. Your weapon is personal defence, empathy, compassion and love. You don't shoot back unless you are cornered, weakened and on your own. Do you hear me?"

"Yes, I am sorry Grandfather."

"Why were you being so cocky with her anyway?"

"Because she has got it so obviously wrong and was one of those people who were greedy and self-centred on the Earth plane. I know I shouldn't judge, but I struggle with people like her."

"Watch your judgements John, they may lead you into trouble. Judgement is a weight we must carry as part of the human condition; you will have to come to terms with its burden. Anyway, enough said."

"OK, I think I understand, you have reminded me of a conversation I had with Monique earlier, sorry, but she did shoot me!"

Grandfather was still deep in thought and rather casually replied.

"Oh, yes and how did it feel?"

"I take it that I am not going to die then?"

I was being a little facetious because I could see Grandfather was distracted by something.

"Oh, I am sorry John, I didn't mean to ignore you, I was connecting to my own stuff and got a bit side tracked. You are not harmed, are you?"

"No, but it was a bit weird and frightening."

"What do you mean when you say weird?"

"Well, when she shot me, I could see a red ball of light coming towards me and when it hit, I felt instantly vulnerable, anxious and depleted in energy. Like being sucked dry. When you put the white light around us, I felt a little more energised again, but I still felt weakened and anxious."

"Why weren't you defended like I had told you."

"When we were with George, he knew I was defended and that had made a difference to him. I wanted to show him some trust, so I lowered the defence. I made an assumption with Pippa and at the same time wanted to show her that I was trusting."

"If you are going to do that, you need to be aware, at any time you may have to raise your defences, I mean in a split second. Can I suggest you practice at this?"

"A bit like the fastest draw in the west!"

"You may need it one day, take a look over there."

I looked up and sitting on a gate about 200 metres away was Simon. I felt a cold shiver go up my back as I caught his eye, but more from his presence than any fear I might have for him. I nodded and Simon nodded back, but he made no attempt to come towards us and then he was gone.

"You have met Simon?"

"Yes, when I was with Peter, just after I had been killed. He came over and spoke to us, then protected us from Clara, this other not so nice Leaf. Peter tried to encourage him to come with us, but he wouldn't."

"Be very, very careful of Simon. Once when I was visiting your grandma he caught me unawares and for no provoked reason he attacked me. It was like being hit by the lowest dreadful feeling and I felt utterly drained. He disappeared quickly, but it took me a while to recover."

"When you say attacked, you mean he shot at you?"

"Yes. How are you feeling now John?"

"Much better."

"Good. Pippa is known for using lower charges, a bit like warning shots. In one sense, you were lucky to experience your first attack from her."

Grandfather smiled and winked, which left me with the feeling that there had been some planning in their encounter with Pippa. I fixed Grandfather with a quizzical look.

"Nothing to do with me!"

Just then I noticed some movement by the gate on the road and after acknowledging Grandfather, I walked over to see who it was. Mrs Daniels had arrived with four of my friends from school. They all looked pretty miserable and I wished I could let them know I was all right. My friend Becky was amongst them and I felt my sadness start to swell. Although she and I weren't an item, we both knew we liked each other, but I had not had the courage to take things beyond friendship. As I looked into her face I could see she had been crying.

"Grandfather, how can I read what she is thinking. Is it the same as splitting?"

"Similar. Just ask your mind to blend with her mind, take a deep breath and as you exhale feel your mind enter hers as the breath leaves you."

As I did so, I was amazed at the depth of her feelings and her genuine grief. I went with her thoughts and found myself sitting with her on a bench at Bretton Country Park where we had once visited to see the sculptures. I remember how hesitant she had been that day and how I had felt she wasn't interested in me, in a relationship way. Her mind told me I had got it wrong and she was in fact waiting for me to kiss her. I sensed how her heart had ached for me to hold her and how she had waited in vain for me to show a sign. She had clearly loved me and had done so for some time. I had missed what might have been, the warmth of her touch and her words. I looked at my grandfather and he raised his eyebrows in a gesture of submission. I had missed my opportunity for the intimacy of love and this made me angry.

"Why didn't I see this? I have wasted something which could have been so precious. I can't believe I was so stupid." I hid my face in my hands and broke the connection.

"I'm sorry, John."

I looked up with crystal tears in my eyes and gazed upon the faces of my friends. All of them, including Mrs Daniels were lost upon their feelings and all of them genuinely loved me in their own way.

"So much love and so much loss, I am hurt so much right now. What do I do with this grief?"

"You have to let it be and accept the pain. Now this may be hard John but work with me, I want you to experience something. Just allow yourself to deny the pain in a detached, 'I can cope, I'm alright' sort of way. At the same time, connect with the love and grief of your friends."

In doing so, I felt as though I was more attached to them, that the only important thing to do was to stay with them, stay with the loving truth, stay with what was real. After all, the Earth is what is really real. All senses, all limitations and an anxiety of the expectations dictated by being solid and grounded. The connections of potential and actual feelings for another, strengthened my love and need for Earth emotion. I could see the uncertainty of not knowing of the afterlife, was part of the essential human condition. It was the essence of being Earth bound and a way of being. I felt caught.

"I think I have decided I want to stay here with them, they love and need me and I love and need them and Mum and Grandma are here too, so I should stay."

As I struggled with my feelings, grandfather linked directly into my mind.

"Come back John, I love you too, but come back, come back to my voice and come back NOW!"

I felt myself being drawn back into spirit and towards Grandfather. I had experienced an extremely powerful pull towards the Earth plane and my friends and had genuinely wanted to stay with them.

"Are you OK?"

"Yes, I think so."

"Do not deny your feelings, open your heart and allow the truth of loss to come through. This truth allows you to grieve and accept the loss as part of the process of letting go. Denying creates an illusion and the reality of spirit then becomes the illusion, because it is a new reality and you are not accustomed to it as yet. The combined power of emotions expressed by those left behind, draws you back to what is familiar and what has been reality for the last fifteen years. It is a powerful draw."

"I was caught; I was really caught. But I can see why. As I have said, so much love, so much truth."

"This is what happens to those people who have passed to spirit and then decide to come back and live on Earth. What they are attracted to is the feeling of love and the open show of emotion which happens particularly at funerals. The reaction to this display is usually greater than anything they ever experienced during their lives on Earth and is something they may have always longed for. They become blinded by the light and warmth and then make a fateful decision to stay. What they don't realise is this intense pouring out of human emotion is a necessary part of the grieving process for those left. It purges the feelings of loss and allows movement to the next stage of the acceptance of death."

Grandfather went on further to explain that a funeral is a ceremony of a rite of passage, which represents a transition and is celebrated as with other comparable rites such as birth, puberty, parenthood and partnerships like marriage. A rite of passage is an occasion marking a life change, with an invitation to accept a new level of personal responsibility which will determine future pathway choices. Within a lifetime, most rites are designed to empower the initiate, however at death, the rite of passage is different because it is an ending and the future of the initiate is uncertain to those who are left behind. Those attending the rite, can only speculate or hope for a positive transition for the person passing. Therefore, they in fact become the initiates themselves and have no choice but to manage their grief, loss and the impact on their lives, in the absence of those who have passed on.

"But people forget, don't they?"

"Not totally. They have no choice but to get on with their lives. It is not as though you have moved to Australia. Earth-bound people are not given irrefutable evidence that life goes on."

"I struggle with seeing why they should not. There is too much unnecessary suffering in this model and for what?"

"Big question, just a mill hand, can't help you there," Grandfather shrugged his shoulders in empathic resignation.

Although I was following what my grandfather was talking about, I also had an eye out for the arrival of Mum.

"I remember a saying which my mum had learned from Dad. 'Water, water everywhere, but not a drop to drink'. I had not really understood the meaning of it until now."

"You mean, so near and yet so far?"

"Yes."

"What's so difficult is, I know how they feel, but they do not have any idea where I am, or whether I exist."

"And you do not want to spend the rest of their lifetimes trying to convince them you are still alive. It is extremely tempting to stay and the truth the new spirit sees has caught many. What many cannot accept is, once the funeral day is over, people start to move on with their lives and the dynamics of sharing a life with the departed soon fades to memories and past tenses."

"Do all spirits like George and Pippa remain with their bodies?"

"No, not always, some follow their loved ones and try to be with them, but they have no way of communicating with them and can become anxious and depressed. They go unheard and remain unheard in the majority of cases."

"Can they become a nuisance?"

"No, not really, but it is possible for them to learn from other Earth-bound spirits, how to project light and emotion like Pippa did. If they project their feelings onto their loved one, this can cause them to feel the same feelings. These can be negative because they are desperate to be heard."

"How do you solve this?"

"The only assured way is to move the spirit forward. If someone becomes aware of what is happening from the Earth plane, they can use prayer or use a call for help to guides or already departed loved ones. In the spirit world, guides are usually aware of their Earth-bound spirits they have a responsibility for and they will continue to visit and encourage the person to pass over."

"What about Simon, he has been here for what must be, maybe, 400 years?"

"Yes, but he has never been over to the spirit world."

"You be talking about me, young master?"

Simon had not even completed his second word before Grandfather and I had raised our defences. We had both spun on our heels simultaneously to face him.

"Excellent John."

"Excellent, what? Don't be fooling yourselves; I could have got you both from a hundred paces."

I knew for some reason, maybe connection, that I had to be bold with Simon, if I was to try and gain his trust.

"Maybe Simon, but over there, they teach you how to see it coming even before its fired. Can you do that?"

"That may be but I thinks that would depend on you seeing me and you didn't see me this time, did you."

"I see you now. This is my funeral why are you here?"

"He didn't see me coming either!" Simon was motioning towards my grandfather.

"Yes, Simon, that's another thing, why did you attack my grandfather?"

"Your grandfather? Well back then I wouldn't be knowing that would I and anyhow, he was trespassing on my patch."

"Trespassing? Do you own this particular part of West Yorkshire?"

"This is my patch and anyone I be catching on it has to answer to me!"

"He had only come to see his wife."

Then thinking empathically, I said, "Probably as much as you want to see yours."

Simon thought long and hard before he spoke again.

"You were very proper towards me when we first met and I respected you for the way you were. You were killed in a bad way and I guessed you must have been sore afraid when it happened. I came here today to see you and ask if you might deliver a message to my Sarah?"

His approach softened my concerns and I reduced the intensity of my guard. Simon, on recognising this gesture, put out his hand to shake mine. In an instant, I heard my grandfather's voice in my head, telling me not to let his energy pass into me. I ignored him and at the moment of touch, I let Simon feel my warmth and sincerity. I passed the thought 'I will help you' to him. Simon was taken aback and dropped his eyes, stepping back from the contact.

"I will be going now young master, enjoy your day in peace. I advise you not to stay on this plane, like those dim witted over there, there is nothing here for them and yet they cannot see."

"And for you, sir?"

"I be still lost and I fear I will remain so. I must go now but perhaps you will be along these parts again. I am sorry for what happened in the past John's grandfather, I remember, that was a bad day for me. You are welcome to visit your wife and I will not bother you."

Simon vanished and both Grandfather and I breathed a sigh of relief. I was trying to translate the message.

"You amaze me John. Simon is one of the renowned lost spirits in this area with a history of aggression and disruption and yet you were able to reach out to him and gain his respect. Also, you seem to have a sense of knowing, similar to which they allow you to tap into, when you first arrive in the spirit world."

"I haven't lost that sense. It is almost as if Tarquin is still facilitating. I have a much greater confidence than I did when I lived here, but I am also being enabled to make my mistakes."

"Extraordinary. What was the message?"

"That he loves her and each day he asks himself why he cannot drink?"

"What does he mean, do you know?"

"I think it is something to do with horses."

A Funeral in Service

The unmistakable sound of the Mumbai Theme tune met my ears. A wooden coffin was being carried by six bearers, followed by Mum and Grandma as they walked along the path from the gate towards the church. I joined my mum immediately and linked my arm into hers. Her face remained the same, distant and expressionless. I had somehow thought my touch would have made a difference and that she would have known I was there with her. She felt empty and unbelievably sad. I looked across at my grandmother to see grandfather walking beside her with his hand on her shoulder. She smiled to herself and crossed her right arm over her body and placed her hand on his. I was instantly excited.

"She knows you are here. She can feel you?"

"She believes I am here. Believing and knowing are on the same scale, it's a matter of allowing yourself to know."

As the piece of music was coming to an end, they placed the coffin on a stand next to the altar. Both Mum and Grandma sat down on the front row in front of the minister. Although we had not been regular churchgoers, I recognised the minister but I did not know him. Following the customary throat clearances, which I thought was amusing, the minister opened the service.

"We are gathered here together on this bright and frosty morning not to consume ourselves with the grief at the passing of this bright, loving and talented young man. We are gathered here in celebration of his life.

"Here is a young man who made himself known in our community. Who always had a smile for the passer by and a cheery word for those who knew him. He was a scholar, musician and a poet. He was also a sportsman, being a keen canoeist and cyclist. Friends describe him as imaginative and loyal and his family, as loving and caring. My feeling is, we have lost from our world, a young man who had much to offer and who will be very much missed from our daily lives.

"There are no hymns today as part of our service, but a collection of pieces of music and poetry that meant much to John. His friend Richard has very kindly arranged the music for us and will be in charge of delivering it. He tells me that although John was keen on 'drum and bass', he has saved us from the delights of such compositions, in fear of our stained-glass windows."

There was a volley of muffled laughter from the members of the congregation and an outburst of laughing from me. I was so pleased my service was not going to be a dreary affair.

"Way to go Richard!"

"Would you all refer to your orders of service so you can follow the proceedings. I would now like to introduce Richard who will conduct the musical score."

Richard came to the front of the church and spoke.

"John was and is my friend. We have known each other for ten years, since we started school together and I hold a lot of love and respect for him. We shared our music and before today, his mum and I got together and decided what we should choose to play. John liked a broad range of music, from classical through to drum and bass. He had a particular interest in Asian-Indian music, hence the opening piece and we will play some more before the end of the service. People enjoy weddings and christenings, but funerals are traditionally sad. John's mum wanted to make his final journey a celebration and I am proud to be your DJ for the day. 'Nuff respect' my friend and if you are listening, this is all for you."

I was pleased Mum and Richard had done this, this was so cool. The first few bars of *Beethoven's 6th symphony in F major 'Pastoral'* sounded out which didn't surprise me. I loved this piece and so it seemed did the audience. As I watched, blue light appeared to collect around people, some more than others. It was as though the music connected with something inside of them. The light appeared to move with the ebb and flow of musical waves,

"…created by the very essence. I am now confirmed in what I see she meant."

As the piece came to a close, Mrs Daniels rose from her seat and walked to take her place at the front.

"As many of you know, I am John's music teacher Isbeth Daniels. I had the pleasure of teaching him music for what was nearly two years. John is, was, a promising clarinet player and for those of you who knew him, you will also know he played the guitar. Today, we have left the musical role to Richard and I am here to read you a poem John wrote and shared with me in late summer. It is called 'Night Wind.' He told me, before he read it to me, to imagine a hot summers night when the welcome breeze blows through your bedroom window and cools your slumbering brow."

"Sounds like a good old fart in bed to me!"

"Grandfather! You sound like a rough ode mill hand."

"I am!"

Turning leaf on up-borne axis
Rippling water dented with a kiss

Cooling brow through open window
Moisture lost in sensation of bliss

Night winds blow 'cross open meadow
Nodding ears in reaching stance

Silently touching crumb on fallow
Lifting web, a spider's chance

No one knows from where they started
Fancy only to where they go

Facing into loose locks parted
Taking with them your temptuous foes.

"You may clap, the credit lies with the author and if he is here I am sure he would welcome the applause."

I started the clapping, not that there was anything to hear and follow and after an unfamiliar pause of people overcoming the hesitancy to clap in church, everyone joined in. The atmosphere was uplifted and people started to relax. *Nitin Sawhney 'Streets'* started to play and its upbeat tempo soon got people making discreet body movements in time with the music. I loved this piece of music as well, as I felt it touched, something close to my soul as I imagined travelling, flying at speed across open tundra in my mind. I reckoned with Richard's help I would have made some converts by the end of the service.

As I was wandering around the church, I caught the eye of my little cousin Melody. I noticed her because her eyes seemed to follow me wherever I walked. I looked at her, smiled warmly and waved. She smiled and waved back to me. She then turned to her mother and pointed in my direction saying, 'John, John.' My aunt looked and then told her to be quiet, so I scratched my armpits and made monkey noises which she giggled at. Walking back to my grandfather's side, I told him what had happened.

"Yes, that's quite common. Melody is about 2 years old. Little children can see spirit but when they get to about 3 or 4 they tend to have engaged so much with what's going on around them in the material world, our world becomes detached from them."

"That's a shame, but I remember being older than that and still catching glimpses of things I thought were there."

"Yes, I think it really depends on how sensitive you are. Were you still seeing things before you came over?"

"Not seeing but sensing stuff like atmospheres in houses or buildings, it was sort of like, I felt people were around I couldn't see. I would also have thoughts about things and have no idea from where they came. I always put these down to imagination, but with the sensing, I thought that they could be ghosts. There were times when I felt quite frightened. Come to think about it, I did see Peter before he caught me."

"You must be sensitive John; in fact, I know now that you are."

"Tarquin told me the same thing."

"Well he would know."

As the music was finishing, Mum got up from her seat and made her way to the side of the coffin. I sat down next to Grandma. Leaning across I kissed her on the cheek and she lifted her hand and touched where the kiss had fallen.

"She definitely knows we are here!"

"Grandma, Grandma, its John can you hear me?"

There was no response but she rested her hand on Jennifer's seat where I was sitting and smiled to herself.

"I notice some of you speak as though John is still here and maybe for you he is. I feel like a limb has been torn from my life's tree and this is so hard for me. Thank you all for coming today. I am sure John would have loved to see you all together, although perhaps not at his own funeral. I am starting to see that my son had some good taste in music and I am grateful to Richard for playing it for us. I am going to read you something I have written for myself and John and I am hoping I will be able to read to you without faltering. If I cry, perhaps you would cry with me and just forget the worst. I think John had got his interest in poetry from me. I have heard 'Night Wind' before of course, but not read in public by someone who knows how to read poetry properly. Thank you Isbeth, you were an inspiration to him. OK, deep breath."

This, was my John…
and only God knows why
he was not with us long

He shone like the brightest of stars
One I plucked from the heavens afar
To become my beloved son

He was my world
My companion
My life

And in a moment
what I knew to be him
has now gone

I picture you upon that icy road
and in your last moments
thinking of home

I ache, that I
could not be there
for you then

But know that wherever you are
You will remain my shining star
And one day I will hold you again

"I miss you so very much…"

The tears came and they wet the faces of all who were present in their grief. I balled my eyes out and hugging my grandma, was aware that Grandfather was keeping a close eye on me, the one that wasn't weeping! Mum wiped away her tears and regained her composure.

"I have chosen the last piece of music because it connects to something in my soul around my journey to hell in losing my son. When I listen to it, I can imagine him lost and alone and that somehow connects with my own sense of being lost also. Some of you will connect this piece to the film, but it has no connection. It is just the music that haunts me in my uncertainty of what is to come."

Grandma left her seat and went to Mum's side to guide her back to hers. As they sat down the music started and not recognising the piece, I connected to Richard to find it was called *'Road to Chicago' by Newman*. It stirred the feelings of being lost and alone for me and I wished I could tell Mum it wasn't like that. Sitting cross legged in front of her, I remembered the many times we had shared music together and how much it had been a part of our lives. Through my veil of tears, I made her a promise. I could now connect to Grandfather's thoughts, as he watched me with baited breath, but knew I had to make my promise without any interference from him. I looked up and smiled at him before looking back into the teary but soft and gentle eyes of a woman who had made my life so much easier to live.

"Mum, I love you more than anything in this, well every world and I promise I will hear your call wherever I am and come if I can, when you need me. But I must leave you to live my new life. In a way, I will never leave you. True, there seems much here to stay for and if I was still living in your world, I would never want to leave. But I have already left and know that for what I now seek, remaining will just be a journey of fading memories. I will always love you and Grandma and I know that I am but one step away. We will meet again."

"Good boy."

I looked up at Grandma and she was looking straight at me.

"Grandfather, are you sure she can't see us?"

"What did you say, Mum?"

"Such a good boy, is what I said, good, good boy."

I looked at her with a doubtful glance.

"Can you hear me Grandma, do you know I am here?"

She said nothing.

The music had the desired effect of allowing people to cry and reflect and they all seemed to know what Mum meant. The minister took his place once again at the head of the church and spoke clearly.

"Would you all join me in saying the Lord's Prayer in order to close this celebration."

Outside, the sunshine was still bright and at head height glinted from the brass like handles upon my coffin. Instead of following the procession in silence, there were little murmurs from people as they followed on. As I earwigged, I could hear that people had enjoyed the service and that it wasn't a conventional funeral and how good it was. I was really pleased Mum had chosen a different way for me to leave. As they lowered the coffin into the ground, a rose was thrown by Becky and Mum looked over to her and smiled. She burst into tears, so I walked over, kissed her softly on both cheeks and whispered I would always love her for what never was. With the words of committal and the ritual over, people turned away from the grave and I followed. I had made the break and confirmed my departure from this world and knew Grandfather was proud of me.

"Grandfather, are we going back for the wake?"

"No, John."

"Why?"

"It's a meeting for fellow mourners to celebrate your memories and support each other's losses before they start the rest of their lives without you. It's not for us and I think you have a very good idea of how much people love you."

"I was only thinking of the cake!" I was trying to make light of the fact that I felt thoroughly miserable.

"You and your cake. You can have anything of your choice at home. Come on, you have a life to lead. Take my hand and –"

"Wait one moment."

I walked over to my mother and wrapping my arms around her, kissed her on her cheek. I did the same to Grandma and standing back from them I said,

"Thank you both, I love you lots. I will see you soon and don't worry about me, I will be fine."

I gripped Grandfather's hand.

"Where to James?"

"Mill Cottage."

"And don't spare the horses." I remembered the one that could not drink.

As the funeral car pulled away from the entrance to the church, Audrey turned to Jennifer and asked how she felt it had gone. Jennifer responded by saying she hoped people had enjoyed the service, the minister had been marvellous and Richard had done a great job.

"I think it was a great turn out and I am sure John and Tom enjoyed it too."

"Oh Mum, you know I don't like it when you talk like that, they have gone, they're gone!"

"Well, they have now, that's for sure, but I could feel them there. I couldn't see them, but I am sure Tom placed his hand on my shoulder when we were walking into the church and inside when you were speaking, it was as if John was sitting on your seat listening to you."

"I don't doubt you feel something, but I think you are feeling yourself wanting to feel something. I want to know too that John and Dad are safe and well, but I can't accept they would come back. I think they could be in heaven now, if it exists, but I just don't know and if there is a God, I am not too pleased with him at the moment."

Audrey bowed her head, sighed, made a wish upon Jennifer's fallen star and slipped into sullenness.

A Time to Play

There was no doubt Mill Cottage and its surroundings were truly beautiful, with its rough cut stone walls, inglenook fireplaces and working water wheel. However, from when we arrived back, I was detached from its natural ambience and tranquillity. I spent the next three days feeling miserable, sitting, reflecting and thinking about the funeral and the people I had left behind. I could hear Mum calling from time to time as she struggled in her void and imagined being with her, without actually splitting. Hazel had invited me to let things be for a while to enable those in loss to adjust to just that, including me. I now felt separate from the Earth plane and in possession of the knowledge, there was nothing to keep me there. I debated with myself over the feelings of emptiness and anxiety for what was to become.

"What next? What happens next?" I whispered to myself, the questions, veiling the real questions of 'what's the purpose of this' and there must be a reason for dying and coming here? I could not find answers to similar questions on Earth and the thought of there being no purpose, added to the hollow feeling already carved out by my grief.

Grandfather and Hazel had left me alone to wrestle with my loss. Although they met me with smiles, hugs and words of encouragement, they let me struggle through my own perceptions and beliefs around what had happened, answering when needed, the best they could.

One afternoon I was sitting by the Mill pond and watching dragon flies dart across the water. Connecting with their symbolism, I compared their metamorphosis with my own. I could not help but to centre my thoughts, which were, that on Earth, we are kept in the dark about life beyond life. Meaning we have no definitive clue as to what is really about to happen. In a similar vein, the dragonfly starts its existence in the darkness of the underwater world and then undergoes a metamorphosis into the light sky world.

I wondered whether the dragonfly nymph had any inkling about how its life would change. At least its change was within the same plane, not a total shift across realms. But then again, dragonflies were present in this realm, so they must also go through the death transition as well. *Two changes in one lifetime*, I thought, which led me into wondering *if I had to die in this realm, if I was to move to the next. Or that maybe I will stay here forever?*

An iridescent green dragonfly hovered above my hand and slowly descended to sit on my index finger. Raising my hand to inspect the creature, I was captivated by the detail in its body and wings.

"What do you think about that two changes thing?"

"I think you should chill out and have some fun," the dragonfly replied.

I nearly jumped out of my light suit. The dragonfly once again settled on my finger.

"I am sorry, I didn't realise that you could talk, that's amazing. What's it like being a dragonfly?"

"It's a real buzz."

"Buzz, ha, ha, you're funny. Do you miss living underwater?"

"Not really. I could never get used to the sinking feeling in the mornings."

I could hear sniggering behind me and span around to see Tony leaning against a tree.

"Was that you? Was I talking to you just then?"

"Me? I thought you were having a conversation with a dragonfly!"

"How are you doing Tony, I have noticed the difference of not having you in my head so much."

"I am most excellent, but how are you, John?"

"A bit miserable to be honest. I thought I would be able to make the break and move on a lot easier."

"Why?"

"Well, because I have Grandfather and Hazel over here and this is a whole new world."

"It's a massive shift John. Firstly, you had no idea about this place other than a 'could be'. You exist differently over here and you are different as well. You have left everything and everyone you have ever known behind and to many of them, you are dead and gone. You can't expect to be able to move on that fast. Your grandfather is very proud of you, he said it was tough at times, but you made it and you got blasted as part of the bargain!"

"Yeah, but I get the feeling he had something to do with that."

"Your grandfather? Never," Tony grinned at me and winked.

"Anyway, are you here to cheer me up?"

"No John, I am here to blow your mind!"

"Sounds fun, but I have always said no to drugs."

"Mr Kenton, pay attention. We are going to go riding and I don't mean cycling. Name your bike."

"You mean motorbikes? Ducati 990, a red one," I said in a flash.

"I prefer Kawasaki's myself."

"I remember you saying that."

"OK, we are going to play in virtual world, or what I like to call virtual virtuality. It's similar to a gaming program you would get on devices and computers on the Earth plane, but with this game, it's really virtual and you create the location and terrain as you are actually riding into it. I will generate the terrain and using a mind link, we will communicate between us, so that you can experience the same thing that I am imagining."

"It sounds incredible but I haven't ridden a motorbike before, can you crash?"

"All you do is imagine you can ride one and we both know you can do that and yes, you can crash but don't worry you can't hurt yourself."

Before my eyes the scenery around Mill Cottage disappeared and sitting on the grid of a racing track, the two bikes were resting on their stands, their paintwork gleaming in the sunlight.

"You do realise you are never going to catch me on that!"

"Yeah, right Kenton, in your dreams!"

We got onto our bikes and Tony explained we would start off slow and simple. Everything was in place, the track, the stand, pits, flags, blue sky and sunshine.

"Helmets?" I enquired.

"Not on your life, I like the wind in my hair!"

As I fired up my engine, I felt a kind of excitement never before experienced, even in my imagination, let alone in someone else's. I revved the engine, let out the clutch and before I knew it, I was at the first bend. I was heading for the crash barrier which suddenly disappeared as Tony expanded the track to match my direction. Having practiced spirit mind reading since I got back, I could hear Tony telling me to slow down a bit and take it easy to start with. The track continued to grow and banked to the left where it re-joined the main track. Tony drew up alongside.

"Take it easy, that duke is a beast. Just ease off a little. We have all the time in the world."

We both released our clutches and took off at speed. Second, third, and into forth. Dropping a gear, I slowed into the first bend and banked to match the camber. Accelerating out of the bend, Tony increased the pace and sped along the straight. Looking forward, I could see the track materialising about a thousand metres in front of Tony. I opened the throttle and powered into the straight, catching him up quickly. The sensation was incredible. I could feel the bike beneath me in all of its power and the wind rushing through my hair, yet I could stare open eyed into it. The speed was awesome and the acceleration was amazing, as there was no delay at all between the twist of my grip and the increase in speed. Tony was slowing down to negotiate a double bend. Before he hit the first bend, he accelerated and took both of them with alternate knees hovering just above the ground, before screaming up the hill and into a tunnel. I followed at a slightly more cautious pace. After two more laps, I was getting a better feel for the bike.

"There comes a time when the bike feels as though it is an extension of you. When you get this feeling, don't be tempted to take the risk and go for it. Allow the bike and you to grow into each other and then integrate with the road. When you have synthesised all three, you will feel more confident and can then take more calculated risks."

"How do you integrate the road when it is constantly changing?"

"That's experience. You gain a feel of what you might expect from the road through you and the bike and then you ride to the road. Here I will show you."

He created different conditions like wet tarmac, gravel, grass and concrete and I started to understand how I had to modify my riding for each. As we came into the double bend again just prior to the tunnel, Tony told me to stay focussed. We both screamed through the tunnel except this time the exit opened into a fantastic mountain range with the road meandering along a ridge cut into the mountainside at an equal contour.

The scenery was absolutely breath taking. Tony's imagination had opened to allow a much broader view of our surroundings and as we made our way along the valleys, I could see all the detail of the rock faces and landscapes. We came to a halt at a natural viewing platform and sat quiet for a moment taking in the view.

"What you are creating is absolutely incredible. How can you hold and project all of this information?"

"It's not information like you would have in a computer-generated scene, it's a projection of thought and feeling interacting with minute energy vortices within the projected spatial plane. My thoughts and feelings organise the energy in such a way that light is reflected back at us from the structures created. Once the pattern is set it repeats itself and I overlay varying detail to create perceptual change. The clever thing is, virtual world fills in the unimagined gaps."

"Where are we now?"

"We are in one of the infinite sub dimensions of the main realm that we live in and we are back at Mill Cottage."

"Two places at one time?"

"Yes, but remember, this is a virtual world."

"Could you make this permanent if you wanted to?"

"Yes, you just press print! No not really, you have to ground it, which is really an Earth plane term for anchoring the scene, so it does not rely on you for its formation. I mean it is almost as though the vortices behave as they would on the Earth plane and exist as matter."

"Could I do all this?"

"Yes, but it takes a bit of practice and quite a bit of meditation."

"Why meditation?"

"Because whilst the mind we come with does adapt to life over here, we still arrive with the same mind, thought patterns, ticks and habits. In order to do this kind of stuff we need to quieten the mind and practice focal creation and holding. It is holding in the sense of maintaining the structures you are creating. You might start off by creating a virtual object, holding it in your hands, studying it and then learning to modify it into different shapes."

"I did manage to imagine up a flower when I was at the rest home. Is it the same process as that?"

"Yes, similar, but you can only materialise real objects in the realm. Whereas in here, your imagination is the limit."

"Will you teach me?"

"Of course, I will, no worries, but let's do it at the end of the ride."

"OK, thanks, Tony."

We set off again and I could not stop thinking about how I might create different things, when I was able to. I now understood how Hazel had created Mill Cottage. As we continued down the valley, I could make out a flat plain below with a straight road cutting across it and disappearing into the distance. As we made our final descent, I started to imagine I was wearing racing gloves, whilst keeping partial focus on the road. I pictured them in my mind and imagined what it would feel like to wear them. To my astonishment, they appeared almost exactly as I imagined. I quickly dematerialised them before Tony detected them as part of our link and continued to think about other things I could create. Tony came to a stop as we alighted onto the plain and I drew up alongside him.

"This next part of our journey is about speed. There are no road limits, so you can go as fast as you like or as fast as you think your bike can go. Just watch for the surprises. I think you will be eating your words about my Kawi."

I did not hesitate and took off. I knew he had a fast bike and more experience, but I also knew this was a virtual world and there didn't seem to be any limits. Plus, I knew my own imagination's capabilities. In a very short time, I was racing ahead doing 150 mph and couldn't sense Tony gaining. However, I knew I must be quite a way ahead because the road and scenery were only defined a short distance in front of me. Suddenly, the terrain in front expanded rapidly. Tony overtook me on a machine that was low, elongated and fast. The only thing I could think of to catch him, was nitrous oxide. Two small tanks appeared either side of my main fuel tank and the connecting pipe work evolved and reached into the fuel injectors.

"Three, two, one, FIRE!"

I overtook Tony in a matter of seconds and accelerated forward towards the extent of his projected and imagined limit. It was an amazing experience to be riding at such a high speed literally on the edge of a virtual universe, seeing it appear in front of my eyes as I flew into what could only be described as oblivion. Suddenly the terrain in front of me expanded at an incredible rate and I knew Tony had upped the game again. I could hear his voice in my head.

"Nitrous Oxide, virtual nitrous oxide? Kenton, you learn too fast, well eat my shorts!"

I looked to my left to see Tony riding a silver machine shaped like a delta wing. He was set snugly in a cock pit and smiling up at me.

"I hope you have good tyres on that thing, otherwise you are going to take off."

"Who said anything about tyres."

With that, he lifted the machine to about 20 metres above my head. There were no wheels, just a smooth under surface. Bearing in mind we were travelling at well over 200 mph, Tony brought the machine down level with me again.

"So, John, if I was to accept that you had a natural talent for creating virtual matter, you must realise and accept that the game now becomes more complex. You now have to be aware of what I am creating, what you are creating, the interaction of the two and the mind link. We both have the ability to block the mind link so we can increase the element of surprise."

Tony looked up to see a 40-tonne arctic baring down on them with about a two second reaction time available to get out of the way. He pulled his machine violently to the left, but not fast enough to avoid the arctic's wing mirror clipping his tail fin. This sent him outwards into a flat spin. He expertly brought the delta wing back under control and instantaneously repaired the damage. His major concern was for John, with old Earth born instincts kicking in, he feared the worst.

I saw Tony veer out to the left and stared the artic straight in the grill.

"Come on then! No truck is going to flatten me again ever!"

I opened up the throttle and screamed into the face of the arctic, my mind splitting it right down the centre as each half peeled either side of me harmlessly. The experience was surreal and exhilarating. An image of a lorry giving birth rather than causing death, flashed through my mind as I shot through the tailgate and back onto the clear road.

"John, John, are you alright?"

"Yes, I am fine."

"What the hell was that about, I don't know what happened, did it hit you? I don't know where it came from?"

"You sound surprised?" I said, with an ever so slight sarcasm.

"You bastard. Game on."

I estimated, I was doing about 240 mph, when the road and the ground beneath me disappeared. Looking back, I could see sheer cliffs rising about 800 metres above the surface of the sea, I was now heading towards. In the short seconds, as I made the spectacular descending arc towards the surface, I thought of my grandfather and the dream. Instantaneously, I found myself sitting in a canoe, which I knew was not the best of ideas. Having created the canoe, I also realised this was not a dream and started to panic. I wasn't sure if I could actually die in virtual world and in that instant, was transported back in my mind to the church, where I had seen myself in the coffin. In my growing confusion, I thought about myself in the coffin and then found myself lying down enclosed by a box.

Tony was watching John making his mind up from his vantage point aloft. It was a temptation to seed ideas into John's mind, as he had done for years whilst John had been on Earth and it felt alien to watch him decide his own virtual fate. Perhaps he had assumed too much of him to introduce interactive play this early. When he saw John's canoe turn into a coffin, he knew he had made a mistake.

Tony blasted down towards him, attempting to mind link and make suggestions but John was blocking all connection. He gave him an extra 200 metres descent and created a massive white air bag on the surface beneath him.

"Focus!" I shouted at myself.

I desperately thought about how I could fly out of this and from the depths of vague familiarity, my mind focussed on an eagle. After a stumbling start, the words flowed from a source I thought was outside of me and yet they felt like a resonance of a distant memory. When they connected, the transformation initiated.

"Sands shift between the rift, hold me when I fall, for I am an eagle, I am the eagle, the eagle's I, eye of an eagle. Through to be, in heart's union see, thee as they, just one step away. So, mote it be."

Nothing happened, so I said the words again but this time from a union of my heart and mind. Feeling myself dissolve, I followed the words into the unknown and a moment later, the brilliant sunshine breathed into my heart and I reformed. The box surrounding me had disappeared and I had in fact transformed into a large eagle with a mind that was my own. Suddenly I was facing a massive white expanse, which I could not comprehend, so I pulled up and soared to the right, wing feathers bouncing off its surface. With all of my strength, I beat my wings to gain some height.

Many previously imagined scenarios blended together as something instinctual was freed inside me. Strangely, in my being, I was the bird, which held a timeless familiarity most difficult to recall. Feeling every sensitive connection between each feather and my mind, enabled a natural confidence of being held by and in control of the air. I thought that it was Tony who had seeded the thoughts and created this new form.

Tony however, looked on in disbelief. He had no idea how this was happening and had only heard of remote incidents where spirit had transformed into an animal form. He was aware spirit could transpose themselves into the mind of spirit animals to experience their perception of the world, and of people transforming into a virtual world projection of an animal, but not to become the actual animal itself.

"Delta wing to eagle man, are you receiving?"

"Yes, delta wing, I am as high as a kite."

"You're not a kite, you're an eagle, except I am not sure how you are an eagle."

"Look below on the sea, you will see a large raft and a cool drink's box on it. I'll meet you down there, let's chill and have a chat."

It was some time before I joined Tony on the raft. I was totally absorbed with the sensations of flying and the memories of what it would be like to be a bird in the freedom of flight. The air tensed each barb of each feather and the slightest of muscle contractions changed my direction. I delighted in imagining and placing thermals rising up beneath me, effortlessly ascending towards the sky.

"John?"

"Yes, I am coming. This is fantastic, you ought to try it!"

"I'd love to, but I don't know how to."

"I'm coming down."

I folded my wings and dived towards the raft, but as I made my descent, realised I had no idea how to land.

"Nose up, wings back, open flaps and undercarriage down," shouted Tony.

The result was little more than a heap of feathers and a beak full of raft, but at least I was down. Tony was rolling around in laughter.

"Couldn't have done it better myself!"

I ruffled my feathers and stood there erect and majestic, before preening myself to straighten some of the tangle.

"What do you think?"

"You look magnificent, I… I am lost for words John, I have no idea how you have done this?"

"Come on Tony, stop mucking around, I am only a virtual eagle!"

"Change back then, if you can?"

I imagined myself to be back in my human light form but it made no difference, so asked Tony to link with my mind and we both tried a reversion. I still remained in eagle form. Tony opened a cold soft drink and took a long draft.

"I would like to see you get your beak around one of these. Sorry John. What I cannot understand, is you have made a shift into spirit animal form. I have only heard of two or three incidents where this has happened and the spirits who have achieved this are advanced beings. I did not think it was possible for those who live on this level. What is weird is you seem to have a natural talent for integrating into this spirit realm and appear to be able to do things which have taken me a long time to do, let alone be able to do some of things that I cannot."

"Why do you think that is, Tony?"

"I don't know my friend, I don't know. I have worked with you for years and yet, although I have always known you thought of yourself as more than who you were, nothing showed itself, not that I could see anyway."

"Whilst I lived on the Earth, I did some reading into Shamanism and I was able to imagine the interface between my world and the world of the spirit animal. I did this by imagining myself standing on the sand inside an hour glass. As the sand disappeared beneath my feet, I felt committed to falling with it. I thought it was my imagination but as I did, I felt no fear as my senses started to link with the animal, I was imagining myself to be. Do you remember as a child at school, running around pretending to be an elephant or a pig?"

"No. I was either a wolf or a lion."

"Well, strangely, I felt like the animal, even then. Tinker and I always had a close friendship. I believed I knew what he was saying to me even without words, but I could not always trust it. I always stopped short of dropping into the bottom half of the glass though, because the feeling became overwhelming and I got scared something might actually happen which I could not change back. I find myself in that place now and I admit, I feel a little scared."

"Don't be scared John, I am sure there is a way out of this. When you were imagining yourself to be an eagle, did you use some sort of incantation?"

"Yes, but I thought it was coming from you. There was a part of it that seemed not to be my thoughts; they just came into my head. Strangely, it also seemed to be a memory."

"Do you remember what you said?"

"Sands shift between the rift hold me when I fall, for I am an eagle, I am the eagle, the eagle's I, eye of an eagle. Through to be, in heart's union see, thee as they, just one step away. So, mote it be."

"And where did the 'so mote it be' come from, it sounds sort of familiar?"

"Rune magik. Do you remember I did the Norse project on Vikings, well I became interested in Odin's symbols?"

"Yes, I remember the project, but I did not realise you had connected with the symbolism. You were a bit young for that I thought, although rune magik can be a very positive form of belief. Did you incorporate the sands, to overcome the fear?"

"Yes, and then I played with the identity and the perspective of me as an eagle and vice versa. It was the other part about union, becoming they and one step away, that just came into my mind."

"They are powerful words which hold the potential belief that one form can become the other through the union of being both. What else? You were in a coffin just prior to becoming the eagle, so symbolically, you were taking flight from death. Why were you in a coffin?"

"I guess, I thought I might die from the fall."

"But I had told you, you could not be hurt in virtual world."

"Yes, but I was confused about what to actually believe. I was starting to panic."

Tony suggested I try to reverse the incantation, focussing on becoming myself again through the heart connection. I spent a while changing and reformulating the words trying to really feel them, but there was no effect. We then explored my fear of becoming myself again after experiencing the freedom of flight and whether I really wanted to give that part up. We played with the tone of the words and the structure of the sentences and then tried to alter my mood to incorporate different levels of feeling. Nothing seemed to work. By this time, I was getting a bit fed up with being an eagle and started strutting about on the raft. As I paced, Tony watched me and then he had an idea.

"Movement, you were in motion when the change happened, you were falling in fear and you were able to overcome it by imagining yourself to be inside of the hour glass. Could you try to perform the incantation whilst you are falling?"

"Yes, I think so, but I know now I have nothing to fear when I am falling and courage seems to play an important part in this transition."

"Ah well. I didn't exactly give you all the details when I told you, you could not be hurt in virtual world. There is something called virtual pain." Tony shaded his thoughts as he lied. "Which, can feel as bad as being hurt in the physical world."

"Why didn't you say?" I was quite shocked.

"The idea was to protect you via our mind link all the time we were in here, so you didn't get hurt. I figured you may have hesitated about playing and we wouldn't have had such fun! Sorry."

This made me decidedly nervous and more so when Tony suggested I fly as high as I could and invert myself whilst collapsing my wings. I would then plummet towards the water, which would stimulate the fear he thought I needed to create the courage to shift back again.

"How do you know this is going to work?"

"I don't, but there is another factor we must bear in mind. We had no mind link when you transformed. It must be the same when you try to turn back. You are on your own. One more thing, you set the mind block, so you will have to do the same. Oh, and if you can recover into a dive position before you hit the water, you will feel less pain."

"What? From two hundred metres?"

"Two hundred? I think you better make it three hundred, more margin for error."

I was very worried, which was exactly what Tony wanted me to feel. His idea would create enough fear to hopefully catalyse the courageous break through. I took off from the water platform and as I circled overhead, gaining height, Tony called to me.

"Remember to shut your eyes on the way down, you don't want to have your concentration broken by the image of the water rushing up to meet you and good luck, I will be waiting for you."

The words, remember to shut your eyes, sealed my fear, I was now afraid. I was going to be plummeting towards the water and would have to somehow suspend awareness of the impending impact in order to focus on the words which were becoming more confusing in my mind. Three hundred metres were gained in no time and I found myself circling and running through my lines.

"I can still hear you!"

"OK, I am just preparing myself."

I severed the link, stalled, folded my wings and dropped.

"One thousand, two thousand, three thousand, four…"

"Sands of time rise from below, reverse your course and temper your flow. As eagles see beyond what's mine, who's I and sense became sublime, then halve our hearts and set me free and allow my being to truly be. In honour of our new-found bond, reflect upon my grace, allowing us as two entwined, to stand about in face. So, mote it be."

I once again, felt myself dissolve and follow the words to emerge again in brilliant sunshine. As I opened my eyes, impact with the water was only four metres away. I wasn't sure if I was still an eagle or not.

"Stop!" The halt was immediate and with the rush of air suddenly quietened, I felt as though time had also been stopped. There was no movement, just stillness and I imagined I could hear my own heart stop beating. The margin for error was one and a half metres. I started laughing.

"What a rush, woohoo!"

"Nice 'n precise, welcome back."

I released myself, dropped into the water and swam over to the raft. I opened a cool can and rested back on my elbows.

"You gotta try that. That was amazing."

"You are amazing."

I felt embarrassed by what Tony had said and tried to laugh it off.

"No, I believe it and I mean it from my heart, you certainly have talent."

"Thanks Tony, I have had a most excellent guide."

"Is that a feather in your hair?"

Touching the right side of my head, sure enough, there was a feather embedded in my scalp, which I thought was a cool reminder of my flight as an eagle. However, it would take some explaining.

"Had enough play for today, Mr Kenton?"

"Yes, I think so Tony, thank you for a fantastic adventure."

"OK, I will see you soon, take care."

"And you."

I closed my eyes and found myself back at Mill Cottage, sitting by the pond. I smiled as a dragonfly settled on my knee.

"You know I used to be a real dragon in my last life, a Sardinian Barking dragon, very fierce."

"What?"

I could hear Tony laughing into the distance. I smiled again and touched the feather. I thought about when I had transformed back from the eagle into human light form. In that transition, I was neither and both at the same time yet, I existed, so who or what was I? Just then, a horse fly started buzzing around my head, I knew what it was by the sound it made. The dragonfly took off and the horse fly took its place. It was funny how I felt cautious about it and yet knew it would not bite me. I wondered how long it would take for me to become acceptant of spirit life and to lose the preconceptions and fears associated with life on the Earth plane.

"Well, horse fly, you are a long way from any horses."

The fly scratched its flanks with its two back legs, cleaned its mandibles and took off, landing by the water's edge. It crouched and lowered its proboscis into the water.

"Sarah!"

I had almost forgotten about the message Simon had given me, but how was I going to find her?

Light Defence

I ran back to the cottage, with a feeling of excitement and a mission building in my mind. On entering the kitchen, I found Hazel and Grandfather chatting, as he was making tea.

"We were just going to sit outside for a while and have tea. Come and join us," said Hazel.

"Yes OK, but I have something urgent to talk to you about."

Grandfather handed me the tray and we walked on to the cobbled veranda shaded by a pergola adorned with beautiful lilac wisteria. I sensed the calmness of their pace compared to mine and placed the tray on the wooden table before sitting down.

Gradually, the blueness of the sky darkened and a billion stars shone brightly from the velvet of nothingness around us. Fire flies danced beneath the trees, nosing Chinese lanterns dangling from their branches and the dragon flies lit themselves in iridescent displays of unimaginable colours. The garden and stone pathways were dimly lit with candles in coloured glass jars. A fire had been lit in the fire pit, the flames dancing within and around each other, teasing the air as if to excite a response from their surroundings. Scents of a myriad of flowers, somehow deepened by the night air, wafted purposefully catching my memories of Earth. I was not disturbed by the change, more excitedly intrigued.

"I wondered if night time would ever come, it comes on quickly when it arrives, doesn't it?"

Tom and Hazel smiled at each other.

"You are not telling me one of you two just did that, are you?"

"Why not?"

"Because it's big to turn day into night! Hang on a minute, is this like virtual night, but I thought you had made Mill Cottage and its surroundings permanent?"

"It is permanent, but there are no rules saying you can't place a virtual night dome over it. You would have got a sunset first, but you said there was something urgent to talk about? The main thing is you look happy, are you feeling better and did you know you've got a feather in your hair?"

"Yes, yes and yes, Hazel. I have been into virtual world with Tony, it's a long story."

"Anyway, what is eating you?"

"I need to ask you how you find someone whose probably been in the spirit realm for about four hundred years, it's Sarah, Simon's wife. Do you remember when we met him in the grave yard and he asked me to contact her, well, I have just remembered."

"If she has been over here that long John, which seems unlikely, she might have moved to the next realm," replied Hazel.

"It would be a bit more difficult if she has. You would need to speak to a high planer to see if they would pass on the message," added Tom.

"I get the feeling she would still be on this plane, because I think she is waiting for Simon."

"OK, take some deep breaths and settle your mind, close your eyes and focus on my voice. Put your feet firmly on the floor and imagine you are growing roots from the soles of your feet which grow down into the earth beneath the cottage. Keep those roots firm. Do you know what a lotus blossom looks like?" Hazel spoke calmly.

"Yes."

"Then imagine a lotus flower growing from the depths of our old pond. It has its roots in the murky bottom and a long stem that reaches up to the surface towards the light."

In an instant, all three of them were literally transported from the veranda and yet were still sitting around the table which was now resting on the surface of the pond. Tom went to speak, but Hazel put her finger to her lips and silenced him before he could say anything.

"Keep your eyes closed John and see the lotus reaching the surface. As it does, a flower is formed, which opens up. It is a beautiful white flower with many golden stamens at its centre."

Both Hazel and Tom could see the flower upon the surface forming and glowing.

"Now, I want you to imagine the flower starts to pour out white light, until it becomes like a fountain. Let the light spill onto the surface and cover the entire pond and then the whole garden. Now place a seed of love at the centre of the flower and with it, a fragment of your knowing of Sarah. Perhaps think of Simon as well. Imagine the light proceeding beyond the grounds like a smoke ring, but as a pulse, moving in every direction, crossing the whole of this spirit plane. Simply allow it to flow as far as you can."

As John did this, they could see an intense ring of white light traveling into the distance in all directions. The thought and heart seed now interlaced the light with threads of gold which reached away with it.

"Keep your eyes closed and tell me how you feel."

"I can feel the light and I am kind of connected to it as it moves away."

"Good, the light is scanning for her. Keep your eyes closed and rest and relax. Feel the roots drawing back into the soles of your feet."

As Hazel said this, the three of them and the table were transported back to the veranda.

"Come back to my voice and come back now." Hazel asserted.

I opened my eyes and focused on Hazel.

"That was fantastic, it really felt as though we were actually above the pond. How long before she replies?"

Both Hazel and Tom exchanged glances.

"It depends on whether she's on this plane and if she is tied up doing something. Also, it depends on how strong the link was that you placed in the flower."

"Are you planning to go and see her?" asked Grandfather.

"Yes, unless she wants to meet here, why?"

"Because if you are going to travel, you must practice protecting yourself. I will help you. You go onto the lawn, by the orchard and I will meet you there in a minute."

"Are you bringing your six shooter, Grandpa!"

"I am not going to teach you how to shoot back John, at least not yet anyway."

I left their company feeling a bit miffed. I had already imagined the feel of my Walther 9 mm in my pocket, however, as I put my hand in to take its grip, nothing was there. I imagined again, but still could not get the weapon to materialise. I thought no more about it and walked over to the tree swing to wait. Grandfather was speaking to Hazel.

"Wait, set a mind block," said Hazel.

"What was that? I have never seen a meditation actualise before to that degree, let alone us become part of it. I thought it was an 'in mind's eye' exercise on this realm. Did you see that light go?"

Hazel was looking thoughtfully into her tea cup.

"We will have to work hard to guide him the best we can. It is almost as though he is unlocking something inside himself, but without awareness."

"Grandfather! Are you coming?" He came over to meet me by the swing.

"I feel very hesitant about teaching you to return fire. I can teach you enough of how to protect yourself through defence rather than the disablement of the other. This practice is not a game. Returning fire is about disabling your opponent, not about doing permanent damage. We cannot kill and it is not about that. It is about creating time for you to retreat from a volatile situation which could result in your psycho-emotional harm. Do you understand me?"

"Yes, I think so."

Grandfather started the exercise and asked me to imagine I was standing on a golden disk. Then to imagine reaching down and pulling up the sides of the disk which were made of a fine golden mesh. I brought it up over my body and head and I tied it on the inside, so it fully enclosed me.

"The mesh acts as chain mail to negative energy, which is diffused and dissipated as it hits the mesh, thus disarming its intent."

Grandfather explained the key to effective defence was to have foresight, based on an awareness of the intent of the other, which could be read in minds or in the aura. One could be defended going into a potential conflict, but the other would be put on guard if they detected the defence.

"Remember George had been aware of our defences in the grave yard. Speed of response is paramount, as you do not want to incite an attack unnecessarily."

The second defence mechanism was to stand facing your opponent and use vortex energy to create a shield.

"You used a crude version of this when we approached George."

Initiating the vortex involved bringing chakra energy up from the base and sacral chakras and down from the heart chakra, to focus in the solar plexus chakra. The synthesised energy then had to be revolved quickly and projected to a distance just beyond the defender. The result being a spinning, but solid shield of blue and white light.

"The shield can be used to deflect negative energy bolts and it is practice that enables you to generate it quickly."

We spent some time coming into contact with each energy centre transferring and summing their combined effect. I found a component in my success of doing this was by believing I could actually do it. What I was coming to understand more of, was my imagination was the key to creating in the spirit world. I found that the shield defence was much more to my liking, but Grandfather reminded me a spirit could shift position instantly and to use the two in combination gave greater protection. I could still create the shield whilst the mesh amour was in place.

"What kind of attacks might I expect?"

"Similar to the one you experienced in the grave yard, which is a solar plexus projection usually emotion filled. It is draining and you feel washed out. Another emanates from the base chakra, again a projection, but anger primed and you can experience the attack as fearful. This one can be nasty if you are not defended because if it is a full-scale projection, it can create paranoia which can overwhelm and unbalance you."

"What should I do if I am caught like this?"

"Raise your defences and lie still. Whoever is attacking will not be able to harm you further. Whilst you are immobile, imagine yourself to be standing under a silver waterfall with the white light infused water trickling onto your head and through you. This will wash out the negativity, cleansing you and re-energising you. When you have recovered enough energy, transport yourself out of there.

"Another form of attack is a creeping attack. Here, the spirit sends out negative energy, usually in a pincer movement. The energy creeps using tiny vortices in the atmosphere to carry the negative energy and is designed to overwhelm you gradually. They may approach you in a friendly manner and initiate the attack without you knowing. The problem is, it is very difficult to detect, so you have to scan the area around you and be ready to immediately engage your defences if you pick up a hint of danger. If someone catches you in a pincer they can hold you with the energy which makes it difficult for you to defend. Then they can either hit you with a direct chakra sourced attack or flood the pincer with any particular negative influence."

"Scan?"

"Yes. Vortices are little energy centres, mostly blue in colour and neither positive nor negative. They are a vehicle for energy. You detect them by losing focus and seeing them in your peripheral vision."

"What would you say the worst attack was?"

I was expecting him to choose one of the attacks already mentioned.

"I would say a head shot."

"What is a head shot?"

I was thinking about splattered brains and lots of blood and dying.

"Not quite John. A head shot involves the attacking spirit radically reversing the natural vibrations of the head and base chakras. Whereas the crown chakra is our connection to the divine, the shot creates the effect of the two energy centres being inverted."

"You mean like having your head stuck up your –"

"Trust you, no…pay attention."

"The inversion temporarily gives you the feeling of being separated or disconnected from positivity and reality. The attacker's ajna serves to provide insight into the victim and acts as a rangefinder and guider for the pulse to be directed to the most vulnerable thoughts and feelings of the victim. When it discharges, the throat chakra produces a loud noise, like a gunshot. This is serious stuff."

"What happens to you if it connects?"

"Some people, if they are more mind orientated have a greater defence because they can counteract the effect with logic. But it is a powerful force in the hands of those who know how to use it effectively. The energy connects directly with your fears, denials and shame and the unconscious counterparts of these. At the same time, it makes your thoughts race and it confuses you. The sound it makes, disorientates you and you feel utterly and irretrievably vulnerable and defenceless. It makes you want to submit because it can disable your will. If it connects, you will be stunned and vulnerable to further attack."

"How do I know it's coming?"

"You will see a pink mist, then a vortex starts to form above the attacker's head. It will hold the colours of a bruise, deep reds, dark indigo and black which move within the vortex like a fluid. As the energy increases, the vortex spins faster and at the critical moment, the centrifugal force creates a tangent for the energy which is guided by the ajna into the victim. Somebody well adept at this can get a shot off in about a second."

I was feeling uneasy and afraid that this sort of attack could take place. I had always thought of heaven as a peaceful place. I felt a little better though, when he told me I was unlikely to experience anyone in this realm, who would instigate a head shot attack. But there were those in lower realms and low fliers between worlds, who could and do.

"Thanks for teaching me about this Grandfather. You do know that I will stay out of trouble, don't you?"

"Yes, I know that and at the same time, forewarned is forearmed."

"John, John Kenton? It's Sarah."

"Hi Sarah, thanks for connecting, I have seen and spoken to Simon and I have a message for you from him."

"Do you want to come over?"

"Yes."

"Follow my voice and…"

I smiled, winked at Grandfather and disappeared.

Wild Horses

I materialised on a hillside overlooking a green and grassy plain back dropped by red and orange tinted mountains. A small homestead lay to the left above a shallow ravine, wood smoke drifting carelessly from its chimney. The river running through the ravine tempered its pace as it slowed and meandered effortlessly across the meadows. Horses of all shapes, sizes and breeds were grazing in the meadows and standing along the riverbank. The scene looked like a ranch except there were no fences or enclosed paddocks. It was a fabulous setting. Suddenly there was a presence standing next to me.

"Thank you and you are right it is like a ranch. When I came over, I hadn't seen a ranch, but I met an American who used to farm in Virginia and when he realised I had a love of horses, he showed me one and I created my own. There are no fences, the horses are free to come and go as they please."

I offered my hand. "John Kenton, pleased to meet you."

"Sarah Johnson, likewise."

"So, you have met my Simon, is he well?"

"Stressed, sad and lonely, I'd say."

"And stubborn."

"Afraid, I think."

"Yes, I feel what he feels from time to time and keep an occasional eye on him. It has been over four hundred years since we were together and I still love him. I could also give him a wallop for not having the courage to take the leap. Anyway, here's me forgetting my manners. Would you like to follow me down to the house where we can relax and talk?"

We relocated to the garden at the back of the house and sat on easy chairs beneath the shade of an elm. The water sparkled and reflected catching Sarah's face and highlighting her deep brown hair. She was about 40 years old, generously slim and beautiful. I thought Simon must really miss her. Sarah smiled at me and offered me a cool drink of dandelion wine and river water.

"Strange combination?"

"The horses swear by it, although they prefer their dandelions fresh."

We both laughed. Sarah, was caught by a slight familiarity in John, but held her thought without pursuing it.

"So, what is the message?"

"He said he loves you and each day he asks himself why he cannot drink? I have an idea what he means, but you will probably be sure."

"What do you think?"

"I think he is referring to himself as a horse, in that you can lead a horse to water, but you cannot make it drink. It sounds like he is starting to soften and wants help to come over."

Sarah retreated into thought and I watched the horses in the meadow. A fifteen-hand chestnut stallion caught my eye as he wandered to the edge of the garden. I walked over to meet him and gently took his head in my hands, scratching his cheeks, before softly blowing up his nose, vibrating the air with my lips. The horse snorted and nosed my shoulder requesting another scratch.

"Hello boy, you are magnificent."

The horse nodded in appreciation as I scratched his neck and underneath his chin.

"I see you are familiar with horses?"

"I had a friend who kept two horses and she taught me about blowing up their noses. I have done some riding, but I am not very good. I notice they don't talk."

"No, they choose not to. They are a bit snooty really, but I love being around them and working with them. They have a great sense of knowing and an incredible ability to channel will."

"I can hear you don't speak with the same accent as Simon."

"No. I have come into contact with many from different cultures and I suppose I have gradually lost the accent. But there, don't you be worried 'bout that master John. I can be likening my tongue to that of old Denby Dale, if I choose."

I smiled at her and kissed the horse on its nose. The horse licked me back, turned and wandered away.

Sarah asked me about how I had come to meet Simon and I told her of our first encounter with my catcher and when I had spoken to him at my funeral. I said I was clear about how well defended he seemed to be and although he had attacked my grandfather without good cause, I also had a respect for him and for some reason I was drawn to wanting to save him. Sarah smiled at me in an acceptance of my sincerity.

"I don't know what it is but, I feel he isn't at all happy on the Earth plane and he is wanting someone to come and get him and show him the way through, but not just anyone. It would have to be someone he trusted. He talks about being sent to hell if he came over."

"Have you saved many people or things in your life John?"

"Things like, bugs and worms from puddles, baby birds from cats, hedgehogs and toads on roads. I freed a fox caught in an old coal shed and I once found a swan tangled in fishing line and I called the animal rescue and stayed with it until they had come to set it free."

I also told her how I took time to listen to people who were upset and would try to make it better for them or if I could, fix it for them.

"Sounds like you are a proper hero?"

"Well, I don't know about that, but heroes seem to have such exciting lives and everybody likes them. They ride into the sunset, giving up the girl and dismissing all thanks for their deeds, because they are strong and –"

"Alone?"

The single word dislodged something in my heart which then seemed to fall into my stomach and for no reason, tears started to fill my eyes.

"Come here John." Sarah stretched her arms out towards me.

"It's alright, I will be alright in a minute. I don't understand what happened."

"Quite the hero."

The tears came with a vengeance and I sobbed deep heart felt sobs. I could not understand what was happening to me, but knew from our mind link that Sarah was genuine and I could trust her. I decided I was being stupid and with a hard sniff and a cough, wiped my eyes in an attempt to regain some composure. What I had not noticed were the horses, who were starting to gather around us, all listening intently. Sarah smiled at me, making soothing noises. Being mindful of my vulnerability, she gently posed her next question.

"Who did not save you, John?"

I thought how I had saved myself during my life but as I sat and thought, the feelings of emptiness emerged around my heart. I knew the hero, who had never returned and spoke hesitantly.

"My dad…my dad didn't come back."

The tears flowed again, although I held my face in my hands in an attempt to hide from them. I remembered the exchange that I had had with Monique and the other kids at the manor and wondered why this had come up again. Sarah was listening whilst maintaining her distance.

"I sense you have visited this sadness recently. Would you wish to also tell me, about what happened?"

The story was as vivid, as if it had happened yesterday. I told her of how my father had been a merchant seaman, an engineer aboard a freighter which operated out of the eastern ports of the Philippines and Indonesia. This had meant he was away for about ten months of the year, spending four weeks at home during the summer and at other times during Christmas and Easter. His visits always coincided with my school holidays, so I was with him a lot when he was home. There were holidays and days out, projects in the garden and a workshop where we would work together. I remembered him as being strict but kind.

Mostly, I remembered the stories of his adventures, of flying fish and singing whales; of sea birds that caught lifts aboard ship and magical water where you could switch off the engines and be taken with the current for hundreds and hundreds of miles. He had fought pirates off Thailand, steered his ship through mountainous seas, had out-run sea monsters and saved stranded yachtsmen on their round the world journeys. It was a world of wonder to me and I loved my dad, the man who braved it all.

"It was just before Easter following my tenth birthday. I had just come in from school and had been counting down the days to my dad's arrival on my way home. Once home, I had found Mum sitting at the kitchen table and she was crying. She sat me on her knee and held me so tightly I had to struggle free. On asking her what was wrong, she told me my dad was not coming home and after my questioning, explained that he would not be back again because he had got a job in New Zealand and would be living out there for good."

"I ran out of the house and into the woods which backed onto the bottom of the garden, retreating to one of my hiding places. There I stayed until the calls of my mother, grandfather and grandmother had subsided. When I eventually returned after dark, I was met by a police officer who gave me a stern telling off. I remember shouting at the officer that my dad had just left, which resulted in him turning to my mother and telling her he expected that he would be seeing me again, because I was the kind of boy who would continue to cause trouble. I remembered feeling ashamed, even though, I was not this kind of boy."

"After my mother had asked the officer to leave, she scooped me up and smothered me with kisses. We cried together and cried every day for what seemed like a long time. Weeks turned into months and the letter I wished for, telling us that my dad was coming back, never came. Summer holidays, Christmas' and birthdays came and went. Whilst these were marked by cards and an occasional gift, there was never a letter really explaining why he had left us or asking me to join him.

"After a while I got used to living with the feeling that he would not return, but I never betrayed the fact he would always be my hero, even though Mum used to call him a coward for not facing us. Mum made me promise I would never blame myself for him going, but other than his job, I never really knew why he did."

"That must have been painful for you."

"I missed him and I waited, but he never came. I always thought he would come back, but he didn't. I was angry too, but I found it hard to be angry with him. I was angry with Mum for a while and was horrible to her, but that was no good, so I just kept it inside."

"Sounds like you were a little lost for a while."

"Yes, I felt empty, like something was missing and I knew what it was but couldn't do anything about it."

"Lost and vulnerable and no chance of being saved."

I thought for a while, whilst the horses were very quiet.

"I used to dream he would sail his ship up to the end of our road. He would call me from the starboard side to come and join him, saying that we would sail around the world and have great adventures together. Mum was there, telling me not to go. I would frantically pack some of my things but, by the time I ran outside, the ship was gone or it had sailed too far away for me to catch up with it."

"Your dad left you and then continued to leave you behind in your dreams?"

I burst into tears again but managed to speak through them.

"I, didn't want to be left. I loved him so much…but…I guess I wasn't good enough for him, or maybe he thought I didn't love him enough for him to stay or come back."

I wiped my nose and eyes on my sleeve and looked Sarah in the eye.

"I am not going to leave Simon behind! I have felt him and his pain, I know he needs my help."

The horses shifted, some of them nodding and snorting.

"You want to save Simon?"

"I know I can."

"Please listen to what I am about to say. If you intend to take on this task you must first release yourself from what has happened to you. The world resonates to the sound of so many intentions which remain intentions, because people falter before they act, or they have not planned or affirmed or get caught in contemplation. Being caught, is what you are in this. Your father did not come back and save you, so it seems you have undertaken a sense of duty to save others. I am inviting you to look into yourself and wonder whether in the course of saving others, you are attempting to save a younger part of you, that at the time was vulnerable, scared, abandoned and alone."

"I don't know, but I was scared and he did abandon me. I managed to make myself stronger and after a while I felt I did not need him, so I moved on."

"How long afterwards did the dreams last?"

"I still get them."

"You still have them?"

"Yes."

"And do you still get the feelings of being alone and frightened?"

"I don't listen to them, I push them away, but they make me feel more intent on helping others. I can't afford to feel those feelings, they are negative and I feel weak feeling them."

"You feel weak?"

"I can't afford to feel weak, there are no prizes for weak people, only failure."

"Where does that come from? It sounds really harsh."

"My dad told me, if you want anything out of life, then you have to strive for it, be single minded and don't be side tracked by silly voices in your head that might take you off your aim."

"I take it; you haven't met the silly little voice since you have been over here?"

The connection had not occurred to me and then I realised. I could not help sense, when I was telling Sarah about being strong and determined, there was a familiar voice in my head, reminding me I was not telling the complete truth. But this was not Tony's voice. These were coming from inside of me. I tried quelling them with strong thoughts, but they were not going to be shut out. I sat down and sobbed. Sarah sat cross legged opposite to me.

"I...can't cope, I can't cope if I listen to them."

Sarah gently asked what I thought might happen if I did?

"They will take me over and I will never be the same again. I will be weak, useless and frightened."

"You will?"

"Yes...I mean no. I don't know what to think."

"Rather than think, what do you feel?"

"Confused, a bit lost and arrgh, vulnerable."

"Are you OK with that?"

I thought and felt for a while. Our conversation had allowed something to emerge and these doubtful thoughts had shifted in some way.

"I'm not sure."

"There are many voices that speak from within. It seems you still listen to the voice of your father and that is a powerful driver, the one that pushes you along to achieve things. He says you must be an adventurer and go out and take from the world without failing. You made him your hero and therefore connect the two, meaning you must be like that to be a hero. The frightened, lonely and abandoned voice is you at the age of ten and earlier, little John, if you like. It seems he has been calling you for years to listen to his voice, but you have pushed him away and ignored him. Please tell me, if you met a small child like him now, who was upset, frightened and alone, what would you do?"

"I'd help him, reassure him and probably put my arm around him to comfort him."

"That is all little John wants from you. You scare him with these big heroic plans to save people and things you don't know much about. He isn't sure anymore if he can trust you. He finds you unavailable and distant. He feels he won't be able to cope and if you fail, it would be too much for him because it would be too much for you."

"But how can he exist in me for me to talk to, isn't it me I would be talking or listening to?"

"He is a part of you and like you listening to the voice of your father, his voice can also be heard. The invitation to you is to be able to respond to his needs, because his needs are your needs."

"This is difficult. How would I know I wasn't making it up as I went along?"

"If what I am about to do could be done on Earth, it would make therapy so much easier." Sarah closed her eyes.

I could feel Sarah's mind enter mine and as I allowed her to move amongst my thoughts and memories, I felt something shift and lift out from my being. I suddenly felt decisive, positive and free. Sarah called my attention to my left and standing about three metres away with his hands in his pockets and tears in his eyes, was a young boy. He was looking down and kicking at the dirt.

"I know him."

"Yes, you do, but not well enough."

"It's me isn't it? Whoa that is weird."

"Yes, it's you. Perhaps you might like to ride together. Go and be. Might I suggest you start with a Suffolk punch. And by the way, little John's understanding, matches that of your own, because he is you."

I looked at the little boy and felt awkward. It was as though I was looking at an old friend with whom I had fallen out with a long time ago.

"Hello, little John, I'm –"

"I know who you are, are you going to be nice to me?"

Little John jammed his hands into his pockets firmly and defiantly. He looked up and fixed his gaze on me through his fringe. I looked upon the younger version of myself and felt how vulnerable he was. It was strange because I was seeing a part of me that I had actively pushed away for so long and yet I had an innate sense of compassion and unconditional love for him, my younger self.

A handsome punch wondered over to us and stood firm and powerfully. He shivered and motioned for us to climb up. I reached out and took little John's hand, transporting us both onto the back of the horse, with little John sitting in front.

"Don't worry; I will be nice to you, to us."

"There is no us in this. It's been you and me separately for a long, long time and whenever I am around, you won't talk to me. Do you know how lonely that can be, to be rejected, ignored and pushed away when all I come with is a feeling of fear for myself? I am little and all I want is to be held and told that everything will be alright."

"You make me feel vulnerable and hopeless. You also make me feel afraid of myself and everything around me. You are dangerous."

The little boy's eyes welled up.

"You are. You overwhelm me with the risks you take, you frighten me. Riding down an icy hill as fast as you could go, thinking you were some kind of invincible special agent. You got us killed for that, you idiot."

I wasn't expecting that and reflected on his words of truth. I could have avoided the whole chain of events and remembered ignoring the thoughts of caution as I was riding. In addition, it did occur to me that I did think I was invincible at the time.

"I didn't know there was going to be a lorry coming along."

"Yeah right. It was a main road. If it wasn't a lorry, it would have been a car. You were caught in some fantasy, with no consideration for our safety. Well, you need to know you get caught too often. You seem to live in some fantasy world where everything revolves around you. Take the time, for instance, when you were in virtual world with Tony, riding through the artic lorry you created. What was that about?"

"I needed to get something out of my system. I had been killed by a lorry and I needed to prove I wasn't afraid, so I split it into two by ploughing through it."

"You needed to prove what?"

"That I wasn't afraid."

"But you are afraid."

"No, you are afraid."

"When are you going to accept that you are me and I am you and it is OK to be afraid?"

"Never!"

The silence of our impasse left us both defiant and strong in our positions, although I felt little John did have a point about the accident, even though it was hard to accept. In fact, it nagged at me, connecting to my shame and guilt, making a compromise more difficult to see. The punch, who had been plodding and listening to our conversation, suddenly took up a faster pace. We were heading towards what appeared to be a deep ford in the river. The horse plunged into the water and in seconds it was at his chest height. Although the current was strong at this point, the horse remained steady and sure footed, pushing through as though there was no resistance.

"You are an amazingly strong horse, aren't you boy?" I said, patting its flank when we reached the other side.

The horse snorted in appreciation, immediately turned and ploughed back into the water immerging back on the original side. It then broke into a canter and headed back towards the garden. Sarah met us and caressed the cheeks of the horse as we dismounted.

"Found your voice, little John?"

Little John thought for a while and had to admit he had been able to be assertive in what he was saying to me.

"Still stuck, John?"

"I just find him annoying and a bit weak and in what he says to me, although it rings true, I can't decide if what he says is the way forward. It's too hard to accept that in any way accepting what he says, will benefit me in the way I deal with things in my life."

"So, you both feel strong in your positions?"

"Yes!" Both of us answered simultaneously.

"Punches, much as shires represent strong will. They were bred to carry or pull heavy loads. In the spirit world, they channel strong will and when you work with them over here, they transfer the essence of strong will into the rider. The transference allows you to engage with a part of you which wishes to assert, but finds it hard to. Hence, little John, who had found it difficult to be heard, was able to find his voice and you were able to defend your position. Let me ask you John, is your position strong, or does little John impact upon your current thoughts and feelings?"

"What he says strikes a chord, but I find that my way pushes through the doubt and uncertainty of failing."

"Let me introduce you to a horse who presents with skilful will. He is a Spanish Lipizzaner and was a dressage and dancing horse in his time on Earth. I invite you to experience his discipline and skill before you talk and allow his energy to infuse with your own."

A beautiful white horse approached the garden. He was broad across the chest, tall, lean and sculptured. Grace exuded from his every movement. We mounted his saddle and settled in awe.

"I suggest you hold on!"

Just as Sarah's words were spoken the horse reared up onto its back legs, kicking its front legs into the air and rotating one hundred and eighty degrees on the spot. Its movements were planned and precise. We came back to earth with a gentle thump and the horse took off at a fast canter towards the meadows. As it weaved and shifted its gait in flight, I could feel the control he had over his movements. Obstacles were transversed effortlessly and taken in its stride. We came to a circular patch of ground which was free from grass and the horse stood motionless at the centre. There was a sense of anticipation as to what might come next.

Shifting his weight onto his left flank, both his front right and hind right legs crossed over his left and he shifted to the left by uncrossing his left legs. He continued to do this until he met the edge of the circle. He then pivoted to face the opposite direction and proceeded to simultaneously lift his opposite front and back legs bouncing from one position to the next as he followed the perimeter.

When he had reached half way, he introduced a skip within the movement and continued around. We were both amazed at the skill and sure-footedness of the horse and how effortlessly he joined the movements together. The energy the horse transmitted to us as riders was received as skilful, each move being planned and then actioned. Unlike the Punch who blasted through the water in an effort of strong will, this horse appeared to arrive at each point of change by a mechanism of predetermined and skilled process.

"I like this horse," said little John.

"Why?"

"Because it feels safe and feels like it is taking us into account in the way he moves."

"I feel like I am part of the movement."

"That's what I just said."

"No, you didn't."

"I think you know what I mean. Why do you give me such a hard time?"

"Because you always try to trip me up, because when I have decided to do something, you are always there trying to stop me, or reminding me of the dangers. I feel you get in the way."

My mouth had over run. I paused and thought about what I had just said and felt guilty. The horse was walking alternatively backwards and then forward through the four quarters of the circle.

"I just want you to hear what I have to say. Are you afraid I might change your mind?"

"No, I am afraid I might become like you and then I won't be able to cope with things. I have learnt and experienced a lot of things since I was like you and I feel I have moved on."

"I know you have, but you must know the expression, 'face your fears'. You really don't have to be afraid of me. Can't you see that having had all of the experiences you have had since you were me, they will stop you from becoming like me again."

"So, you don't want me to be like you?"

"Of course not. I want us to work together, for us to acknowledge each other without being afraid and for us to be able to love and hold each other when we need or choose to."

"Even though I have found you annoying, I do recognise you come with a lot of power. You are right, I do fear you will be able to overpower me."

"I don't think it is right to say you fear me John. I feel what you fear are the feelings that I bring. These are feelings we both have and you have chosen to deny. If you deny something, it does have a tendency to come back and bite you at some stage in the future. I am asking you to consider my feelings too, that's all. I think you will find that in time, it will be better for both of us."

I thought for a while and settled with an inspiration that came to mind. 'The whole is greater than the sum of the parts.'

"I think it will take some practice, but I am willing to try. Just you remember I can control you if I have to."

"Just you remember I can make you feel anxious and vulnerable when I have to, too."

We both recognised the humour in our last statements and felt as though we had reached the first point of understanding each other better. The horse had returned us both to the garden and after dismounting, we both thanked him and returned to where Sarah was sitting.

"How did you find the horse?"

"He was fantastic, there was real skill in his every movement."

"And what sort of effect did he have on you?"

Both of us looked at each other, both in that moment, allowing the other to speak first. I spoke first.

"Let little John say, he has been explaining a few things to me."

"Thank you, John. Well, with the first horse, I agree he represented strong will as you said. Whilst riding, I noticed John became more assertive and defiant but I also noticed that I was able to find my voice and get my point across. The Spanish horse was different. It wasn't a strong energy which made me push through my fears, it was more of a skilful energy that somehow brought together my thinking and feelings."

"Nicely observed!"

"It wasn't so much forcing my view as with the Punch, but finding ways in which I might be heard and felt in my fear."

"What did you feel, John?"

"I think I have heard a lot from little John over the years. I have chosen not to listen to him, because I was afraid he might overwhelm me and I would remain overwhelmed. The energy from the Spanish horse combined with little John's words, kind of let me acknowledge what was being said. So instead of blocking it out, I was able to be with the fear, or what I thought was fear, instead of pushing it away."

"And does little John make you feel overwhelmed?"

"No, not in this situation because he is here. If it was another situation where he was inside of me and impacting on me then maybe it would be different."

"And if you were in that kind of situation and he spoke to you, would you respond to him differently?"

"I would try."

Little John and Sarah exchanged glances and smiled at each other.

"What?"

"You are missing the point John. Little John is you! He is not a separate being that exists inside you. You have separated yourself from him to a point where you feel he works against you. He doesn't, his voice is your voice of caution and vulnerability. You can't be whole until you integrate him within you. The term 'freedom of choice' also means setting your choices free."

"How do I integrate little John?"

"How would you make friends with someone?"

"Talk to them, get to know them…?"

"Yes, as simple as that and taking on board their views, even if they are fearful, without judging their choice."

A thought sprung to my mind from the espionage memories: 'keep your friends close and your enemies' closer.'

"I'm not your enemy, whaart brain!"

"Take on board their views and judge not, their choices," I said sarcastically, smiling to myself.

"Anyway, who taught you that?"

"I wouldn't know?"

I could see that Sarah was smiling to herself listening to our exchange.

"I have another horse for you to ride. This one is a mare, she is an American Quarter horse. She is calm, if not a little docile, but highly intelligent. Being gentle and steady, she is good at what she does. Go and enjoy."

As we rode away into the meadows, the energy that came up through the horse was calm, light and uplifting. I could feel us both relax more into being with each other.

"Hey little John, do you remember when we were about nine, before Dad went away and we did the thing with the petrol and the ants?"

"You mean when we blew up the drive way?"

"That's the one. That was funny and a bit scary, but we got away with it."

"I did, you mean," said little John laughing to himself.

I remembered the course of events. Dad had gone into town one afternoon to get, amongst other things, some ant powder because there were so many of them in the garden, garage and coming into the house. Mum had been preoccupied in the house doing some sewing and I was milling about in the garden. I had noticed there were a lot of ants moving to and fro from the cracks and joins in the drive. Suddenly, I had the brain wave that if I poured paraffin into the cracks, I could burn the ants out, thus solving the problem.

What I didn't realise was, the can I got from the garage, contained petrol. I very carefully tipped, what I thought was paraffin, into each gap and crack and went back into the garage to get some matches. By the time I had returned, the petrol had seeped down into the spaces beneath the drive. I had thrown the lighted match into one of the cracks and jumped back. The petrol ignited and there was an almighty thud, which visibly lifted a section of driveway, pushing up all the dirt and ants beneath onto the surface. There were ant bodies everywhere.

Hiding behind the garage, I waited for Mum to come out, but she can't have heard. I had then crept back and brushed up the evidence. The driveway didn't seem any the worse for it. When Dad got back, he could smell the petrol and I had to own up to opening the tin and spilling a little on the drive because I wanted to see what it was like. He gave me a stern telling off and I was made to promise never to touch it again. The secret was never revealed.

"You know little John; we really did have a tough time back then when Dad left."

"Yes, I know and it is still very real for me. My fear is it will happen again, something will go wrong with someone we love and we will be hurt again."

"Do you hurt now?"

"No, I just feel wary. You don't seem to want to take me into account when you are doing risky things. When I do start to get worried, you shut me off and push me away. I feel the same feelings that I did back then when Dad left."

"Yes, I'm sorry, but I don't really understand what you want."

"That's because you won't listen to me. If you listened, you would hear my side on something."

"Yeah but I feel you are trying to stop me from having fun."

"I don't call getting killed having fun? Don't you think that I miss Mum and Grandma?"

Little John's comments connected more deeply and I felt an overwhelming feeling of responsibility and guilt for what I had done. The tears of sadness welled up from a depth not yet touched and I sobbed. Little John turned around in the saddle and gave me a hug.

"You know, what's done is done and if you let it, guilt fades to a point where you can live with it if you choose not to deny it. But responsibility is a constant and that responsibility is to all of who you are."

I hugged him back.

"You are quite wise for a ten-year-old, thank you."

"No, thank you."

"No…thank you."

This carried on for some time in a light humoured and joking way. The horse led us to an ox bow lake, overhung by a huge tree. A thick bow jutted out over the water and made a natural platform from which you could jump into the cool clear water below. We both spent time jumping and bombing each other and splashing around playfully. The horse munched the grass and looked on contentedly.

On the way back, we talked about heroes, aloneness, loss and about saving people. In the place in which we arrived, there was a feeling we had saved each other and ourselves at the same time. By the time we got back, Sarah could see something had shifted in our relationship. She nodded to little John, who winked and mouthed back a thank you.

"Was that horse a 'good will' horse?"

"Yes, John. Did you notice the difference from the previous two?"

"Yes, I really felt my heart opening and I was able to hear and listen to little John's view and he's got a point."

"The change you have experienced is based around conscious choice. The choice is about allowing yourself to be caught or not, by what drives a decision. By being more aware of yourself in that choice, you are less susceptible to make decisions based on old and fruitless behaviours, beliefs or defences. Most importantly, it is about listening to the Self in relation to the voices which come from within and not denying their existence, when by doing so, what is created, is a sense of betrayal."

"I can see now how considering my fears and worries and not denying them, will help me to make a more informed choice and without little John's voice, I accept now, I cannot achieve that."

I looked around for little John's acknowledgement, as I made the comment but could not see him anywhere.

Glimpses of Awareness

"Where is he?" I was agitated.

"Back in you."

"But I didn't get the chance to say goodbye or give him a hug!"

"Are you feeling a loss?"

"Yes."

"Do you think you will listen to him now?"

"Definitely."

"Well he is a part of you and you can speak with him at any time."

"In the same way that we have been doing this afternoon, in conversation?"

"No, not through heard words, through feelings and thoughts and suggestion."

"But that is harder to accept it is real!"

"That's the point. Before we become doers, we can choose to be deciders John. To learn to accept and trust that each part of us has a role or has had a role to play, whether negatively or positively, we must first become aware of its needs."

"Sorry?"

"You have been in conflict with little John for some time, because he speaks of fears that you don't want to accept and you feel they will have a negative impact on the way you have chosen to be. Having listened to him are you less afraid?"

"Yes."

"Why?"

"Because we understand each other more?"

"Yes, but how?"

"Through will?"

"Yes, through will, but it is also because you are now aware of him or that younger part of you that feels vulnerable. Many choose not to be aware. It is your sense of not choosing to be fully aware of little John's needs that creates your conflict. However, it is the effective use of the three striving wills, strong, skilful and good, which can bring greater awareness and internal harmony, because that brings you more in tune with the forth type of will, universal or divine will. Divine will, is not generated from us, it is an 'allowing' will, meaning that we allow it. But in order to connect with it, you need to create a place inside you, which is more still and reflective. This is a place in you that with awareness and will, you can understand more of who you are and the way others and the universe impact upon you. How do you feel about what you experienced this afternoon with little John?"

"I feel a lot more at ease with myself and him, because I understand what he has been trying to say to me."

"And do you think he is more at ease?"

I listened for little John's voice and was surprised to hear him say he was. But I heard him not in thought form, I actually heard him speak. I smiled and said nothing to Sarah.

"Yep, I think he is feeling much better."

"I think you will find you are both feeling better because you are more realigned with each other. When you are in conflict with yourself, it is difficult to find a true direction in life and be in authentic relationship with others. If you are in agreement and accept the needs of the other parts of you, it is more possible to make decisions that benefit both when in a relationship with another. The most important building block in any situation is relationship and it starts with 'I'. Know yourself and in doing so, you will truly know others."

Sarah explained her theory of the development of who we are, in comparison to a compass. If a child is loved and supported, it has the best chance of understanding its own and other's needs. However, should it have to endure negative impacts and these are not soothed by others close to it, it will internalise the fear, blame, guilt and shame and take responsibility for circumstances it can do nothing about. I remembered, back to the rest home when I had told Monique I thought it was my fault for not keeping my parents together.

"Imagine the child, who has been best supported and who understands about negative responsibilities from consequences, as holding a direction of 'true north.' True north represents living a life being true to your Self and others. Others, who may have been impacted upon negatively, who have internalised unjust responsibilities, face and proceed through life in a direction at an angle to

153

north. So, there is a gap between the direction a person may actually take compared to the one where you are true to yourself and others."

"Mind the gap!"

"Yes basically, where did you get that from?"

I explained to Sarah about the London underground announcement whenever a tube train was in the station and how it repeatedly warned commuters to mind the gap between the train and the platform. It felt ironic that millions of people a year were reminded of this message whenever they were travelling in a whole host of different directions.

Sarah explained that the gap contained the tension, like an anxiety between what is almost instinctual or pure relational, versus the negative thoughts or defence mechanisms that justify the behaviour which keeps the person away from that truth. Human beings are instinctively relational because they are spirit in matter and spirit comes from the one source. The instinctual or pure relational aspect of them is the most divine of all human wills. This Will, humans have translated as the compassionate, empathic, loving, nurturing and a more moralistic aspect of themselves. It provides purpose, meaning and values when combined with divine consciousness. This is the link between the spirit that we are and the more than, the greater spirit, the Collective. The more we are aligned to the Self, the true north, the more divine will and consciousness acts through us. Divine or Universal will, is the sum collective of such Will in all beings that exist on the Earth plane and in spirit.

"Is this why we have conflict on Earth?"

"Yes, because someone, or a group of 'someones', want something from someone else and feel the solution to their anxious tension, lies outside of themselves. When really the solution lies inside, if only they listened to and accepted what they really needed."

I thought for a while and spoke quietly.

"I have battled for years with little John, when really if I had listened, my life would have been less confusing and less fearful. I am glad you and the horses have provided the opportunity for me to speak to little John. I think and feel my gap has narrowed."

"Luckily John, as with a compass, the needle always wants to point to north, so there is a draw or attraction back from the direction or pathway of fate, so to speak, to the unified true direction, as determined by what the majority of beings want."

"Which is what?"

"A fifteen-bedroom house with a swimming pool, a mobile phone which automatically upgrades itself, a supercar, gym, big TV, maybe a yacht and a paddock full of horses."

"That's funny! How do you know about all that stuff?" I said smiling widely.

"Well, if we get into a discussion around consciousness and how there are many who are unaware of their own and others' needs, we would be here all day. I do listen to those coming over and what their lives have been like. I think what most want, on the Earth and in spirit, is something to do with 'knowing' and the more you are able to tap into knowing, the intuition that comes from the Collective, the more connected to everything you feel, as the gap closes."

There was no doubt in Sarah's mind that John was able to shift quickly and authentically. Although there was no trace of deception, she wondered about his ability and how old he actually was. She told him to imagine into the same space where Divine or Universal will meets his own divine will, but experience it as a large cavern containing a still water lake. John tuned in and probed in search for his own level of knowing.

"I can't have much yet."

"It's not surprising. You have not been over here long. But you really learn quickly, try this. Echo sound like a ping or a bell into the cavern void and see what comes back?"

I used a similar method as I had done with the cottage garden meditation, but this time resonated a bell toll out in all directions but inside of my own mind. Nothing happened. Just as I was about to try again, the first echo sounded back. I linked with Sarah so she could hear the tone. It was then followed by another echo and another. Nine tolls in total echoed back. Sarah was very surprised.

"That was nine echoes or bells, do you feel any level of knowing?"

"It feels like a blockage, like a glimpse and I can't clearly see. I guess I have far to go and that's fine, learning is good for me. When I come to think about it, I know from my dad that bells signified the end of 'watches' and eight bells can also be a nautical term meaning a sailor has 'finished his final watch' or died. Well that makes sense because I just have, but with a ninth, I have no idea?"

Sarah knew the meaning to be different but closed her mind quickly as if to appear deep in thought. A young spirit would not be able to tease the elements of divine will and know where to still themselves into it, in order to echo. This was a technique for ascertaining knowing, something more developed spirits

155

practice. The toll echoes represented lifetimes and they confirmed nine. It was more likely that John, was an evolved spirit who had returned from his ninth and final Earth watch and yet he was not aware.

"There is always time John. OK, the big question, who saved you in your meeting with little John?"

I thought back to the beginnings of our conversation and remembered how energised I was towards Sarah, in wanting to go in and save Simon. It had made me think like I was intending to go on some sort of courageous mission. I realised how important strong will can be for energising a state of mind and getting a point across and then, sensing internally, re-experienced the wills of the other two horses.

"I think we both saved each other and I can see how will works in building awareness and about awareness in choosing will. There is also something important I have learned about saving too."

"Which is?"

"Wanting to save others because there is an unconscious need inside you to be saved, only serves to make you feel more of a victim of your own fearful thoughts."

"Good and…?"

"I am not going to save Simon; I am going to help him escape."

"OK, before we speak about Simon, let's talk about another type of will which uses the qualities of the three host wills. It is called, transitional will. This is the ability to move between the types of will, at will, making a choice between the ways in which you may make things happen or communicate thought and feelings to others or parts of yourself caught in the gap. It is not really a will in itself, but it adopts the qualities of the will it is about to engage with. Used as a skill, it can help you communicate empathically with others you are with as well as in transformation."

"Sarah, do you mind if we chill for a while, I need to rest my mind, too much frontal lobing."

"You do know, what you are feeling is all in your mind. Your mind thinks it's tired because it has tired during all the years on the Earth plane. It's because you are new over, your imagined body still resonates the physical feelings into your consciousness. I think I may have something to purge the dust, follow me in my mind."

156

In the next moment, we were standing next to a tiered waterfall. As I looked up, I could see the crystal water cascading from above into a hollowed bowl before it continued its journey a further 200 feet into the lake below.

"This is my take on the Havasu Falls, perhaps with an extra tier. Come, stand in the flow and let the water run through you rather than over you. Imagine the coolness and clarity washing through all of your energy centres and taking with it any tiredness or stuck feelings in its passage. As you see and feel the water enter and leave you, let the energy that connects the water light together, collect within your form. It will re-energise and refresh you. Watch me."

I stood in the fall and did what Sarah had suggested. Playing with the sensations of flowing through and flowing over, then settling for the flow through, I imagined the water cleansing and invigorating me. When I looked across to Sarah, I could see tiny light crystals were forming inside of her now, very apparent light suit. She sent the thought to me and I too started to collect the crystal points. She then took my hand and as we entered the sunshine, both of us lit up as the light collided with every infused facet. It was like we were both filled with diamonds and at the same time, it filled me with a tingling, ecstatic energy.

"Trust me?"

"I do."

Sarah led me to a flat rock which divided the water's flow before it fell to the lake below. We both stood on the edge of the rock facing the waterfall we had both just stood beneath, with the drop to the lake an inch behind us.

"Follow me."

She stretched up and arched her back into the void. I followed an instant behind her. I was held in my mind by her tranquillity and trust as we dived backwards towards the surface of the lake. On entering the water, the crystals momentarily trapped inside of me escaped simultaneously firing upwards and into the structure of the splash. As they left my form, I felt an ecstatic sensation of release and renewal in my being.

"Cool eh!"

"Well that certainly beats jumping off a log with your little self."

Sarah took us back to the ranch. As I sipped my dandelion wine, which I had subtly changed to the 'and burdock' variety, I thought about the ranch and perfect surroundings which were similar in ways to Arizona in the United States.

"What do you do here other than looking after the horses?"

"This ranch is a sanctuary, where others come to learn about themselves, much in the way you have today. There are many people who come over from the Earth plane who have lived their lives in an isolated, selfish or defensive ways. When they find themselves in spirit, they struggle with adjusting to what their sense of purpose, meaning and value is in a world, they had nothing more than inkling might exist. The horses help them find their path."

"But what is the point in learning though?"

"John Kenton, ask yourself the question!"

"No, I don't mean what's the point in learning, I mean will you die here and move on to the next realm?"

Sarah glazed her mind and thought about how and why he would have no idea he had revolved so many times. Then for whatever reason it had remained hidden before, she caught sight of his feather.

"Are you hiding something from me?" I asked.

"No, sometimes I confuse myself and don't want to look stupid, so I pivot my thoughts in a different direction until I've worked it out."

"Yep, I know that one quite well."

Sarah let out a long sigh and asked me if I was in agreement that I had brought my knowledge and personality with me over to here from the Earth plane. I nodded.

"In the time you spend here, you can increase your knowledge and knowing, but it is not the same as the experience you gain developing it on Earth. On Earth it is hard edged. It hurts, risks are real and as a being, you are always sitting with a feeling of being separate and alone, but somehow being part of a much greater thing at the same time. What you learn here you can take back with you, but you cannot access the learning until you learn it again on Earth. Then, it is like an affinity, rather than actual knowledge."

"I didn't experience it that way when I went back for my funeral?"

"No John, when you are reborn onto the Earth plane."

Sarah knew she was cruising close to what was being withheld for some reason from John and she knew it was not her responsibility to tell him about the nine bells or what the feather really symbolised. He was visibly shocked by her disclosure.

"I now have a million and one questions!"

"I know you do, I can hear them and I cannot answer them all for you."

"Well, let's start with you and Simon. How old are you?"

"In Earth years 486 and Simon is a couple of years older."

"How many times have you gone back?"

"Six times, I waited for about a hundred years after that life for Simon to come over, but he never did."

"Did you ever come across Simon when you went back?"

"How could I, I was alive on Earth and he was between the worlds low flying."

"What happened to Simon, why didn't he decide to come over?"

Sarah explained, Simon had a brother called Jim and they were both farm labourers working for a well to do land owner in Denby Dale. It was late May in 1553 and they had almost finished clipping fleeces from the flocks. One afternoon as they took a break, they were discussing what they might do with their wages. Simon had decided he was going to buy a new apron for his girlfriend. Jim had been seeing a girl for a while and teased Simon that his supposed girlfriend, was not his girlfriend at all, as he had made no advances towards her. It was also unlikely she would accept an invitation to the bale gathering dance from an oaf like him. With Simon being a hot headed and sometimes brash man, he hit Jim and a vigorous brawl started. What Jim did not know, was the girl had agreed to go to the dance with Simon. A final blow was struck and Jim fell backwards hitting his head on the corner of a stone drinking trough. The blow killed him outright.

Witnesses confirmed how distraught Simon had been and what had happened was an accident. He spent two days in a pillory or gaol, while the parish constable discussed with the parishioners in the village, as to what to do with him. There was genuine sadness in the village and regret at what had happened and the majority of the villagers grieved with Simon at the loss of a brother he truly loved.

"He never forgave himself for what had happened and he blamed what he had done on the fact that his life was barren of children."

"I take it, you were the girl in the story."

"Yes, and although we were together for another thirty years before Simon died of pneumonia, he turned his back on the church in fear of judgement, believing he had sealed his fate and would be sent to hell for his crime. Blamed or not, I loved him and a part of me still does, but he is a pig-headed man with a bit of a temper. What he did love, was to work with horses. His master as such, would let him work in the stables and occasionally ride. When the master was away he would sneak me into the stables and I grew to imagine the horses could understand me when I spoke to them."

"If you have been back six times, have you ever visited him in between worlds?"

"I went back once when I was in spirit but did not disclose my presence to him."

"Why not?"

"He was in the midst of a fight with some other low flier and they were shouting and screaming at each other as to who owned a patch of ground and who had rights to it. I thought he was lost and really, it is him that needs to set himself free not me. He knows I am here. If he believes the other spirits he has had contact with over the years, he has nothing to fear. I will, they will, it is up to him."

"Did he buy you the apron?"

"Yes, he did a little later. He had asked one of the women in the village to embroider little blue flowers on it and all along the strings. It was lovely, I wore it a lot."

"What were the flowers."

"Umm, I remember, they were forget-me-nots."

"I am not sure how I am going to persuade him to come and even if I do, where is that going to leave you. Do you want to be with him?"

"Four hundred years is a long time and I feel he has punished himself for so long when he did not have to. It's complicated because I have had time to develop and I am not sure how such differences work. I have a feeling we should be together, but I am not sure. However, even if he does return, he or I might decide over time, it is not the best that we are together."

"I hope I can help him to return and then I suppose, fate will take its course."

"It is not for you and me to decide, it is up to him."

"Have you ever met Jim, his brother over here?"

"No, I never saw his brother again. When do you plan to see Simon?"

"I don't know yet, I need to find someone who can explain the revolutions and why they are necessary. I was thinking that –"

"Tarquin could."

"Yes."

"I am sorry, but I cannot provide all the answers you need."

"That's OK Sarah, I have had a great time shared with you. I can see why Simon loves you."

Sarah smiled and made a final request before I departed.

"Instead of just transporting back to where you came from, take a final ride to the tops of the ridge above the canyon. I have a horse who will match your will for freedom and adventure. He is a Mustang and represents 'Free-Will'. If you accept my final gift, you will find he will meet your passion and give you a most determined run for your money."

"Then loan me a tenner, you're on!"

Free Will

I said my goodbyes to Sarah and thanked her for her insights and guidance. I promised to contact her when I had worked out a way to help Simon free himself and also that I would look after little John. I mounted the horse and settled into the saddle.

"Don't run before you can walk John, you have all the time to learn and find more about who you are. You are intelligent and have a strong free will running through you, the same as this horse. Mustangs still run free in a number of states in America. They are feral and even when tamed, retain a big part of themselves that is untouched by human influence. Temperament wise, they are known to be difficult due to their streak of fierce independence. It is as though, they will serve, but only on their own terms and they will never betray what is true to themselves. Sound familiar?"

"I'm not that awkward, am I?"

Sarah smiled and winked. I remembered back to my short life and to how I had wished that I was something different and, in my imagination at that time, I was. Even if I could not make the wishes happen on Earth, being over here was different, but I still felt restricted in some way as I didn't know about laws and how this world balanced, let alone my future purpose. I wondered if I had revolved, but guessed not, as I could not remember any previous lifetimes.

"Bye Sarah, thanks again, I will send him back to you."

"See you John. Don't worry about Scout, he knows the way home."

The horse plodded steadily along the track which slowly inclined towards the way leading to the waterfall. I settled towards him to feel his energy.

"Giddy up!"

It was a real shame that horses chose not to speak, because if this was his pace, the journey would be a bit boring. I remembered the thrill of Blackpool donkeys, not. Scout coughed and farted loudly.

"Charming, do you think you could speed up a bit, so that it doesn't catch up with us?"

"Neighhh…"

"Yep, thought as much."

Looking around, I was truly out on the range. Sarah had done fantastic work to create the surroundings and the views were awe inspiring. Arid red and orange rocky outcrops stood and reached skywards from flat plains which contained canyons and caves, supposedly cut from centuries old rivers and streams. As we crossed the waterfall where Sarah and I had stood, I looked down into the basin containing the open lake. To the north, the inflowing river had carved a snake winding slot canyon, the sheer walls and cliffs striated with various levels and colours of rock. I thought back to the old westerns' Grandma liked to watch and something nagged me that I could not quite remember. The horse stopped and took a drink from one of the streams. He was ever so calm and unhurried and I wondered if I'd got the wrong horse. Comparing this to the day with Tony was a massive contrast in stimulation.

"Tony, it's John, you OK?"

"Yes, you?"

"I am out riding on the range on this very nice horse called Scout. I have a question for you?"

I felt something change and looked down to find I was wearing a pale blue cowboy suit and hat, with a cream lace trimmed fringe and cuffs to match. I laughed and using my thankyou speech as a deflection, imagined Tony in a bright pink leotard and tutu.

"Oh, thanks, mate, I am out at a market and have just got the strangest looks from a bunch of people. Anyway, what do you want?"

"I haven't got a thesaurus with me and I am really trying to understand what free will is in relation to this horse?"

"What dictionary definition you mean? umm, it's about free and independent choice, like the power of voluntary decision where you are responsible. So, expressing free will is to do so, out of personal choice and not simply determined by physical or divine forces."

"Is it like doing something that perhaps goes against or challenges the accepted, expected or known and you take the consequences?"

"Yes, I guess."

"Thanks, Tony."

"Catch you later Kemosabe."

The nagging, yet elusive memory dropped in. Scout was Tonto's horse out of the Lone Ranger.

"So, Scout, you won't yield if you feel you are having to do something or give up something that goes against your grain and if you want something strongly enough, you will risk the outcome, even though you may not end up gaining?"

I thought about the consequences of my free will decisions on others and felt that mostly they affected me. This was apart from my last ride on Earth, but it wasn't my decision to get run over by a truck. The last thing I wanted, was for others to be affected or hurt. In a moment, I felt the energy of the horse shift and gripped tighter with my legs. Scout descended a steep rocky slope, shifting his weight onto his back legs to avoid falling forward and slowly made his way down to a narrow ledge. When we got to the ledge, I could see it was a rocky shelf cut into the sheer rock face which ran along the canyon, its path ascending and descending along the route. The canyon turned at a point in the distance, so the end of the track was obscured.

"You will have to take it steady along here Scout, or we will be swimming home."

Scout squared his stance widening his gait. I could feel the ground energy move up the horse's legs and into its body, to be met by energy he was channelling from above. As they blended and amplified, I felt their effect on me, like an archer making ready to release an arrow. Scout whinnied at the top of his horse lungs and took a small step forward. I was already standing in my stirrups in expectation.

"I thought…"

Scout took off along the path like a racehorse leaving the stalls. I was out of synchrony with him and bounced and pitched on his back as he cantered along the narrow track.

"Slow down, I am going to come off!"

My request went unheeded as Scout rushed forward into the sunset and although I knew I would not be harmed, I felt unnerved and out of control. A small wise voice from inside my head asked me why I thought I should be in control and to relax into the horse beneath me, not to think, feel.

I evened the reigns, leaned forward and adjusted the angle of my hips to compensate for the changes in his centre of gravity as Scout shifted his weight from front to back and side to side. I followed and mirrored the movement of Scout's body with my own and looked up to the trail ahead instead of to the ground, the edge or what lay below. As I relaxed and matched the fluidity in Scouts momentum, the feeling of synchronicity built until we finally slotted together. Scout sensed this immediately, powering his own energy up into me to seal the bond of horse and rider becoming one. I felt the hit of adrenaline at the same time as Scout accelerated quickening the pace to a full-on gallop.

As the power built, so did the sensation, the familiar feeling of cold ecstatic energy coursing up through my body and into my spine. As before everything around me connected together and my weight in the saddle lightened. It was as if we were flying, perfectly poised in movement, and then the idea hit at lightning speed:

"Sands shift…"

The transformation had already started as the idea gained shape and my form melded into my eagle. Throwing the caution of a difficult reversal to the wind, I stretched out my wings to catch the wind rush of our momentum and was lifted from Scout's back and upwards to the canyon ridge. Scout ploughed on along his course, as if he was unaware of my departure. I tuned in from above.

"Scout look up to your left, I am the eagle. Do you want to race?"

Scout looked up and back to his course as I spiralled upwards, inverting and spinning on a longitudinal axis, cutting through the air in a helix of precision. I dropped to the same level as the ledge and matched Scouts speed, each of us casting glances sideways to check the others position. Scout lowered his head and pushed for another burst of speed and I matched his pace.

"You do know I am a golden eagle and can fly at 120 miles per hour."

"Show off and that's only when you are in a dive."

"So, you can speak!"

"I can speak eagle and it seems, although it is you, you are in fact an eagle. I feel you run deeply with animal spirit but you are the first of your kind I have met."

"First of my kind, what do you mean? Can we stop for a moment?"

"See the falls coming up, land there."

Scout slowed to a canter, then into a trot and on reaching the falls, dipped his nose into a pool of cold water and drank. I alighted gracefully upon a rock beside him, my large wings creating a back draft to slow me down to a point where I could step off the air. I shook my feathers and straightened those in my tail.

"You were saying, Scout?"

"I have heard of your kind, you are a shaman, a shape shifter. In North American Indian culture, shamans used totems, which are objects or animals which hold a special spiritual significance for a tribe. Their medicine, women and men would embody the totem to take on its powers."

"I have heard of this, as I have about Shamans in English Pagan culture."

"What's rare is that over here many can imagine, but few can shift. In shifting, you are becoming the animal in its light structure, make up and traits, whilst retaining your mind and personality. You must be taking from some source of power to do this."

"None I am aware of, other than I use a chant to evoke it, although just before, all I needed to do was think about changing."

"Once you have first evoked, the power will know if your intensions are for good. Have you tried shifting into other forms?"

"What you mean like a horse?"

"Well, it would make it a fairer race."

I thought for a moment and then had an idea.

"What is it like for you when you are galloping at top speed?"

"When ground meets sky energy and I am the one held between, my own energy fires, running along my spine and into my legs, lifting me to a place where I am galloping almost on air. Almost as though I do not feel the ground, almost like –"

"Flying?"

"Yes. There have been many times when I have gazed at the birds and wondered if I could step off a ledge like this at full speed and be supported by the air."

"Rather than me be a horse, do you want to fly?"

"How could you make me fly? With all the will in the worlds, I am not a shaman horse, nor can I create temporary worlds like I understand you humans can."

"Let me think about this for a moment, Scout."

I perched on a dry fallen tree trunk and realised I had just stepped over my known limit. I did not know whether I could help Scout fly, by virtual improvisation or by transformation. I knew what I had seen and experienced in the spirit world was done so at will, so maybe? After all, I had just spent a day experiencing the different kinds of will. Perhaps this could help hone my understanding of transition from one state of being or feeling to another through choice. I wished I had learned more about shamanism on the Earth plane. As I thought about nothing, a seed dropped into my consciousness and started to take form. In questioning its source, it felt like it belonged to me, not coming from outside of my own mind.

"Scout, tell me what it was like to roam free as part of a herd when you were on the Earth plane?"

"I was, as I am now, at one with all in the natural world and what I know of this world. As a herd, we would communicate with each other in our minds or through movement and expression. There is a wisdom that links us all, that maintains a balance both socially and with our surroundings. It is like we just know and use this to support and guide others, like we do on Sarah's ranch."

"So, in harnessing this energy at will, you are spiritual in your own right?"

"Yes, we are spiritual, sentient and aware creatures."

"You must know then, that horses are shamanic creatures and would help or carry shamans or medicine women and men into the spirit world?"

"My ancestors, after the Spanish humans freed them, travelled north and were captured, ridden and cared for by the Crow Indians. There are stories about medicine men, women and horses being involved in rituals, where they would both travel into the spirit world to gain knowledge or healing practice. One day, there was a raid from other tribes and some of the herd escaped back to freedom. There were a number of generations descended from these, who had little if any contact with humans after that. I was also born in the wild. What I am saying is, I know of these stories, but I have not seen it myself."

"Do you believe the stories?"

"I don't know."

"Do you think you could fly?"

"I do fly, but with my hooves on the ground. To be as a bird and lift from the ground, I do not know of the will to get me there. However, you are able to change for flight at will."

"Do you trust me?"

"Well, if it all goes wrong, I do swim you know!"

I enquired of the place Scout found himself in, when at full gallop. When Earth energy shifted, and a different energy filled him as he became one with his surroundings.

At this point there was a change, a just noticeable difference or a transition between the limited and the apparently limitless. When I made this transition, I believed I could transform into my eagle and allowed my imagination to weave into the transitional energy to deliver me to this desired point. I demonstrated at a different level by transporting myself a short distance away and back to make the point. Scout explained that spirit horses did not do this as a rule, although he had transported himself in the past.

"I think it is possible, to fly I mean."

Scout shuddered his shoulders and let off an enormous fart.

"What the hell do you eat to generate so much wind?"

"Nothing much. All horses fart, it's a horse thing. Sometimes we snort and fart at the same time, it's fun, we call it snarting. It confuses the rider as to which end it is coming from."

I squinted and recalibrated my vision to check which end was the culprit and could see Scout was becoming slowly enveloped in a greenish-yellow cloud.

"Now if you were a horse and snorted whilst squinting like that, I would know you were unsure about something, which would make me nervous."

"I'd be nervous if I knew that was creeping up on me! I've got an idea. And I would step a few paces forward if I were you."

"Rocket power?"

"Not quite, give me a moment."

My idea was to create a virtual world sphere around Scout with me riding on his back in eagle form, where the sphere could travel in the spirit plane. However, the challenge was that virtual world was a world within the spirit plane separated in their context of reality and non-reality. I knew there was a transition point though and a process of the shift from the spirit realm into virtual world. There was also the process when the creator could realise a virtual world creation, like in the case of Hazel, manifesting Mill Cottage. However, there seemed to be laws limiting animation, imagined creatures or changes to form being brought across the boundary. What's more, how would we be able to see from inside a virtual sphere into reality in order for Scout to experience his reality world with authenticity. I would need to create a window or a transparent sphere to enable this.

I had learned from the horses, their living and being is done so authentically, whether sharing a life in a caring and authentic herd, authentic telepathic communication or in the following of an authentic path. A flight in virtual world would negate an authentic experience, therefore be contra to horse principle and it was unlikely that Scout would agree to it or trust it.

We practiced galloping and extending the sensation of when Scout felt energised enough to feel like he was flying. I did this in both my eagle and my own form to compare the different perceptions and slowed down the transition process required to change my form to determine the stages of the process. I also practiced moving back and forth and between the real and virtual worlds to feel the boundary. I then shared my understandings with Scout to help him unlock his heritage of between worlds travel. We then practiced being inside the sphere. However, although I was able to project the ground moving from front to back as Scout galloped along, we were still unable to see through the sphere into the world around us.

"Maybe this is not supposed to happen John, I feel firmly grounded on all fours. I cannot bridge the gap of authenticity between what is real and what isn't."

It was becoming apparent; Scout was getting frustrated with the whole situation.

"What I think is, by looking back at your heritage of being able to move between worlds, and your species' ability to accept spirituality on the Earth world as a part of everyday life, your perception of a boundary between worlds is different from humans. Perhaps because the boundary is more permeable for horses, or just not important."

"We are just connected and accept it is the way it is."

"And it is different for Earth bound humans, as the spirit world is firmly a non-reality because we cannot experience it. Therefore, it is easier not to believe in it and the boundary remains impermeable to the majority, because there is little evidence it exists. If your existence back on the Earth plane was to naturally exist between the two worlds, do you experience the same here?"

"The spirit world is what it is. We are not like your breed, we accept the natural and real as it is, we are not looking to understand it more or change it."

"For me, there is the spirit world and virtual world and from what I can see, virtual world is like a parallel within which you can create and change the imagined into reality. Within limits though it seems. If I can transform the imagined into the real why wouldn't that be authentic to you?"

"The problem with you humans is you are never satisfied with things as they are, you want to change your environment to suit you. You consume the natural world constantly and squeeze your co-species into smaller existences or force them to adapt around your will."

"Yes, but your kind has helped us achieve that, even if it is negative in some ways."

"Yes, but under threat. We have had to adapt to survive. When my ancestors had the opportunity to escape, they did not hesitate because they longed for the freedom to engage their own free will. Humans think they tame or break us, but what they don't realise is, in each of us, there is a place that remains whole and unbroken. As Mustangs, we have a resilience which further defends this place. That is my reality, so what you imagine and transform into the real is not real enough for me to feel, it is authentic."

"I did not mean to upset you Scout and I am sorry if I came over as arrogant."

"Apology accepted. I know you are trying to help me achieve what seems impossible and I have come to know part of you as well. I also would trust you enough to accept you as an honorary part of the herd."

"Thank you. You are also helping me to understand myself better too."

I looked up and surveyed the scenery around us in all of its beauty and magnificence. Engaging skilful will in a conscious effort, I turned to Scout.

"I accept you as my friend also, with much respect for your knowledge and wisdom. Tell me, what do you like most about living here?"

"It's beautiful and un-spoilt. The earth smells good and the water is sweet. I am happy to share my life with my herd."

"How long have you been in the spirit world?"

"About twelve years now."

"And how long here now?"

"About seven."

"I take it, you do know it was Sarah who imagined and created this whole place."

Scout shifted uneasily and snorted.

"So, it's not real then?"

"Oh yes, it is real alright. Let me ask you, is it authentic, because if it is not authentic, why have you accepted this place as your home and how have you been happy here?"

"I thought it was real and I did not question its authenticity."

"How would you anyway?"

Scout dropped his head and admitted he wouldn't. He explained that Mustangs could be naturally stubborn, which some see as arrogant and he thought it was something to do with his strong sense of freedom and independence. I asked him if he wanted to experience virtual world and assured him he would be safe and could get back. Whilst it took him some time to reason with the offer he finally relented to his trust.

He told me he would like to go to a place of mountains, trees and water and whilst he described a land where his ancestors had lived, I created a reconstruction of the Yellowstone river valley before us. My thoughts had allowed me to somehow access images of the Crow Indian home land, as it was. I mounted Scout and patting his flanks, told him to link into my mind. As we walked through the veil and were enclosed by this new world, Scout snorted in delight.

We were on a trail in the depths of a coniferous forest on the shallow slopes of a mountain. As we rode forward, I created the woodland smells, improved the detail in the trees and plants and imagined birds and animals visiting our locality. As Scout thought about other detail, I created it so he could increase the authenticity of his experience. In the distance were mountains and water and trees as far as the eye could see. I was not entirely sure where these new abilities were coming from, because, yet again, as before, they seemed to be coming from the depths of my own memory.

"Come on, let's get to the top. Can you imagine being me as I gallop. I mean link into my movements so you synchronise with me exactly, even down to the level of me anticipating the next shift or obstacle. I want you to feel a different level of riding where you with me, are as one, but to a deeper level. Let me remain in control of where we go though, because this is also an exercise of trust," said Scout.

We took off at speed and as I further detailed the path of the journey, I was also able to remain locked into Scout's consciousness. Twisting and turning, our joint movements were perfectly choreographed as we worked together to anticipate approaching features in the track. The sensation was one of just knowing, a step beyond trust. It was almost like I had melded with him, his limbs becoming mine and yet I maintained the perspective of the rider. The feeling was exhilarating and delivered the familiar energy surge we both knew so well. Joint awareness heightened and Scout pushed hard. It took ten minutes to reach the top and as we burst through the tree line, we found ourselves on a small rocky plateau with magnificent panoramic views.

"Are you creating all this?"

"Yes, I think so."

I showed Scout how I could change the detail and project further into the horizon if I willed it and how once created, the structure remained in semi permanency, until the creator decided to deconstruct it or make it permanent or real.

"This place is beautiful, could you make this permanent and if you did, where would it be?"

"I think I could make it permanent and yet, to be honest, I have not created anything this size before. I think it follows models and laws which are quite straight forward. On Earth, things alter state like water changes to ice or darkness turns to light, so, there is a process, but there is always a catalyst or facilitator. Things over here seem to be based on the same principles."

"I feel there is another kind of will at work."

"Exactly and I have been thinking about the types of will I learned about at the ranch. Sarah told me there is a transitional will, but it's not a will in itself. It's like a glue or something that fills the gaps between wills which facilitates the change between those forces of will, like strong, skilful or good. I think it is this will or something very similar, that enables the shift between the imagined and the real."

"But, I am a horse, I think I would know about this type of will, so it can't be one."

"I think you do, but it is so innate in your species, perhaps you take it for granted, well, sort of, if you let me explain. You've told me you are spiritual and even on the Earth plane, you sort of live between spirit and matter, but just accept this as the way you live, connected to everything around you."

"Yes, that's true."

"As humans, the majority do not do that, or we have lost that attachment. Therefore, as horses, you seem to be able to make transitions between these states of being or consciousness without effort. It seems, in the main, effort is required to change things, but you would naturally accept it is what it is. After all, you are the masters of will."

"I think I know what you mean, most humans just don't know. In fact, present company and Sarah excepted, we think humans are a bit stupid and definitely irresponsible."

Scout looked up to be faced by a large black stallion. Immediately, his tail went up and he jumped backwards raising his front legs off the ground.

"Calm down you donkey it's me!"

"You frightened me! I had no idea what was happening and I didn't sense you approaching. How do you do that, because I know it's not real?"

"It isn't real, I transformed into a virtual horse. You can do that in this world, have a go, change your colour."

Try as he might, Scout could not make the shift however, when we connected minds, we were able to start to alter things. After a while I asked him to close his eyes and trust any feeling of transformation that came, without breaking the mind link. In the next moment, we were both sitting on a tree branch, five metres up in the air as a pair of blue jays.

"This is strange, I am not sure about this."

"Just spread your wings and float down, don't flap, glide."

"I don't want to be a bird, I want to fly as a horse, but I will try."

Scout launched himself into the air and glided down to the ground, with me, quickly following. I hovered above him.

"See, it wasn't that bad, but I hear you."

We linked minds again and concentrated on the formation of a pair of wings which would support Scout in the air. Gradually two fully fledged wings of a six-metre span took form embracing his flanks. I momentarily guarded the mind channel, whilst I contemplated whether or not I could maintain the mind link and flight, orchestrate an unfolding virtual scene and concentrate on my own experience. I decided it was worth a try.

"Now, flap those wings and get used to the way they move at your command. Remember, I have no control over them, what I am doing is facilitating them being a part of you. Try not to take off."

Easier said than done, Scout lifted into the air with one strong flap, descending back to the ground with a large horse grin on his face. He spent the next half an hour practicing cantering and flapping, to enable him to judge the power to weight needed to feel confident enough to get the lift.

"How do you feel about flying off the edge of the plateau?"

"I am worried I might fall."

"Well if you do, I will create a massive pile of hay before you hit the deck. Don't be worried, you cannot hurt yourself here."

"You don't have to question my bravery, Mustangs are brave. I know how I am going to do this. I am going to trot back down the trail and time my pace with the distance to the edge, so as I hit it, I will have energised to ground flight. If you know what I mean?"

"Yes, I do, but give yourself a bit more track to allow for the wing flapping. I will be up top watching."

Scout cantered off along the path. He was nervous, but in engaging strong will, he managed his doubts and on approaching his start point, reared up and span on his back legs to face the trail back to the plateau.

"Are you still with me?"

"You know I am, up, up and away. I'll see you in mid-air!"

I took off and spiralled upwards to a point where I could see Scout, the trail and the plateau edge. Circling, I created a warm air thermal beneath me so I could float and focus on the task at hand.

"One small step for a horse, one giant leap for horse-kind."

"Did you watch telly when you were on Earth?"

"No, everyone knows about Louis Armstrong."

"Neil?"

"Whatever, I am about to go…!"

Scout balanced himself with an initial canter and let rip. He was aware of me in his mind, but he had asked for silence during the approach so he could focus all of his energy and internal synergy. I could feel the wind rushing through his mane and along his flanks. Markers flashed past in a blur as his energy built and powered to his limbs. As he hit the tree line, the ever so familiar cold ecstatic sensation ploughed along his spine fully energising him in readiness for his leap into the unknown. With all his current motion in automatic, he unfurled his wings, first raising them high then bringing them down and in front of him until the tips touched beneath his chest. With two more cycles, he had lifted from the ground and flew over the lip of the plateau and into the air.

"Breathe!"

"Whooooo-hooooo! This is amazing, I can't believe this is happening."

"Well done Pegasus, but you seem to be flying in a straight line, can you change your direction?"

"No, how?"

"Use your tail."

"No, makes no difference."

"Well, I wonder how Pegasus managed it. That's the problem with these myths and legends, they are just not real. I am going to give you some tail feathers."

I explained to Scout that in doing so, he would be able to change direction and height and would also help him to land, but to be gentle in the movement. If he swished it like a horse tail, he might end up, upside down. After some rocky movements, Scout gained his confidence and was able to manoeuvre in different directions. However, he quickly established, that unlike me in my eagle form, he could not slow down too drastically in flight as he would drop quickly. But could he soar?

With minds linked, I was captivated by the awe and thrill Scout was experiencing with his new-found freedom. I found that as time passed, my own ability to hold all of the variables in this experience for Scout was becoming much easier to control. Except it was more like orchestrating. I wondered again where all these abilities were coming from.

"I can hear your thoughts you know. Your head is full of questions and reasoning. You should learn to just be or chill every now and again."

"I have always been like this, ever since I was little. I cannot switch it off, but since coming over here, I just increasingly know so much more and I find myself playing with and linking the new information with past and present experiences. It's like having one light bulb moment after another."

I flew alongside Scout and as we talked, I could feel the bond of friendship and trust building between us and with it, Scout's sense of self belief. There was a noticeable shift in the link and in the next moment Scout's coat had changed to glistening white. I was taken aback.

"Well, the stories speak of him being a white horse, don't they?"

"Who?"

"Pegasus!"

"But, I didn't do that!"

"I know my friend, I did, because I can now see how this place could be real."

Scoutasus soared upwards engaging the full power of his huge wings with me in quick pursuit. As we climbed, I created a small bank of white cloud which we flew through at full speed. On emerging from the surface, Scout decelerated and rearing up on his hind legs, beat his wings in an unsuccessful attempt to hover.

"You are a horse, not a hummingbird."

"I am trying hard here, a little help would be good."

I accessed one of my documentary memories and placed a slow-motion video of a humming bird beating its wings in synchronised figures of eight. Scout copied the pattern and remained stable. Another shift in the link alerted me.

"I know you are not flapping fast enough to maintain the lift, how are you doing that?"

"I thought about being as light as air and I am."

I solidified the cloud and as we rested, we talked about Scout's new experiences and what had changed for him to enable him to make changes on his own. It became apparent that Scout's understanding of transitional will had come to a point where he himself could see the connections. This was because it was not dissimilar from the energy of acceptance of being at one with his surroundings and if he thought of something and allowed the will to connect to it, it seemed to change things. Since being on the cloud, I had transformed back to my human form.

"Do you think you can fly on your own?"

"You saying that and us sitting on a cloud, makes me nervous. Hey, I have just realised I have been talking to you and you are in human form."

"Yes, I know, but this is virtual world and things are different in here. Think free-will and combine it with all the other wills. It is your kind who are the masters of will remember. I think your whole and unbroken place holds the key, I think this is the source of your power."

Scout thought for a while and I could feel him exploring himself and saw the merge happen.

"Ready? I will disengage the facilitation link so you can make your own changes, but we will maintain communication?"

"Yes, I am ready!"

I mistified the cloud and transformed back into my eagle. As we came through the bottom, Scout had changed back to his chestnut brown coat, but his wings were still attached.

"Tail feathers!"

"Yes, sorry."

Scout opened the full extent of his wings and spanned his tail feathers and floated down for a while before banking hard left towards a lake.

"I am OK, let me fly on my own and learn. I will meet you back on the plateau."

I flew upwards floating on the breeze. As I hung on the thermal, I watched Scout twist and turn, bank and dive, mastering his new skill. When he reached the lake, he dropped within centimetres of the surface, held his level and started to gallop. Dissolving his wings and tail, his hooves touched the surface and he continued to race across the lake's expanse.

A sad memory had emerged from when he was on Earth, where trappers had cornered his small herd with their backs to a lake. If it had not been for his uncle putting up a tremendous fight, the others would not have escaped. He remembered thinking at the time, if they could have run on water they would have all got away. The next memory was of him looking backwards to the sound of a gunshot and his uncle laid dead on the ground, next to a trapper with a smashed in skull. I felt his tear fall upon my own cheek.

Scout powered out of his sadness and at full speed reformed his wings and tail taking off and banking hard right to return to where I had settled on the edge of the plateau. Seeing Scout come into land was spectacular as his large frame reared up with wings facing forward and tail feathers fanned. He was treading the air with his front hooves in readiness to land and then gently stepped onto the ground dissolving his wings and tail.

"Text book landing, Scout."

"Oh yeah, and where is the text book that shows how a flying horse should land?"

"I could not help but hear your memory of your uncle, I am sorry, that must have been awful?"

"I accept some humans are cruel and brutal and I also accept some humans are kind. Horses forgive, but they never forget and that makes up a part of our wary and inquisitive nature. You are apart from most humans I have known and you are kind, giving and patient."

"Thank you."

"And thank you for believing in me and showing me the path to my centre of power."

Scout thought about a bucket of cool water and took a drink. As his head came up he snorted and shook his mane. As he did, I glimpsed something white amongst the thick black hair. A tingling sensation rose up my neck and arms.

"You have a white feather in your mane, that's weird. Is it real?"

"What's real and what isn't. You know I feel like I have regained that Earth horse feeling of accepting the existence of the two worlds. What has happened has reminded me of my heritage."

"I think that is a good thing, but we will see what is real when we leave here."

"Yes, about that. Can you make this permanent so I can come here and fly and maybe bring some of my herd to visit?"

"Well that's if I can make it permanent, it's pretty big. Plus, if it is permanent you won't be able to fly in it."

"I was wondering about this. Could you keep it as semi-permanent, like right on the cusp of being virtual, so it would stay formed and yet retain the elements and qualities of being virtual."

"I don't know, but I have an idea. I think if we can create a physical opening to this world so it's entrance is in the real or actual spirit world, that links between the two worlds, then fill the entrance with a transitional will energy field, it might work. To be honest, I am not sure what I am doing enough to keep it as semi-permanent?"

"OK, let's go for permanent, trust me. This place is beautiful and I want to be able to return, but where will you put it?"

"From what I know, it does not matter where you put it because the spirit world seems to exist as worlds within worlds. It is a really neat way to conserve space, if that exists over here. But we will make an entrance. When I was in the waterfall with Sarah, I noticed quite a deep cave at the back of it. Why don't we place the entrance at the end of that?"

"Perfect." I thought back to the time when I had sent out the message pulse to Sarah and how I had sent out the energy. Except this time, I replaced the energy with combined will energy with the intension to transform. I closed my eyes. Scout watched as the hoop of green, blue and violet light energy was projected outward towards the boundaries. In an echo, the ring met with its limits and returned to me to reconnect. The transition to the real had given the landscape a different quality; more lush, detailed and sharp. The quality of the air was different and water shone in familiar multifaceted crystal reflections.

"Master!"

"On yer bike. Did you not feel me link to you for the added extra? Come on, let's go back to reality world."

"Can we go back to where we were at the start of the ledge in the canyon?"

"Yes, if you want."

"I thought we would have one last ride together, at least until I see you again."

The thought of one last ride unnerved me. I narrowed my gaze towards Scout and snorted my best snort. I flashed the last bike ride memory to Scout and he nodded his head.

"Now, if you had been riding a horse, it would have been different. We will be fine, trust me as I have trusted you."

As we stood in human and horse form at the beginning of the ledge, Scout looked around and was pleased to be back on familiar ground. It did seem real to him and he played with the experience of the virtual world in comparison with this one. He explained to me he wanted to experience flying on all fours connected to the ground again, so he could compare the feeling between this and virtual world. He wanted me to ride him, so we linked minds and having climbed on Scout's back, Scout accelerated away into a canter and then a gallop.

"Synchronise, like we did before, when I tell you, transform to your eagle and fly above me!"

I locked in and engaged my movements in harmony with Scout's. We moved with each other perfectly towards the point when I knew Scout would power up. As I looked down, I could see the white feather twisting in the wind and had a dread filled feeling.

"Fly!"

"Scout I am…"

"Fly now!"

I took off and beat my wings hard upwards. Scout had broken the mind and communication link and continued to power along the ledge above the drop to the river. At full gallop, he rode off the edge and disappeared from view.

I could not fly fast enough in my concern for my friend. I banked hard into the canyon and almost crashed into Scout who was flying brown coated in the opposite direction.

"You, mad horse!"

"Well, I guess that makes two of us shaman?"

"I think you are correct in both senses."

After we landed, I hugged Scout's neck and rubbed his shoulders.

"You scared me!"

"You scared me too, in your black stallion costume, but I knew what I could do!"

"That was quite an adventure, brilliant in fact and I am glad we were able to help each other. Free will seems to be about wrestling with the process and edges as well as facing and owning the consequences."

"For me, free will is about engaging the courage to become who you believe you are too. I am going to head back to the ranch now to re-join the herd."

"Are you going to fly?"

"Would you?"

"Yes, I would."

"So long for now shaman, I know I will see you again."

"Adios shaman, be you."

"Oh, by the way, I think we should become a tribe-herd, in honour of our ancestors and call it the feather-mane tribe?"

"Nice idea. Founder members."

"One more thing…"

Scout reared up flapped his wings, snarted, then took off. I looked up following his ascent and shouted, "I can see some of your endearing qualities haven't changed."

"I just wanted to see if it made any difference to the lift."

"I repeat, mad horse, see you later."

Having watched Scout fly beyond my view, I sat on a rock and thought about the time we had just spent together. The feeling generated within me, when Scout had mentioned the last ride, then had ridden himself off the edge into the canyon, had stirred something emotionally deep within me. I remembered what little John had said about getting us killed and mulled over my decision to take such a risk.

I had not wanted to kill myself, that was for sure, but my actions had resulted in my death and the pain in others I had left behind. *Free will was something to be bridled*, I thought, but not broken.

Scout flew from the canyon and over the waterfall, before descending into the open paddock. As he flew closer, the herd shifted uneasily snorting and whinnying until he touched down amongst them and retracted his wings. Within a few seconds he had spoken to all of them and they settled quietly, although with a quality of excitement in their silence.

180

Sarah was in the kitchen of the ranch when she heard the commotion and looked out of the window in time to see a flying horse looking like Scout, land in the paddock. She walked quickly over to the herd and spoke to him.

"Did I just see you fly down into the paddock?"

Scout raised his eyebrows and shivered his shoulders. He walked towards her and nuzzled the side of her face. Sarah caught sight of the feather and stroked it knowingly.

"You have been gone for a while, just what have you two been up to?" Meanwhile, I linked into home.

"Grandfather, it's John, are you OK?"

"Yes, fine, are you? You have been gone for quite a while, but we knew you were alright."

"I think I am; I just feel a little low for some reason. Don't worry, I will be home soon."

"Right you are. Just link in every now and again. See you later."

Ultimate Choice

I leaned back against a smooth rock, closed my eyes and thought about how much more I had to learn about myself and for that matter, about others too. I wondered mostly about the things I seemed to be able to do over here and then about what I had imagined I had wanted to do, back on Earth. These talents, if that was the right term, appeared to emerge with a familiarity and yet I could not seem to anchor them in any previous experience. I thought about déjà vu and the possibility of seeding. *But if déjà vu was also the result of occurrences in previous lifetimes, when in a past life had I transformed and flown like an eagle and what was I? If it was seeding, who would be placing the ideas to enable such transitions and to what ends?*

These unanswered thoughts added to this low and almost repressed feeling I was now experiencing, even in the light of all the recent euphoria. This was something to do with the responsibility of my choices and felt similar to the depression I had suffered, which I did not want to sink into further. Will as I might, nothing changed.

I imagined I was sitting on a cliff top looking out to sea. Staring at the horizon for a while and appreciating how the water and the sky balanced themselves, I thought, it may just help with my internal balance. Strangely, there seemed to be a lot of cliffs in his spirit world journey so far.

With eyes still shut, I sensed a change in the air and temperature and upon opening them, found myself in a place that looked vaguely familiar. Peering at the scenery, I realised I was at a place similar to Beachy Head in East Sussex, England. I recognised it because I had been on a caravan holiday to Hastings one year with my mum and grandparents. Thinking I had accurately recreated the scene from a random memory was settling, but the world around me appeared very real displaying different qualities to a virtual scape and I started to feel vulnerable. I sat down a little way back from the cliff edge and watched the seagulls floating on the thermals. Connecting them to my own sensation of flying, I no longer felt envious of their ability to do this.

As I lay back, I noticed a man walking up the cliff path towards me. I might as well have been invisible, because the man almost brushed past me then walked over and stood on the edge of the cliff. I knew immediately, I was invisible to the man and was in fact, back on Earth at Beachy Head. My anxiety heightened. The man sat down, right on the edge, put his head in his hands and burst into tears. I watched him intently as he muttered to himself and was only able to catch the odd word like useless, failure and hurt. At that point, I feared very much for this man's life.

Very suddenly, two spirit people arrived and stood right next to him. One was a woman in her forties, the other a young man in his early twenties. Both were angry and vitriolic, barraging the man, goading and chastising him relentlessly. Even though they were standing 30 metres from where I was lying, I could see the anxiety, hatred, and chaos emanating from their two spirit auras. Within seconds, another spirit appeared, but he was of a different nature. I realised the two earlier arriving spirits must be low flyers from this world, whereas the third was from the spirit world. I guarded myself immediately.

The third spirit, placed a shield around himself and the man who was still sitting. He spoke firmly to the other spirits who appeared to be working together. There was an angry exchange of words between the woman and the third spirit and as the woman distracted him, the young man launched his first attack. It was fruitless because of the guard being in place.

"Don't waste your time on me, or your effort. Leave…this…man…in… peace! Can you not see he is troubled and desperate?"

"And that is what I want him to be."

"And I want that too," said the woman.

I remembered back to my own passing and the scene of the accident. It seemed that low flyers were attracted to traumatic and actual death situations. I wondered whether the attraction was based on an instinctual call to seek an opportunity to pass over. Or perhaps facing the opportunity to pass at the same time as experiencing the dilemma of trusting to go or not would perpetuate their own suffering as part of this painful existence. They did however, seem to take pleasure in witnessing another's suffering, which could provide some justification for their own fear and anxiety. This was probably why they chose to torment the desperate man, victims turned perpetrators.

I also felt compassion for them in their confusion, as the deliberation must be a torment. It was obvious to me this Earth man had come here to kill himself and these two low flyers were here to witness this and connect with the trauma. As well as compassion, I also felt anger and sorrow for them at the same time and for the man who I hoped was unconscious to their interference. I also hoped they were incapable of seeding.

The man stood up and looked over the edge. His spirit helper spoke gently to him, saying he did not need to do this. There were people who would miss him, there was a chance for him to re-engage with his life and work through his issues. Things were not so bad. The man responded in a melancholic voice as if hearing the spirit. He said he was done, he could never recover or regain what he had lost and life was too painful. In his failing, this was all he deserved.

"Come on, get on with it!" the two goaded.

"Back off! Vultures, that's all you are!"

I could see a glow forming around the third spirits head and recognising the threat, the two low flyers moved back. In all that was happening, I could see the decision to end his life was the man's choice, regardless of the spirit person's presence. The spirit could do nothing other than offer guidance or perhaps seed new thoughts, that's if the man was at all receptive. The reality of the situation unravelling itself in front of me, suddenly connected to my recent learning.

I wondered why we have such a power of free will which allows us to reach the point where we can throw the gift of life back into the face of the universe. Perhaps living is all a matter of choice and free will, which even allows us to take the decision to sacrifice the ultimate.

To understand the process more, I decided to intercept the communication link between the spirit helper and the man. At the moment I connected, the spirit turned and faced me, immediately powering up his defence. However, realising I was no threat, he calmly spoke to me through his mind.

"I don't know who you are, but please stay out of this."

I continued to listen and could feel the intensity and pace of the conversation increasing. The Earth man, although not conscious of the conversation with the spirit guide, believed he was talking to himself and was doing his utmost to defeat all of the positive thoughts coming into his mind.

"I have had enough, it is not worth it, I cannot stand this anymore. I have failed. I am no use to my family as a man like this."

I could feel the depth of the support from the spirit shift in an attempt to soothe. Then all of a sudden everything went quiet. The man stepped forward and calmly walked off the edge of the cliff. I immediately went to his aid, not really knowing what I could do and found myself at the bottom of the cliff watching the man fall towards me. There were no screams or shouts, just a riveting silence apart from the sound of the air rushing against his clothing as he fell. He hit the rocks with a sickening slap a few feet in front of me. Micro seconds later, the spirit guide materialised next to the body, closely followed by a second man, not present previously. The latter turned to face the fallen man, whilst the guide turned towards me.

"Who are you and why are you here?"

"I am sorry? He just killed himself! I have never seen anything like that. That was awful. Why were those other spirits harassing him so much, and why couldn't you stop him? That was unbelievable, I feel so angry that this can happen?"

The spirit guide linked into my mind.

"Calm down, I know you are no threat, and I understand this must be quite a shock to you."

I introduced myself and said I had come from the spirit world and had somehow arrived here unintentionally. The guide asked me if I was new into spirit and I confirmed I had only been over a short while. As we were talking, I could see the Earth man had appeared outside of his body and was standing amongst the rocks staring down at his own lifeless physical form. Bewilderment and fear were caught in his expression and he looked around in all directions, hunching his shoulders in anticipation of the unknown. The guide explained the other spirit was a catcher called Stephen, who would help him and take him over to the spirit world.

"Who are you, sir?"

"My name is Arthur, I was the Earth person's guide, or one of his guides."

"Did you know this was going to happen?"

"Well, I had my fears that Philip, the man yonder, was moving in this direction as he was unstable and vulnerable. Sometimes, you cannot tell whether they are actually going to make that decision to cross by their own hand. For some it can be premeditated, but for many it can be spur of the moment, although there are quite a few who don't actually mean to go through with it. In Philip's case, it was a spur of the moment decision and as you heard, he overpowered his rational thinking."

"But did he have to kill himself?"

"No, he didn't have to. Philip has been suffering from a lot of stress and from mental and emotional pressures, which have been building up lately. It got to a point where he felt he could no longer cope, even though the problems could have been solved if he had had the right kind of support. But unfortunately, he didn't."

"So, is it his fault he has taken his own life?"

"John, you are asking lots of questions, I just need to sort this situation out with Steve and then maybe we can have an opportunity to talk about this."

I sat down on a rock and watched the scene. The catcher gently approached Philip and explained to him where he was, what was happening and what was about to happen. I remembered back to how I felt when I had died. The jolt, the immediate loss and the perplexion of being in a new world. It then occurred to me that Philip's future may be different to that of my own; in terms of how he would be treated because he had willed his own death. I thought this must influence the process of events and wondered what might happen.

Out of the corner of my eye, I caught a movement on the rock face. The two low flyers were stealthily descending towards the group at the bottom of the cliff. Both guides had their backs towards them and seemed unaware of the immanent intrusion. As I watched, I could see the woman starting to power up for an attack and it seemed obvious to me, they intended to immobilise both guides and probably interfere with Philip.

I did not hesitate and although I wasn't sure what I was doing, other than instinctually, I guarded and powered all chakras from my throat to my base and violently forced the energy downwards into the base chakra. The downwards force projected the energy mass beneath me and as it connected with the ground, I inverted it. Like a cork released from under water, the ball rose increasing its energy through each chakra, as it ascended at rapid speed. The feeling was cold and exhilarating and in the same moment I fixed my ajna sight on the woman.

At great velocity, the bolt accelerated to a point behind my eyes and blasted out from between them. There was a terrific bang as a bolt of red light was delivered. It hit the woman flat on the side of her head. She was immobilised immediately and fell to the rocks. The young man behind her, disappearing immediately. Both guides span to face me instantly guarding and powering up to execute a response. I was left with a smoking gun, a resonance of pink light as a halo around my head. The questions came thick and fast.

"Just who are you, no newcomer knows how to project energy in that way. Why are you here, state your intension or we will open fire?"

"I have told you, my name is John Kenton, I am here because I imagined myself to be here. Look, I didn't have a choice, the low flyers were coming down the rock face, and the way I saw it was... I haven't done this before, I haven't shot at anyone before, nobody has taught me how to shoot. I had to take the decision, you two were tied up with what was going on there...and that woman was powering up and she was going to get a head shot off. I had to make a decision to stop her and I did! I don't know how I did it, I just had an idea because my grandad taught me how to defend myself and I just reversed the defence action and imagined the rest and that's what I did. I thought I was helping that's all, I didn't mean to cause any damage! Look, I don't know why I am here, I don't know what the situation is, I have only been in the spirit world for a short time and all of these things are new to me. Nobody has sent me, I don't know what's going on, I really don't!"

"OK, we know you are telling the truth. Calm down, Steve is going to take Philip over and then we will talk about what is happening here. Wayne, is it?"

"No, John?"

Arthur smiled at me.

I was a little confused, although vaguely familiar with the last comment. I sat down to watch.

Both Steve and the new spirit disappeared as an opening created and they stepped into it. Arthur came over to me and apologised for the intensity of his response to me earlier. He explained it just seemed odd that I was here at this specific time and he wondered why it was perhaps necessary for me to be exposed to this type of passing. He did not know, but sometimes it feels there is a greater plan and we can be involved in situations which provide us with useful knowledge and this maybe what was happening here.

"John, do you want to stay here, or go back to the spirit world and chat or what?"

"I think I will come back over with you. I would like to talk." Just as we were about to leave, I saw the woman stirring amongst the rocks. I protected myself and watched her as she rose to her feet.

"I hope you died a really horrible death and if you have any family left here, they live their lives in pain and misery. Although, I should think they were all really happy when you died, you little shit."

"And I hope you find the strength to join us one day, take care of yourself."

She spat on the ground and disappeared.

"You meant that, I felt it, how old did you say you were? OK, link into my mind and we will go back over."

Lighthouse

Interestingly the context hadn't changed much. Arthur and I had re-materialised in the top story of a lighthouse sitting on the coast. I was looking out onto a lazy azure sea, with the familiar colours, tones and blushes of blues and greens held within the spirit spectrum.

"Wow, what a view!"

"Yes, I know, spot on, isn't it?"

"It seems odd you are living in a lighthouse and your Earth person has just thrown himself off a cliff."

"Yes, very painful."

"Sorry, I didn't mean to be unfeeling. What will happen now?"

I had ascertained from our initial meeting that Arthur was a serious and intense individual and predicted our discussions were going to match his character. Arthur explained that his mentor, who supervised him, was already aware of what had happened and there would be a debrief later.

"Suicides are always sad and the motives and deciding circumstances have to be clarified for the victim to enable them to move on from it. It can take a long time for them to accept what they have done, especially after realising that life continues. Anyway, we can talk about this later, tell me how you came to be at Beachy Head?"

By now I had learned how to vary the porousness of my mind and to moderate the amount of information another could see. The alternative was to block my thoughts completely on a subject which could be perceived as deception. Although spirit dwellers accepted the privacy of blocks they were still able to truthfully translate general intent. However, I wished to obscure my recent adventure with Scout and swept my hair to the side to bury the feather.

"I was working with a lady called Sarah and she and her horse herd were teaching me about different types of will. When I left them, I thought about my own passing, felt miserable and wanted to be alone for a while, so I imagined the

189

cliff top. What I don't understand is how I was transported from the spirit world back into the Earth plane without meaning to do so."

"It could be a number of things, depending on what was on your mind. Were there any regrets around your death?"

I told him about the circumstances leading to the accident and if I had not been so blasé about the risk, I might still be alive. I said I felt responsible and was struggling with the impact on my family and friends. The suicide I had just witnessed for some reason seemed to increase my guilt.

"Does a mountaineer, with a passion for climbing, who falls one day and dies, commit suicide in that act of risk? No, it is called misadventure or an accident because you did not intend to die. Another reason is something or someone had enabled you to be transported to where you were, for a reason. Like you were supposed to experience what you did as part of a bigger picture, you are not aware of yet. Do you have a mentor or someone who was working with you in your development?"

"No, not that I am aware of."

"It seems odd then that something like this would be created, unless of course it comes from a larger power, which is something we do not always have control of."

"When you say larger power or something, what do you mean?"

"Sometimes, the universe or Collective may transport us into different situations when it feels it would be beneficial for us to experience it. These teachings are for future journeys and it is like you are being forewarned or provided with knowledge you will need later. Another is, you are transported to meet someone who will be able to provide knowledge you might need."

"So, I could be here to meet you?"

"You could. These are the main reasons, but as to why you need to know these things, I do not know? I mean, look at it John, you are in a situation where you experience somebody killing themselves. You have an encounter with low fliers, you launch your first psychic attack and you are now here with me in a lighthouse. A lighthouse is symbolic of giving a message out to the surrounding world, or a warning perhaps. I am not sure what part I have to play in this, but I will answer your questions the best I can. The spirit world works in mysterious ways and we are not always aware of our developmental pathway and why things happen to us."

"OK, thank you."

I asked Arthur why low fliers gather where people are dying and why in Philip's case, they were pushing him to kill himself when he was so obviously distressed and vulnerable. He explained it was a form of torment and that suicides were difficult for all involved. The Leaves wanted him to take his own life because of the risk involved in the actual decision. In many societies, cultures and beliefs, taboo surrounds suicide and in some it is illegal. On Earth, many believe, if you kill yourself, you will go to hell or be eternally damned. The Leaves, are not sure what happens either, so they goad the person into taking the risk, with a possibility the victim may suffer eternally. In short, the low fliers suffer in their existence, so to help create what could be a greater suffering for another, the inflicted torment brings them some sort of macabre persecutory power over their victims.

"It is also to do with the perceived contempt, the victim has for the gift of life. Whether people believe in a God or a universe which provides life, the act of suicide is seen by many as throwing the gift back into the face of creation."

"That's what I was thinking."

"The low fliers enjoy the contempt when it is present because it justifies their own for staying in 'between worlds'. Not all low fliers are menacing and some are developed enough to be more respectful of passing's, even though they may find it difficult to break their attraction to the Earth and go over with the catchers. We accept Leaves are part of the Earth world and only protect ourselves against them if they threaten."

"Was I right to do what I did today?"

"Yes, they could have overpowered us. It is unusual for you however, to have mastered a perfect range finding head shot on, as you say, your first attempt!"

"A lucky shot, I think. And if they had overpowered you, what would have happened?" I had to admit, I was pretty impressed myself.

"We would have been alright, although they might have continued to disable us, whilst they worked on Philip."

"How do you mean?"

"They could have persuaded Philip that he would go into hell eternally for what he had done and to stay on the Earth plane with them. If they had, he would have missed an opportunity to go over and once they had taken him away, they would more than likely have rejected him and caste him out on his own. He would have been well and truly lost and could remain so for years or more."

I told Arthur about my encounter with Clara, before Peter arrived and how easily I could have been persuaded to go with her.

"I met another at that time called Simon. Who was more developed and said he had been dead for a long time. By his clothes, I would have said he was from the mid-16th century. He has a wife in spirit, I have met her and he misses her."

"That is a long time and there are few of that age. It's also very unusual for his wife to still be connected to him after that long. Most Leaves have a personal link to spirit but unfortunately, it isn't always strong enough to free them. They have to learn to trust and to be able to surrender to themselves, to the big S."

"Big S?"

"The Self. The part of you which is spirit in matter on Earth, which we retain in spirit. It is the part that is made from the Collective which connects all beings. When we are spirit in matter on Earth, we are semi separated from it at the moment of conception, however, there remains a magnetism between the part we hold and the whole."

"I understand this is why humans can feel an internal conflict and a sense of not quite belonging on Earth. I felt that when I lived there."

"Yes, that's right."

Arthur explained on Earth, many learn to turn away from the Self or spirit, thinking they are just physical matter with a consciousness which helps them to survive, adapt and navigate, before they die and cease to exist. Depending upon our experiences, even as an infant, we develop a schism within which we struggle to know who we are and our role in life.

"It sounds similar to what my friend Sarah told me, except she describes it as a compass, where true north represents the unblemished direction the Self strives to take. It sounds like a battle to me."

"It can be and many are un-blissfully unaware of it! Psychiatrists call it neurosis, or an anxiety that something unknown is displaced."

"When you say in order to pass, Leaves have to surrender to themselves, why do they find it difficult to surrender?"

"Can we take a breather? Would you like a drink?"

"Yes please, it is so easy to forget we do not have to eat or drink over here."

"Yep but doing so for pleasure makes it even better! Look out there, what do you see?"

I looked out of the window facing inland and across a sea of powder blue flowers. As I watched, I saw tiny droplets emerge from each of the flower heads and suspend themselves in a uniform layer just above the petals. Ever so gently, a wave in the air rippled across the blanket from the far side of the expanse, collecting and carrying the droplets. As the wave approached, the droplets were funnelled into a wooden container, like a pail. A small tap on the side functioned to decant the contents.

"One, moment."

Arthur left my side and returned immediately with two half-filled glasses.

"I take mine with spring water, as it is a little heady on its own."

"Yes, spring water for me too."

I could smell the liquid as Arthur diluted it. The aroma was of nothing I had ever smelled before. Struggling for a description, I thought it was like elderflower with a hint of mandarin and something else which made it lift and burst as if part of a song inside my nose.

"Wait till you taste it!"

I took the glass and allowed a small amount to trickle upon my tongue before letting it run into my throat. It was cool, refreshing and strangely musical. As I let the taste settle in my mouth, I closed my eyes and became the gentle breeze teasing every petal of every flower, each one responding with a crystal chime in my mind. When swallowed, the intensity of sensation cascaded towards my stomach ending in a crescendo of scales, notes, flavour and tingling.

"This is heavenly, there is no other word. You could make a fortune selling this on Earth, I would call it tune juice."

Arthur laughed.

"Everyone on Earth would be a millionaire if they could experience the riches of heaven. The sad thing is, they could experience many of them on Earth, if they chose to look simply enough."

"Simply enough?"

"The paradox is simplicity can be many facetted, multi levelled and connected to everything else. However, it has the quality of knowing which overrides the complexity of your expectation and which delivers an understanding and beauty in perception."

"Simplicity is then, cheers."

"Yes, basically. Were you a Mensa member or gifted child on Earth?"

"No, transitional will, the horses taught me, it's like an etheric glue, it connects ideas and concepts and helps me to see and think through the motions needed to understand how things join together to create schemas and models."

"Anyway, where were we? Ah, yes."

I did find Arthur a bit wordy but was able to keep up and hold his interest with reciprocated wordiness.

He continued by saying that Leaves find it difficult to surrender because they don't trust or believe in themselves enough to move away from the familiar material world, even though their continued behaviour serves no positive outcome in staying. Their behaviour is no different from those still physically alive who cannot change their behaviours, which keep them in the negative familiar, kidding themselves that coping is the same as living.

"In most cases, there is a fear of what might happen to them if they decide to go over. It does not always depend on what they have done or the way they have treated others, it is the perception of how they think they have behaved and what has been premeditated and intended."

Arthur's experiences had shown him there were a lot of Leaves who were under a misconception, placed there by others whilst they lived, that they faced punishment in the world afterwards because they were not good enough. However, there were those who had good reason to fear what might come next, even though they were unaware there always remained the opportunity to eventually change their perceived fate.

"So, in the case of Phillip, if he had been persuaded by the others to stay, he could then have decided not to go over because of what he had done?"

"Yes, because of what I said about throwing the gift back. The taboos and beliefs say, committing suicide is a course of action against God's or Divine Will and it is unforgivable and punishable. The fact of the matter is, it is not punishable, but there are consequences. The act does not always have a defined outcome in terms of what happens to the individual after they leave Earth. There are so many circumstances around it and so many reasons why people choose to kill themselves. One could argue they weren't in their right minds to take such a decision. Therefore, if you are not in your right mind, it is your mind that needs to be eased and healed in the spirit world, rather than be punished."

I felt it was those who chose to die as a way of purposefully avoiding the consequences of their actions leading up to the decision, who cause themselves problems as to what happens next.

"Many spirit guides believe, people can tackle their problems and things are not always insurmountable or unforgivable. It is a really difficult grey area and as spirit guides, we support life. We don't want people to give up their lives, so will work with them on this brink to try to seed and guide them otherwise. Guidance is not always successful, as you have witnessed, because people have free will and free will is unconditionally given to us and never taken away, whether in body or in spirit. It is a fundamental paradigm of human existence to have free will and choice and suicide is also about choice."

"What about belief?"

"Generally what religions and belief systems teach is, don't commit suicide because you will be punished and will suffer in the afterlife. On the whole, this does act as a deterrent for some people. However, if people knew they were going to continue to live afterwards in the spirit world, they may also think they may be able to avoid the consequences. However, it does not work like that, the outcome is not guaranteed. A person could find themselves living in a darker realm for centuries because of the motive behind of the decision."

"Dark realm? I have a basic idea of what they are, but I don't know much about them."

"Has anyone explained the structure of the spirit world to you in terms of realms and moving between realms?"

"Basically, but it is very vague. I get the feeling people are not sure how it all fits together. They seem to accept they live in this realm, know high planers come from higher realms, are aware of lower realms and see the Earth plane as being sort of different because it supports physical life. I do not know much about the realms, how it all fits together and about dark realms especially."

"Come with me."

Arthur transported us to the outside of the lighthouse.

Infrastructure

"If you look up as you walk around the base, tell me what you see."

"There are no windows at the ground level."

"Yep."

"But at the second level there are two. Then three and so on until you reach the sixth where there are six windows. At the top it is totally glazed."

We then entered the base through its doorway.

"Now look up."

The inside was designed with a helical staircase ascending in a clockwise rotation. With the door at the bottom closed, the base was the darkest and as the staircase ascended, so the light became brighter.

"Light brings information, knowledge and awareness. But how do you get to the top?"

"Climb?"

"Yes, that's true and to climb, you need?"

"Will."

"So, with will and awareness you become more of who you are, enlightened so to speak and in doing so, align more with the Self and the Collective. If you do this, what is the benefit?"

"You increase your knowing."

"You have been working hard since you have come here! This lighthouse is a model of the structure of the spirit world from popular belief, as nobody seems to know the exact layout. The two lowest levels are the dark realms and the seventh is the highest in terms of housing those with the greatest sense of knowing. The third is a reflective realm. This houses those who have achieved a stabilised and reflective sense of genuine Self. Such as those who have emerged from the dark realms, who reside there to acclimatise to a way of lesser self-tortuous existence than being in the dark."

"So it is like a sort of purgatory?"

"Yes, if you like. If you think about it, progressing through it is no different from being in that time of our lives on Earth when it takes nothing more than focus, dedication and self-belief to achieve something that is better for ourselves. It is an inherent concept."

"Do people go directly from Earth into the third?"

"Yes, this third realm also serves as a location for Earth leavers who judge themselves authentically and responsibly for actions against others, creatures and the environment and who caused intentional suffering. They would spend time here considering their responsibility and actions until their own sense of Self was satisfied and the individual could live in the next realm. The forth is where we were living now, where the majority of Earth dwellers come to. The fifth, sixth and seventh realms are the higher realms. In the highest realm, the connection with the Collective is at its greatest and so individuality becomes unimportant."

We made our way back into the viewing area.

"Those in lower realms cannot travel upwards until ready to, but those in higher realms can travel downwards. The Earth plane is semi-separate because as you know, the spirit world is hidden from the Earth. There is much on Earth, however, which can be termed as symbolic or having hidden meaning, bringing us insight as we struggle to understand the balance between matter and spirit. That is, if we choose to see. I think the Earth is like a green house where souls develop their own sense of being in the world and upon death are transplanted into the spirit realms. The realm they come to reside in, depends upon their own developed sense of awareness and will in relation to the other. The other in this context, meaning life in all of its forms and its right to develop without negative impacts which would create suffering."

"Who really decides which realm, you are transplanted in?"

"You do."

Arthur explained at a point shortly after death before you reach the spirit world, you are connected to the truth of your actions as enabled by the Collective consciousness of all spirit. The process is set up to enable self-judgement and in some cases the person splits and faces themselves. In that moment of dual analysis, where both the personality and the spirit Self know the truth, the personality is shown the impacts and consequences of its life including all the ripple effects on others connected. I thought for a moment this was similar in some way to the encounter I had with little John.

The split enables judgement of what the person has done to satisfy their own personal gains. It is our awareness and will and the choices made based on these, which define who we are and the 'supportive or rejecting' relationship we have with the Collective spirit consciousness, either consciously or not. Being judged by the part of you who knows the truth, cuts through deception and denial and allows the individual to accept responsibility at that moment.

"The Collective already knows the truth. Even though people may deny everything after the judgement, they have already placed themselves in a realm which will manage their risk or support towards others. Meaning they will share the appropriate realm with others who have lived their Earth lives in a similar way. Self-reflection is the appraiser on Earth and in spirit and denial or harmony, the product of our actions."

"I don't remember judging myself when I passed over?"

"Judgement can happen in a moment. After death, it is the ego or personality that remains co-joined with the spirit in the spirit realms and remains so, until much higher development in the higher realms."

"What happens after judgement. I obviously know I arrived here?"

"On leaving the judgement process, they hold the seed and hence the key to their further future development. It's like a gift which can be accepted graciously, used or rejected. Again, it is a matter of choice."

"Who goes into the dark realms?"

"Dark realms are worlds of existence containing those who commit moral crimes. They are those who supress collective spirit until their individual will becomes disturbed and perverted to a point where their own assumed power impacts on other being's lives, causing suffering and fear. We are talking about those who create awfulness knowingly and their existence after bodily death can be impoverished and self-tormented for what can be a considerably long time. They are not on their own. There are others around them, who will impact upon them in both positive and negative ways and there are visits from those in higher realms who try to help them."

"So, it's like a prison?"

"Of sorts yes, but they hold the keys to get out. Denial is one of the most powerful inhibitors of truth and even though many are shown the truth in judgement, they still deny it and reinforce past behaviours with victim or perpetrator mentality. They will not be able to release themselves until they face the truth and take responsibility for their actions. Then they can choose to move up a realm. The system is developmental. What would be the point of operating a system based on choice unless it was available at all levels?"

"Are they dark?"

"I have never been to one and I do not have the experience to work with those in dark realms. I hear they are dark, subdued and cold. There is no virtual world and imagination does not have the same power as it does over here."

"You say spirits can descend through the realms, but they cannot ascend upwards. Why is that and does that mean people are restricted to their self-allocated realm?"

"The movement between realms is based on perception, light, resonance and spiritual development. Have you ever faced into a powerful light and been blinded by it?"

"Yes."

"Well, you could not live in an environment where the light stopped you from orientating yourself. Higher realms are said to be lighter, containing energy we cannot navigate through. We cannot move up to the next realm, without gaining a sense of spiritual development. As on the Earth plane, we perceive ourselves as separate and exist separately, although our spirit essence is shared. Here, we have the ability to directly link into each other's thoughts and emotions, which cannot be achieved on the Earth plane. This is a facility which enables us to increase our knowledge. Spiritual awareness, knowledge and will form and progress a sense of knowing. To 'know' appears to be the prize of existence, to know without doubt. The Collective is all encompassing, all wise and all-knowing and it is believed we can progress through the realms to be more like it or to become part of it."

"So, we develop to be like Gods?"

"No, we develop to eventually become one with the Collective or the Divine. We become more God like in being, less individual and less separate and re-join the divine energy, becoming the Collective. The opposite, if you like of when we were semi separated from it and placed in matter on Earth."

"It seems like a sacrifice, where the prize of development is to give up individuality and identity?"

"There is no sacrifice in knowingly surrendering to evolution. Surrender is not giving in, it is the wilful acceptance of the inevitable choice."

"It's like death then!"

"As I have said, the models are the same."

"This is massive stuff! Do you actually know this, or is this your interpretation?"

"This is what I have learned and have heard through snippets from high planers and what I believe to be true. It seems to make sense, but there is nothing concrete to substantiate it, other than the existence of these more developed beings coming into our world and my belief of course. You will notice how belief is still important in the spirit world even though we are sort of living a belief."

"What's beyond the seventh realm and what happens after that?"

"We don't know. My theory is, everything is beyond the seventh. Everything, that is beyond our perception and imagination. If you look in every direction at the horizon from the top of this lighthouse, you will get a sense of this."

"In essence then, the entire spirit world is built upon the dark realms or hell, as a lot of Earth dwellers would term it and it is hierarchical?"

"You seem surprised? What model or structure on Earth isn't built on, or has its foundation in darkness and is not hierarchical? Plant life rooted in darkness; human history in darkness; in fact any living thing is continually evolving from a darker, less aware history, to give it a better chance of survival in a hierarchical chain. The models are the same across worlds for the reason of maintaining security, stability and continued progression for those moving through it."

"Security, stability and progression? Apart from the evolution of Earth-bound humans."

"Yes, but that is because, as a race at the top of the chain, they have misinterpreted the balance of nature as requiring competition at the expense of cooperation. The Earth-bound humans still have a long way to climb."

"In my view, hierarchies are positive but corruptible. Misinformation creates the illusion of greater control and power."

I could hear Arthur's thoughts questioning my agility to debate.

"How old are you John?"

"Please stay with me. Hierarchies create competition, which is fine, but on Earth they also create fortresses which covet to the detriment of the whole race."

"Yes, but that is why we have the Collective. It is not at the top of the hierarchy, it comprises of a network of every life, at every level, in every hierarchy."

"But it's not the same on Earth."

"It is. The Collective is networked across all worlds."

"With one big difference. We know about it over here and I think the Earth bound are misinformed. Without the guiding information, they are left to their own devises and what are they doing? They are destroying the very world they need in order to survive. They are heading for the dark. There is a problem with the network. You are a guide, you must see this?"

Arthur paused.

"Every day," Arthur spoke quietly. "There are a growing number of us who feel like you do, but we are dealing with immortality in the Collective and our life experiences and personalities are forged in the mortal context of Earth. We also, do not have all the information."

I guarded my mind and wondered if it was Arthur's intensity that was catalysing my capacity to intra-connect the system's shortfalls. I did however, think that it was good to see that everything was not just blindly accepted over here.

"I am fifteen, but I felt a lot older and very different to others around me on Earth and that made life lonely. I trained my mind to run scenarios, to consider all possible outcomes and in doing so, tried to predict everything. Since being over here, I just see things emerging and I work hard to connect everything together."

"You must have had to face some difficulties early on?"

"I did and my mind kept me as free from them as possible, which I have since found has been detrimental to my development."

I heard an internal fanfare of trumpets and a 'yeah' resonate in my head.

"What's it all about then?"

"What, life? I do not know, although it seems to be to do with investing and creating energy as well as knowing. If you follow the garden greenhouse analogy, we appear to hold a divine seed which we have a responsibility to nurture and develop, whatever the plane or realm. Its growth comes from our relational experiences. We individually have the potential to develop knowing and in so doing, develop and create more energy that can be shared."

"But when is it shared or collected and do we lose the knowing we have acquired?"

"We share knowing whilst on Earth with others and when we die and return to spirit, we surrender the energy but retain the ability to know. The channel remains open, if you like."

"So, we are like ants or bees?"

"There are many similar and successful models which operate throughout the evolutionary chain."

"What happens then when we have progressed through all the realms?"

"We re-join with the Divine and willingly sacrifice individuality as I have said, as it no longer serves the growth of knowing. Whether the Divine energy as a whole grows, as a result of the process or remains static, I don't know. If it grows, I do not know how it uses that growth and what it uses it for. The possibilities are too far reaching. If you think about it, Earth world populations are continually growing, so perhaps the Collective's additional energy is invested in additional human life."

I guarded again and thought if this was what was actually happening, someone ought to tell the Collective that if it carried on, it would not be long before the Earth could not sustain further population growth, then what would happen? Even I knew, following Arthur's greenhouse analogy, if you plant your seeds too close together, you get a poorer yield.

"We are like hosts then?"

"I think that sounds a bit like a science fiction horror movie! Maybe we, our personalities or ego created by our experiences, is the real host or symbiote for the Divine. The body is a vehicle only. It is the experiences that are needed with which the Collective can interact and so grow, the result being increased knowledge and developing knowing."

"Maybe the divine needs us in order to exist, but do we need the Divine?"

"Woah John, where is that coming from? You learn and think around corners quickly, don't you? In my opinion, we are all the same thing, but as we develop, for some reason, we do so with a sense of separation, so as to individually create opportunities and further knowledge. I think individualism is essential to create progress and difference through creativity and volition. How else would comparison take place because without comparison, how would we learn we are all different and similar at the same time?"

I felt I had contemplated this line of thought before, but was at odds to know when.

"Have you ever thought about being a teacher, Arthur?"

"I was, in history and philosophy at Durham."

"Ah, that makes sense."

Arthur scrutinised me closely.

"Hang on John, I have a call coming in. Yes, I know, yes, I am OK. Yes, he is here with me now. Yes, he should be alright with that. We have just chewed on the meaning of life over a glass of tune juice. Yes, tune juice, I will explain later."

"John, that was my supervisor, she is coming over to check to see if we are alright after today's events. Her name is Sasha."

In a matter of seconds, Sasha was standing in the room, smiling a warm greeting. She was not what I expected at all. Tall, slim in build, high cheek bones, almost Elfin, with long dark hair. I thought she was very attractive and her image stirred me.

"Dobriy den John, Kak pazhivayesh?"

"Zdrastvooyte Sasha, Spaseeba preekrasna! Eezveeneete Ya plokha gavaryoo pa rooskee."

"Well your Russian is not bad, however, perhaps a mind block would save you from further embarrassment?"

I did not know where to look. This was the first time, since I had come over, that I had encountered a psycho-emotional arousal based on an attraction to the opposite sex.

"Yes sorry, no practice with that."

"Well, I am honoured and thank you, you are also beautiful, although perhaps a little young for me."

I put my face in my hands and asked politely if we could re-wind and start again. Although it took me a short time to join in the laughter, I managed to regain my composure and relax.

"I was worried about you and I am here just to check if you are alright. A person killing themselves in front of you is one of the most helpless and disturbing acts of free will we can experience. Although in our work, it is a common occurrence, it is doubly hard for us as spirit guides, because there is nothing physical we can do to prevent it, even when all reason has been exhausted. Arthur has told me you transported yourself, so you actually witnessed the impact."

"Isn't there a way you could physically act in situations like this?"

"There are two factors which govern this. Scientifically, we are light oscillating at a frequency far beyond the spectrums perceivable on Earth and our frequency cannot affect matter. Our wavelength is much more complex because it has information diffused into it and we can travel at speeds beyond light speed.

You have probably experienced thoughts and emotions as light here and perhaps you have wondered about the comparable speeds of light and thought?"

"Yes, I have seen emitted thought and feelings as light. I don't quite understand the time difference though and not specifically considered speeds."

"The speed of information via light is fundamental to the existence of the Collective. The web on Earth is a similar model except very rudimentary in comparison, but like the web, all information is there to be accessed. Not all are developed enough to fully access it, apart from the Collective itself."

"So, the Collective is a thing in itself?"

"We think it is both. It is diffused into all life. Without it, we would cease to exist and many think the Collective could not exist without all of us."

"We?"

"Those who search to understand the nature of things," added Sasha.

"I would have thought everyone coming over from Earth, having survived death would search for meaning." Being aware I had asked this question of Monique.

"Sadly no, John. What makes you think people over here are any different to how they were on the Earth plane, they don't suddenly change. There are many who accept this must be the next stage, but still continue to behave according to their personalities, knowledge and beliefs that they had on Earth. Yes, there is the self-judgement filter to rightfully place individuals, but most carry on as they were before. Anyway, we have digressed. The second governing reason is we honour the overriding principle to not interfere with choice."

"But you do. You attempt to seed and sooth, I have seen it."

"There is a difference between informed choice and a choice consciously or unconsciously filtering out reason and right relation. We try to help people to see how they have arrived at a choice point. We accept people are not always receptive but, attempting to save a life that may go on to help others, makes it worth it."

"Where is Philip now?"

"He's in three, the reflective realm."

"Why, it wasn't his fault! Did you know about his father and how he used to tell him if he had a problem, he must deal with it on his own, that it was weak to seek help from others. He was ashamed to admit he could not cope. I would say that kind of shame was pretty good extenuating circumstances!"

"Did you know about this Arthur?"

"Yes, I did and Philip was developing slowly."

"The thing is John, Phillip, on judging himself, chose to go to the reflective realm even though, he could have come here."

"Well he would have done, wouldn't he? People who suffer shame, self-punish, don't they? He probably thought he deserved to go there. I think there is a flaw in this system somewhere?"

"No, he faced himself and his truth must have seen the value of a time in reflection. If he is in the wrong place, he will soon set himself free, but this time, with direct help and support from others working with him. I have a couple of questions which are intriguing me," said Sasha.

She told me that she had been in spirit for a long time, with many years spent, involved in this kind of work. It had also taken her a lot of practice and study, to be able to cut through all of the emotional-mind turmoil being experienced by a spirit person in crisis, let alone an Earth person, to get to truth. However, I was able to access such wounding experiences fundamental to that person's make up and was a young fledgling spirit. Her second question was: When I was on Earth, where had I trained in psychoanalysis, to be able understand and communicate the orientation of personality due to its wounding affects?

"I have explained to Arthur; I have been learning about transitional will. I seem to be able to understand the gaps in processes and it may also have something to do with this."

Without warning, I transformed into my eagle right in front of them. I had never seen anybody jump back so quickly as they crashed into the furniture. I then changed back.

"You are a spirit shape shifter. I have never met anyone like you before. You can command the transitional. That explains your ability! How long have you been here?"

"I don't know, two or three weeks and yes a horse friend of mine informed me that I was."

"You can speak with horses. You are so lucky, I would give anything to be able to talk with horses."

"It's all a bit new to me. I am learning how others experience their internal and external worlds in relation to my own."

"Yes, but you would have had to revolve many times to develop this. It is an ability present in one who already has a strong sense of knowing."

Sasha then heard a gentle but firm voice speak to just her, in her head.

"Enough for now."

The directive silenced her.

"Are you alright?" I asked.

"Yes, that was a bit of a shock and I have to say meeting you has been quite overwhelming as well as an honour. So, how do you feel about Philip's passing, are you disturbed by it?"

I was a bit puzzled by the halt in the conversation flow. Yet again there was this question around revolving. Even with my shamanic abilities I had no idea of past lives and left my own enquiries at the level of possible, but unlikely.

"To be honest, I am settled with it. I think it's because of my own and others experiences we worked through at the rest home which changed my perception, but mostly because I know Philip is alright and alive."

Sasha thought otherwise, whilst suspending the link.

"I must get off now, I know you are centred Arthur, thank you for your efforts and I will see you later. John, it has been a pleasure to meet you and I hope we will be able to meet again sometime. One piece of advice. I mentioned about our ability to travel at speeds quicker than light, well, it can play havoc with time. Although we cannot time travel, time elapsed here can be different in relation to Earth time. I think you may have been here longer than two or three weeks. Good luck John, *do svidaniya*."

"Bye and thank you."

"Good bye Arthur, thank you for all your guidance and thoughts and of course the tune juice. I know we had a difficult start but, I feel that it was you I was supposed to meet. I must head home, bye for now."

"Absolute pleasure, I learned too. I hope to see you again John." Caught in my own thoughts, the transition enabling me to step onto the patio of Mill Cottage took a millisecond longer than my expectation. The thought of the governing system in all of its knowing, unknowingly undermining itself, was a huge concern. As my heroic sense of responsibility kicked in, it was accompanied with a small voice. 'Careful John, that thought might just be a huge delusion of grandeur.'

"Arthur, it's Sasha. I think we would be wise to remain quiet about what we have just experienced. It's just a feeling that we should let John find his own way in this."

"I agree, interesting sensation though, jumping out of your skin again when you haven't had one for years."

Stirrings

"Is that you John?"

"Yes, it's me, are you in the kitchen?"

I walked in and found Grandfather and Hazel sitting at the kitchen table drinking tea. It occurred to me they spent quite a lot of their time doing this. I thought back to the adventures I had just experienced and the different pace of ongoing events during the time I had been away. I was not judging them, but there were so many things to do and see in the spirit world and yet they seemed content to spend their time close to Mill Cottage, with occasional visits to their friends.

"What are you up to?" I asked, as I rested both hands on the back of an old wicker chair.

"Just relaxing and thinking about folks back home. Your grandad is a bit worried, as Grandma Audrey has not been well. He has been back to see her and she is worried herself that something is wrong," said Hazel.

"What do you think it is, Grandad?"

"Well, she has been to the doctor with pains in her stomach and he has prescribed something for it, which seems to help a bit, but to be honest, she has suffered with stomach problems for some time now and has done nothing about it. I am just worried it could be something serious."

"Shall I go and see her?"

"No need, I think she will be alright, she is tough and has had good health for most of her life."

"Did you see Simon?"

"Only fleetingly. He did not speak to me, but he waved a greeting, which I returned."

"Good, I am glad he kept to his word."

"When I came away from the house though, I saw him in the distance. He was with another man of similar dress and they were arguing. When I saw this man power up to attack Simon I came back over quickly."

"You left him?"

"It was none of my business John and I do not get involved in trouble over there if I can avoid it. Anyway, you have been away for weeks in Earth terms, what have you been getting up to?"

"Weeks! It only feels like a matter of days to me, I don't really get the time difference thing."

Grandfather explained that time in the spirit world seemed to pass slower than on Earth and time in virtual world, even slower. People over here tend to mark time in Earth days. It appeared that I had been over in spirit now for, two months. I found this confusing, as from my conversation with Sasha, spirit could travel at or beyond the speed of light, however, he confirmed that Earth world physics were different from those governing the spirit world.

Adjusting my mind filter to semi porous, I told Grandfather and Hazel about my adventures with Sarah, the horses and little John, leaving out the details of my extra adventures with Scout. My intention, was not to be deceitful or dishonest, it was just that I knew from their minds they had little understanding of a Shaman and I did not wish to give them cause for concern. I did tell them however, about Beachy Head and the suicide I had witnessed and my time with Arthur and the tune juice. They listened intently making little remarks about my safety and thoughtfulness around my actions, although on the whole, they were pleased I had made my first steps into experiencing this world. What I was concerned about, was including details which would draw many more questions than I could fully explain. Although they were my own family, I struggled with the difference between my view of life and theirs, which was, in my kindest thoughts, a bit dull. I felt guilty about this, but then, they were my mother's family so I must take more after my father, who was the man of sea adventures.

"What next our John, perhaps you would like to experience one of the spirit towns where many folks live together?"

"Yes, I would definitely want to do that. Everything here seems separated. We travel from point to point or from one person's little bit of heaven they have created to another and nothing seems to join it up."

They both smiled and explained that nothing needs to be joined up. An example Grandfather used was that the garden is outside the cottage and we can walk from one into the other. However, if he thought about being in the garden, he could transport there, so the garden could be a thousand miles away and yet he could get there in the same time. So, would it matter if it was not just outside the door or joined to the cottage?

"Thank you for explaining it so simply, I get it. I suppose on Earth, every location is connected to the one next to it, so you get used to seeing actual horizons and as it's a sphere, you are able to keep travelling until you end up at the same place you started. The spirit world must be massive?"

"Why should it be? How large is light? Physical form and matter on Earth is determined by the environment, nothing restricts light in that way, not our wavelength anyway. We could be infinitely small inside our cottage and if so, how many of our cottage universes could you get in say, the size of a tennis ball. On the flip side, if the whole of the spirit world existed in another dimension to Earth, let's say suspended in space with lots of room to expand, it could be massive."

"Yes, I see it could be both."

I realised my relatives were perhaps not as simple as I had thought. I hugged them both and said I thought I might rest in the garden for a while as I wanted time to reflect on my travels.

"If I might, I would like to take you both up on your offer a bit later."

I sat alone by the pond. Grandfather and Hazel had decided to visit friends of Hazel's instead and save the trip to the town when we could all be together. I relaxed as I watched the water play with the reflected shards of light, as dragonflies displaced the meniscus with sharp but meaningful indents. I was thick with 'Arthur' thought but much happier. I let my mind wander and drift to different places connecting with the actual of what was and then rest in the ether between the angles and folds of intention, anticipation and being. I lay back in the afternoon sun, my head softly cushioned by a small clump of easy grass and listened to the grass hoppers tuning their forks.

Of all my experiences, my mind reconnected with my meeting with Sasha. Although it was really embarrassing for me, it was the attraction that had affected me. I had never had a close relationship with a girl on Earth and hoped it was possible to meet someone here. I thought about Becky back on the Earth plane, the girl who I had liked and she had liked me. Our friendship had never blossomed beyond a shy smile and an acceptance of a fondness between us, but

I reminded myself I had wished for more and remembered her thoughts at my funeral.

Settling into myself, I wondered about love and what it must be like to be in love. As I did so, I felt my heart warm and noticed an ache laced with a sense of missing something, or someone. The name Alana entered my mind, yet I could not place her, nor understand why I would be missing a girl named Alana.

The softest and sweetest of voices then spoke to me in my mind.

"Hello, I am Alana."

I tuned into the voice and waited for her next words.

"Umm, excuse me?"

I opened my eyes and sat up with a start. Sitting next to me was a girl with eyes the shade and depth of burnt copper and hair as dark as flaxen but shot with warm walnut strands. She was beautiful and her image stirred me deeply. I found my mind waiting for my smile, and the delay between thinking and doing it was not fast enough for me to create the impression of seamlessness I was after. Alana laughed, and knowing she had read my thought, I blushed and laughed as well.

"I thought you were in my mind. I didn't realise you were here. Who are you?"

"I am Alana."

"I was just thinking about you, but how is that possible?"

"You opened your heart, just long enough for me to pick up your very distinct vibration and I gave you my name."

"How do you know my heart?"

"I have known your heart for a while. John, isn't it?"

She was smiling sweetly and I was being drawn into her with a familiarity I could not understand. My sense was I had somehow felt very strongly about this girl before. She smiled again at me as she encountered my thoughts.

"I have been looking for you, you disappeared, I didn't know you were over here. I figured you must have died, but I could not locate you in this world. It was when your heart opened again, I knew you were here."

I started to feel a little confused and unnerved.

"But how do you know me. Who, who are you?"

Alana smiled again.

"Well, I have known you for a little while now. Tell me, is it John, or is it James?"

"No, it's John. But come to think about it, I always fancied being called James, not that I ever wanted to be called Jim, I just like the name James, James Kenton. It has a nicer ring to it than John."

"I think James suits you as well. Can I call you James in this world?"

I nodded a little hesitantly, but her voice and the use of my chosen name, seemed to ease me. I felt I knew her, but could not understand why? I thought she was someone I should know, who would be easy to know. I liked her very much already and could not fathom the depth. Whilst I was thinking, she was beaming away as if caught in some rapturous resurrection of a secret exquisite memory and I felt teased.

"You smile a lot, don't you?"

"Depends on who I am with."

"So, Alana, how long have you been here? I mean in the spirit world?"

"Well, I have been here for about twenty-six years now. I lived in Harrogate in North Yorkshire."

"Harrogate wasn't that far from me, I lived in Denby Dale. I remember going into Harrogate on a couple of occasions to have tea in a tea shop with my mother and grandmother."

"I know."

"What, what do you know?"

"I know you used to live in Denby Dale."

"But Alana, I don't know you, how do you know so much about me? Have you been one of my guides? Is that why you are so familiar to me?"

"Yes, I think so, I think that is probably why you know me."

"Ahh, I understand, but I don't. Well I feel as though I know you, but I don't, I feel as though… I know you in a different way, but I don't understand. This feels like an unravelling déjà vu. Oh, I don't know."

I shrugged my shoulders and Alana smiled widely again. There were no mind guards necessary as I wanted her to know.

"Maybe you do," she said.

"Anyway, one thing's for sure Alana, when I feel around this, if I am honest, I feel I have missed you, even though I've only just kind of met you, or feel as though I have."

"I've missed you too James. Can I join you for a while?"

"Yes of course you can. That would be really nice."

"What were you doing anyway?"

"Well I was lying here just relaxing. I was thinking about the dragon flies and the water and how they play upon it and how short their lives together must be."

"Life maybe short James, but lives are not short. Come on, I'll lie back with you and we can both be dragonflies."

I felt Alana come into my mind and join with me. Her softness, her beauty, her love and her essence mingled with mine.

"How old are you Alana?"

"Oh, I think I'm the same age as you really."

"What, about 15?"

"Yes, sort of 15. Let me ask you James, do you not feel older than your years sometimes?"

"Well yes, I've got to say my mum always used to say I was…well, before I died, 15 going on 45 or more."

"Older I'd guess. May I?" She said softly and before I could speak, she slipped her hand into mine.

"I've missed you James, so much."

And without thinking, I replied,

"I have missed you too."

Alana was holding my hand and I was not resisting her. It was she who conducted the transformation of the two of us simultaneously. All of my senses shifted as I felt myself shrink in size, transforming and minimising into the light form of a dragonfly.

"Ever been a dragonfly before James?"

"No."

"Wait for the speed and the turning power, I am channelling their skills and behaviour patterns so you can fully appreciate what incredible creatures they are."

I took off vertically and hovered. Lifting my abdomen, I tilted my four wings and immediately shot off in the direction of the water, touching my tail onto the surface. Looking back through multifaceted eyes, the display of the light displaced, was like a multi-coloured firework show. Tilting upwards, I stopped in an instant, turned to hover and appreciated the resonance of the colourful trench. Alana, hovered beside me.

"This is amazing, absolutely incredible. It's almost as good as being an eagle."

"Eagle? And come to think about it, why do you wear a feather in your hair?"

"Long story, but I will tell you."

"It's OK, I can see it in your mind. So, you can shape shift, even on this world. That's rare you know?"

"So, I am led to believe, but I don't understand why I can do it?"

"Catch me if you can!"

My uptake on her action was instantaneous and the acceleration specific. We chased each other, twisting and turning upon imagined anchors and shifted direction in an immediacy, precisely honed to execute exactness, choreographed within a shared wing beat. Our synchronicity within movement was seamless as we danced and displayed our skills and colour to each other.

Finally, Alana settled on a reed and I rested beside her. We admired each other's beauty displayed in bright green and bright blue, iridescent colours and talked about the dragonfly and how its transition is of one from the darkness into the light, across the mediums of water to air. Alana explained how she thought, as a symbol, the dragonfly mirrored the transition between our lives and the shortness of lifetimes. How moving from the darkness into the light was like waking from a previous existence with no idea but an echo of foresight of what was to become. I agreed with what I knew and felt already, but met her without arrogance. I felt very comfortable with this spirit and trusted her presence. We returned to the grassy bank and transformed back into our own light forms.

"Thank you for the dragonfly experience, it was perfect. I have to say though, whilst I have been over here, I have transformed into my eagle a number of times and know that most spirits can only transform when they are in virtual world. When you took my hand and led us, we both transformed into dragonflies here at Mill Cottage, not in virtual world."

Alana smiled and shook her hair. A small brown and white striped feather surfaced from the depth of her locks. I was not shocked, but my feelings met me with a mixture of surprise, delight, intrigue and strangely, a sense of belonging.

"I am the same as you James. That is why we feel we know each other and if we were to become friends, you would see what I see and feel what I feel, if you chose to. Our kind seem to have the ability to link with each other, sensing and anticipating into levels and between levels of emotion and thought. Whilst you can do this with others, it is never to the same depth."

"Have you met anyone else like us since you have been here?" I asked.

"No, but it does not mean I have been lonely, I have just been missing something or someone."

"Hence the missed me bit?"

"Yes."

Alana's ability to manage the intricacies of her own mind guard had been finely tuned, even though John was also a shaman. She sensed his probes and questions and carefully responded with a projected openness to build his trust in her intentions. If she chose to be fully honest at this stage, her efforts to draw him close, would probably be wasted and he may run. She smiled her warmest and most genuine smile.

"I am dying to know?"

"You are already dead."

"Ha, ha, you know come on, what kind of bird are you?"

"Well, I am warm, funny, genuine and quite pretty…"

"Yes, very funny, which feathered variety?"

"I am an Osprey."

"Bloody excellent! I was afraid you might be a goose or something!"

"Careful James, my talons are very sharp!"

"You want to see mine."

"I think we ought to get to know each other a little better, before I do."

I blushed on purpose in an attempt to show my vulnerability and was pleased she responded with intrigue. I knew she was guarding, but could not see what it was. This was turning into a game, but with an adversary who could meet my skill and need for instinctive mental agility. Alana warmed to the introduction of humour and banter. It had been a long time since she had played like this.

"James, what say if we took a trip to the zoo this afternoon?"

"The zoo. I didn't think we had them here?"

"We don't, I mean animal world."

"Can we do that, because if we can, the answer is, definitely! Let me just check in with Grandfather and make another quick call." I spoke to him, just to let him know where I was going and following the customary, take cares and be responsible, I told him I was going with a new friend and would be back soon. Quick descriptions later, I managed to end the call. Alana listened in and smiled to herself.

"Tinker, it's John. Are you working in the realm or are you back in animal world?"

I explained our plans to him and wondered if we could visit, but Tinker was working with fledgling blind spirits. Evidently having spent their lives on Earth with guide dogs, his presence and temporary companionship, helped them get used to their restored sight. It was something to do with trust and suddenly seeing in spirit, following in some cases a lifetime of imagining what it was like to see.

"Anyway, when are you going to get a job?"

"I'm busy."

"Teenager!"

"Fleabag!"

"I'll bite ya!"

"Ha, ha, catch you later."

"So, you have mastered the dog language then?"

"I thought everyone could communicate with them?"

"Not quite to that level."

Alana described the animal world as one of zones, much like Tinker had explained. It was not a massive continual expanse, but habitats within habitats and with links or kinds of corridors which enabled different species to mingle and socialise. It included sea worlds, again interlinked and as with all animals they could transport themselves between habitats. I asked her about insects and smaller creatures that lacked a consciousness and it appeared their life essence returned to Earth quickly after they had died; but she did not know whether they changed species.

"Are there any dinosaurs?"

"Dinosaurs died out millions of years ago!"

"Yes, but they have died, so, where are they?"

"They revolved back to Earth as other species after the world's climate changed. Extinct animals do not suddenly reappear; they would have to go through the whole evolutionary process again. The spirit world is not a living museum for everything that dies."

"Can animals revolve back to be humans because I have seen some pigs and donkeys in my time on Earth?"

"That's a bit harsh, James, but no. Species tend to remain as they are, unless they become extinct as I have said."

"Is that the same for humans then?"

"Yes. Where do you want to go first?"

"I would like to go to the tropical rainforests, like the Amazonian one, because I am worried about them."

"If we transform on route into a couple of macaws we can visit the canopy. That's where the majority of the animals live together. Take my hand."

The heat was the first thing that met us as we landed in the top of a Ficus Tree, surrounded by other macaws and parakeets. The chitter chatter was quite noisy and they all seemed to chatter in unison.

"We know you are different, yes, different, not the same, yes, not the same, why are you here, why are you here?"

Alana calmed the birds with a wave of feathered empathy and explained we were here to visit, not to disturb and we had come in macaw form to be amongst them and be in the forest without causing unnecessary alarm or attention. The birds told her they were not afraid of spirit humans and we could be as we are. She asked how else we could be in the canopy and enjoy the freedom of flight as they did, when we could choose.

"You are different to others, but you are welcome here. Keep an eye on the Harpies. They are a bit grumpy and chase us a lot."

"Thank you for your welcome and we will."

"What is a Harpy?"

"It is a rainforest eagle with an interesting hair do. They hunt macaws on the Earth plane and they have even larger talons than yours. For some reason, they must still enjoy the chase."

"Okay, we will avoid them then!"

We settled down to take in our surroundings and watch the activity around us. In the distance, cloud forests floated above the main canopy, suggesting a separate world of mystery and legend, with the tallest trees reaching skywards from their misty collars. I had seen films of rainforests before, but in spirit the shades of green were almost limitless.

Blue Morpho butterflies danced about us floating on light as they eased upon their beats as if resting in flight. It seemed every animal which might be there, was. Howler monkeys and tamarins played in the branches, stepping over sloths who hung without a care in the world. Chameleons changed colour and tone in tune with that of the branches they walked upon. Birds of all different species squawked and sang to each other as if catching up on exciting news. A pair of hornbills gently knocked their beaks together in a display of affection and hummingbirds of all kinds buzzed between flowers collecting their nectar and showering those close by with crystalline pollen.

"Wait here, I need to try something. I will be back in a tick."

Alana watched John transform into a hummingbird and head for the nearest flower. Somehow expertly hovering, I inserted my beak into each of the nectary's, my tongue working like a sewing machine needle to empty their contents. My head was filled with musical notes in a crescendo of varying tempos.

"What on Earth, well you know what I mean, are you doing?"

"Tune juice! Scan the memory, you will see why, I am going to try another."

The same delight, although by a different composer met my mind and expectations. Transforming back to a macaw, I re-joined Alana with a broad beak-like grin going on.

"You are mad, James Kenton."

"Not mad, you should try it."

"May I."

She leaned forward and nuzzled her beak against mine and licked her lips. Little notes and tones reverberated upon her tongue and she shivered in her feathers.

"Was that the tune juice or the effect from our first kiss?"

Alana blushed on impulse and put her face under her wing.

"Got you back Miss Alana Macaw."

She scuttled towards me, shouldering me playfully saying she could not quite make up her mind. As we perched next to each other, we drank in the beauty and diversity of the surroundings and shared our concerns for the Earth, an Earth without rainforests.

"I wish the people of Earth would realise there were somethings which must remain whole, unbroken and protected. That there are somethings on Earth that sustain the global habitat and you just leave them alone."

We both agreed every nation should jointly take a far greater responsibility for the body of the Earth, much as every individual has a responsibility for their own body. This was not an ideal, it was a necessity. If the Earth decided to wash its decks, if taken beyond the balance, all the passive-aggression and denial on Earth, would not help the survivors remaining, to restore even a basic level of existence.

We also felt sad with the people and nations who continued to miss the point, on the basis of trying and continually failing to satisfy their own insecurities. Insecurities that had now infected the most natural of all balance.

"When you think about it James, all humans are insecure, if they are honest about it. Even in spirit. It is an innate liability and yet seems to be the most difficult of our qualities to share."

"Yes, but I wonder if it is a flaw in the system, the Collective now cannot put right?"

"Meaning?"

"Insecurities lead to a choice. If we do the opposite of deny and protect and accept them, we learn and can share the knowledge. This can lead to knowing and compassion, which is what the Collective wants. But to saddle a species with insecurities in the hope that it will overcome them and become productive, is risky and slow. Risky, because the reward remains hidden and humans are driven by reward, even the basic promise of the sun returning to the sky. Slow, because in the face of the imminent threat, the design cannot react fast enough in the current circumstances, to right the balance."

"You don't know if the saddle is by design. Free will and choice leading to knowing, is the reward, surely?"

"In a world that chooses to narrow them? Maybe this system needs to reboot once in a while?"

"And sadly, maybe it is about to and we don't know if that is in fact the design," added Alana.

"You have been here for a while now Alana. Do you know what the people in the spirit world think will happen to the Earth?"

"No one knows, that I know of. The majority are worried, because the two worlds are dependent on each other. If the Earth world is destroyed or seriously damaged by the current guardian generation's thinking and lack of effective and timely action, what might happen to us all, is unimaginable."

"I think it comes down to power and affect and yet power is not a negative thing, it is what it is until a motive is applied. I mean why doesn't the Collective or Divine enable the Earth to know of our existence? I am sure Earth leaders would sit up and take more co-operative action then!"

"I don't know."

"Global warming and over population, all happening in front of their eyes and they continue to join up their individually woven carpets to create one massive one, so they can hide the ever-growing elephant beneath it. Good grief!"

"Cool your jets hero, you are always trying to find the solution to things that frustrate, which you can't solve yourself and sometimes, if you had some faith in the hidden agenda and focussed on what is within your power to change, you might just understand it better!"

"I want to know what's on the agenda."

"My point exactly!"

"You know me. I am just passionate about things. Sorry for ranting."

"And I am sorry for snapping at you."

We both perched and remained silent for about ten seconds, minds locked. Alana was worried about her outburst of 'you always' and I was searching around my 'you know me.' We turned to face each other at exactly the same moment and asked each other the same thing.

"Where did that come from?"

We laughed and commented on old married couples and frustrations and the moment was put aside. We then wondered if we fitted in well with the other birds, with all of their chit chat.

"Come on Alana, let's go high and look over the expanse of the canopy. I would like to get a feel for the size of this place."

"Sounds good to me."

Wing tip to wing tip, we flew above the canopy and climbed higher to increase the view of the surrounding horizon. There was no end to its expanse and the sight that met us was an undulating sea of complex greens and rocky outcrops. It was like flying across a massive broccoli head with the tree tops packed so tightly together.

"We are so lucky to be able to see things like this."

"That's why they call it heaven!" said Alana.

The Howler monkey alarm call boomed out in low frequency from a point in the canopy below. It was Alana who recognised the warning and focussed in sweeping arcs across the air space beneath us.

"Harpy at 3 o'clock, 40 degrees' ascent, 400 metres and climbing fast."

"Got him. Were you a fighter pilot in your last life?"

"James, let's get out of here!"

"Let's split, you head for the canopy. I will draw his attention and go higher, I know he will follow."

"James, remember the hero bit of our conversation?"

"I will be fine. I have an idea."

"Oh no. I think I have heard that one before."

Alana banked hard left and folding her wings back, plummeted for the tree tops. I continued to fly ahead and upwards, periodically looking backwards to check the closing gap between myself and the Harpy. Twisting and turning I lay doubt in my anticipated flight path to no avail and beat my small wings as hard as I could. At 300 metres I applied all of my breaks at the same time as spinning to face my adversary and with my claws facing forwards, I evoked my eagle.

Shock was not the description for it. Wings back, open and high and tail feathers fanned and forward, the Harpy decelerated quickly. I knew with this manoeuvre the Harpy's talons would be projected forward. Using the element of the surprise and just before impact, I locked the Harpy's talons with my own. Arching backwards, I drew hard with my right wing and holding on with all my strength put us both into a downwards spiralling spin. I tuned into the bird's mind.

"Not quite a macaw then. Ever whirled before Mr Harpy?"

"You were a parrot, what are you and what are you doing?"

"I am a golden eagle and we are whirling towards the tree tops."

I knew the Harpy had the weight and power advantage, but I knew what the game was about and I held more stamina. There was no doubt this bird had a powerful grip.

"We are going to hit the trees!"

"Do you want to let go? You first?"

The Harpy released me with enough height to recover our flight. However, he maintained his intense interest and continued to fly after me. I, headed upwards again, powering my wings in an attempt to climb quickly. Having uploaded more information on the Harpy from a worried Alana, I knew I had a speed advantage and especially a dive speed advantage.

"Slow down, I can't catch you."

"I am not sure if I want you to. Why, do you want to go again or something?"

"Yes, definitely!"

"Excellent! OK then, this time lets climb to 450 metres."

"And we will see who let's go first, I felt your grip, you grip like a Cotinga."

I mind blocked.

"Hi Alana, what's a Cotinga?"

"Having fun up there? It's a good job you are not on Earth, otherwise, he would probably eat you. A Cotinga is a pretty little blue bird with a plum coloured cravat. Play nice!"

"A Cotinga hey, at least I haven't got a hair do like a cockatoo, but more importantly, we will see which one of us is a chicken!"

"Chicken, what is a chicken?"

With the planned height achieved, both of us engaged talons and whirled towards the trees. This time the Harpy mastered his rotation technique and the increasing centrifugal force stretched our forms and increasingly tightened our grip. The sensation was thrilling in its whirling, speed and dropping. I had a flashback to when as a young child, I had whirled around with a friend in a tight hand grip, both holding on to avoid the tangent spin off and inevitable fall.

"You are a human eagle, aren't you? It's OK, don't let go."

"I am a shape shifter; I can transform into animal forms."

"Is your mate like you?"

"Yes, but she is not my mate, she is a friend."

"My name is Audaz."

"I am John. Audaz, as in bold? So, you are a bold eagle?"

"That is me, not bald, not with a crest as magnificent as mine."

"We will see just how bold you are shortly."

Both of us narrowed our eyes in a joint focus of defiance, talons tightening. The canopy was ascending rapidly.

"Going to let go bold Audaz?"

"Never, shifting Joao."

The canopy was eerily quiet as we smashed into the tree tops at high speed, talons still locked tightly. Our display had not only drawn numbers but had silenced the mesmerised watchers.

"You can let go now Audaz."

"No, you first Joao."

I burst out laughing followed closely by Audaz and an eruption of chitter chatter, howling and a whole plethora of excited rainforest voices joined in. Alana flew in, in Osprey form and perched on a branch as we disentangled and sat preening our feathers. Alana caught my eye.

"Very handsome eagle, I must say."

It was Audaz who answered.

"Oh, thank you, but I am sorry, I only date Harpies."

Alana and I erupted in laughter.

"Oh, I see, you were referring to him. Handsome, no, he's too brown and you are a bit brown too, but I see you have a white under belly like me, so you are definitely more good looking than him."

"Thank you Audaz, pleased to meet you, I am Alana."

"Like wise Alana, any friend of Joao's is a friend of mine. I see why you cannot mate now."

Alana looked quizzically at me and I mouthed, 'explain later,' in my best beak-lish. Audaz took us to his favourite resting spot, which gave us a rich view of the forest. He explained his mate was still on Earth and he had been here for two Earth years he thought. I asked how he had come to be here and Audaz told us that his territory was being cleared for cattle farming and as he flew towards the people one day, he was shot.

"It was a wing injury and I could not fly, so I hid in the undergrowth and bled out for two days before a rat found me and killed me. Although I was weak, I took his eye before he took my throat. I was so frightened hiding there. I had done nothing to these people. I do not know why they take our forest for their cows?"

"Nor do we really understand why they have to. It's about short-term gain, for long term pain."

"Harpies mate for life don't they," asked Alana.

"Yes, we do and I miss her. We used to play together, but I avoided any fights as she was much larger than I. She could carry two Howler monkeys in her talons and a beak full of Macaws, at the same time, she was so strong."

"Two Howler monkeys?" I questioned.

"Well, maybe it was one big one. I am bored here really."

"Is that why you chase the Macaws?" asked Alana.

"Yes, I suppose. It is hard to deny an instinct, but I mean them no harm."

Alana understood exactly what he meant.

"You know Audaz, if you ask the macaws nicely and were less grumpy, as they say you are, they might play with you," said Alana.

He shrugged his wings and said they were a little slow.

"Then what about other Harpy's. There must be quite a few in the forest and you could make friends with them and perhaps show them what you have been doing today. I know what it is like to miss someone, you could do with some company."

"We do not usually mix with our own kind Alana, but it is worth a try. Thank you for playing with me today Joao, I knew I would win."

I finished my conversation with Audaz, whilst Alana transformed back to a macaw and flew to have a few last words with the smaller birds, before returning.

"You didn't let go until last because you were so frightened!" I teased.

"No, it is because my grip is so powerful, it demands great strength to release it."

"Boys! Anything else you want to compare?" said Alana, as she arrived back.

Alana and I gave our best wishes and said our goodbyes, having thanked Audaz for his hospitality.

"Will I see you again in my forest?"

"We will say yes."

Setting a mind lock for Mill Cottage garden, we disappeared to find ourselves once again sitting by the pond.

"Your eagle is magnificent."

"And your Osprey is beautiful."

"We are lucky, are we not James?"

"Yes, and I wonder where the gift comes from?"

"John, I hear you are back again, is that your new friend with you?"

True Intentions

As we walked up the garden towards the cottage, there was something different about the grounds. The addition of a flower meadow struck me both visually and in fragrance. The scent was fresh and heady and combined a mixture of freesias, orange blossom and jasmine. On walking in, instead of tea, Tom and Hazel were drinking from wine glasses.

"Tune juice I presume?"

"A delightful symphony, I must say. Pond water or fresh mill stream in yours?" asked Tom.

I could see Grandfather was enjoying the senses, as he had forgotten to transform back to his older self and was projecting as his thirty-five-year-old.

"Alana, this is my grandfather Tom and my great-grandma Hazel, this is Alana."

"Hello Alana, pleased to meet you, are you a friend of John's?"

"And you and yes, we only met very recently."

I could sense Grandfather's mood change quickly, when he realised, he was his young self and increased his years. He had also detected the Earth years of Alana.

"You are a bit old for him aren't you. You must be in your seventies in years of life on the Earth plane? Can I remind you John is just fifteen, or do you have some weird grandma-grandson thing going on?"

"I am older yes and you were about thirty-five when we entered the room. My intention is not to be disrespectful in pointing that out to you."

"That may be, but he is my grandson and young enough to be yours as well. What is your intention?"

"Excuse me, I am in the room and in the words of one of my mum's CDs recorded by a very talented woman, Aaliyah, who is now on this side too, 'age is nothing but a number'. And if you haven't yet noticed, it seems that since being in this world and the last, I know that choice is the deciding factor."

Alana smiled inwardly with a sense of pride for John who had defended his and her choice. Tom had never been repositioned by someone as young as John before and although the eloquent rebuke prickled his pride, he had to admit, especially in the spirit world, what John said was true. Tom rose from the table and placed his arms around both of them in a gesture of acceptance.

"I am sorry. In my old fashioned kind of way, I am protective because, although this might be heaven, you still get some funny folk over here. I can see Alana, your intensions are true and you come with love."

"Thank you, Tom, we have done nothing but play together all day and you have a very special grandson who is young at heart and wise in words."

"Tune juice you two?" Hazel asked.

"Yes, I will have mine with pond water. It has a nymphy kind of flavour to it which seems to lighten and transform things."

"Me too," added Alana.

The four of us took our drinks outside and settled around the fire pit. Whilst Hazel dimmed the lights and lit up the garden walk ways, I built a fire in the centre of the sunken circle. Cushions and blankets appeared to soften the seating and guard against Hazel's cool night air. We talked for what seemed hours, reminising about the small towns and villages of West Yorkshire and our lives just passed on the Earth plane and became friends. It was important to Alana, she gained their trust, as her next journey with John was going to test their belief.

With the fire reduced to embers, Tom and Hazel bid their goodnights and made way to retire to the cottage.

"In bed by ten, Grandad?"

"You know me, creature of habit and it is hard to change the habits of a lifetime."

"Do you actually sleep?"

"Sometimes I do and sometimes I travel in my mind to all the different places I can think of."

"Do you sleep Hazel?" asked Alana.

"No, not really, I travel too. I am making my way around the Pacific Rim at the moment. I started off in New Zealand about six months ago and I have got as far as Hokkaido in Northern Japan. I was there last night visiting the Ainu. They have a really interesting belief culture. Did you know they thought and some still think animals are visitors from the spirit world?"

Tom was silent, even though his mouth was open.

"So, you go back to the Earth plane to travel?" asked Alana.

"Yes. This may be a beautiful realm, but there are many things I missed when I was on Earth. In fact, pretty much everything outside of West Yorkshire, well apart from a couple of trips to London and Blackpool."

"You haven't mentioned this before?" enquired Tom.

"You have never asked. Do you think I am going to stay in the cottage and listen to you snoring? And besides, time is too short over here to sleep. Anyway, I will bid you farewell for now, I am off to Sakhalin tonight. They have a number of interesting Korsakov Churches there with some beautiful icons in them."

We all bid our goodnights and watched as Tom and Hazel still tied in dialogue, walk up the path to the cottage. I placed another log on the fire and watched it take flame. Spirit light fire was interesting as it twisted and danced, as if holding a life of its own. Alana showed me a game where you could guess the animal shapes made in flame by each player. We closed our minds to each other and created our creatures. It was I who spoke first.

"Going back to Hazel and Tom. It is funny how you can share your life with someone and not really know them."

"We all have our private times and that is a good thing. It is trust that smooths over any cracks and makes it alright for those close, not to always know."

"Is that why you shade your mind from me at times, to smooth over your cracks?"

John's last comment sent a ripple through Alana's own trust and she knew the time had come.

Awakenings

"Are you tired James?"

"No."

"Will you come with me to another place, I wish to show you something?"

"Yes, of course, where are we off to?"

"Just follow my link."

I took Alana's hand and we appeared next to another pond. It was ornamental compared to the one at Mill Cottage and much larger. I looked around the surroundings and behind us stood a large country house fronted by symmetrical and regimented flower beds and a fountain. All carefully cultured and cared for. I squinted and looked around inquisitively.

"I know this place, but I've not visited it on the Earth plane. I recognise it from somewhere though."

Alana smiled.

"Alana, are you creating this? Is this virtual world?"

"Umm, yes sort of. It's created from an actual memory. It is a virtual world replica, an exact copy of a place on the Earth."

"It's rather posh and I would imagine the owners must have been very rich to have built such a beautiful place?"

"Yes, it is beautiful. So, what do you remember about it James?"

"I don't know, it's a strange feeling really. It's almost as though I've been here before and it feels like I was with you, but that's impossible."

"Umm, interesting, shall we explore?"

We walked across the lawns, making reference to the flowers, the trees and the layouts of the garden. To our right was a cedar tree. Within its limbs hung a rope swing.

"Come on I'll race you."

Alana took off and with no shoes on the grass, we ran together and arrived beneath the tree at the same time. Both laughing, I turned, smiling into her and said,

"Gosh I haven't run for ages."

"I know, good, isn't it? Come on you can push me."

She climbed onto the swing and I started to push her. I could feel the warmth of the sun on my back, travelling through me and radiating from my heart. The sounds and scents reverberated in my head and I felt happy, a state which had seemed to have often evaded me upon my Earth journey. I found myself connecting to the very simple movement of pushing Alana away and then catching her again as she returned to me. There was something very powerful about this. I felt a small link and with it an increase in the sensation of what I was experiencing, except this time, when I pushed her away there was an anxiety and when she came back to me, a real sense of relief. It was as if I had endured this pain and joy for a time longer than I could remember.

"When was the last time you pushed a girl on a swing James?"

"You mean you?"

Although her back was to me, I could hear her smile. I flippantly continued and said I didn't know and perhaps it may have been a couple of hundred years ago.

"You reckon," Alana replied.

"I have to say though Alana, I have never pushed a girl on a swing."

"Ah, what a sheltered life you've lived John Kenton."

"Well I have, I was quite shy on the Earth plane, but I don't feel shy around you at all. I feel very easy, very comfortable. You must have been a good shaman guide."

"Well I learned things from you too."

"So, when were we together? When during my life were you around then, guiding me?"

"Come on let's go up to the main house."

I noted the avoidance. "Did you say this was an exact replica Alana?"

"Yes."

"So how do you know it? where do you know it from?"

"Well it was a place I visited a number of times, it's like a stately home."

"When you say visited, is it somewhere you visited when you were on Earth or you visited, you know, since you've been over here or what?"

"Both really."

"Well, where is it?"

"It's in East Sussex."

"That's amazing. I was in East Sussex a little while ago at Beachy Head."

"Well this place is closer to Hastings."

"I've been to Hastings, I went to Hastings. That connects with Beachy Head because I was…well it doesn't matter."

As we looked together at the house, I realised where I had seen it before and explained to Alana.

"One day it was raining when we were on holiday in Hastings. We were supposed to look round the gardens of this house and we decided it was too wet to actually do it. I recognise this house from the picture on the pamphlet, so we almost came here. I remember thinking it was a real disappointment we were unable to visit. Not that I was interested in gardens and things, it's just that the house looked interesting historically and there was some kind of draw to it. It is beautiful and yet there is something sad here. So, what were you doing in East Sussex then, because you were a long way from Harrogate?"

"I was with my husband and we were in East Sussex one year on holiday when we visited this home. I really got the feeling I knew it, that I had been here before. You know sometimes you get a funny knowing feeling and I came to the swing and swung on it and had this strange sensation. My husband didn't want to push me so I swung myself and whilst I swung, I felt a little lost and a little alone, as if I was missing something, or somebody. I felt sad, but it wasn't a sadness of total loss, it was just a sadness around something that wasn't yet completed."

"So, you were married?"

"Yes, why?"

"I don't know, it just feels a bit odd. I was too young to marry in my life, so I don't know what that's like. Did you have children?"

"Yes, I did, I had two girls who are now in their early 60s, Janice and Angela."

"J and A, same as our initials?"

"Yes, although when I named them I wasn't too conscious about it!"

"Why would you be conscious of it anyway?" I was bemused.

"No reason, really."

Alana smiled at him wondering how long it would take him to wake up, but she knew that this was about patience and if she was to hold her love again, she would have to allow him to awaken at his own pace.

"So, if your kids are in their 60s now and you've been here 26 years, that means you must have died when they were in their 40s?"

"Yes, that's right, but I didn't have them until I was in my mid-30s. I was 75 when I died."

"So, you are presenting yourself now to me as a 15-year-old? Why do you not decide to be older? My grandfather for instance, was well into his 70s when he died but he presents in his mid-30s as you have seen, so why do you decide to present as a teenager?"

I found this age thing difficult to comprehend. Having met Sarah who must have been four hundred and eighty odd years old and presented as a forty-year-old, I could see age didn't really matter, but in Earth terms, I would not generally hang with a seventy-five-year-old, unless he or she was a grandparent.

Alana heard his thoughts and although concerned, held the real reason and told John that when she was 15, this was about the happiest time in her life. At that time, she was carefree and adventurous and loved by her family, so this was the age she decided to remain at. I was a little sceptical.

I could pick up the guardedness Alana was using, but it remained nothing but intrigue, because I knew her intentions were not with malice. She just seemed a bit shy and there was an air of mystery around her. What was strange to me, was that I knew she was an adult and had led an adult life and yet I had no experience of this because I was only 15.

"Is your husband still living or is he in the spirit world?"

"Yes, he is in the spirit world, but he didn't die until he was in his 80s. He was my second husband anyway. My first husband and I didn't have children and I lost him when I was still very young."

"Is he in the spirit world?"

"Yes, he is."

"So how do you decide which husband to be with in the spirit world, if you lived your life with two on the Earth plane?"

"Well I don't want to be with my second husband because I choose not to be. We had a journey together on the Earth and we loved each other. We had children and a life, but he's not somebody I would wish to spend more time with. I feel as though what we did together was enough during that Earth time."

"That sounds a little harsh though really."

"Why, why do you think it is harsh James?"

"Well, you marry somebody and hopefully you'll be with them for the rest of your life."

"Exactly, but not necessarily lives. You might choose to be with somebody after your life but you don't have to be and he's fine. He feels the same way as I do, is living his life and is happy."

"What about your first husband then, do you see him? You say you lost him early?"

Alana recounted the story, where they were married just before the start of WWII. She was 20 and he was a bit older. They were living in London and he was connected to the admiralty, working as an agent, which meant she didn't really know a part of his life. She accepted he used to have to disappear and would come back at strange times having been away for weeks on end.

She knew his work was very important to the country and he would be working behind enemy lines in very dangerous situations. At this point my skin prickled. They had been married for 4 years and every moment counted. Every moment together was like their last moment and they were so much in love, they could have breathed for each other. They both knew the life expectancy of agents during this war was not very long and he lived and survived until 1944 when he was caught and killed. She did not know where he was or whether he was going to come back and after 6 months she received a letter from the admiralty saying he had been very courageous, dedicated his life to his king and country and had died a hero.

What she did know, was for 4 of those 6 months she imagined speaking to him every day in her head and then suddenly one day she knew he was dead. The tears rolled down Alana's face.

"I missed him so much he was my absolute world. There were so many things we were going to do, so many places we would have travelled to and so many experiences we wished for. Yet, when we were together during those 4 years, although much time was spent apart, the intensity of our relationship was beyond what I could have ever wished for. We talked and talked and we had such a knowing between us. It was almost as though we had been together a lifetime, even though we had only been together for a short while. He was a beautiful man or I should say is. Very talented, very sensitive, loving and romantic. He used to play the clarinet to quite a good standard and would play in an amateur orchestra. I used to watch him. I was so proud of him when he played."

"I play the clarinet or I did do."

Alana cried again and said: "Yes, I know James, I know you do."

"How do you know?"

"Because I just heard you, thank you."

"I don't hear you thinking at the moment Alana, why do you hide?"

"I guess these are my emotions James. I think they come with a lot of pain and sadness and I suppose I am holding them close to me."

"But your first husband, you said he is in the spirit world. Did you see him? Have you found him again?"

"I did and we were together again for a short while, but he decided he needed to go back."

"Revolve, you mean?"

"Yes, revolve and I understood he needed to go back to complete or experience something and so he did. We had three years together in the spirit world and then he returned. I decided to stay here because I wished to and because there were things I wanted to learn here. What I didn't know was how long he would actually remain on the Earth plane before he came back and neither did he at the time he went back."

"So how long was he on Earth?"

"Another 15 years."

"So that must mean he has only been here for a short time?"

"Yes, that's right."

"And have you seen him again?"

"Yes, I've seen him."

"And is he alright and do you see him often?"

"Yes, he seems fine and well and I hope to."

"Does he want to see you? Does he want to carry on seeing you?"

"I'm not sure John. He seems a little unsure at the moment, but I'm sure he will make up his mind either one way or the other."

"Gosh Alana, it must be so difficult for you to be so in love, not that I really know what love is. But I have a feeling."

"I'm hopeful James that things will be alright. Anyway, we'll see."

Alana smiled to herself and was amused by John's naivety and his inability to connect things up at this level, but deep down she knew he loved her and she loved him and time would tell.

I was a little bit confused by my feelings towards Alana. As I spent time with her, I grew to like her even more and we seemed to have something that connected us together. I struggled with the past lives' situation, because this was the first time I had really come across it with examples. I had heard people talk about it, but I still couldn't understand what its function was and why people went back, or how in fact they actually managed to get back. It opened up quite a wide field for me as I thought about the implications of who organised such things; who you might go to see to discuss the situation; whether you decide on your own that you go back and what you go back to achieve. It seemed strange to me that in some instances, life on Earth can be so short and sometimes very painful for the person. I thought about small children who are born and then suffer at the hands of their caregivers and wondered the purpose of their lives. The complexity grew and I knew I would have to discuss it with somebody who could unravel some of the mysteries. Alana was listening to my thoughts.

"Do you know Tarquin, James?"

"Yes, I have met him."

"He might answer your questions. He is very approachable although he is a high planer and perhaps you can contact him through one of the sanctuaries he visits to help new people coming in."

I remembered what Sarah had said and thought Monique might be able to contact Tarquin.

"You can always contact him direct if you can remember the pattern of his vibration."

"Yes, I think I can do that, but I would want to collect my thoughts before I dared to speak with him, as he seems to be an important and busy spirit."

"He seems like a good soul, I think he would make time for you."

"You speak as though you know him Alana."

"Not really, I have met him and he does help people."

"Come on James, let's go into the house."

As we stepped inside, it was an amazing feeling because it felt as if it was ours. There was nobody else around and because Alana had created this and it wasn't permanent like Mill Cottage, then nobody could gain access to it unless it was at the invitation of Alana. As we walked from room to room, things seemed more familiar to me.

"Are all these rooms exactly how they were?"

"Well yes. I mean I imagine they are like how they actually were because this house dates back to the 1600s."

As the familiarity grew, which I could not fully understand, I wondered whether it was a link from Alana's memories causing this. We turned into a music room furnished with a large piano, stacked bookshelves, comfortable seats and sofas. Very large windows of panelled glass spanned almost from the ceiling to the floor, their doors opening out onto an ornamental terrace I had seen from the gardens.

"I'd like to create something, if it is OK with you, John?"

"Yes, go ahead," I said hesitantly.

"What I'm going to do is to create a scene from a long time ago, as I see it. You and I will be in it and there will be others around us, but they will not be able to see or detect us as we are in our time now. Just close your eyes."

I closed my eyes for less than a moment and opened them again to find I was in the same room but with other people around. Music was being played by a string quartet and harpsichordist, with the tempo complimented by the chatter of ladies being wooed by courteous gentlemen. It was like a party but judging by the clothes and accessories of what surrounded us, I guessed the eon was in fact around the 1700s. Long frock coats, waistcoats, A-line dresses, lace frills and cuffs, sideburns and ringlets, appeared to be the fashion for the time. It was an interesting situation because although I knew everything was buzzing and going on around and people were interacting, Alana and I remained the observers.

I looked at my own clothes and they fitted in with the surroundings as did Alana's. Alana was beautiful, she was slightly older as well, now in her 20s. Catching a reflection of myself in a mirror I was amazed to see I had aged by about ten years.

"How many years do I hold Alana?"

"One score and five, sir. And I, one score and six."

"I am amazed and impressed. You are creating an illusion through my own perception of my reflection in a virtual world, where I actually see myself as older? That is clever."

"Why thank you, this is a blend of the two."

"You are very beautiful."

"Well thank you again James, you are very handsome yourself."

"So, what is this about, is this a party? And who are we in this? And why are we here in their time?"

I was starting to get confused and a bit nervous. Alana felt my anxiety.

"Well this is a memory John…James, based in a virtual world situation, framed by a reality setting I have created. Please bear with me. All of the people around us know we're here but can only interact with us in the eon of the then period in the 1700s. They may see you but only see you in terms of their own memory. We cannot talk to them and they cannot talk to us in the context of now, but they might acknowledge or speak to your presence because that is the memory they have of us from then."

"So, you have created a scene from one of your own memories and within that memory there are others who have their own memories and their memories are of me, or this older version of me back then. So, we were here back then?"

"Yes, but their own memories of course cannot encompass what is happening in the here and now from our observer position."

"So, what you see them play out, is your own memory of us?"

"Yes. Please let it run through, I promise it will become clearer."

"So, if this is a memory, Alana May, and I guess that's your name because it seems to fit?"

"Yes, it is."

"Then that means you were here in 16?"

"1685."

"And from what you are trying to explain, somewhat confusingly, I was also here in 1685 too?"

Alana hesitated and looked down. I tried to link with her mind and feelings. I was sensing she was not only hesitant, but there seemed to be something she didn't want to open just in case the moment might be lost.

Alana was feeling vulnerable. She felt as though she had brought John into a past life context where they had both been together, hoping he might remember something, but rather than let the memories stimulate his own memories, he was trying to work out the context and the reasons for him being there. She really wanted him to discover through coincidence and intrigue rather than for her to risk explaining to him and for him to back away and question her intentions.

"Not exactly James…John."

"And what does that mean?"

"James can you let me run the memory, please?"

She held both my hands in hers, as if to implore me.

"There is something that informs me, I should trust you and I am willing to take this chance with you. This is not because I know you cannot harm me, this is because what you hide seems so important to you, that it should remain hidden until an exact moment, I realise your intentions within this revelation."

"You always did have such a way with words James."

"Thank you, I surprise myself sometimes."

"There are two ways in which we can observe this. One, we can actually sit outside of the memory and observe ourselves interacting with those around us and see the events unfold as they did in 1685. Or, we can be as observers positioned within our own selves as memory beings, so we can observe their minds and sense their feelings as the memory plays out what actually happened. We would be aware of what was going on from an internal point of view as we would also be looking through our own eyes at that time, but we would be unable to change the words or course of events. If we choose the second way, there is a feeling of powerlessness which comes with it and the emotions can be a lot more intense. This is because things might occur that you have no control over, which you might wish to change now, but you can't do because they are all memories."

I felt a little bit hesitant. I wasn't sure of Alana's motives, but I knew enough to trust her and to feel this was necessary, for her at least. I was also venturing into places and situations I hadn't encountered before and this spurred on my inquisitiveness. There was no doubt I had a strong feeling towards this woman or girl and wished to go along with what she was choosing. However, I was a little worried about the second scenario of the observer position from within.

"OK Alana, let's play this memory from within."

Alana explained the background to the scene. At that time, we were not married and had been seeing each other when we shouldn't have been. There was some difficulty with regards to my station or prospects and Alana's father was not happy with our liaison. The problem was, we had been seen in embrace, by one of Alana's father's friends and on her father's return from London tomorrow, he had requested counsel with her to discuss the matter. She knows what he will do. She cannot disobey him because of her position and the family's reputation in society and she would not betray her father.

She could run away with me to set up a new life, but her sense is that this would create great difficulty for her and I. She also knows I would be in danger, because her father was owed favours by many and any one of them might seek an opportunity to repay her father by betraying us or hurting me.

Alana has to make a decision to say we cannot be together because she knows really, I will be under pain of death if I do not leave. We both know we are very much in love and we both sense we have been together before in lifetimes. We understand we will be together again, but it is Alana who is the stronger of us and she is the one that says we must part. In feeling we will return and be together again in the next lifetime, we know not to seek each other again during this one. It seems I end up going to sea and travel to become a merchant. Neither forgets the other. Neither falls out of love with the other, much as we have never done through our lifetimes and although each of us has our future separate partners, neither loves them with the same passion, nor the devotion with which we have loved each other.

Having heard her words, I felt that I had suddenly become a character in a book, who had just had the majority of the plot revealed to me. I searched desperately for the realisation of the meaning behind Alana's motives, trying to add weight to my decision to trust her intent.

"Alana, I am not entirely sur…"

Choosing not to let me finish my sentence, Alana engaged the memory and my speech and consciousness melded with that of James, speaking and feeling from a previously forgotten eon. In that moment, I considered transporting to protect my heart and yet instinctively, I was compelled to remain. It was the seventeenth century James who spoke first.

"Alana, I don't want to be here and yet I want to be here so much because of you, but my fear is the feelings you hold for us right now. My fear is the feelings that were a result from our discourse today. If I could shout it from the very turrets of every castle in this kingdom, I would say that today and every day, it is my love Alana May, whom I live for and would die for."

"James hold your peace and temper your pitch for there are others around who speak closely to my father. They are closer in loyalty to him, than any loyalty they may have for me."

"Do you think I fear these people? Do you think I would let anything come between us?"

"I fear that you do not fear now, for it is perhaps our love that blinds you and it is necessary you listen to me in this moment."

I connected to the feelings of James and sensed what was about to be spoken was going to reduce him to utter despair.

"Why do I fear your words Alana? How is it that I love you so much and yet my sense is your words would create the greatest of pain within my heart?"

"James please, please, I implore you to let me speak."

James' eyes welled as did mine, as he focused intently upon her face. Both of us wanting and wishing what was about to be spoken, would not be.

"You know I love you with all of my heart. You know we have loved before and will love again across centuries. You know as part of this delight and as part of this responsibility, we cannot always be together, but we will always return to each other one day."

"We live this curse of life path crossings you and I and it is always the partings that are the very hardest. It is never knowing when or where. It is sitting with heart ache within the same life time as knowing you. And sitting with displacement in the lifetimes where I have not yet met you, holding a feeling there is a love somewhere that I cannot quite find."

"You know James, sometimes we may spend years together and in others just months, but it is the love and intensity which bonds and binds us together. You know we do not always choose our own path."

"God, do I know this? Of course, I know this. My heart breaks each time, as if it was the first time, for I love you so much and my desire is to be with you forever."

"We will be James. As you know there are times when neither of us are on the Earth plane and are residing in the realms beyond and during that time we can be together."

"I know Alana. Why is it we must part this time?"

"Your life is in danger James. My father has discovered our liaison and because of station, reputation and loyalty, I cannot be with you."

"So yet again we are divided because of others' thoughts and because of others' feelings. Why is it we cannot have a lifetime where we may forge our own course? Why is it we cannot have an eternity where we make our own decisions and we choose to be together whatever? Why do you not run away with me this time Alana? We will live wherever?"

"You know why I can't. We do not choose our lifetimes totally and there are others within them who rely on our presence in their lives and the consequences of our presence within their lives. Paths are not always as easily set or understood, as we would wish they were. You and I both know there are experiences associated with lives which we do need to experience separately. Do you know we cannot get around these circumstances? Do you know James? We always know, because we know!"

"Alana, I don't want to leave you."

"You know you must James."

By this stage in the conversation, I was in tears within my older self. I was lost and distraught, confused and vulnerable. I sensed from the Alana within Alana her complete and utter sadness connected with this scene.

"James look around, there are others who are now aware of our discourse. We must draw this to a close."

"And a memory of you Alana to take with me?"

"A lifetime back in a hayloft after the thunderstorm, we made love with an intensity and a knowing which will stay with me for an eternity. I have never forgotten and nor shall we. Goodbye James."

"Goodbye my love."

James left the room with me still within him and both Alana's watched us go. Alana dissolved the memory and followed me outside.

Dawning

Alana found John sitting on a garden wall with his head in his hands trying to make sense of what had just happened. She approached him slowly, wondering at the suffering that was of her making, his resurrection task and the pain they must go through, in order to awaken. She knew at this point, he may reject her, which would change the course of their lives. She asked the Collective for strength.

"I…I don't understand. There are so many feelings and thoughts. It was like watching a movie for the first time and then realising that I have in fact played a leading role. I just feel that…I don't know Alana; I am a bit lost."

"Yes, I know. It is always hard. It is always difficult. Do you know who you are now?"

"Yes, I do, I am James in the scene inside and I am your first husband, aren't I?"

"Yes, you are. Do you remember our words?"

I looked up, wiped the tears from my eyes and sniffed.

"I too, to be with thee, I too, to be set free. We two, to be as us, through the dawns of our lives and into our dusk."

"Do you still want me?"

"More than anything else in the entirety of worlds, more than time itself."

I stood up and walked towards her and with tears rolling down our faces, we held each other tightly and lovingly, in the realisation of who we were and who we had always been.

Although I knew I would be confused for a while, I also knew, without doubt, I was exactly where I was supposed to be.

"I hate awakenings James. I know we do it, we part and we do it again and again. I can never ever get used to what it's like to feel so alone for such a moment, not really knowing and wondering whether this would be the last time you would accept me back into your life."

"Or you into mine, Alana."

"How are you feeling?"

"Yes, yes, I'm OK. A bit like a dragonfly emerging into the light."

"God, it's just so good to be back with you. James, I love you so much, I have missed you so much."

"Where've you been all my life?"

We looked up through the veils of our tears and smiled at each other, replying in unison…

"Looking for you."

The kiss was long and searching.

"Hey Alana, it's going to take me a little while to adjust back into things. You do know I need to sort this out in my mind a bit?"

"I know James, think away."

"It makes me think about some of the times when I have found you and it's been you who has not been sure and I could not know for a while. How painful those times were? We always seem to come back together though, don't we?"

"We do and we're here."

"I'm still John, though, aren't I?"

"Yes, you are. You are a part of every person you have been. You are you. It's just James has always been the name that you have held and Alana is mine."

"I notice that you are the age of Alana in the memory, and must be, as you said earlier, 26?"

"And if you were to look at yourself James, you would find yourself to be about the same age now. This is our form and this is the age we chose to hold all those years ago. This is how we decided to be and this is our balance."

"I think Grandfather's going to have a shock."

"But if you remember James, we are not like a lot of others. We have more of a consciousness of our lifetime travels as you know. Many others don't accept their previous lifetimes and therefore stay in connection with their last lifetime. Your grandfather probably has no idea of the inter-lifetime links."

"Why is it so few remember or broadcast knowledge of their past lives?"

Alana explained to me, that past experiences are embedded onto the light spirit form as well as into the memory in the physical body form. When we pass over from the Earth plane, the memories, knowledge and wisdom remain with us. For most people, past Earth life experiences, remain inaccessible, apart from the previous life time. What allows access to them, is an ability to strengthen the power of recall at will, which requires a degree of Self-awareness and it seems a transitional catalyst also.

Not everybody on the Earth plane or in fact the spirit world can tune in to them and even those who can, some choose not to face themselves from the past. Everybody has the ability, but as we both knew, it takes a focus towards a motivation to know beyond the evident. Also, there are many distractions that stop people from even wanting to know themselves because they see no value or are afraid to 'drag up the past.' Again, it's all about the choice to know and the perceived cost to the individual for choosing it. Alana continued.

"For some reason we are different. When we meet during lifetimes on the Earth, we trigger an awareness in each other. The more time we spend together, the more we glimpse our past lives and realise who we are and yet the depth of knowing is not always achievable. When we find each other in the spirit world, we still have to go through awakenings to activate our complete history and it seems whichever of us arrives in spirit first, has the responsibility of waking the knowing in the other."

"I suppose, because you were not around in my last life, I had no idea you existed."

"Yes. You were young though and had not had time to access knowing on your own. There is a responsibility that comes with it. Not all people choose to receive it or in fact find a way to it as it has to be linked with Self-belief, awareness and a will to see and do things differently. The aim for everyone is to understand and know themselves and others on more levels than just the actual past and present within that lifetime. For some unknown reason, we seem to be wired that way without a choice."

"Arthur gave me some insight as to how it is all supposed to work and I can see now, he was not far off. So, I was only on the Earth plane for 15 years the last time, what was that about?"

"That's for you to know and remember in time James. As you know, we return for our own needs and development. We go in directions which take us away from you and I, to actually achieve these things and to live life for other people to reflect upon us, as does everybody. Perhaps you need to think and feel around why you were there. It could be for a whole number of reasons, perhaps for someone to experience something you brought, or for you to live out a particular emotion or way of thinking or knowing. You may have needed to top up an experience you part experienced in a previous lifetime to give you a greater sense of completion. It may have been as simple as the feeling of being born again or to generate sadness in somebody else's life for their own journey, where sadness is needed in their life to perhaps help another who is also suffering from sadness. It's a myriad, an absolute myriad of reasons, of connections, of possibilities and we just don't know why?"

"But Alana we know the reason we go back before we leave here."

"Yes, but once we're back on Earth we don't remember why we've come back and in our case, do not remember any previous lifetimes, until we meet each other. I think it is more about our own developing sense of knowing. It is about the experiences we have on the Earth plane which add to that and give us a greater sense of completion and knowledge about who we are in relation to others and the Collective. I think there is a hope we gain experiences that can build knowing, because that is the only way forward to collectively survive as a species."

"To what?"

"Come on James, you can't have forgotten all this stuff."

"Yes, I know."

"I know you know," Alana laughed.

"Oh, give me a break, Alana I've only just arrived, well, only just woken up."

"Do you know how boring it is waiting for you? I have scanned the universe for 15 years looking for a surrogate mirror who reflects only half as clearly as you do."

"Did you crack any?" I took her in my arms again and kissed her fondly. "I love you so much, it's so good to be back with you. You are the best thing that has ever, ever happened to me."

"And you to me James."

"Have we ever had any children, Alana?"

"Come on, think James," Alana said in a soft voice.

"I can't feel any?"

"We have no children James. We have never been in a lifetime where we have ever been able to have a child. Either one of us has not been able to, or time has forbidden us or age has made it impossible."

"That's sad, isn't it."

"We have this discussion every time we're back together again James. It's part of it. Maybe one day we will, but I don't want to leave you, I don't want to leave you for a long while and then, only if I have to. I don't want to go back yet, to lose you again would be so difficult."

"I feel the same way and I don't know why, but I feel as though we have got some time here, if time is what you call it. If you've been here 26 years, have you been thinking about going back or do you have a sense of where you are going? I mean have you thought about what needs to be developed next and stuff?"

"I have an idea of what needs to be developed next, yes. There are some things I am missing but they are not massive, so I am not driven to return. What about you James, do you have a sense of work to be done?"

"Well, I need to go back to the Earth plane, but I'm going back as spirit."

"Yes, but that's a different matter, that's not about going back into an actual Earth lifetime."

"Yes, I know. No, I don't know yet. I haven't been in a state of mind to think about it. It's all been very fast paced since I arrived and I keep losing track of time. How many times have we revolved back to the Earth?"

"You have been back nine times now and I have had eight journeys."

"Does it ever end and when do you know when you have done your time?" The ninth bell resonated from my memory of Sarah.

"All I know is, that it is an instinct or angst which has drawn me back to what I would call, the experiential world. It is much like the existential angst for the meaning of life, that can happen part way through your lifetime on Earth, but much stronger."

"So, you have studied existentialism, have you?"

"After you died and the second world war ended, there were a lot of people searching for experience-based meaning and I got involved. Why are you impressed?"

"Totally and thinking about lasting impressions, as much as I have really enjoyed the day out to your country manor, I've just had a deliciously nostalgic thought."

"I have seen that look on many occasions James, and know exactly what you are thinking! Come, take my hand."

Our joined-up world was not a place for doubts, hesitations or anxiety, it was a world of the depth of understanding and respect for each other. We were not beings of one mind, although we could choose to be. We were separate, very individual and independent spirits, who had chosen to know through each other.

Alana led me through her mind to a beautiful place of rest. An isolated beach house on a distant shore far from where we were and transported us both to it. We made love through the afternoon and into the evening, resurrecting, caressing and loving ourselves back towards full awareness. At the end of the day, as we lay upon the sand, we watched the sunset tease the ripples of the water with its amber warmth. Folding into each other's arms, we thanked the universe for our lives and for our re-joining. It was always the sweetest of moments, one that was ours and had been for nearly 500 years.

"Will you still love me when I am 500?"

"More than anything, ever, anywhere."

"Good. Shall we sleep, you must be tired after today?"

"Yes, thank you, I am. Being enlightened is draining."

Just as I was falling into rest, Alana blanketed my mind with her loving thoughts and transported us, without me knowing, to a place of comfort and familiarity. I sleepily spoke to her.

"This sand is soft, it's like a feather bed…good night darling, I love you."

Alana snuggled herself back into James's lap and smiled to herself. She was happy again, happy and complete. She was once again together with the man whose light shone with the same intensity and knowing as her own.

"Good night my hero, you are the best."

"No, you are."

"Hush, go to sleep."

Revolutions

I awoke in the morning to feel the softness of the sheets and the fragrance of jasmine in the air. On opening my eyes, I found myself in an ornately designed, white washed room, with pillars, arches and high fan vaults. Walls were adorned with beautifully coloured silks gently rippling in the breeze and tapestries ornately embroidered with scenes of lovers through ages. The floor, a complex mosaic artwork, sparkled and reflected colours of gold, copper, burnt umber and mother of pearl. The sunbeams captured by these many facets reflected the richness of the colours onto the walls and domed ceiling. As the coloured messages reverberated within the dome they ascended towards a crystal pyramid spinning slowly in the breeze at its apex. White light splintered from the crystal, back into the room creating a vortex of rainbow shards and bathing objects with slithers of an exquisite spectrum unique to this world.

I gazed across to the source of sunlight and saw Alana sitting in a large open bay terrace window looking out onto a clear blue sky. Her form was silhouetted by the light which outlined her curves through the gossamer like fabric of her gown, capturing the beautifulness that was her. As I rose and softly walked towards her, I was met by the sight of a sea, islands and mountains choreographed to perfection before me. Blues, greens and silver reflections undulated and dimpled to the songs of the breeze on the water's surface.

"Don't think you can creep up on me and catch me unawares."

Sitting down next to her, I slipped my arms around her waist, pulling her close and feeling her relax into me. I kissed the nape of her neck as I breathed her in, intoxicating my senses with her fragrance mingled with the jasmine and spices in the air. We both daydreamed on the happiness and contentment that was ours and the bliss of being.

"I am so in love with you Alana."

"I know you are and me in you."

"Where are we, it looks familiar?"

"Well, I thought you would have liked to have woken up in our home in Capri."

"We created this? Yes, I remember it took me ages to design the mosaic pattern and get the lamp shape right. Do we have many homes?"

"Let's say, we have a few in many different types of locations, but this is our favourite."

"I feel I am coming back to me slowly. There are so many glimmers and memories, but they are a bit mixed up at the moment."

"Don't worry and be patient. It will take you a short while to readjust and order things. Then we will see the true you again."

Alana turned and kissed me sweetly on the lips.

"There is one thing about living in spirit. It certainly solves the problem of morning dog breath."

We both laughed out loud and at the same time remembered the 16th century, when we used to chew on a bunch of parsley and rinse with water in an attempt to deal with the problem.

"I remember waking next to you sometimes and thinking, now shall I kiss your lips or kiss you on your bum, it was always a tough decision?"

Alana picked up the nearest silk cushion and hit me squarely on the side of my head. As I fell, I transformed the stone seat into soft satin pillows. At the moment of rest, as her shining chestnut hair fell about my face and she gazed deeply into my eyes, we both knew without doubt, we were one again.

"You are good James, so good."

"No. We are my love, simply the best."

After we had made love and cuddled into the morning, I stood on the edge of the balcony holding the pillar and surveying the scene. Mountains touched sea and sky, colours blended and the sun shone and reflected from the waters. Alana joined me by my side.

"Come on James, let's fly, but this time, instead of dragonflies or Macaws, let's be us. We can tease the fish if you like."

We both linked into each other's minds to meld the experience. Having been a virtual creation, but made permanent some time ago, the universe had assimilated and synthesised its own natural blue print on our representation and injected life into it. The result was a perfect world within worlds which followed the laws of spiritual manifestation and Earth plane memory.

Holding hands, we fell forward from the balcony in our human forms and down the cliff face. In moments, Alana engaged the transformative and stalled her descent changing into her Osprey. Her eyes immediately followed my descent, still in my spirit form.

"James!!!"

My mind was caught back at Beachy Head, imagining how Philip must have felt as he plummeted to the rocks below, about to lose his life. Alana's voice cut straight through my distraction and I changed to my eagle form arcing upwards violently. I skimmed the boulders and victory rolled at great speed centimetres above the surface of the water.

"Show off!"

"Not quite Alana, I was caught for a moment. Link in to this."

I showed her the Beachy Head scene in my mind.

"That is so sad and yet a scene I have seen before myself and luckily, we have never lost each other that way."

"And never shall we."

"Come on James, up top and let's float and bring you up to speed on our lifetimes."

We had travelled through lifetimes together since both being born onto the Earth plane in 1539. During every Earth lifetime we would meet at some stage and in most revolutions, have a relationship with each other. However, fate would play its part and our being together would not always last long.

As we floated, we talked about life paths, locations, jobs, meetings and the cruel circumstances of our partings. Alana then reminded me of our times in the spirit world. Our adventures, of love, friendship and intimacy and the homes we had built together. We remembered friends we met up with from time to time, including the high planers like Tarquin. As her stories unfolded, I was able to piece together my own awakened memories with those of hers, each fragment triggering the emergence of an expansive schema of knowledge, experiences and wisdom collected over the last 478 years.

Although we both knew when we were first born on Earth, neither of us were able to remember our first lifetime, nor the first time we lived in the spirit world together. We accepted this as part of a grand plan, all were subject to. What we did know was my first life ended in 1562, making me 23 and Alana's 1577, when she was thirty-eight. I revolved into my next life in 1582, which meant our first spirit 'rest' together was for five years. In this lifetime, it was the longest of our relationships, where we had been married for twenty-five years, but had no children.

We were only together for six months in the one following, when Alana had to send me away from where she lived in the East Sussex country house.

In the fourth and fifth lifetimes, Alana revolved as a male and me as a female. This was always a choice open to us and others and was seen as an opportunity to experience not only child birth, but also to engage with the joys, opportunities, restrictions, taboos and suffering when living within another gender. My reason for revolving as female consecutively was because I had been unable to have children in my first female lifetime.

Alana joked the real reason was because I enjoyed being a woman more. However, I reminded her that being female and of African descent in England and in service, in the mid to late 1700s, was not an enjoyable time. In fact, both of us, during this lifetime experienced cruelty, hostility, prejudice and extreme poverty. We had been reduced to begging on the streets of London in order to survive, having absconded from our masters to be together.

The length of each Earth visit varied considerably and there were difficulties such as age difference to contend with. The most difficult time was during my seventh life time. We had just spent seven years together in spirit and I revolved back first in 1910, with Alana following in 1911. Living in London, our parents were educated and professional and we were children of different families, however, we attended the same nursery together. Even at this age, we were inseparable until Alana contracted scarlet fever and died in her fourth year. For me, even at this level of development in Earth terms, Alana became someone whom I continued to miss and this event led me to further develop my heroic, saving tendencies. Perhaps because I could not save her.

Alana revolved back to London in 1920 and finally met back up with me in 1939. At this point I was working for the British Intelligence as an agent on active duty. We were married quickly afterwards and although we would be dangerously apart at times, we lived happily together until my death in 1944.

Having lost or been lost to Alana twice in this lifetime, I impetuously revolved back in 1945, thinking I could catch Alana up, who was now twenty-five years my senior. The alternative was to wait for her in the spirit world, which could have been for decades and during this time, I knew my urge to revolve would grow stronger. It took twenty-two years before we met again in 1967, when Alana was forty-seven. At this time, she had two teenage daughters and a second loving husband.

We saw each other for two years, but our responsibilities, the era and with Alana being much older, made it difficult for us to be together. Regretfully, we went on our separate pathways, me to Ceylon to learn the tea trade and Alana remained in Harrogate as a teacher. Alana died aged 75 in 1995 and me, early from a heart attack in 1999. Following three years of catch up in spirit, I returned to the Earth plane and to Denby Dale in 2002. In our total 478 years, I had spent 387 years on Earth, Alana 380; we had shared just over 52 years on Earth and 50 years in the spirit world. Although we had not had children together, with other partners, Alana had 18 and I had 10.

Moving from thermal to thermal, interlocked into each other's minds, I thought about the way things were between us in the different worlds.

"There is a massive difference between what you know on Earth compared to here. When I had revolved back to Earth, I have had a blank slate. I have always found whilst living my Earth life, I can imagine being able to do things or know things, but have no idea about past lives. It is only when I have met up with you, I experience this powerful connection and past events start to emerge."

"Then as time rolls on, we believe we know we have had time together in previous lives, but we don't remember as many details or knowledge from those lives on Earth compared to when we are together in spirit," added Alana.

"In my eighth life time when I lived in Sri Lanka, I had a greater understanding of people and relationships. I felt I understood how the world worked and how it was limited. I also felt I had a natural ability to do certain things or was more comfortable with situations I had no previous experience of. In the short time I lived as John on Earth, everything was potential or seemed like fantasy."

"That was probably due to you not being old enough to have really experienced life."

"Yes. When I look back, I wish I could have had more access to what I had learned through all of my lives."

"But then you would have been distracted from the reason you went back. People tend to stick to what is familiar and you probably would have done the same things you had done previously."

"It seems all very slow being reset each time you go back. It makes me wonder who designed this system. If the aim of the system is to generate knowing, it appears flawed because 'blank slating' people, in my view is handicapping the pace of the progress of world relations."

"Hello James, welcome back!"

I laughed as Alana smiled at me.

"If you increase the access to previous knowledge, I think people will stick to the familiar, having more knowledge resource to fuel their own ambitions and will drift towards those who can reward them. Them, I refer to as those countries with the greater resources and influence and what do they do presently?" reflected Alana.

"Don't share and everyone else covets?"

"Pretty much, so I think you would make the situation worse. Ours is not to reason why, ours is but to do and die."

"Yes, but we are doing that already and we keep doing it. I think the Earth is in trouble. I think we should enable everyone to have insight into the importance of right relations in the literal meaning of the term."

Alana, slightly frustrated with me, banked right and bumped into me.

"I'll tell you something about you. You have always been an idealist, all the way through your lifetimes, which I think is one of your most magnetic qualities. However, just how do you intend to impart the ideals of this world on those of an experiential Earth world, where they are finding their own way because they feel they are on their own. Earth is a learning centre for us all, injecting too many spirit ideals, may upset the reality balance."

"Umm, I am thinking about it."

"How are you doing James?"

"I think I am back. I have that familiar frustrated feeling and all cylinders are firing."

"We have been up here for hours; shall we go back home and I'll let you preen my feathers?"

"What a splendid idea and I will do. I just fancy a speed blast to let the wind blow through my mind and dislodge the cobwebs."

"Excellent. I know that's one of your sayings and I will see you a little later." Alana flew above me, landed on my back and pecked me lovingly on the back of my head, before rolling into a high-speed dive.

"I am so glad you are not a goose."

Icarus, This Is Me

I climbed upwards, then gracefully piking, came to rest in mid-air at a 30-degree angle. My senses were acute and energised, perhaps from the renewed access to previous lifetimes. What seemed to manifest was a feeling of greater potential, possibly from the actual awakenings transition itself. It was like once again having access to the accumulated energy, with the additional energy supplementing it from my last lifetime. I was keen to see what was now possible. I imagined the whole potential of all of my knowing and experiences moving from the tip of my tail up towards the base of my skull. The sensation connected each of my vertebrae, until I felt a powerful tingling coursing along my wings to their feathered tips and through my legs to my talons. Sensing each feather standing on end, I let my mind flatten in intense stillness.

"Let go, letting go…"

Balancing the accumulating power between latency and engagement, filled me with an anticipated, but unknown expectation. Poised in the tension within this gap, I teased the growing power with transitional will, creating the all familiar feeling of a release from all limitations and into the limitless. In a slight of a second, I remembered my final Earth journey and knew this had been what I was trying to recreate back then in my limited awareness. I had become all I was and more and yet it seemed on Earth I thought I was only playing at something, however, the fantasy had been real for me.

"What is reality then, if it is not first imagined?"

"All is real," the words echoed into my consciousness. "All is real."

I purposely cut through the bonds between the poles, the effect like an elastic band retorting from an eternity of tension.

Whoooooshhhh…I accelerated away at high speed and in no time, was at the boundary of our Capri landscape. Rather than switching into virtual world, I elongated my form, minimising my dimensions to a ray of light to transverse the gap between the current and the adjoining spirit space. On emerging and whilst maintaining my speed, I returned to eagle form. Again, and again I hit and went through boundaries as the frequency of my transitions became so fast that my form appeared to flash on and off like a beacon.

"James, I keep losing you, you must be at an incredibly high speed. You are not going for the realm boundary, are you?"

"Trust me."

"James, you are going to get yourself in trouble!"

"I'll be OK."

Alana knew James was fully up to power again. Whilst she was the stronger and more resilient, James was the driven, sensitive one who always had to push the boundaries metaphorically and sometimes literally, to find the edges to things. His consciousness was driven by connections, what ifs, why nots and possibilities. She had to admit, this was a powerful attraction for her, however, his inability to find the 'that's just the way it is' switch, taxed her patience at times and had drawn unwelcome attention in the past.

The second voice took me by surprise as I was about to hit the next boundary at beyond light speed.

"You are doing it again, aren't you?"

"Is that you little John?"

"John, James, whatever your name is now, why are you doing this?"

"That's it, I just want to know why."

As I hit the boundary, everything slowed down. It was unlike others as the light frequencies were different, more acute and although I was still travelling at speed, the resistance of this different light made it harder to make progress. I was also finding it increasingly difficult to focus, as the brightness of this light interfered with my perception. Transforming back into my eagle form I softened the acuteness of my vision and looked around. There was no ground to this place and with the sky striated with high lilac coloured cirrus clouds, it had an unnerving feeling of emptiness. I was losing power rapidly and started to fall. My mind grasped the suddenness of my vulnerability and with it, a fear of falling into continual nothingness.

With no warning and from no apparent direction, I was joined at either wing tip by two fantastic birds, both having the mythical look of the phoenix. They were translucent, shifting in density, and coloured with reds, oranges and yellows, as if they were ablaze. However, their beaks were fashioned in the form of birds of prey and at twice the size and wingspan of a golden eagle, had the talons to match. Both birds arrested my decent and stabilised my flight. The bird on my right-wing tip, spoke to me gently but firmly.

"Don't fly too high little brother before the knowing arises. Remember Icarus?"

I said nothing.

"Look James, we can read you like a book, mind guards and all. So, we know you are testing your limits, having just awoken. Most would spend some time in their own realm regaining their centre, not trying to blast into the next whilst trying to prove something."

"Who are you?" I asked respectfully.

I was unable to fully read these beings, like I could with other spirits. It was the left-wing tip bird who answered.

"We are Realm 5 border patrol."

"Caicias, you so dramatic at times?"

"Oh, come on Circios, I've always wanted to say that."

"Well James, have you anything to declare?" said Circios with serious humour.

"I wasn't expecting to get in. I just wanted to see if I had evolved enough to nose the edge."

"Your declaration is truthful enough. We can't let you in anyway, you must know, if the time comes for you to reside in this realm, you will do, or you can choose to. As you can see, you cannot fly in here and this is just the border. You are not supposed to be here."

"I know, I am sorry and thank you for helping me."

"It is clear you have a talent for moving between the levels, but that's always been an issue with you Harpies. You have mastered transformation and are swift winged but, you are continuously in search of your purpose, who you are and where you fit in."

"I am not a Harpy; I am a golden eagle."

The two guardians looked at each other and smiled.

"Oh yes, my mistake. It's the light on your feathers," confirmed Caicias.

"We know where you have come from and your partner is in some distress because she has lost contact with you. We will take you back and James, come back, when you know, you can fly closer, to the sun."

Alana in her Osprey form, was perched on a mountain top calling desperately as she had lost all sense of where James was. The two birds lowered him gently to the ground before her.

"Where did you go, I totally lost you, there was no trace, I have never lost you like that before."

"He strayed too close to our realm and lost his power. It's OK, we know who he is and who you are Alana."

Alana greeted them as the high planers they were and felt safe and honoured to be in their presence.

"How has he been able to do this?"

"James has tapped into a way of transversing this realm and into the gap in between. You both know you cannot move into the fifth realm until you are ready. It is not advisable to explore the gap and get caught by the light, as a moth does to the flame."

"I am sorry Alana," I said sheepishly. "I was interested to know what was out there and whether I could get to it."

"Might we invite you to connect to tortoise energy once in a while. Centre in this realm and pace yourself. There is much to be learned here and from the lower realms. Build your base James, you can be all you wish to be when you have learned to be. Use the gifts you have been given to gain insight wisely, or you may lose sight of the true purpose for which they were intended."

"Thank you, I will try to slow down and thanks for the lift back!"

"Duck."

"No, I am not, I am an eagle!"

"Thanks for flying, Firebird Air, have a nice day!"

"Caicias!"

There was a forceful down draft as the two beat their huge wings and took off from the ground. At 200 metres they joined wing tips and began turning at high speed before accelerating away at a velocity beyond the perception of either of us.

Very nice birds, I thought!

"You don't change, do you James. Always cruising edges, but don't either, as I love you just the way you are, although I wish I could find that switch. Please stay within range of me next time, I really thought I had lost you and I never want to do that, ever."

"We will never lose each other, Alana, I promise."

I transformed myself into a tortoise, with Alana doing the same. We looked at each other and rubbed noses.

"This could be interesting!"

"Don't get any ideas!"

Five hours later we reached the beach.

"I think I get the point."

"Well, the prize of patience, is in fact patience!"

I remembered the wisdom from a lifetime away.

"Tune juice on the veranda?"

"Perfect!"

We transformed simultaneously, took off and flew across the inlet.

Becoming

We both rested after our tortoise adventure and spent more time travelling through memories, endings and new beginnings. On reflection, both of us shared the thought that this recent re-joining, held a sense of some kind of completion. The culmination of eight and nine lifetime's travel, union, absence and hope.

We marvelled and despaired at the experiences we had had and the learning accomplished, which had created both our degree of knowing and sense of Self. The mirrors gazed into, reflected upon and at times unknowingly scorned, had over time enabled us to shed a great degree of our own selfish and self-motivated behaviour. Our varied experiences on Earth had put us in many situations where we had learned much about ourselves and others. This consciousness collected over lifetimes now appeared to have purported us into a position of much understanding of love and of existence itself.

"You know, it's funny Alana, it does not take long after an awakening to come back to power. You know my meaning of power, don't you?"

"Yes, of course I do."

"It's like a resurrection of all previous thoughts, all meanings, of all knowing and their connective synthesis into a revelation of what is."

"And of what is for us as well, you mean."

"Yes. In light of what we talked about yesterday, have you thought anymore about where we are going from here?"

"Well, you know I said I had been in spirit for twenty-six years now? In joining with you again, I do feel that sense of completion, almost as though we have done all we can do and we have learned enough from Earth."

"I think we need to talk to Tarquin about this."

"I think you do! Hi, kiddies, how are we?" said Tarquin materialising on the veranda beside us.

"You know Tarquin, you always take the mickey, when we come back. That's the problem with you high planers, you think you are all adults, but you are not really."

"I am well aware of that, being a high planer!" All three of us joining in the laughter.

"Nice to see you again, Tarquin."

"Nice to see you James, Alana."

"That was quite impressive Alana, it only took you two and a half months to find James this time. How long was it for you on your last time James, a year wasn't it?"

"Yeah, alright."

"So how has the joining been?"

"Well as you know Tarquin, from your knowledge of such things, it was as difficult and nerve racking as usual, but we are here and we are back in the knowing. Anyway, how is your lady Patricia?"

"She is fine and doing well. Working on some pocket of collective consciousness at the moment, so she tells me."

"You know what she is doing anyway."

"Yes, of course I do James, but convincing myself I can momentarily forget, kids me into a sense of engineered surprise. Anyway, down to business. You are back in the spirit world together again and you are correct Alana, about this new feeling of completion. Neither of you are complete, but, both of you are reaching points where parts of your knowing are starting to match that of high planers. However, there are a few points I would like to raise before we talk about what might happen next."

"I was obviously aware it was you at the rest home where Monique was mentoring you. In knowing you, I wondered how long it would take you to awaken and engage that endearing quality of yours, where you become the proverbial pain in the backside, who pushes the limits and exposes others in the realm to situations they are not ready to accept or deal with." Tarquin purposefully did not pause in his deliverance, just to make his point.

"I list a few. Sending out a location echo wave to find Sarah, which spanned and reverberated across many a concerned spirit's homesteads. Aiding and abetting a wild Mustang to retrieve his heritage and grow a pair of wings. Leading to his entire herd wanting to be like Pegasus. Gunfights with low fliers at Beachy Head, whilst interfering with a catcher and guide who were trying to manage a difficult suicide case. Scaring the wits out of that particular guide and his boss, by using your transformational powers to turn yourself into a golden eagle outside of virtual world. Again, alarming homesteaders by crossing boundaries in the form of an eagle travelling at Mach 881,000 and beyond."

"Whilst these have all met my attention with some concern, it is the final and most recent endeavour of yours, to breach the boundary to the fifth realm that takes the biscuit."

"In my defence, a lot of those incidents occurred before Alana awakened me to who I am."

"And who are you James, in relation to the realm status quo and spirit laws?"

"I don't know and I think that is the issue."

"I do not doubt your intentions are for the greater good. I know you have lived lives in humility and patience and have learned from them. But your issue is acceptance, because, as you say, you do not know all."

Alana was starting to feel anxiety rising. She knew this was James's issue, but it was also her own. The difference as it manifested, was she had learned to play the game throughout her lifetimes on Earth and in spirit, whilst James refused to temper his quest. Strangely, she could feel a part of herself communicating with a part of James, then little Alana and little James stepped out from their adult light forms, stood defiantly holding hands and addressed Tarquin in unison.

"We have never been accepted. Who are you to lecture us about acceptance? We can sense your journey has never had to endure the persecution, isolation and loss which has been entwined with ours. We know we are different. Many spirit call us rare and we have had to hide, always hiding and never being together long enough, to what, to get to know who we actually are?"

Tarquin, a little taken aback by the synchronised delivery was silent for a while, as if in deep thought. He knelt down to eye level to meet the two children, whilst James and Alana stood at their backs with their hands on their shoulders.

"I know it has been very hard for all of you. Yours is a difficult existence because you are of a kind most spirit and Earth plane humans fear through ignorance."

"We know we are shamans or shapeshifters, is that it?"

"When you were at the fifth realm boundary, what did Circios say to you?"

"He said I had a talent for moving between the levels, but that had always been an issue with 'you' Harpies. Then he said, we had mastered transformation and were swift winged but, we were continuously in search of our purpose, who we were and where we fitted in."

"And what did you say to him?"

"I said I am not a Harpy; I am a golden eagle."

"And what are you Alana?"

"I am an Osprey."

"You are saying we are Harpies, as in the mythical bird people from Ancient Greece, who were hideous creatures sent by the gods to punish, snatch souls and conjure storms?"

"It wasn't just Greece. Harpies scattered to Italy, Egypt, Scandinavia and central Europe. However, there are myths and legends in many cultures all over the world of bird featured men and women who were seen over centuries. As a species they were fear mongered, hunted and then exterminated because they were seen by humans as a threat to their power and control. They were a small race of souls who had evolved differently and difference causes Earth born spirits or at least some of them, a problem. Do you remember James, your discussion with Alana about dinosaurs, their extinction and the return of their souls to Earth as other creatures?"

"Yes, I do."

"Well, the Harpy spirit lived on, but with most deciding to revolve back to Earth as humans because there were none of their kind to be born back into. However, they always revolved with hidden potential and some have manifested as shamans and even witches. The Earth people did their best to kill them off also or at least drive them underground. When you get back into the spirit world between lives, that's when you become more of who you are and you two did so on your first spirit rest."

"But we don't remember our first life time or time in spirit," added Alana. "It was hidden from you because it was a most distressing time for both of you and as part of your ongoing development, it was felt the power of what happened, may follow you into subsequent lifetimes. You see, you were new spirits born as decendents from a Harpy spirit line and you two are a pair. And Harpy pairs bond for lifetimes."

"What happened?" asked James.

Tarquin explained. We were both twenty-one when we met and started a relationship. A year and a half later I was killed in an accident by someone else. During that time, we had established a link of immeasurable depth and I had wanted to stay on Earth to be near Alana, but had been persuaded it was better to come over to spirit. After my death, it seems Alana was distraught and became unwell, some thought with deep melancholia. She was never the same after recovery and isolated herself to the edge of the village and gained the reputation of being strange to others in her study of herbs and potions. Evidently, I would not leave her alone and kept travelling back to see her and although there was no materialisation, I was able to show her signs I still lived and warned her not to kill herself.

In the spirit world, I had mastered my eagle, but with no significant development of the Self, made selfish decisions and upset many spirits in my path. Most were totally shocked and unsettled by my abilities. I also delayed revolving for fear of missing Alana. As time went on, Alana had mastered some of her abilities and became known as a healer woman, who helped the ailing in the village and at the same time learned about the pagan beliefs.

It was not long before and in her late thirties, she was skilled enough to cross the veil as a shaman and visit the world between worlds where the low fliers reside. It was here she met up with me again and we continued our relationship. Unfortunately, Alana was seen by a young woman who claimed she had disappeared into thin air. With witchcraft becoming a capital offence, fourteen years previously and Alana's choice of lifestyle, she was tried by the local people and hung in November 1577. Tarquin continued.

"For me, Alana's death was a blessing in disguise, because at least then, the suffering had ended and you were back together in the spirit world. Here, I could sooth the situation and mentor you both to a greater understanding. It was me who decided, with your agreement, to obscure the first part of your journey from you."

We, with our little selves now re-integrated, looked at each other with a sense of resigned acceptance of what was and what had happened.

"So, James and Alana, this is who you are."

"Why couldn't we have children?" asked Alana.

"I know you have both had children, but as to why you two have not had children together, I do not know. It is not always by design. I know what you are going to say James and I do not think it is a matter of fairness. You two were created, like everyone else. What is different about you two, other than your spirit line, is the connection you both have and your ability to locate each other and awaken yourselves. So many other spirits and spirits in matter, spend lifetimes in search of someone they cannot find and sometimes, they fail to accept in fact, they have already found them."

"So, the magnetism between us is there because we are the minority and it is important to preserve the minority even if it cannot be preserved in matter on Earth. Therefore, there should still be dinosaurs?"

"No, animals are governed more by instinct than consciousness and choice, that is other than those who are evolving consciousness. Animals who are made extinct on Earth revolve as other animal species."

"But, we have met animals over here who appear to have a consciousness."

"Yes, and the truth lies in who you are. You are descended from beings who held features of birds and so you have a more advanced level of instinct blended with consciousness. You have a developed sense of the intuitive and you can enable their language. Even as a so called high planer, I cannot communicate with animals in the same way you two can. I would lay a bet you can communicate with all shapes and sizes of birds and horses for that matter."

I was suddenly caught by what he had just said.

"You are not telling me, without saying, that flying horses are an ancient species as well, are you?"

"There were a few of your kind who revolved as horses. Legend tells, one in particular, like Alana in her first life time, managed to cross the veil and fly in the world between worlds. He was somehow seen in that form back in your homeland in Greece and became a spiritually symbolised icon. There were no more. Well not until you got back here, but there have been no more on the Earth plane."

"It wasn't too difficult to help Scout free his wings and he obviously had them in him."

"Think about it, who magnetises you?"

"What you mean Scout is one of us?"

"At core, yes. He is descended from the Harpy horse lines, those with a particular sense of free will, whilst you are from the human lines."

"What else did the Harpies revolve as?"

"Come on James, think. You do know this!"

It was Alana who spoke.

"Where would I go to escape persecution? which up until recently was one of the most inaccessible places on Earth and yet the richest of hunting grounds.

I would live in the rainforests and become one of the most powerful eagle species in the world."

"Exactly!"

"It makes obvious sense that Audaz is one of our line also. He said their species mates for life as well?" said Alana.

"I think he told you he was waiting for his mate, so, that suggests, lifetimes, does it not?"

"OK Tarquin. If Harpy eagles are descended from Harpies and the species still exists, they must be able to have children. So, how come we haven't had children?"

"I don't know; I have told you. Have you tried?"

"Oh, we didn't think of that."

"Seriously, I do not know how to answer. The Harpy eagle is a current Earth-bound species. Not all of these eagles are of Harpy spirit descent."

Alana was troubled by the situation. She hated it when she could not satisfy her heart and it resonated ever so slightly differently whenever the subject arose. I detected her disquiet in the 'just noticeable difference'. I veiled our minds, linked in and wrapped her heart with my own. Tarquin looked at us quizzically.

"What are you up to?"

"You mean you don't know?"

"He was just soothing my heart, because it holds a sadness."

"Yes, I can see it is sad for you both."

Again, there was a slight scrutiny in his look and I noticed Tarquin did not know, even though as a high planer, all was supposed to be visible to him.

"I have a question for you. Why is it that you are making connections with Harpy descent lines and then attempt to breach the realm five boundary?"

"I admit, I wanted to see how close I could get to realm five, just out of curiosity, but the attraction to Scout and Audaz is unconscious. I did not know they were descendants at our time of meeting and I feel safe in saying, they are not aware of their ancestry. Take a look in, you must see this."

"Yes, I can see. Please do not think I do not trust you."

"You have never said that to me before, ever. Let me help you here. It seems like both Alana and I have evolved an ability to veil some of our thoughts and feelings even from you, as a know all high planer. It happened just then. Your reaction suggests that our relationship must now change in some way, perhaps because you no longer have the advantage of the all-knowing perspective. I see not as to why the relationship need change and I am a little sad because I know you think it might need to."

"Wise words James. Seeing all negates the need for trust. I think you have just reminded me of the importance and responsibility of the act. Thank you. May I just ask, can you see my thoughts and feelings?"

"More than before!" We both responded in unison.

"At the risk of sounding condescending, you two have come a long way in your development. I am amazed just how much you both grow when you are back in each other's company. From my own selfish viewpoint, I welcome the new level of meeting and I look forward to what it might bring. Now, we must talk about practicalities and what might happen to you next."

Tarquin explained that as individuals, our sense of knowing would enable us to ascertain other spirit's levels of development and self-awareness. In addition, we would be able to sense their feelings, thoughts and fears and the way they see everything around them. Essentially, we would be able to see others for who they actually were and would be able to do this without the other knowing. What would also change, was the way in which others saw us. People tend to gravitate towards wisdom, because it affords the potential of a different or true path. With this gravity comes the expectation of guidance and the responsibility for that operates with one simple rule:

It is Self-realisation in the person which makes any change authentic and binding. If a guide rushes an outcome, where an individual cannot link the steps to realise the path, no progress is made. The responsibility of the guide is the ability to hold the balance between will and awareness in the person. The process provides the guide with the opportunity to experience the free will held by another as it engages to shift. Guiding is about tempering the pace to change things and being aware of the true motives involved in the person's engagement with you. Pace is integral with authentic change and the awareness of other influences which may affect change, have to be realised by the individual before it will become possible. The guide learning that the prize of patience is exactly that, patience, is also integral to their own ability to successfully guide. Alana gently nudged me.

"If you look at your last lifetime James, you struggled with your sense of purpose and who you were, at the same time as living in a context of humility. Your lesson was to experience and accept humility, but instead of incorporating it in your search for your sense of purpose, you fought it because you saw it as a weakness. It wasn't until you experienced little John at Sarah's ranch, were you able to translate the learning's intention and accept little John's message."

"I thought it held me back but I understand it now."

"You just did not see its power in the parts becoming the whole."

"Alana, you say you learned to play the game on Earth. In fact, there were many occasions when others in power learned from your mirror and altered their ways of being and yet there was nothing but compassion and skilful will in play."

"Thank you."

I obscured my mind and linked to Alana: "Smarty pants!"

Tarquin revealed the three guiding contexts, which we could choose to work in if we wished, included working as Earth guides, guiding spirit in the fourth realm and working in the dark realms.

"The work as a spirit guide is rich with concentrated opportunities to further Self-develop. Whereas in previous lifetimes on Earth, experiences accrue as they occurred, guiding provides the context to encounter experiences at greater frequency, due to the diversity of people worked with. A guide can therefore obtain the detail and depth of knowledge, creating a collective and knowing resource. In terms of the guide's own experiences gained through Earth life times, these combine with the growing resource and help to create meaning for the individual. This also helps the guide move towards a point of actualisation."

"What is actualisation exactly?" questioned Alana.

"Actualisation is the product of Self-realisation in authentic balance with the self or personality, with others, the world and the greater spirit context. It is becoming your potential through the drive for the pursuit of knowledge, creative expression and spiritual enlightenment. It is knowing where all you have become, resonates with spiritual intuition provided by the Collective. What comes with it is peace, but it is far from inactive."

"Why guide Earth or spirit people towards it though?"

Tarquin explained there are many distractions on Earth and without free will and choice, life would be controlled and lifeless. Developing awareness of will as an individual in relation to others and the environments we exist in at all levels, promotes a greater understanding of existence itself. Without guidance and understanding, there is the fear of the unknown and where there is fear, there is destruction. He said that we were living examples of this.

"Therefore, guidance, whether it is Self-guidance or catalysed by another, is there to maintain a balance between fear and understanding."

"I partly know this, but I want to debate it. Why not blend the two worlds? Why not provide Earth spirits with concrete proof of the existence of this realm, revolving lives and the whole self-judgement process?" I asked.

"Because you would take away choice. You would over balance in favour of understanding."

"But isn't that a good thing?" asked Alana.

"Earth is a learning centre, a place of semi-disconnection from the Collective, a place of acute senses and experiences, both positive and negative. As humans, we compare and judge in relation to others and we all seek relationship in many forms to ascertain our place in it all. On Earth, we learn from one another and also from those who lack understanding, same as we do here. The Earth experience is a hard experience and one of mortality. If you take away the question of mortality, you not only take away the focus on the here and now, you take away concept of: 'we are alone and yet, we are all in this together and we must find a way resolve our differences'. Which is what you need to Self-develop, develop as a collective and increase understanding."

"But why the quest to grow understanding?"

"Because understanding promotes a belief in yourself which comes from the connection to the Collective and enables connection to others and creates knowing."

"And why does the Collective need knowing?"

"Because knowing, which is aided by spiritually guided intuition, promotes spirit growth, which can be donated by the individual to create new spirit life. Hence the reason why the Earth population continually grows."

"On a planet that cannot sustain it and is using up its natural resources in an attempt to manage that growth. Not to mention warming its atmosphere, killing its rainforests and plasticising its oceans. I stand by my concerns. The Earth is in trouble and it suggests that your balance of understanding is not only imbalanced on Earth, but in the spirit realms as well."

"Listen to me openly. Can you see why you are considered to be a pain in the arse and at the same time, can you see why your non-acceptance of 'what is', is crucially important to us?"

"I am not sure what you are saying. You have described me as a pain in the backside in my previous incarnations and in spirit as well. Just what are your concerns?"

"Please don't get me wrong. My description is based on your drive. You incessantly drive for change and in terms of your own development, that is applaudable. Those of Harpy descent are inherently the fastest to develop and are incredibly motivated. However, the pain bit comes with the need to constantly challenge and push the limits and boundaries. At times you demonstrate a need to test the ways that are and have been so for thousands of years. It can be irksome and it makes me wonder if this way of being is a selfish need, rather than a selfless one motivated in favour of the Collective."

Alana responded immediately. "Good grief Tarquin, I think what irks you is you cannot control it and find it challenging to work with it! We possess something that you never will. Our kind have been hunted and exterminated and if that does not make you question the motives of who now is in control, when extermination is on the list of Earth possibility outcomes, what would?"

"My sentiments exactly Alana! How else are we to evolve and spiritually develop like the Collective wishes, when the Collective is resistant to change initiated from within?" I added.

"And from within we mean, by those who have become the product of the Collective's design, who can authentically see what needs to change!" summed up Alana.

"I see your views exactly. If this is a model or a system, it needs to be challenged from within and something needs to change, as you both say. It's either that, or collectively, we let the Earth crash and burn, with all of the short-term suffering and that might put its development back thousands of years or more. In addition, we have no knowledge of the impact this could have on the spirit world's future. James and Alana, we need you not to fight against us. We need your creativity and drive, so we may all learn from what you can bring. And Alana, whilst James is usually the voice, your knowing is equally abounded and together you create more than just the two of you."

"We both wish to help, but why not seek the help of other high planers?"

"We are, but I need front liners who have completed their revolutions, whom I believe have not fully achieved their potential, visible and hidden and who come from an extinct line that has given them a clear understanding of what extinction means. We need to work together to attempt to combat this looming Earth catastrophe, otherwise we may all be facing extinction."

"So, what do we do after breakfast?"

"I am so pleased somethings don't change," said Tarquin smiling. "As high planers we are formulating ways in which those in heaven can come to the aid of the Earth-bound, whilst upholding our non detection. I will approach you again when we know more. So what might you do in the meantime, if you choose to?"

Alana said she wished to work as a guide to spirits in this realm and she would talk to Monique about any referrals for those who were needing re-settlement support.

"James, I hear you have a mission going on to help Simon one of the low fliers, to help him free himself. I don't know much about the low fliers; they seem to have slipped through the net somewhat."

"Yes, he is someone I feel I must help."

"I'm going too, you know?"

"That, I do not doubt! I will see you both again shortly. Thank you for being with me and the heat of our discussions aside, I relish the challenge you both bring. Before I go, there is something I do know about Simon, in that he obviously did not recognise you when you first met. He was your brother in your first life time."

Tarquin disappeared, leaving us with jaws ajar.

"Well, that makes it more interesting, Alana."

"That means Simon must have known us in our time there and what happened to me?"

"If he hasn't forgotten?"

"Oh, and the other small matter he mentioned as well?" included Alana.

"You mean saving the universe. I don't think we are supposed to do that on our own. That would be too much."

"James, you are learning!"

"Thanks, you old goose!"

"If I am a goose, that makes you a turkey!"

I pulled her close and gave her a cuddle.

"At least we have a better idea now, as to why our lives have been so weird. I do struggle with the concept of being extinct though."

"And I with the necessity behind why." Alana reflected.

"Yes, you have a massive point. Changing the subject, I think there are some people we need to see, like Tom and Hazel and then I would like to go on a reconnaissance mission to Denby Dale. I wouldn't mind seeing my mum and grandma, as well as catching up with Simon."

"Well, I think Tom and Hazel are going to find this interesting, if not a little hard to believe," added Alana.

Tuning In

I tuned into my grandfather's frequency and spoke to him in my younger voice.

"Hi Grandfather, is Hazel with you?"

"Yes, she is. Are you still gallivanting or are you coming back home for a while? You have been gone for ages again, I am starting to think you have a place of your own."

"I am with Alana, we've been travelling and I think it's important for us to come back and tell you what we've been up to. We will be with you shortly."

We had talked about our explanations and would materialise back to Mill Cottage as our younger selves. I thought it unwise to tell them about the Harpy connection and Tarquin's request for help. Our older selves, revolving lifetimes, shamanism and increasing knowing, we thought, would be enough for them to take in, in one go. We transported to the patio and walked through the kitchen door.

"What, no tune juice?"

"No, tea at this time of the day. Anyway, I have been searching for a flower, that sounds like jazz."

"Have you tried trumpet honeysuckle or the yellow trumpet vine? The honeysuckle is particularly good," advised Alana.

"Thank you, Alana. No, I haven't, but I will imagine some up and have a blast later. Anyway, you have some news. You haven't decided to run off together, I take it?"

"Not quite, but this might be difficult to get hold of."

We started with revolving lives, of which both Hazel and Tom had an understanding of. It was Hazel who had heard of connected spirits, whom she termed as those who chase each other through lifetimes because of their love for each other. Again, it was Hazel who knew her time was approaching to revolve and had heard of shaman spirits and their abilities, but had never met one. Tom, it seemed was quite a young spirit who was in the early stages of his journey and was more preoccupied with just being in the spirit world, without an interest in the mysteries it was entwined with. He found it difficult to accept we were 478 years old and had revolved numerous times, let alone were birds of prey and could transform ourselves into various animal forms outside of virtual world.

"Grandfather, this is John you are talking to. You know it is me, why do you find it difficult to accept?"

"Because you are my grandson and I know you have a very active imagination and can make stuff up. I was concerned this might happen, where some older woman gets hold of you and fills your head full of wondrous stories because you are so impressionable."

Alana squeezed my hand under the table and whispered, the prize of patience into my mind. Hazel acknowledged Tom's previous comment and exposed his real concern.

"I think, if you are honest, it is a fear John will be taken away from you and you find it hard to accept someone in your descendant Earth line, may perhaps be more than who you might have thought."

"Why, do you believe them?"

"Why shouldn't I? Even I can feel their intentions are true. But what would convince you?"

Tom thought for a while before speaking.

"The bird thing I think, because I know that no one can transform outside of virtual world."

"Well, don't jump out of your skin Grandfather. Both of us together or separately?"

"Together, would make it harder to fake. Keep your minds open."

We both transformed into our eagle and osprey forms. However, it was not until we had subsequently changed into cats, goats, barn owls, rhinoceroses, which we had to go outside for and armadillos, before Tom relented and accepted, we must be shamans.

"It is hard for me to accept all of these changes and different aspects of the spirit world I am not aware of. I sort of understand the revolving thing. But for me, being here in spirit is about getting on, meeting with people, waiting for loved ones to arrive, reconnecting with them and eventually, in time, going back to Earth to do it all again for some reason. All of this knowing stuff is beyond me because some people have wisdom and others don't. It is as simple as that."

"Nobody is forcing you to learn about yourself. It's not like there is an exam at the end of it. You achieve it at your own pace. What I am wondering is whether 'non-acceptance' is a family trait, because I have struggled with it as well."

Alana cringed anticipating the response from the veiled criticism. "I said patience, James."

"Look John, James, whatever your name is now. I am not having you come into our house, telling me what I am and have passed down the generations. Just because you now think you are all knowing and wise and can turn yourself into a bird. I am off to my allotment to be amongst my friends who live in reality instead of cloud cuckoo land."

Tom disappeared.

"Hit and run, or what?"

"James, that is unfair, it's a lot for him to take in. You will need compassion as well as patience, if you are going to guide."

"I know, I am already sorry for saying it. Sometimes old wounds from childhood, like not being believed, seem to overwhelm my sense of compassionate relationship."

"You are right, Alana. Tom is a straight forward man. When he first came over, it took him a long time to adjust. There were days when he thought he was in a dream and I, his departed mother, was some sort of hallucination. There are some folk over here that just don't accept this is the next part of the journey and dying on the Earth plane and coming here is not the end of it."

"How many times have you revolved, Hazel?"

"Twice, I think. The feelings of wanting to go back are getting stronger by the day and as I explained last time you were here, I am travelling and exploring, because I am hoping I will be able to choose my location."

"What do you want to go back for, do you know?"

"Yes, it's simple. I want to learn how to risk and not be afraid to take chances. As for Tom, he will come around. Since he was a child, he has struggled with change and clung to the facts as he sees them."

"This is difficult for Grandad and me too, Hazel. Growing up with someone you love, respect and admire and then being able to see and sense them from the inside makes me want to look after him."

"That's just it, John. What has happened to you has taken his role away from him and his choice is now to either accept this new you or deny his feelings of loss and remain at a distance. He can be stubborn you know, so don't hold your breath."

"Thanks Hazel, I will let him be for a while, so he can think. He is still my grandfather."

"James and I are taking a short visit to Denby Dale. Shall we bring you a pie back?"

"That would be wonderful and if only!"

"See you soon, Hazel. Bye for now and thank you for listening, lots of love and take care."

In that moment, I linked to Alana to follow my thoughts as I wanted to talk to her before going back. We materialised on a hillside in common space, overlooking a small village where we could see other spirits going about their business. Common space were areas where spirit people could live in community if they wished, which was a popular choice for many. Although outwardly the villages or towns looked small, within them were pockets and folds of tailor made homesteads built by the inhabitants from virtual world constructions.

"I just wanted to touch base before we go over. I don't think it's wise to try and bring Simon back today. I want to see how he is and whether he has thought anymore about coming over. I suggest we go back as our younger selves though."

"I agree, but I would like to know more about us in our first lifetime."

"I would like to visit my grandma first and then my mum, then see if we can find Simon."

"I must admit I am a bit concerned about the Leaf who was giving Simon grief. Hey that rhymes!"

"Wonders never cease!"

After leaving Denby Dale nearly three months ago, it was strange to go back and I was drawn to the thought of how my friends were. I took us to my grandma's house where we could see her through the kitchen window sitting at the table, listening to the radio. She looked older than I remembered and could see what Grandfather meant about her being unwell. We sat at the table with her, without reading her thoughts.

Grandma looked up from her paper and switched off the radio. She sniffed the air almost detecting a scent that was not there before. Taking a blue exercise book from a pile of magazines, with 'Tom Visits' written on the front cover, she entered the day's date and wrote: Oranges, Freesias and Honey Suckle, then crossed honeysuckle out and wrote jasmine.

"We must be carrying the cottage scents. She is sensing us."

"Is that you, Tom?"

Audrey squinted her eyes and looked around the room in an attempt to catch a glimpse of her husband. She sniffed the air again and placed the book to her left.

"Grandma, it's me, John."

She looked up and stared in the direction I was sitting.

"Thank you spirit for visiting me in my home. I know you are not my Tom, but you seem friendly and for that you are welcome."

"She knows someone is here, that's impressive. Way to go Grandma!"

"This is like one of those séances. I went to one in the late 19th century. At least she hasn't asked 'is anybody there' yet?"

"I am going to try something."

I moved the energy down from my throat to my base chakra, letting it rise purposely through each of my vertebrae.

"You are not going to shoot her, are you?"

"No, of course not, I am going to fizz her up."

I reached across the table and placed my hand on her hand. As all of the energy reached my shoulder, I bounced it back down to my heart chakra and let it flow through my arm and into Grandma's hand. The slight flinch was unmistakable with the tiny hairs upon her forearm all standing on end. She shivered.

"Thank you for making contact with me kind spirit, I know you are here with me now. Can you tell me your name?"

"Let me try!"

Alana followed the same energy process as I had and touched Grandma's other hand, with the same result.

"So, there are two of you. And thank you to you too, for also visiting me. What are your names?"

"John, Grandma, John!"

"And Alana!"

Audrey sat and mused for a while before speaking.

"I am happy you are here, but I cannot place a Joan and Alan in the spirit world?"

We looked at each other in joy and agreed that was close enough. Whilst I knew my grandma had an interest in life after death, I had no idea she was an amateur channeler. I powered up again except this time I pulsed the energy emission coinciding it with my name John.

"Not Joan, John, John!"

On the last pulse I sent her the combined image and word, bike. The tears rolled down her cheeks and she looked up to where we were sitting.

"John, our John? Where ever you are in this room I need a big hug from you right now. We have all missed you so much."

I hugged my grandma as tightly as I could and she imagined me holding her close. No dry eyes were spared and Alana was touched by the closeness I had experienced during my time on the Earth with her. Grandma dried her eyes and said she would offer us tea and biscuits, but we probably wouldn't be able to manage them.

"If you send me pictures into my mind, like symbols, I am better at guessing what you are trying to say. Words are harder to place, because we all know a John, but when you showed me a bike, I knew it was you. I will not always guess right as Earth memories are all connected in some way and it is easy to get confused."

"How is your grandfather, Tom?"

"Donkey, Donkey-shoe, Mule!"

"Stubborn, yes that's him, takes after his dad."

"What does he do over there?"

"Vegetables and fork?"

"Gardening, an allotment? He has an allotment. I was hoping we could have a big garden with a vegetable patch, that's a shame?"

"Does he live with anyone?"

"Nut? Not sure about that one, brown and green, eyes, bush. I get it, Hazel, his mum? Not sure if I want to live with his mum when I get over there either!"

"How are you getting on, John?"

"Sun shine, well, bucket, ahh, well, good. And your friend Alan have you known him long?"

"Doll, no, dress, err, Alan is a girl?"

"Sunshine, lollypop, heart. She is your sweetheart. Sunshine."

"Doll, Dress, Alan, A, chain…links, I get it, the girl version of Alan, Alana?"

"Sunshine."

Just then, the doorbell rang and the person let themselves in.

"Hi, Mum, it's me are you in the kitchen. No radio?"

"No need, I have visitors, come through."

"Visitors, who?"

"Wait and see."

As Jennifer entered the kitchen, Alana knew who she was and acknowledged James's concern for his grandmother as his mum was pretty sceptical about the spirit world. She could be a little short and dismissive with her at times.

As I quickly read into her mind, I could see she had become more tolerant of Grandma's beliefs since my passing. However, she remained unconvinced. I was happy to see Mum again, but the difference concerned me. She looked weathered, more guarded and sadly, bitterness, quite understandably, had caught part of her heart.

"There is no one here, Mum. Oh, let me guess, it's Dad again, is it?"

"No, not this time Jenny, there are two of them and I think they are still here."

"Pinky and Perky then?"

Alana giggled and Audrey smiled.

"Jenny, I know you don't believe in this kind of thing, but this is the first time I have had quite a strong link. Please humour me, this might be a shock."

"Who do you think it is, then?"

"I think it is John and he is here with a girl called Alana."

Mum started to well up and as she turned to leave the room, raised her palms to the air.

"No Mum, no. I cannot believe John is here. He has been gone now for three months and I have never felt him around as you think you feel Dad. I am sure I would have felt him. God knows I have called for him enough times."

In that moment, I did not feel guilty for not coming back to visit. I knew she needed time to grieve, to feel her sadness and solitude in order to move on. I had also had much to do since I arrived in spirit. Although I now had the choice to provide some information that might alter my mum's perspective, I felt cynical about her having any acceptance. This acceptance message which had come down the generations was indeed powerful. At least I had learned to turn it from denial into challenge. Alana was listening to my thoughts and echoed the 'P' word and told me to keep the link positive.

"Jenny, please give me a chance, sit down, there's tea in the pot."

"Loose or in bags, because you might find it more difficult to read bags? Alright. Sorry, I will have a cup of tea and nod along with you, if it makes you happy?"

"She's funny."

"Alana says you are funny, Jenny."

"Tell her thank you. So, you can hear them?"

"You just did and no, they speak in pictures because I am not good with words. John is talking with me now; he is showing me a picture of him as a baby in a blue jacket with his dad's cap on."

"You know this picture, that's coming from you! Oh, come on, Mum, you'll have to do better than that."

"Lock, he is showing me a padlock, but it's not that, it does not feel right. I can see coloured glass, like a church window. Locket, it could be a locket, but I know you wear a locket. Scissors, he has shown me scissors."

Mum took the chain from around her neck upon which hung her locket. She placed it on the table in front of Grandma, put her hands to her face and burst into tears. Grandma moved towards her and put her arms around her as she sobbed. Alana and I also held each other and joined in.

"Open it, please open it."

Grandma gently opened the locket to find a small lock of blond hair bound with blue cotton.

"Only I knew about this and it seems, so did John, if it is him."

"I feel it is. I have never been this clear before and it feels right."

I powered up and placed my hand on my mothers'. I released the pulse and she shivered.

"He just touched you, he did it to me earlier. I think it's his way of letting you know he is here."

"I miss you, John."

"He misses you too and he gives you his love. He is showing me pictures. He says he is only one step away and will see us both in time."

"James, look left through the window. Is that Simon?"

"Yes, we better go."

"Jenny, James, sorry, John and Alana must go now, I feel the link is fading. They say bye for now."

I placed my arms around my mum and generated a wave of power that made her shiver and take a sharp intake of breath. Grandma grasped her hand.

"I guess he just gave you a big hug. More tea?"

"Bye for now, John, I love you. Tea, blow the tea, got any gin?"

Stalemate

"Decided you would return then and who'd be this, your sweetheart, is she?"

"Hello Simon, my name is Alana and yes, you could say that we are sweet on each other."

Simon furrowed his brow as if trawling his memories and Alana went with his search. I caught her thoughts and interrupted them gently, requesting we should not read him just yet and to let him talk of his situation and how he had trapped himself. I could sense her zeal and reminded her of the patience word she so often bestowed upon me.

"I knew of a girl called Alana once, a long time ago. I remember she was a troubled soul, not like you, young missy, but, there is a likening between the two of you. Sad, it was, a sad time back then."

"I am sorry it has taken some time to come back. There is so much to do when you first go over, like finding out what it is all about and meeting up with people."

"You have seen Sarah then, did you give her my message?"

"Yes, she shares her life with horses and between them, they help people who find it difficult to solve their own problems. She knew what you meant by your words, 'I cannot drink.'"

"Always was a smart girl, my Sarah. Sounds like she has done well for herself owning horses."

"She doesn't own them. They choose to live with her on her farm because she is kind and they understand her work is important, so they help her."

"Horses don't choose to live with you, you must stable or pen them, unless you be riding them. I have heard this kind of bull-scutter before from know-all other-worlderers. Seems like you have turned into one young master."

"We are not know-alls or high planers as they are known. They are the ones who live in another plane because they know more than we do. We cannot go there," added Alana.

"So, there be different heavens then, for folks who be gooder than others? Then there be a hell too, for those who are not so good?"

"There are other planes where people go whose deeds have been harmful to others, but they are not called 'hell', they are called dark realms and they are dark. The people in them torture themselves and others like them. They are helped though and can leave when they have accepted responsibility for their deeds and seen there is better in them."

"So, they trap themselves by their deeds. How long do they remain there?"

"Some, hundreds of years, some less, but there are those who refuse to see and have been there much longer."

"That would be where I'd be going if I came with you. That is why I stay here."

"Even if I said to you, that would not happen, you are not going to believe us. Why do you not believe? There must have been hundreds of spirit people who have told you the same thing?"

"There is a term I have learned. I think you are like bounty hunters. You encourage us, who are here between worlds to go over because in doing so, a debt will be paid and you gain somehow. I took life from my brother. In my ledger that is a large debt to repay."

"Look, I know you would not go to the dark realms. Sarah told me it was an accident and you were cleared of any blame for his death. If you came over you could work with Sarah and help others and repay any debt you may think you owe."

"Do you think I don't help others here?"

"Well to be honest Simon, I do not know what you do, other than sit around wallowing in your own self-pity."

"Watch your tone with me young master. You are not beyond my anger if I so choose to deal it. But I am pleased you have chosen to show me one of your other sides."

"Sarah says you are hot headed and stubborn as well."

Simon caste his gaze to the ground. We could both see the shifting colour in his aura as he struggled with the accusations and his sense of shame, but at no time did he start to power up. Alana mind-linked and understood that I was trying to evoke a reaction to gain a better sense of him.

"She is right in what she says. I have learned during my time here to use my anger and direct it to serve others."

Simon explained there were many low fliers in between worlds and their numbers were growing. He had noticed over the decades how the personalities of new Leaves had changed and many over the last seventy or so years had trapped themselves because they did not trust the catchers. He had decided all those years ago to turn his back on the church, but his reason for not going was because of what happened and he feared hell.

He experienced more and more people who refused to accept any kind of idea of a heaven. This made sense because with an absence of belief, what would make you follow a light being into a glowing tunnel with a promise of heaven being at the end of it?

When he talked to new Leaves, a lot had said, they preferred to stay and make up their own minds, rather than trust an apparition which was probably a consequence of dying. He had heard tell of films and programs that had affected people's view of what could happen after death and how dark spirits tempted and manipulated to reach their own ends. Even though he had been stopped by his own deed, he had helped many who were obviously not bad people, to follow the catchers through.

"So, you could be seen as a bounty hunter yourself?"

"I only help those who have misjudged themselves and do not have debts to repay."

The other thing worrying Simon was that Leaves were becoming more organised. There were those who bullied and threatened others to follow them, it seemed in the main for territory. With over four hundred years of experience as a Leaf himself, he understood his kind and was regularly having to defend his peace of mind and defend spirit coming over from the other world to visit their loved ones. These spirits had become a sort of sport to the angrier Leaves. He also said, he was drawn to defend more vulnerable Earth people from antagonising Leaves. He felt they should not worsen people's conditions and would open fire and ask questions later, getting them to leave them alone.

"It didn't stop you from blasting my grandfather though, did it?"

"I'd been havin' a bad day. I had just been jumped by three Leaves without warning. Your grandfather just got in the way and I have apologised for that. Unfortunately, I have made enemies. I think being here so long, I have seen many changes and I have kept myself from becoming bitter, spiteful and pitiful. I am not full of self-pity, I just find it hard to trust."

"You are a warrior. We could do with someone like you in our world and I think there are others who may learn from your knowledge and experience." I encouraged him.

"You have to fight in heaven?"

"No, not exactly, but there are things in your so-called heaven, that need to change and we have to fight for them."

"Your comments bring warmth to me. You and Alana's growing familiarity sooths me."

"Incoming!!!"

The ball of red light hit Simon between the shoulder blades and he fell to the earth immobilised and defenceless. In an instant, Alana created a dome shield covering all three of us, protecting us from further attack. Two further light balls hit the perimeter without effect.

"So, there are at least three of them."

"We are safe in here. Is Simon alright?"

"Yes, I think so. He is just dazed. I will fizz him up, that should bring him around."

I touched Simon's arm and sent a combined chakra light charge into him. He opened his eyes wide and attempted to get up.

"Stay down a minute, you are safe, we have this covered, well Alana does."

"What is this shield, how do you do this?"

"We pack heavy from where we come from."

"Hero!"

"Oh, come on Alana, I haven't been in a gun battle since I was in Germany in 1943."

"1943, but you are young people and you died here only a few months ago."

"Just here, just right now, trust us."

Alana mind-linked and asked me why they couldn't all transport back now. I reassured her and said I felt the decision must be Simons. Both of us transformed into our older selves.

"I am not sure whether it is safer out there or in here with you two?"

"Simon, you are not in a position or at power to transport out of here."

"But you could transport us to a safer place?"

"You must be joking; we are going to stand our ground."

"Hero," repeated Alana.

"You really love me, don't you?"

Alana shrank the dome to fit our separate forms and each took control of the power to support our own defence. Three equally defended forms came into our vision and remained standing at twenty paces. Alana took pole position.

"What is your problem, bumpkin Bill?"

"I'd be wondering what kind of a man let's his woman speak for him and my name is not Bill!"

The resultant crack was unexpected and incredibly fast. The red ball smacked into the man, right between his eyes and although he was guarded, he flinched and took a step back.

Alana stood her ground defiantly.

"He is the kind of man who trusts his woman to fight beside him and as for me, I am man enough to blast your ass standing right in front of you, rather than shooting from the cover of the trees, you wandought coward."

I mind-linked – "I really love you too."

"Impressive shot fustylugs. But if you'd been on your own, it would have been a different matter!"

"Excuse me, Bill, as the lady said, what is your problem?"

"He goes by the name of the governor; he thinks he owns the rights to Denby Dale," said Simon.

"You are trespassing on my territory and you will be leaving now!"

I mind-linked into Simon.

"You may not be aware of this way to talk, it is John. Is this the man who has been hassling you? My grandad said you were arguing with someone the last time he was here."

"Yes, I know this linking talk and yes, that's him. I have to watch my back, if I want to remain around these parts. This has been my home for centuries. His name in fact, be Leslie."

"I was right to call you wandought then Leslie. Was your mother not sure whether you were a girl or a boy?"

Alana waved her little finger at him. Leslie was visibly disturbed by the gesture and started to power up. I asked Alana to trust my next line, because I had picked up a disturbing thought from the man.

"Hold your tongue woman, that is enough!" I said to her.

"That'd be more like it, know your place fustylugs."

"Look Leslie, Simon has been here much longer than you, this is his home. Why can't you leave him in peace?"

"He's a do-gooder. I have lost men to his interfering, but I hate him most of all because he persuaded my woman to go with a catcher, leaving me alone. I don't care who you are, all of you are leaving."

"I should say we have a stand-off here. We are equally matched and nobody seems to be going anywhere."

Then the disturbing thought was spoken.

"I think you are leaving because we've been watching you since you arrived. You visited the old lady in the house yonder, the one who thinks she speaks to the spirits. You might have somehow changed to an older version now, but you must be the boy killed on the road a while back. Which means, she must be your grandmother. You cannot remain here all of the time and mark my words, as soon as you are gone, she'll be talking to us."

Leslie stood with his hands on his hips and his chin jutting forward.

"Another thing, we know an old man visits her often. We will be overjoyed to share pleasantries with him as well."

I kept a thought link open to Simon and Alana. I was thankful for the awareness of my anger and did not rise to the bait. We were not going to win this battle.

"You know governor, you have a good point and I will appeal to your sense of fair play, not to harm my grandfather or grandmother. I would also kindly ask you to consider letting Simon live here in peace."

"You are not in a position to ask for any terms. I want him gone from here."

"I do not like to be threatened, nor do I like my family threatened either. We know what it is like to be hunted and from that, we also know how to hunt. Let me be clear, if you harm my family, you will be hunted."

"Whatever, now go!"

I linked into Simon and Alana and transported us all to high ground in Upper Cumberworth.

"We were not going to win that one. Gosh, he is an our soul."

"Our soul?"

"The place where bull-scutter comes from Simon."

Simon laughed.

"I am liking you more young master, even though you are not so young now. And missy, you pack a punch worthy of a collier and dare I say, you have a mouth like a fishwif!"

"Well, thank you, kindly sir."

"But, why you be calling him James, when his name be John?"

"It's a nick name. He reminds me of a famous character in a book of our time."

"He also reminds me of someone from my time, in fact you both do, but my mind is old and can play tricks on me, like other things."

Simon was getting visibly agitated.

"Simon, you have no cause for concern. Sarah, sent a message back which was, it is up to you to free yourself from this place, if you choose to. She visited you once and you were fighting with what must have been Leslie and she was sad because she thought you had not changed."

"She came to see me? I have not changed in some of my ways. I will fight anyone who be a bully to others or do others an injustice."

"And yet you do an injustice to yourself by remaining here and not coming over to where you really belong."

"I know where I belong. Well, it may not be where I belong, but I know that it be, where I shall be sent."

I explained to Simon the process of Self-judgement, stating there were not others who judged and condemned. This was met with his concerns that he had already judged himself and if he was to a second time, his pride and guilt would condemn him again. It was his pride that killed his brother and guilt is what he had suffered since.

"You know, there are Earth people in these modern times who intentionally kill others for a whole host of reasons. They are then imprisoned for life. However, on average, the majority stay in prison about seventeen years of that life sentence. You have served over four hundred. Do you not think that is fair payment?"

"The debt is never repaid. It seems to me the justices have gone soft. In my time, you would have been judged and hung."

"But that's it, you were judged and the judgement said there was no crime."

"I was judged by men, not God at that time."

"Are you afraid of the 'eye for an eye' teachings?" asked Alana.

"Yes. God said to Moses: 'If anyone injures his neighbour, as he has done it shall it be done to him, fracture for fracture, eye for eye, tooth for tooth; whatever injury he has given a person shall be given to him. Whoever kills an animal shall make it good, and whoever kills a person shall be put to death.' I refused to go with the catcher who came for me, because I feared God's, not man's judgement.

I knew I was dead when I came here, which was a shock. Then I thought, I am not really dead because God is saving me for a greater punishment and I have proved my guilt before him by turning my back on the church."

"Good grief Simon, you should fear man more than God, or the Collective, as we call it. There was a great soul whose wisdom said 'an eye for an eye only ends up making the whole world blind," said Alana.

"I can agree with that and there be still some of man's actions, I think be better changed on Earth and in this place, even when that wisdom is spoken. It appears to me, all of us on Earth are threatened in one way or another and we are all well versed in the language and meaning of threat. Why do you call God the collective?"

"Because it is whole yet divided amongst all of us and all of us have a responsibility to keep it whole in the separateness of what we are."

"It'd be like God then?"

"Pretty much. In the spirit world, like here on Earth, there are many names for God and in our experience, the Collective does not threaten. However, the presence of threat is for us to experience and overcome, so we can know ourselves and others better."

"Wise words, Alana."

"Know thyself, Simon."

"We have company. Down there in the hedge rows. They must have tracked us somehow."

"Simon, please come with us."

"No Alana, I'd be better off here and I can keep an eye, the one I have left, on John's grandmother. I can remain hidden as I know every shadow in these parts."

"What weapons do you have in your armoury?"

"Base and head shots that's all and I can guard."

"Let me show you how to use a stun grenade."

I mind-linked to Simon and demonstrated how he could draw energy from the base and solar plexus chakras and spin the combined energy around his mid line until it hummed. Once he had sighted his target in an expression of giving with his arms, the orange ball could be projected up into the air and arc down onto the target.

"Why not use a shot?"

"The grenade will take out more than one adversary at the same time."

"I could do with spending more time with you two. This makes me imagine flying like a bird of prey and bombing them from above. I have always wanted to do that."

We both guarded and mind-linked at the moment the energising thought connected.

"Do you think he could be one of us?"

"No, too much of a coincidence."

"Now, you two be off. I will draw fire. I hope to be seeing you again. My sense of ease grows, but there is work to be done here."

"Simon, you know the dome shield I used, you can place an Earth person inside it with you," Alana sent him the link.

Simon left us and travelled down the hillside towards the Leaves who were growing in number at the bottom. Half way down, a shot rang out which was deflected. I then recognised the sound of a grenade launch and the unmistakable thud as it exploded at the centre of the gathering, stunning the group.

"I'd be liking that, very much!"

Simon disappeared.

Maiden Flight

"Come on hero, we should go. We do not want to antagonise them anymore having just chucked a grenade into their midst. Did you not think about that?"

"They are going to go for Grandma anyway. That's why I planted a thought in Simon's head to watch out for her. We have to learn from this threat. This Leaf situation has the potential of becoming more of a problem. I want to try something, link in."

"You cannot transform into your eagle on this plane!"

"Who says, I still have a feather in my hair and so do you?"

I energised my body and channelled transformative imagination into my form. There was a small flicker and then nothing.

"Runes, do you remember runes?"

"Yes, I do, but not in my lifetimes, unless I am remembering from the first one."

"As above, so below. All reality is reality in whichever level of reality."

"You mean, all is whole, even though the realities are separate."

"Exactly. So, if we can transform in at least two of the realities, the spirit world and virtual world, we should be able to transform here. Tarquin said we used to fly here when we met up, when you were veil crossing during your first lifetime."

I tried the runic incantation, but to no avail.

"Let's get out of here, I have another idea."

I took us to the summit of Scafell Pike.

"That's a bit random, but I have always wanted to visit the Lake District and wander lonely as a cloud and all that. Shame we are a month too early for daffodils and yet because of the global warming, we may be in luck."

"Oh well, it is handy we have that, isn't it? Good grief! Come to think about it, I have had another idea as I do not think we are going to find what I am looking for here."

"Umm, never seen you in a kilt before James."

The next moment, we were in Mull and it was not long before we had spotted a golden eagle being mobbed by crows. Eventually and with more skilled manoeuvres, the bird came to settle on a crag and preened its feathers.

"What are you going to do?"

"I don't know, go and chat with it, or get the feel of an Earth-bound bird. It will not be able to see us, so we can sit right next to it. I am wondering if we can feel its Earth-bound energy and somehow incorporate it into us. If so, we may be able to materialise our birds."

"OK, sounds like a plan."

We sat either side of the majestic bird and although she looked from left to right in the instant of our arrival, she appeared to be unaware of our presence. We could see she was scanning for her next quarry. Although it was lambing season and these were easy prey, Alana was aware of her hesitation and fear of trawling the flocks. I gently stroked the bird along it's back, imagining the feel again of Earth-bound feathers and she shivered and rustled her feathers as if sensing my touch.

"Try. I can feel her. There is definitely a different type of energy coming from her, almost like she is tolerating the ground. I bet it feels different when she is flying."

Alana stroked the bird and agreed there was almost a tension to want to fly again which perhaps was because she was poised to lift and hunt at any time. We both engaged with the transitional whilst touching the bird and felt her energy come into us. We watched each other's forms flicker again with a stronger magnitude, however, could not maintain our bird forms. The eagle turned on her perch and flapped its wings, before settling again. Both of us flickered.

"What do you want?"

"Can you see us?"

"I can feel and hear you, but you are like bird-men, some of both. I am not afraid of you."

"We are bird-men and bird-women spirits. We wish to fly here, but we cannot change to our bird forms. We wondered if being near you would help?"

"Your energy is strange to me, I feel in you, what I feel in myself and yet you are grounded and free at the same time. I also do not understand why I can talk with you. I have sensed other spirits, but never talked with them before."

"That is us. We can talk to birds and animals where we come from, but we have never spoken with one such as you, who lives on the Earth."

"I am James and this is Alana. What is your name?"

"Sealgair. How can I help you?"

"We know there is a difference between how you feel when you are perched and when you are flying. At the moment of take-off, you require an energy and determination to lift."

"I know this."

"We want to share that energy with you as you lift off, because I think it will help us to transform. You can lift great weights and I am thinking, as you take off we might hold your talons if we can and you might be able to pull our bird forms free."

"I can lift lambs and small deer; I am not sure I can lift both of you."

"Do you know when you skin a rabbit? You pull the skin and the inside, it's body peels free?"

"I think, I know what you mean."

We practiced our one, two, three's and were confident to try the experiment at the next attempt. Alana pointed out that if we hung on with their hands, these would transform to wings first and our grip would be lost. We decided to sit with legs facing forward and direct the initial transitional force into our feet and so talons, so they could latch on.

"Legs in the air, like I just don't care. I hope no-one is filming!"

"I didn't get to where I am today by worrying about throwing my legs in the air."

"James, you are mad."

"One, two, three...lift off."

Transitional energy was engaged and focussed upon our feet. As we connected with the eagle's talons, our own emerged and were grasped into place. Sealgair beat her wings hard to take to the air. We watched in amazement as our human forms peeled away, revealing our raptors. At twenty metres we released ourselves, falling slightly before regaining a flight path to catch up with her.

"We are not back in the Earth world, are we?"

"No, that's impossible, we are still in the world between. Come on, lets wing-tip her."

Climbing, we sat on Sealgair's wingtips. She scanned left and right.

"So, you are an Osprey Alana, and you James, one of my kind."

"OK, you can see us now?"

"Yes, but you are surrounded by a brighter light. I am pleased I could be of service to you. Funny, but you cannot be mates then."

"James is my mate. We are of the same species, but we fly as different birds, we come from a line that is sadly extinct."

"You must be Harpies; I have heard the legends told. You have endured much. Well, if I have helped you all I can, *Tha mi a guidhe gach sealg dhut*."

"And to you Sealgair. Talking about hunting, have you seen that rabbit down there?"

"James, in case it has escaped your notice, I am also an eagle!"

"Thank you, you are perfect. Fair well!"

The video taken of a female golden eagle rising into the air, lifting a male eagle and osprey with her, had gone viral within twenty minutes.

"Let's go back home. We need reinforcements to help us in Denby Dale and I am wondering if Scout and Audaz would be up for an Earth-bound venture?"

"Capri?"

"Fine, I'll follow your link, but before we go, let us transform into our human forms and then attempt to transform back into birds. I think we can both replicate the energy we need to do this."

We touched down on a rocky outcrop and underwent the transformations.

"Good, that has solved that. Come on James, it's freezing here in Scotland, I need some sunshine. Maybe, we can do the kilt thing next time we are here. Quick flash perhaps?"

"Go on, then."

"Excellent, I have always loved your knees!"

"But it falls below them?"

"Do you not think I can see through it and in doing so, have I somehow missed the true Scot in your ancestry?" Alana remarked in a Scottish accent.

"Go on, off with you, you are dreadful."

"Ha ha, follow me, Hamish MacDoobrie."

Making Ready

We both landed on the balcony of our home as raptors. As I put a call into Scout, Alana linked with Audaz. We explained we wanted to meet up as we needed help and that it would be an Earth mission to help a friend and protect part of my family. Without hesitation, it was Audaz who swooped in first, slowing at full wing span to alight on the balcony edge, followed closely behind by Scout. Scout came in low across the water, before beating hard to rise to the level of the balcony. Alana projected out a wide extended platform to enable enough space for him to land.

"Joao, Alana, a pleasure to see you. Is that what I think it is?"

We both laughed.

"Yes, it is! This is Scout."

"But it is a horse, it has wings. Horses do not fly and I cannot speak with horses."

"This one is special, he can fly and you will be able to talk with him."

"In the myths and legends of my ancestors, there was a story of a flying horse. Some say he was like us for some reason, but he gave up his wings to live just as a horse because he no longer wished to work for the gods. Too much god's will and not enough free will, I think. I have never been able to work out why they thought he was like us. We are eagles?"

There was a massive down draught as Scout came into land.

"Scout, how are you? This is Audaz, one of our friends from the realm's rainforests and this is Alana, she is my mate."

"I keep telling you, she cannot be your mate as she is an osprey and you are an eagle."

"Audaz, this is Scout my dear friend, who has taught me much and you are quite right, he is a flying horse."

"John, Alana, Audaz, I am pleased to see and meet you."

"It has been a while since I have seen you both, so to sort out any confusion, in our human forms Alana and I have progressed our years and Alana calls me James, which is my old name."

"OK, but to stop my confusion, I will call you John, if that is alright?"

"And I will call you Joao."

"I think that is fine, as there will be no mistake in who is calling me!"

"I can read from your mind Scout. You have connected with your heritage and now know where you have descended from."

"I have, yes, and it makes perfect sense now as to why I can transform and fly. I am indebted to you for enabling me to free this part of me."

"You are more than welcome, have you done much flying?"

"At every opportunity, away from eyes and I have met two other Mustangs who have only just found their wings. We have had much fun. It is like belonging to real family."

"How is it, you can fly Scout? You are like the legend, the Pegasus horse."

"It was John who showed me how to connect with my ancient line. The one I now know to be of Harpies."

"No, I am a Harpy, you are a horse, Joao is an eagle and Alana is an osprey."

"Where did you find this rooster?"

James mind-linked to Alana and Scout.

"Audaz, remember what you were telling me about your legend of Pegasus, of 'some saying, he was like us?' Was there any other part to the legend?"

"Something about human-birds, but I never believed it because humans hunt us as you know."

At that moment, Alana and I transformed back into human form and Scout dissolved his wings. Straight after, we all transformed back.

"Audaz, you are a Harpy, you are obviously descended from the Harpy lines as per your legends. We are all of the same line except our ancestors took different forms."

Audaz then transformed into handsome grey-black stallion and then into a tall elegant grey-haired man, before returning to his Harpy eagle form.

"Forgive me. I do not show all of my colours until I know I am held by trust. I know who you are, I did when we first met, but you did not know at that time my friends. Scout, it is an honour to meet one of my kind as you are."

Audaz and Scout bowed to each other. All of us took time to pool our knowledge of the Harpy line and it coincided with what we had been told by

Tarquin. Although the ancient information was sketchy; tales told of beautiful bird men and women, not monstrous creatures. The race had been labelled as foul, cruel and violent, female monsters who snatched food and people whom they took away and tortured. It appeared, these majestic and peace-loving creatures who embraced all of nature, were captured, imprisoned, abused and killed by humans. As a result of their persecution it became necessary to scare the humans away by transforming into ghoulish demon-like forms. It was mainly females who were sighted and were involved in conflict, as like the current Harpy eagles, they were larger and more powerful than the males. It appeared that after they scattered across Europe and to other parts of the world, they were finally extinguished in the 1100s. There was a sadness amongst our group as we reflected on how it is difference that breeds fear.

"So, why the call for help? This Earth adventure seems intriguing, if not concerning for your kin. But where do we fit in John?"

"We need some fire power. We are outnumbered by angry Leaves who have trapped themselves in between worlds and there is a real threat to my grandparents, which I wish to change. However, the other reason for going is a Leaf called Simon who is caught in this issue. We think he is on the brink of coming over. What he does not know is, he was my brother from my first lifetime and when we were on Earth together, we fought and I was killed by accident. He has misjudged himself and fears he will be sent to hell for that reason."

Alana and I explained the history of the situation, the connections with Sarah and how the low fliers were becoming increasingly threatening and organised to control territory. I felt what was most worrying was their threat to interfere with the Earth-bound, as in the case of my grandmother and just how impactful this threat might be to others. I also told them of how Simon had worked for some time to help others.

"When did this happen and what are your aims Joao?"

"About two days ago. I should wish to take away the threat to my family somehow and convince Simon to come with us to his rightful and true place. He has been alone unnecessarily for too long."

"Can we be ourselves on Earth? Are we capable of transforming and are we allowed to do this?"

"Alana and I found a way to transform into our bird forms by connecting to an Earth-bound eagle. We know how to recreate this energy ourselves, which we will now link to you to enable you to do the same. It worked for us, so there should be no reason it should fail you. As to whether we are allowed to do this? Tarquin, the high planer, is aware I am working to help Simon, and that I have made contact with you two. We are edge riders, those who live and work in the interface between realities and I feel, if we cruise close to a few edges, that's what I call creative intervention."

"So long as we are not locked up and tortured! What is the plan then, John?"

We briefed them on how Simon was keeping an eye on my grandmother to stop any Leaf interference and how the house was being watched for visitors. Leslie was the main leader of the Leaves and if he could be separated from the others, they may lose their impetus to continue their quest for territory. It was very unlikely Leslie could be persuaded to come through to the spirit world, therefore, he would have to be deterred from remaining in the area and carrying on his activities to control others.

"It may be possible for us to persuade other Leaves to come back with us. If they were enabled to see there was no real truth to their fears. There may be women amongst them too, who are taking part against their will and I can help them," Alana added.

"So, why firepower?"

"They use light defences and project to disable others. Although they are not as skilled or aware, or even able to use the light in a way we can, they have numbers on their side and can come from different directions. At least with four of us, we can defend the four quarters of our stance more effectively."

"What are they using, Joao?"

"It seems to be the two basic shots from head and solar plexus, whilst we have anxiety grenades, aerial foreboding mines and pincer creepers if needed, in addition to their two pacifiers."

"We also have hypnic topplers, it is a bird thing. It makes the recipient feel as though they are falling, even when they are lying on the ground. I will show you."

Once briefed on Audaz's weapon, Scout informed us of his technique of rapid fire where he could follow a chest shot with four further bursts at one second intervals. He then needed a five second pause. The downside was, he was unable to keep a shield in place at full power whilst doing this. On demonstrating, he sounded like an anti-aircraft gun from WWII.

"A while back, I met a guide called Arthur, who teams up with a catcher called Stephen. I am hoping they will be able to join us, or at least Stephen. I am thinking, if there are any Leaves who can be encouraged or decide to come over, we need someone to open the veil and help them through."

I linked in to Arthur and Stephen simultaneously.

"Arthur, it's John. I have got you on group chat with Stephen, I really need help from both of you."

"Group chat?"

"Arthur, how long have you been in the spirt world? I am linking to both you and Stephen at the same time. Are you both linked in?"

"Yes."

"Yes, hi John."

I explained the situation and what we were intending to do.

"I must say John, this is highly irregular, but I think your cause is true. Do not expect us to join your conflict. We will act as observers, help others and defend if necessary. Does Tarquin know what you are doing?" Arthur enquired.

"He knows I am working with low flyers and with Simon in particular."

"OK, when are you planning to go?"

"I think, within the next few hours."

"We are both free at present, but as you know, our services can be called upon at any time," stated Arthur.

"Well, if you can delegate, that would be great, but if you can't, we will work around you."

"You don't delegate death John, but we will do our best, so call in when you need us," Added Stephen.

"Thank you, both."

"Are you alright John? You seem pretty energised at the moment and your vibration has changed somewhat. It's just I still have quite a strong guide link with you. I was scanning the guide waves and knew you were on."

"Tony! Link in."

"Ah, I see. You weren't thinking of leaving me out of this, were you Kemosabe?"

I suddenly found myself wearing a chicken outfit. Much to the surprise of the group standing close by me.

"Cheers mate. That would have been even funnier if I had been in human form."

"You think that, do you? Can I come then?"

"Yes, most definitely. Link and follow, come and meet the group."

Within a moment, Tony had joined us and acquainted himself with each member. He spent some time talking with Alana, as he had no idea, I had revolved so many times and that she and I had chased each other through life times. In the meantime, Audaz, Scout and I talked tactics, which Tony and Alana caught up with after their conversation.

"John, it's Hazel. Something is badly wrong."

"Who, where, what is it? Is it Grandfather?"

"Yes, I cannot reach him, he is in Denby Dale."

"Don't worry, I will go and see him and get back in touch."

"Saddle up, we are going in. No wings to start. Audaz, can you arrive there in your handsome grey-haired man guise? And quarter stance when we land, Tony you take the middle. Link in."

"But I am a Harpy eagle. I suppose so, if I must."

"Arthur, Stephen, we are going in now. There seems to be a problem involving my grandfather."

Clean Sweep

Our group materialised in defence formation in the garden at the back of my grandmother's house. It appeared the activity was happening at the front, where three Leaves had got Grandfather pinned to the ground. His defences were weakened and they were repeatedly targeting his shield which was not strong enough to repel the anxiety and misery of their intent. As soon as he showed any sign of recovery, they would blast him again and knock him back down, whilst they laughed at his struggle and chatted amongst themselves. As we came around the corner to the front of the house, the link was fast and direct.

"Audaz right, Scout left, me centre!"

The head shots rang out in quick succession hitting their targets efficiently and the Leaves fell to the ground. Hypnic topplers were tossed in for good measure to increase their disorientation and decrease their communication to others. Alana transported herself to Tom and placed a shield above and around them. There seemed to be only the three Leaves on site, so whilst the others in the group stood watch over them and looked out for other activity, I also attended to Grandfather. Although he was groggy and miserable, he was recovering slowly.

"Alana, what are you doing here?"

"John is here too, we heard you were having problems, so we came to help you."

"Thank you. They just didn't let me get up, I could do nothing."

"Grandfather, how are you? That was quite an ordeal."

"John, thank you for coming. The Leaves have been getting more aggressive recently, but this is the first attack in a long time."

"You stay with Alana for a while, I am going to check on Grandma. Come in as soon as you are able to. And don't worry, we have friends here with us."

297

I entered the house and found Grandma in the kitchen. She was ringing a handkerchief nervously and as I entered the room, she looked up and put her face in her hands.

"Please leave me alone. Can you not see I am frightened enough?"

I energised and fizzed her up. Intertwining feelings of love and calming thoughts with the wave, I sent her a bike image at the same time.

"John, oh John, is that you?"

"It's me, Grandma, don't worry you are safe. Come, let me give you a hug."

She got up from the chair and took two paces towards me. I was surprised, thinking she could hear me. I wrapped my arms around her and sent wave after wave of loving energy into her. As the hairs on her arms raised, I knew she could feel me.

"I cannot hear you, send me pictures."

Mule.

"Tom, is he here?"

Sunshine.

"Yes, where is he?"

"Standing in the doorway darling."

"I can feel Tom, is he near?"

Tick symbol.

"She knows we are here, John. How do you link with her? I have never been able to communicate with her."

"You are brighter than Tom, your presence is stronger and I can almost feel tingling on my hands and face."

Ghost, house.

"There have been a few spirits here. One is kind, he has been around a lot, but others have frightened me. It is like being filled with dread. I have not called your mum because she will think I am just imagining it all, but I am not."

I looked at Tom and sent him the link for contact. He walked across the room to Audrey, cupped her cheeks in his hands and kissed her on the lips.

"Hello darling, I do so miss you, I have been in a bit of a pickle lately, sorry."

Tom kissed her again and she held her fingers to her lips.

Ghost, smiley face.

"The kind spirit?"

Tick.

"He went, I think, earlier this morning. There were others, not so nice. When they came, it was awful. Then they all disappeared. There have been a couple of not so nice visits since then. The house has felt horrible at times."

Blanket, hot water bottle, z, z, z.

"Sleep. I wish I could, but I am very scared."

Box, coins.

"Box?"

Box, coins, key.

"Safe. But I haven't got one, I have nothing to steal?"

Blanket, box, coins.

"Oh, safe, as in safe and sound."

Tick.

"You mean, I am safe now?"

Tick.

Blanket, hot water bottle, z, z, z, x.

"Sleep?"

Tick.

"What is the cross for?"

I leant forward and kissed her on the cheek and she touched her face with her fingers.

"Thank you. I love you both, you are my knights in shining armour. Will you stay with me a while?"

"I will darling, John has something to do."

Mule, tick. Bike riding away.

"Tom will stay, you must go."

Tick.

I briefed Grandfather to update his arsenal and linked the methodology into his mind. I then showed him how to construct the shield dome within which he could protect both himself and Grandma if they received company.

"If they come in, shield dome over and toss a grenade into their midst. Any stirrings from them, repeat step two. Keep me updated. If they come and once you have neutralised them, try and get Grandma to Mum's, she should be back from work in about half an hour."

"Soldier in one of your past lifetimes, I take it?"

"Sort of. Intelligence."

"I can see where you are going. Take care and thank you John, I am sorry for being an ass."

"I love you, always will."

I left the house and returned to the group in the garden. The three Leaves were still sitting on the ground, looking decidedly anxious. By reducing the level of the repeated charges, we were able to communicate with them, without them being able to communicate out to others, raise shields or escape by transporting. I linked to the others saying we could not leave them here as they would tell their comrades and we could not spare anyone to keep watch.

Upon questioning by Alana, they confessed they were following orders and did not want to be mixed up with the Governor, because he was persuasive and threatening. Alana and I could read from each of them that they too, had misjudged themselves and were unsure and hesitant, rather than fearful about going over.

"Who are you people? You do not come from around here. Are you friends or family of the old man and woman?"

"We are messengers, we come from the spirit world beyond. Those who watch over the Earth plane, this world in between and our world, are displeased with what you have been doing and how you have been interfering with others who try to live peacefully."

"Messengers, my arse! You are just ordinary spirit folk and you've brought your old nag with you for some reason."

"Mind link – Transform."

In a microsecond, the three Leaves were faced with two eagles an osprey and a Pegasus. For added drama, Scout raised up on his back legs, powerfully flapping his wings and treading the air with his front hooves. In our winged forms, we had the added bonus of being fringed with blue-white light. I could tell from the faces of the Leaves; they realised they were in the company of a different kind of spirit.

"Are you angels or something?" asked the younger member, so visibly awe struck.

"Angels are a myth; they use us these days," said Scout, drumming the ground with his right hoof.

"A talking, flying horse. OK, I believe you. Please do not harm us, we are sorry, aren't we lads!"

"Yes, sorry."

"Me too. Sorry."

"This osprey spirit has already read your histories and minds and it seems you ought not to have any fears about coming to our world, unless you would like to carry on living here serving your governor? Choosing to stay here between worlds is not a crime, you will not be punished, in fact you punish yourselves unnecessarily by staying here. However, carry on doing what you are doing and you will eventually end up in a dark place."

I linked into Arthur and Stephen, who materialised almost immediately.

"Hello Ted, Brian, Henry, haven't seen you in a while," said Stephen.

"You know these three, I thought you worked down south?"

"We have known each other for years. They are regular spectators to catches. This is my usual patch; I was on call the day we met."

"I thought Peter worked this area?"

"Yes he does, we share it. So is it you three that want to come over."

"Well, I am glad it's you, Steve. Are these guys legit. Are they angels?"

"I should not think they called themselves angels. They are more like messengers, but warriors also. In our world, they stand apart from most of us and are held in the highest regard for their knowing of matters."

"Messengers, he said messengers, the Golden Eagle one. I'm gonna come, I'm fed up of this place and angry people. Are you coming Brian, Henry?"

"I am," said Henry.

"I want to say goodbye to my mates and I am gonna tell them that they can come too, if that's OK?" Brian added.

"Young master, you will do that when we say. Heed my words, not before," ordered Audaz.

"You are going to fight them, aren't you? Let me fight with you. I can go behind the lines and spread the word of what has happened to us. I think quite a few will come."

Stephen had opened the veil, with Ted and Henry, stepped into it. Alana smiled into my mind. She was wondering about Brian's potential to act as a double agent perhaps. Alana transformed back to human form with the rest of us following suit. She spoke softly to Brian.

"You were never good enough for your father, were you and you so wanted to be loved by him. I see you tried and tried, but whatever you did, it was never good enough."

Brian shifted uneasily and nodded.

"You stayed here to punish your father, telling yourself, you hated him and did not want to see him ever again. I see you look at Leslie as a father figure and also try to please him so he might look after you. But he doesn't and in truth, he is like your father."

Brian burst into tears and sobbed saying he'd tried so hard.

"You do not need either of them to make you who you are. You can forge your own way and gather and give love along the journey. I can see you have a warm heart ready to receive. And Brian, your dad's name was Trevor, wasn't it?" he nodded. "He has changed a little and knows now, that he was unable to let go of the way he was also not loved. He would like you to fight true to yourself. Do what you believe is right for your heart, regardless of him and yet he would be honoured to meet with you, if you decide to come over. He owes you a lot."

Brian disappeared.

"Damn it, he is good. You and he had us all mesmerised with love and knowing and nobody topped up the charge. What are the chances he is going to blab?" asked Tony.

"We cannot wait to find out Joao."

"Simon? Link in."

"John, I am sorry, they came in force. I had to leave your grandmother and go with them, otherwise they said they would worry her further."

"They did anyway. How come you can communicate, although you are very feint. Why aren't you immobilised?"

"They have me held by a power of sorts. It takes four of them to hold it. I cannot leave."

"You are under the viaduct, aren't you?"

"Yes."

The viaduct in Denby Dale was a favoured place for the Leaves to hang out. Sadly, there had been two Earth-bound souls who had chosen to take a final fall from the heights and the desperateness of their passage had left a resonance of trauma energy, to which the Leaves were drawn.

"How many Simon?"

"One score and four."

"We are coming in."

After Stephen had returned, he and Arthur maintained a safe distance, whilst Audaz went up top to perch on the viaduct. Tony stayed out of sight, but ready to transfer in at a call. With all wings hidden, Alana rode Scout and I walked along side, as we approached the Leaf gathering straight through their front door.

"Tony. When you get an opportunity, can you get close to the energy they are using to hold Simon. We need to know if we can recreate it and use it for ourselves. Keep your head down, you are the stealth member of the team."

"I'm on it."

"Audaz, aerial mines at the ready? Can you shield in flight?"

"I can drop two at a time and yes, of course I can, I am a Harpy eagle."

"Good luck, and everyone remember, we are the ones who risked our all, who fought the odds to rebalance the heavens and fight as soldiers of spirit, who –"

"Oh, shut up James."

"Sorry, couldn't resist the temptation of delivering a rallying battle speech!"

"Yes, shut up John, or I will do the charge of the light brigade one. I am sure some of my ancestor herd were there that day."

"Open fire on my call."

We were thirty metres out when the Leaves ran from their hiding places to front and centre, opening fire in quick succession. The shield Alana was holding to cover us deflected the barrage of fire as we proceeded to approach. At twenty metres we came to a halt. The shots continued for a short while and then stopped.

"You do realise Leslie, with two of us powering this shield, we could quite happily sit here for three or four weeks whilst you popped away and we carried on yawning. You broke the agreement and you harmed my family."

"You went, but he didn't. He's been hiding at the house with your grandmother. I said all of you should leave."

"Who the hell do you think you are," exclaimed Alana as she held her fingers up and slowly counted them towards her smallest one.

"Listen strumpet britches. I don't care what you do or say, I own this village 'n all the Leaves in it. They'd be all loyal to me and I say who stays here or go's. What have I ever done to you, any of you? So, your granny got a bit afraid and we had a little game with your grandfather. So, what, what are you gonna do about it?"

"John, the trap that's holding Simon is pretty simple. Anyone of us could generate it on our own. It operates to dampen transitional energy. I think they are using four Leaves because it takes quite a bit of cognitive linking and maybe they are not overly bright. The four are also not shielded. The thing is, they are probably under strict orders not to let him out, so it might be better to leave him there until we have wrapped things up."

"Thanks Tony. Can you get high for a clear line of sniper fire into their group? Also, see if you can project one of those cognitive cages. We must all try, as they will be invaluable."

Tony mind-linked the information to the others.

"A young trooper of mine told me you were in the village and also tells me you are some sort of messengers."

"Mind link – Oh no, here we go."

"What I'm wondering is why you have brought dobbin, unless it's for carrying you all out of here once we have seen to you?"

The group of Leaves joined Leslie in his laugh. Scout snarted loudly and shivered his flanks.

"Our message is clear. You must disband this outfit of yours, cease your personal activities and leave the Earth-bound folk alone. Is that clear enough for you Leslie?"

Audaz reported twelve of the Leaves powering up including Leslie.

"Scout, hold your form because they think you are a horse. Alana transform and everyone, open fire!"

The element of surprise shocked the Leaves. Two aerial mines exploded amongst them as Audaz took flight. The distraction enabled Alana and I to transform and transport to a hundred metres in the air. We banked simultaneously into high speed dives, both screeching and firing head shots as we sped at incredible speed towards the group. Tony honed in and surgically took out the dazed and disorientated amongst them. With Audaz joining me and Alana, all three of us, swooped and dived, dropping mines and firing shots with great precision. The Leaves were confused as to the direction of fire and it seemed that having no experience of shooting at flying targets, were shooting randomly into the air.

"John, let me out, I want to join in."

"Alright Simon, hang on."

"Scout, power up and transform. Free Simon."

It appeared young Brian had not given us totally away due to the expression on the Leaves faces when Scout took off with his powerful wings, shining in his brilliant whiteness. He opened fire at the four Leaves holding the cage, the unmistakable cannon fire blasting into his targets. Simon, now freed, came out shooting at the two remaining of the four and threw a stun grenade at a group running for cover. With twelve immobilised and eight who had fled the scene, there were four Leaves standing, including Leslie. Brian stood at a safe distance with Arthur and Stephen.

"Tony, keep those who are down, down. Reduce your charge, I want them to hear what I have to say, but don't let them power up or transport."

"Yes, sir!"

"On yer bike."

"Umm, could do with a delta wing right now, I wish I had wings."

Alana and I landed with shields engaged, transformed and stood continuing to fire at the remainders. Audaz circled and dropped topplers before coming to rest. He shielded and perched on Scout's back who was surrounded by a red haze from his rapid firing.

"Leslie, I am starting to yawn again. I think you can see, you are out gunned and eight of your loyal followers have decided to, oh yes, run away. And by the way, we have a man up top who is sighted in to keep the others down. Now let's talk."

"Not for long."

Leslie disappeared.

"He is going for Tony, I'll get him." Audaz took off and disappeared.

There were three bright flashes then silence. Audaz appeared over a tree line carrying Lesley in his talons.

"He is caged and Tony is holding his post." Audaz dropped Leslie in front of where Alana and I were standing.

"You are not going to give up, are you? I would if I were you, you could always come back with us if you wanted."

Alana let me know that Leslie was a likely candidate for realm two. Sporadic shots continued to ring out targeting the immobilised as they started to recover. This seemed to unnerve Leslie. The remaining Leaves although still shielded, had raised their hands, once they saw their governor was captured.

"Let me shoot him John. This idiot has made my life a misery for years."

"No, you can't Simon. I need to talk to him."

"Maybe I will not, then."

Simon walked a few paces away, turned and tossed a grenade at Leslie's feet. Whilst the blast was minimised by his shield, the shock wave caused Leslie to take two paces back and cower, hands protecting his head. I looked at Simon who shrugged his shoulders.

"You said I could not shoot him. He had it coming, he's full of bull-scutter."

I gave Leslie a few moments to recover, before I spoke.

"So, Leslie, what are you going to do?"

Leslie straightened himself and arrogantly replied.

"As I see it, nothing has changed. You still won't stay here, I won't be leaving and your grandmother and as I have learned, your mother, still live here for us to visit."

Audaz linked in privately to me.

"Your young follower called us messengers. As you can see, we are a bit more than that. We have been assigned as the new between world's border patrol (Alana giggled in her mind), so we will be here more often to deal with Leaves like you, who think they can control others for their own gain."

"I have seen enough magic in my time. I am not afraid of you! So, we just have a gun battle every now and again, so what?"

Audaz asked Alana to hold the cage and flew from Scout's back to stand in front of Leslie.

"What do you want? You, tufty chicken."

"I know what a chicken is and that is not me. I am different from the others, you see. The spirit world is not all angels and harps and my job is to track and target people like you and do so relentlessly."

"Get lost."

"Look into my eyes and learn more of what awaits you and will hunt you on this plane."

As he looked, Audaz's eyes glowed red and his body grew to eight feet in height. Eventually, the skin on his back split and two huge, skin covered wings emerged. With legs contorting and talons growing to fearsome lengths, his face transformed into a hideous monster. The creature flapped its gruesome wings and screamed into Leslie's face. He cowered uneasily. Audaz spoke with a hissing and gravelly dialect.

"Do you want me to take you now? Because I have the power to do so. I do not report to anyone other than my master."

"No, no, I don't want to go with you. I must have a choice?"

"You have limited your choices. You could go through yourself at any time and face your fate, if I decide not to take you. I have tasted cowards like you before. If you remain here between worlds, you will live away from others and I will track you from my world to make sure you do. If you break our pact, I will find you and I will fly you to a place, drop you and you will fall for centuries."

Audaz hissed and screamed again, projecting a hypnic toppler to demonstrate his promised effect. When Leslie had recovered enough to hear him, Audaz spoke with cold intent.

"Do you understand what I have just said?"

"Yes. I will remain between worlds and you will not need to track me. I will stay away from others."

"You will be tracked regardless!"

Alana released the cage and Leslie disappeared.

Coming to Light

Audaz turned to us, transformed back to his Harpy eagle form and took a bow. He was met with a rapturous round of applause and counts of genius.

"Well, thank you my friends, it was no big deal for a Harpy eagle like me."

"What I want to know Audaz, is can James, Scout and I do that too?"

"I should think you might be able to, but it is a talent from my line. I may perhaps show you how to at some future time."

"Err, excuse me, what the hell was that?" linked Tony.

"That was a Harpy in ancient battle dress," I replied.

"That, was impressive."

The three remaining Leaves who had been caged by Tony, were standing with their hands still in the air. Three other Leaves were standing with Brian, Stephen and Arthur. I told them to put their hands down as we were not arresting them and gave them the opportunity to come over if they wanted. Tony released the cage, one joined the group and the other two disappeared.

"I beg your pardon. It is John, is it not? You look a little older, but knowing people like I do, because I am special, as you know, I know it is you, or is it?"

Pippa's pseudo cultured tones were unmistakeable.

"Hello Pippa, how are you?"

"Perfect of course, but I was just wondering. You see, since your funeral, there do not seem to have been too many visitors and frankly, I am looking a little grim these days."

"You look fine to me."

"No, you silly boy, I mean, down there in my grave. George and I were wondering if we may, you know, go over as well? I am sure there will be plenty of people there who would love to have me around and we are just a tincy bit bored. Oh, and very sorry for shooting you that day. You must learn how not to be so irritating. I could give you some tips if you like?"

George was standing a few paces behind Pippa. He had his chin on his chest and his hands rammed into his pockets. I connected to the recent memory of little John when I first met him and thought how young George looked.

"Hello George, are you sure you wish to come?"

"Well, I figure I can be grumpy and miserable anywhere and like Pippa, I am hoping there will be others who are like me, you know, start a grumpy club."

I smiled at him and a fleeting glimmer of a smile danced across his lips. I linked to Stephen to make sure he could transport seven at one go. He had already opened the veil and the Leaves were stepping into it.

"Brian, lots of love to you and thank you for not giving our game away," Alana said, smiling warmly.

"Sorry, I had to give Leslie something, so I could speak with the others, but I did not betray you. I am going to find my father."

"You are a brave soldier, more than good enough. I think you will find that your dad is waiting for you. See you around."

"Bye for now."

After they had all stepped from between worlds into the shimmering entrance to the portal, the veil closed behind them.

"Tony, would you mind checking on Tom and my grandma and tell them the coast is clear."

"Yes, no worries. You do realise, I am going to boss you around when we get back."

"Well, you did me for five years. Perhaps, a taste of your own?"

Tony raised his palm to his face, pulled his middle finger and acted surprised when it stood there on its own. He laughed and disappeared.

"Where is Simon. Has anyone seen him?"

No one had and as I linked in, I located him sitting on the top of the viaduct where he had been watching the group.

"What are you doing. Come down."

"That devil creature has come for me. You have brought it for that purpose and who might you all be? You are birds of prey, not ordinary human folk and that is a flying horse."

"So why are you still hanging around then?"

"Because there be something about you and that Alana girl, I feel I should trust."

"If that is so, then trust us. I promise, you will not come to any harm and Audaz will not be taking you to hell."

Simon materialised next to Alana and I. Each member of the group, greeted and introduced themselves to Simon in their natural form.

"These are our friends. We would not have been able to have done what we did here today, without their help. We are all from the spirit realm, the nice part. It is just that we are different from other spirit folk, as we can transform to bird and animal forms if we wish. Just because we are different, does not mean we should be feared."

"I know what it is to be feared and different," said Simon. "After my brother died, although they said it was an accident, many were fearful of me because I had killed a man and I knew I was not trusted."

"You are trusted Simon and it is time to come home. Please come with us?" Alana pleaded with him.

"Alana, you are so kind and gentle, even though I have heard your tongue with its lash. You remind me much of the Alana I knew from these parts when I was alive. She was a strange one."

"Oh, thanks for that!"

"No, don't get me wrong. We knew she was a medicine woman and a healer who helped many. She used to keep two birds of prey and an owl for company. The village elders did her a great cruelty."

"Yes, I know. They hung her."

"No, before that. She was my brother's woman. Jim and her were lovers. When he died, or when I killed him, she became sick for months and months. You know, almost as though she had a demon in her head. She had many fevers and many dark and troubling moods. There were times when Sarah and I thought she was going to die."

"You looked after her?"

"Yes, me and Sarah did. Her parents thought she was possessed and to them, she had brought shame on the family. You see, they were loyal church goers."

"Shame, why shame?"

"Jim did not tell me, or perhaps he did not know, but Alana gave birth to a –
"

"What!" exclaimed Alana. Alana and I linked into each other immediately. Which Simon sensed.

"A baby girl."

"Where is she, what happened to her?"

"Alana, it is almost like I am talking to the same woman. This was over four hundred years ago. She died like everyone else does. But she lived until she was three score and fourteen years. I watched over her, after I died."

Alana was absolutely shell shocked and started to cry. Simon placed his arm around her.

"I have heard stories about spirit people who come back to Earth again as they have unfinished business."

"Yes, this is true," I confirmed.

"I am reckoning that you are her. You are that Alana."

Alana fought back the tears and quietly answered.

"Yes, I am the Alana you once knew, although I look a little different now."

Simon turned to me and dropped his brow.

"That would mean, I am guessing, that you John are my brother Jim. Is this not so?"

"You'd be guessing right older brother. Come here."

I pulled Simon into me and hugged him tightly. Simon burst into tears and sobbed. I could tell Alana was desperate to know more about our daughter and so was I, but what was happening was equally as important.

"I am so sorry Jim. I did not mean for it to get out of hand. I was hot headed in those days and it was the last thing I wanted to happen. I am sorry for all of the trouble I have caused."

"Simon, you are my big brother. There is nothing to forgive, but just for you if it helps, I forgive you."

"Thank you, brother."

"Simon, about the baby, we both do not know much about that lifetime, did I look after her?" Alana interjected.

"That was the cruel bit. The village elders were guided by the church to take the baby from you back then. It was not possible for you Alana, to look after her at that time and your parents wanted nothing to do with you. Because it was my brother's child and they knew that Sarah and I would probably wed, they told us we should look after her and not say anything to you, under pain of threat. They told me I should hold my peace because I had already done a dreadful deed and God would look favourably on me if I met this task and so we kept our mouths shut."

"What was I told?"

311

"The incumbent of the parish told you after you had recovered, you had been possessed and the child you were carrying was still born. What happened to you at that time was used against you when you were hung for witchcraft to strengthen their judgement against you. They said at your trial, which we heard afterwards, that the child died because you were evil."

Alana was visibly subdued and I cuddled her.

"What did you call her?"

"We called her Neve and spelt it as 'Nevaeh'. It was Sarah who thought of the name, as she could read more than I could. Nevaeh was a pretty little girl and very bright. I would say, wise words beyond her years. We loved her as our own. You became her aunt and shared a lot with her in her lifetime before you died. I am sorry Alana, it was a hard secret to keep, we did all we could. Nevaeh was in danger during your trial, as the same incumbent came to our house, with two women from the church. They stripped Nevaeh and searched her for marks which might show that she could also be a witch. It was odd but Nevaeh had a tuft of hair that would never straighten with a comb and when cut off, would always grow back. I remember cutting it off before they came. Strange really as it was a bit like a feather."

"Definitely ours, then."

"Most definitely ours," added Alana.

"Thank you for looking after her Simon and allowing me to be with her. We have never been able to locate her in the spirit world or on Earth. I think there is someone who has a lot of explaining to do!"

"Next question brother."

"Am I going to come with you, you mean?"

"Yes."

"I think it be the right time for me to leave here. Excuse the play on words. Yes, I believe you are telling me the truth."

Whilst the three of us had been talking, Scout and Audaz, apart from listening in, had been watching out for any residual activity. Two women had arrived on the periphery of the scene and were watching patiently. One of them was Clara. She caught my eye and with palms upwards, smiled and nodded. I smiled and nodded back to her. Audaz transformed to his human form and established that they also, would like to leave in between worlds and go over. He linked into Stephen who after a short while, rematerialised. Whilst Alana spoke with the two women, I left the others to check on my grandma. When I arrived, I found Tony, my grandfather and my grandma, in deep symbolic conversation.

"Getting the hang of it, hey Grandfather?"

"Yes, except she keeps referring to me as a mule! I somehow feel it is you who is facilitating this link I have with your grandma?"

"Yes, it is, but it is possible for you to strengthen yours yourself, plus Grandma seems pretty sensitive and tuned in."

"It must have been passed down to you from her then?"

"Maybe you could make a request for the next time you come back here?"

"Maybe I will. Thank you. I can see you are much, much more than just my grandson."

"I always will be though."

The two of us hugged each other.

"John, is that you back again? I hear you have been busy."

Broom leaves.

"Sweeping up leaves, but it's not autumn for months?"

Tick. Bike riding away.

"You have to go, I know, it sounds like you have much to do."

Bird x.

"Bird x, lark, sparrow, no sorry not with you."

Small bird, woman in blue uniform x.

"Small bird, RAF, wren, it's a wren."

Tick, label, label, tick.

"Name, name before bird. Jenny wren, ah my Jenny, you mean your mum."

Tick.

Xxxxxxxxxxx.

"Lots of kisses."

Tick.

I held both of her hands and fizzed her up as strongly as I could, then kissed her on both cheeks. She shivered and touched her face with both hands.

"Bye John, love you lots and see you soon."

Tony and I left the house to go back to the group. Tom told me he would go back directly after a while. When we got back Stephen had returned and was preparing to open the veil once more. Simon and the two other Leaves were looking nervous, but still keen to make the short journey.

"Stephen, can't we take Simon with us."

"No, sorry James. He must come over and through with me, it is part of the process. Here are the coordinates, we will see you on the other side."

"By the way, was it you who caught those two souls who sadly jumped from the viaduct?"

"Yes, it was me."

"Good. Where did they end up?"

"Safe and they are both in our realm."

"I am pleased about that because as we know, not all do. Thanks for all your help today, you and Arthur have been great. Please send my thanks again to Arthur."

"Hey James, thank you for calling me in. I haven't taken so many over at one time before and I have learned a lot today. If you ever need me again, just call in."

"I will. See you around."

Audaz was perched on Scout's back, with Tony and Alana flanking him as I approached the group.

"I just want to thank all of you for a brilliantly executed mission. We have done a great job here today and I think that we work well as a team."

We all gave each other a clap and laughed and joked about how each of us had fought and at the same time, recognised we had helped many Leaves and many Earth dwellers as well.

"I am off John. Work to do, folk to guide, you know how it is. Catch you for a race someday."

"Cheers Tony, see you soon."

He said goodbye to all of his comrades and disappeared. I gave the link to the others and for good measure and a final symbol to the Leaves who had decided to stay, suggested we take off and fly above the viaduct before disappearing.

The sighting of a Golden eagle, a Harpy eagle, an Osprey and what looked like a white cloud, flying in formation over a small West Yorkshire village, went viral within 45 minutes. There was some conjecture however, concerning the cloud, which some thought could have been a weather balloon or marsh gas lit up by the extraordinary bright moon.

Lost and Found

Alana, Audaz, Scout and I landed at the meeting place in human and horse form. There was quite a gathering of loved ones and relatives who had been informed by Arthur that their kin had decided to come over. I called into Hazel, who told me Tom had already been in touch. Alana spotted Brian and his father waving at her. She gave them the thumbs up, which they returned and then disappeared. I could see George, who whilst hugging his wife, had a grin like a Cheshire cat and Pippa was chatting to her sister, remarking on the lustre of her new spirit world hair. Simon however, stood on his own looking forlorn and alone.

"She didn't come."

"She doesn't know you are here. We left in such a rush to get to Denby Dale, that I forgot to tell her. Come on we will fly in."

"I cannot fly!"

"We will see."

"How do I look?"

Alana linked in and helped Simon tend to his clothing and he give himself a shave. She recommended a pair of jeans, a checked shirt and a pair of cowboy boots, which he was very pleased with.

"Do they have flowers here, they must?"

"Just imagine what you want and place them in your hand."

"Sarah, I know this is a bit short notice. We have Simon with us."

"Bring him home John and thank you."

We materialised above the ridge with Simon riding on Scout's back. Alana, Audaz and I flew beside them, each of us calling as we flew towards the ranch. Two mustangs transformed and took off from the paddock, flying to meet us.

"I cannot see her."

"Don't worry, she will be there."

A large bald eagle, swooped in on my wingtip.

"Shhh."

"Sarah?"

"Who else?"

Alana, Audaz and Scout linked in.

"You are one of us. Does that mean that Simon is as well?"

"Of course, he is. I think that is why you were drawn to each other when you first met."

"But you never said and I could not sense you?"

"You have had a lot going on and it was important to keep it under wraps otherwise it might have affected Simon's return. And you Scout, keeping secrets hey, didn't notice a bald eagle flying around whilst you were practicing with your mates?"

"But, I did not know. That means you must have heard us too."

"I have been listening to you snarting and chuckling for years, all of you, but I respect your silence and presence. Not sure I am a crazy old woman though?"

"Very affectionate pet name, sorry. I don't think you are old really and only a little bit crazy."

Sarah laughed.

"Still no sign," reported Simon.

"She's here alright, she must be inside."

Sarah disappeared and walked through the front door waving.

"There she is, there's my Sarah!"

All four of us touched down in front of the paddock, with the other two horses and transformed back. Simon dismounted and slowly walked towards Sarah, the flowers materialising in his hand.

"Made it then, you stubborn old fool."

She was smiling.

"Hello lass, sorry, been a long time coming, but I never did."

"You never did what?"

Simon handed her the flowers, a bunch of bright blue forget-me-knots.

"Forget you!"

With matching tears rolling down their cheeks they stepped forward and hugged each other for the next four hundred years, or so it seemed like to the rest of us. As we all sat around a table outside, the stories were told of the day's events, including those, slightly exaggerated ones from Audaz, when he flew as a huge Harpy and darkened the skies. Simon was quietly taking everything in and twiddling something in his hair.

"What's this in my hair lass, can you pull it out?" Alana and I looked up.

"No dearest, I cannot. Now you have returned you seem to have your feather back. See, I have one and so does John, sorry James and Alana. Audaz has loads and if you ask him nicely, Scout will show you his. We are all part of the Feather-mane Tribe."

"No really, what is it?"

"Simon, when some of us return from the Earth plane, their partners choose to take them through something called the 'Awakening'. You see, you and I have been back to Earth a number of times and when we go back we do not remember being there before. When Jim died, you were so traumatised you could not remember me from previous lives, but I remember all of our lifetimes. I told John a little fib when I met him as you and I have been back and forth seven times and I have waited for you for over four hundred years."

"That's true Simon, remember me from when we first met, I was fifteen? Alana woke me up. We have both been travelling together for hundreds of years too. Don't worry everything will become clear, it did for me."

"The feather reminds me of Nevaeh. Do you know Sarah, that this is Alana, our Alana?"

Sarah turned to Alana quickly and hugged her tightly as more tears were shared.

"I am sorry Alana. I did not pick up it was you. You look beautiful, it is so good to see you again. There is so much going on."

"That's fine Sarah, we will have plenty of time to catch up. Thank you so much for looking after Nevaeh and me. I heard it was an awful time for us all."

"Yes, not the best one."

"Do you know what happened to Nevaeh when she left the Earth plane?"

"I, I am not –"

"And the between worlds border patrol have returned!" announced Tarquin.

"I have got a bone to pick with you Tarquin, why lie to us about Nevaeh?"

"Yes, Tarquin, why did you tell us we did not have a child?" I demanded.

"Calm down, there are reasons for this, let me explain."

"Well, they'd better be damn good. I thought we worked on truth and trust over here and our trust in you is severely dented. I have been brushing shoulders with you for the last twenty-six years and you have held this from me!" Alana seethed.

"Please let me set the context. Trust me if you can for this."

"I know you, don't I?" asked Simon.

"You do old friend, although it has been many years now since we have spoken."

"You told me you did not know him. This gets better," I interrupted.

"Please, wait James."

"How are you?"

"Can't grumble, except I feel I have been foolish by staying so long between worlds."

"You fought well today, you all did and helped twelve Leaves to return. You may not know but the energy brought by Leaves freeing themselves is much greater than Earth incarnations. And Simon, you have helped many over the years too. The task of gate keeper is a hard one and one of much sacrifice. You have served this realm well."

"Gate keeper?" I questioned.

"One who lives between worlds and helps those confused souls to find their way over by becoming one of them."

"You speak as though I chose to do it?" asked Simon.

"You did choose and when you and I made the plans, you were supposed to only spend one lifetime as a Leaf guardian. Unfortunately, you had not come into awareness when James was killed. His death affected you so badly, you isolated yourself, even from the guides and nobody could reach you. Even though Sarah was with you and Alana and Nevaeh also, as part of your support before you went into between worlds, you would not link to them. You would not use the combined consciousness of your kind to awaken you, nor listen to any of the catchers."

"My kind, you mean my family?"

"Yes, your ancestral line. You, Sarah, James, Alana, Audaz and Scout are all descended from the ancient Harpy line, the one that is extinct."

"You mean the one I saw Audaz transform into today, you mean, we are monsters?"

"Sarah, can I awaken him just a little. I will provide none of your shared lifetime history?"

"Yes, be my guest."

Our heads were darting back and forth keeping pace with the unravelling information. I sensed Simon could feel his thoughts and memories reappearing, which were starting to clear and make sense for him. Simon reassured the group, everything disclosed so far was the truth after he had received the authentic history of the Harpy line. I searched Tarquin's mind to see if he was altering Simon's consciousness to make his story more authentic.

"James, please. Sarah and Simon are as developed as you and Alana, except when they went back all those years ago, you were in your first lifetime. Because of what happened, Sarah has remained in spirit and waited, as this was an option open to her and in truth we never knew when Simon would come back. Your last lifetime James, was not totally to do with learning patience and humility. You did not know on the revolve, but it was also to make contact with Simon and establish a knowing link that neither of you would be conscious of, but would be bound by. It turned out your lifetime was shortened by your accident."

"Shortened? Did I shorten it unconsciously?"

"No, that seed was never sown and we do not have such power to cause such effect. It was a Collective action, beyond our control."

"Come to think about it, I used to watch you ride down that hill on many occasions and think, I bet he wishes he could fly. It makes more sense now," added Simon.

"Audaz and Scout, thank you for helping these three. It always surprises me how those of the Harpy line, find and support each other."

Both Audaz and Scout nodded in Tarquin's direction.

"Simon are you catching up?" asked Tarquin.

"Yes, it's a bit hazy, but I am remembering and following."

"Good, let's talk about Nevaeh."

"Yes, lets," Alana confirmed.

"Nevaeh, was on her final revolution, her eighth when she returned to Earth and was born as your child. You have all heard the saying where some children appear wiser than their parents? This was one of those occasions as you and James were fledgling Earth-bound spirits. Part of her role was to grow up and support both of you and Simon before he undertook his Leaf assignment. It all went wrong, as you know and although Sarah grew in consciousness, she was powerless to help either Simon or you Alana, in the directions you had decided to take. You were out of control Alana, flitting back and forth into between worlds from the Earth plane to see James. Between the two of you, you stirred up great uneasiness with the Leaves at that time and you were both engaged in regular battles with them, because you were different to them. James was beside himself, behaving erratically because he would not risk you being in between worlds alone."

Alana squeezed my hand and whispered, "Hero."

"When you met your end Alana, Neveah was fifteen years old and unbeknown to Simon and Sarah, you had already begun to teach her in the ways of herbology, magik and seership. She, being who she was, but not being aware, was a natural. The last thing all of the sensitive, caring and wise women in Yorkshire needed, was the presence of a young girl who might transform and fly like an eagle and who would have caused a certain witch hunt. As you know, that sadly came later."

"After, you were hanged, Neveah told me about what you had taught her and I had to make her promise on your soul, she would never practice the arts and to my knowledge she never did. I remember that my suspicions came one night in a dream," said Sarah.

"I remember the day of the hanging as told by others, as we did not wish to see you die. They said when they placed the noose around your neck, you were _"

"Smiling?" interrupted Alana.

"Yes, that's right. The church people said it was because you were happy. Happy because you were going back to hell," said Simon.

"No. It was because I knew who I was going to see next."

"Can you see why we decided to erase your memory of your first life? It was an unbearable time for everyone, me included," asked Tarquin.

"Yes, we can, but where is Nevaeh. Even now we cannot trace her?"

"After she came back, I told her what we had decided to do and she agreed. She knew, even as young Harpies, you would be able to trace her, so she guarded when you returned between earth lifetimes until you returned to the Earth for the next. After a while, she went to a place more out of your natural reach."

"She is a high planer, isn't she? No wonder there was no sign," said Alana.

"Yes, she is a high planer and one of my closest friends. Your instinct is to hunt and protect and your perceptions are incredible. We had to give you a fair chance to carry on with your lifetimes and grow to be the spirits that you are. We are sorry this was held from you and your rewards have been gained on a hard and challenging path. However, we were guided by the Collective, as well as our own knowing."

Every one's eyes were on Alana and I as we searched each other for forgiveness and found it for all to see.

"Can we meet her, Tarquin?"

"Look up."

A large Sea eagle, with brilliant shining white tail feathers descended majestically and came into land. She shook her wings and transformed into her human form.

"Mum, Dad, Aunt Sarah and Uncle Simon. It has certainly been a while."

Believe It or Not

This is not reality, for reality remains the imagined until it is revealed. On our Earth world, we are well aware and acceptant of the imagined becoming reality. We see this in the majority of cases as progress and nowadays science dominates most of these transitions. However, even in science, the scientists have to believe that what they imagine can one day become real. Although not reality, we live each day facing this imagined reality and it will always remain imagined to us, until for good enough reason, we need it to be true.